MW01132830

BRUTAL ENEMY

ALSO BY RONN MUNSTERMAN

FICTION

Behind German Lines – A Sgt. Dunn Novel
Operation Devil's Fire – A Sgt. Dunn Novel

NONFICTION

Chess Handbook for Parents and Coaches

BRUTAL ENEMY

A SGT. DUNN NOVEL

RONN MUNSTERMAN

Terrance M. Phelan

January 2019

BRUTAL ENEMY – A SGT. DUNN NOVEL

Copyright © 2014 by Ronn Munsterman
www.ronnmunsterman.com

Cover Design by David M. Jones and Nathalie Beloeil-Jones
www.beloeil-jones.com

Printed in the United States of America
1 3 5 7 9 10 8 6 4 2

ISBN: 978-1-505-82035-5
BISAC: Fiction / War & Military

Acknowledgments

Thank you, dear reader. Your support inspires me to create better and better stories for Tom Dunn and cast. As usual, I have an Author's notes section at the end of the book. Beware: it contains spoilers, so please save it until last.

My FIRST READERS happily take my first draft, which is always full of errors and plot holes. They helped me create the book you are about to read. They make great suggestions that end up in the book, sometimes for plot or characters or equipment. They force me to provide more clarity than a writer sometimes does in a first draft, mostly because we are too close to the story. They are true friends, who encourage me when I need it the most, and kick my ass when I need that, too. Thank you, my friends: Steven E. Barltrop, Dave J. Cross, David M. Jones, Nathan Munsterman, Robert (Bob) A. Schneider II, John Skelton, Steven D. White, and Derek Williams.

David M. Jones (Jonesy) and his wife, Nathalie Beloeil-Jones, deserve a special thank you for creating the great cover, which captures the mood and essence of the story in one image. This is Dave's second cover for Sgt. Dunn, and Nathalie's first. She created the beautiful freehand sketch.

For this book, due to the tactical complexity of Dunn's squad's actions, I had to draw a couple of military-style maps so I could keep things straight as I wrote the scenes. For one of those scenes in particular, I asked a good friend to critique the attack for military accuracy. A big thank you to Robert A. Goerdt, SFC (U.S. Army Retired). Any errors regarding that scene are mine alone.

Thank you to Greg Schluter for allowing me to use his name for a despicable Nazi character. More on this is in the Author's Notes.

Thank you to the veterans of World War II. May the memory of your service and sacrifice always remain with us.

Every day of the year, our modern day service men and women work tirelessly for our security. Thank you to those who are veterans and those who are currently on duty.

To Elijah L.

Your arrival is a blessing,
Welcome to the world.

You are a beautiful little
boy and we love you.

In addition to bringing us
joy, you brought a World

Series to Kansas City, just
like your dad did for

the Kansas City Royals in
1985.

BRUTAL ENEMY

Chapter 1

Airborne – 5,000 feet altitude
2 miles south of Turin, Italy
31 July 1944, 1935 Hours

Colonel Frank Rogers realized two things simultaneously: aircraft are flimsy things and he may have made a terrible mistake today.

German anti-aircraft rounds slammed into the two-seater Lysander. The small airplane shuddered. The rounds striking her sounded like a giant attacking the plane with a sledgehammer.

Rogers, sitting behind the pilot in the tandem seat, flinched.

More rounds struck the engine compartment. Smoke immediately bellowed out, streaming behind them.

The pilot, Lieutenant Doug Watson, immediately hit the throttle, pushed the stick forward and left, and stamped on the left rudder pedal to speed up the turn. The maneuver worked as the tracers swept behind and above the smoking plane. His plan was to go lower and count on the mountains to obscure the gunner's view then, when out of sight, head back to Corsica. However, one look at a gauge told him the plane was mortally wounded.

"Sir, we're in trouble here. Losing oil pressure."

"Can't make it back?" asked Rogers evenly, although his guts were churning.

"Not even close, sir."

"Well, do what you can."

"Will do, sir."

Watson guided the plane into a southerly direction, heading for the coast. Maybe there'd be a chance for a submarine rescue. Ten minutes passed and he somehow kept the plane at the same altitude, just under five thousand feet. The bottom of the clouds appeared to be within arm's reach.

As they approached the next set of mountain peaks, the engine coughed, almost quit, then resumed running, but at a lower RPM. Airspeed fell. Watson knew they would have one chance to find a place to land in a narrow valley between the ragged ridges of the mountains.

Banking the aircraft to the left, he pulled back on the stick slightly. Grudgingly, the nose lifted.

"Sir, we're going to have to set down in the next few minutes. We can't clear the range after this one."

"Okay," replied Rogers as he turned his attention to the camera hanging around his neck. He unlatched the back cover and yanked out the film, unspooling it to completely expose it to the light. Next, he slid open the small window pane on his right and air rushed inside. Taking the camera sling off his neck, he wound it around the camera body, then flung it out into space. Crinkling the exposed film into a little ball, he tossed it out, too, then closed the window pane and sat back.

Soon, the plane reached a gap between peaks, just where Watson had been aiming.

To Rogers' untrained eyes, it looked like they might not clear the jagged rocks, but he didn't say anything. *Don't distract the pilot*, was what he was thinking.

The rocks flashed by, seemingly just under the wheels.

"I see a clearing. Some farmland," Watson said, relief in his voice.

"Very good, Doug."

"Sir, are you strapped in as tight as possible?"

Rogers quickly checked his harness, tightening it some more. "I am now."

"Okay, sir. We're about two miles out."

"Roger."

Watson worked to bring the plane in, slowing her, getting the nose down. Everything looked good. The plane suddenly jumped a few yards to the right and down.

"Wind gust!" Watson fought the stick and used the rudder pedals to get the Lysander back on the right line. After a moment, things smoothed out. He'd heard about wind problems in valleys; they could be swirling, nasty things.

The British Lysander only needed one hundred fifty yards to land. The field Watson had selected was at least five hundred yards long, but was surrounded by thick forest. An east-west road ran along the north edge.

The pilot picked his touchdown spot and activated the flaps.

The field was bare of crops and appeared to have grass growing all over. There was no way to know whether there were old furrows under the grass. Watson had to choose one direction and he picked the one that ran the length of the field rather than across, believing, hoping he would be coming in parallel to any furrows. He knew it had rained for several days recently and hoped the ground wasn't so soft that the wheels would dig in and cause a nose-over.

He dropped the airspeed. The plane began to drift closer and closer to the ground.

"Almost there, sir."

"Roger." *Do a good job*, thought the colonel. Rogers leaned to the right so he could see where they were headed. Off in the not-so-far distance lay the mountains they would have to cross on foot. Forming a large sweeping curve, a river wound first southeast then west where a bridge crossed the churning white water.

Watson didn't force it and just let the plane land itself. When the wheels hit the dirt under the grass they bounced and the plane rose five feet before settling down into a nearly smooth roll. To Watson's immense relief, there were no furrows. He pushed gently against the brake pedal and the plane quickly came to a stop. He switched off the engine and said, "Welcome to Italy, sir."

"Thanks, I guess."

Watson rotated the radio frequency dial, but heard nothing at all, not even static. He flipped the power switch on and off a few times, but still nothing.

"Sir, the radio is a dead duck." He tore off the headset, and said, "Best get out now."

Both men unstrapped as fast as possible and climbed out of the dead airplane. Standing several yards away, they examined their surroundings. The thing that struck Rogers the most was the silence. Without the engine noise, the world seemed a peaceful place. Then he began to discern subtle sounds: the grass rustling in the wind, a few birds, a cow or two mooing far off to the north, back toward a village. It made Norfolk, Virginia seem very far away, a place found only in fading memories.

"Sir, give me a hand? I want to make sure the bird is gone. I don't want to hand it off to the krauts."

Rogers came back to the present. Watson was pulling knee-high dry grass out of the ground in great clumps.

"Sure."

Rogers followed suit and soon they each had large handfuls. In turn, they climbed up the permanently attached ladder and dumped the grass in Rogers' former seat, repeating the process several times.

When they were done with the grass, Watson unscrewed the fuel tank cap located just to the left of the ladder to allow the vapors to rise outside the aircraft, and stepped back.

Rogers understood that the pilot had to destroy the aircraft and assumed Watson was going to ignite everything with a tossed Zippo lighter, but instead the pilot pointed to a spot a good distance from the plane.

"Better hightail it over there, sir." He pulled a Very pistol from his belt. The pistol, named after its inventor, a U.S. Navy officer named Edward Very, carried one flare round. Instant fire.

Rogers nodded and took off. Watson bent over and grabbed a rucksack he'd taken with him when exiting the plane, then ran. After ten yards, he stopped and turned around. A wistful expression crossed his face, then he lifted the Very pistol, aimed at the open cockpit, and gently pulled the trigger. His aim was true and the round flew right into the back of the cockpit and went off in a blinding flash, followed by a larger one that engulfed the interior. Watson turned and ran, peeking over his shoulder every few steps. Flames roared out of the inferno and, seeking more to burn, raced along the side of the plane and into the fuel vapors.

Watson saw this on his last peek and he reached Rogers at the same time. Diving, he tackled the superior officer. Behind them, the plane exploded with a *whump* that both men felt. The resulting fireball shot skyward.

The two men disentangled themselves and rose carefully to their knees to watch the plane burn.

"Sorry about the tackle, sir."

"Don't worry about it. I'm sure I felt the heat pass right over us. So thanks."

A moment passed, then Rogers got to his feet and Watson joined him.

"Best we get away from here, Lieutenant."

"Yes, sir."

"How's your Italian?"

"I know pizza and parmesan, but that's about it."

Rogers smiled ruefully. "Me, too."

"Well, sir, if you'll pardon my French, we're fucked."

"Indeed. But for now, let's get away from this beacon. I saw a river and a bridge to the west, maybe a couple of hundred yards."

"Yeah, I saw it, too."

"After we get across, we head toward the tree line at the base of the mountain." Rogers pointed toward the south.

"After you, sir."

Rogers turned away and strode off.

The flat field yielded to the trees living off the river water, right on the banks, and they followed them to the road leading to the bridge. Stopping twenty yards from the road, and fairly deep in the woods, they knelt and examined the road in both directions. Nothing moved. No worrisome sounds came their way.

"What do you think, sir?" asked Watson.

The bridge was about fifty yards long. On the far side, the road went another fifty yards and broke off to the southwest, out of their sight. Any vehicle coming from the other way might be on top of them before they could react.

"I haven't sprinted for a long time, but that's what we're going to have to do. A 50-yard dash at top speed. You up for it?"

"I am."

Rogers nodded and then stood up. Edging out onto the road, they stopped once more. Still no sounds.

"Let's go!"

Rogers took off and Watson easily kept pace, right behind him. Rogers looked down at the rushing waters beneath them and thought, *be a bad place to fall in.*

They hit the end of the bridge and leapt into the woods again. They walked steadily and quickly reached the first slope. The brush and trees grew thicker and the ground steeper with each step. The men began to labor under the strain of going uphill and after a hard thirty minutes of climbing, an out of breath Rogers said, "Let's stop and take stock of our situation."

"No argument here."

The men sat down, then lay back against the hillside, hands folded behind their heads. A few minutes passed and Rogers' breathing returned to normal. At thirty-eight he was still in pretty good shape, but it'd been a good long while since he'd walked this far in rugged country.

Rogers said, "I've got my .45. What about you?"

"Same here, sir, plus two extra clips in my pocket. I have a compass and I've got a couple of days' worth of mystery spam and a full canteen in my rucksack."

"Good man. Thank goodness we ate before we took off. I could use a bit of water, though."

Watson opened his rucksack, removed the canteen, unscrewed the lid and handed it toward Rogers.

"No, you first, Lieutenant."

Watson smiled, then took a short swallow.

After the colonel took a drink and handed back the canteen, Watson said, "I figure we're about ten to fifteen miles from the coast. We make it there, and maybe we can make contact for a pickup to get back to Corsica."

"Due south?"

"Yes, sir."

"How high are these mountains?"

"We were at thirty-five hundred as we went over, so I'd say a good three thousand feet."

"Have a map in there, too?"

"Yes, sir." Watson dug into the rucksack and pulled one out. He opened and oriented it in his lap.

Rogers moved closer to see.

Watson found the valley they'd just landed in and located the river. The town they'd seen was too small to appear with its name, but another larger one, Calizzano, was less than a mile away to their southwest.

"Looks like we'll have to head east to avoid that town," Watson said.

"I agree." Rogers looked at the darkening sky, then at his watch, which showed 2015 hours. "There must be only another hour of light at the most. How much ground can we cover in that time?"

"A mile or two an hour is the best we'll be able to do in this terrain."

"Best get started, then."

Watson got to his feet, and held out a hand to Rogers, helping him to his feet. Watson slipped the rucksack over his shoulders and snugged it into place.

Rogers took the lead and they strode off, each man wondering what the next few days would bring.

1/2 mile south of Caragnetta, Italy
31 July, 2020 Hours

The understrength four-man Waffen SS squad made it to the burning aircraft about thirty minutes after the two American officers had left for the mountains. The unit had been on patrol when they'd received a radio communication declaring a U.S. plane being shot down along with its last known heading.

The squad leader, *Oberscharführer* Otto Nieman and his men were already heading in the general direction by chance and stopped in the village of Caragnetta, where Nieman had questioned the owner of the lone cafe. At first, the man pleaded that he knew nothing. Then Nieman had grabbed the man's seven-year-old son by the arm, pulled his Luger from its flap-covered holster and pointed it at the boy's head. The man immediately said he'd heard an aircraft not long ago, but hadn't seen it. The sounds had come from the west.

Nieman pushed the boy away, who stumbled and fell. When the man tried to help his son get up, Nieman kicked the man in the face, breaking his nose. With rage in his eyes, the boy jumped up and started to take a swing at the German, but his father got a grip on the arm just in time and yanked him back.

Nieman laughed, turned and kicked over a display table of breads, and stomped out the door and into his truck.

Walking around the airplane's still hot carcass, Nieman and his men looked for anything to help identify the plane. The wings, constructed of metal and fabric, resembled a bird's skeleton. The metal fuselage had begun to sag from the heat and the engine had fallen from its brackets to the ground face first. There was nothing to indicate its nationality, but Nieman assumed the men who shot it down were correct and that it once had U.S. markings.

The struts that connected the wings and lower fuselage were warped, but still intact. This helped Nieman determine that the plane was no known fighter, as all modern fighters were low-wing monoplanes, while this one was a high-wing, plus they all had retractable landing gear, while this one had fixed gear. That meant it was likely an observer type of plane. Nieman knew he could contact the firing unit and get a better description, but he wanted to solve the problem himself. Something to make the day more interesting.

The fuselage just below the now empty frames for the glass of the cockpit sagged from the intense heat and Nieman could see inside enough to tell that no one was on board when it had started burning. He gave a brisk order and his men fanned out in all directions, looking at the ground carefully. A short time after, one man called out, "*Oberscharführer*! Foot prints!"

Nieman ran over to join the man. He immediately saw the mashed down grass and farther away in a relatively bare spot, the clear marking of someone's shoes. Kneeling for a closer look, Nieman noticed a foot print that seemed to be on top of another one. Two men, not just the pilot. Was this an intended insertion of an agent, like the British and their damned SOE had done so often in France? What aircraft was that? He searched his memory and came up with Lysander. Capacity of two and famous for its short takeoff and landing distances.

He raised his gaze to the mountain off in the distance, to the south. That's where the men would be. Judging by the foot prints' spacing, the men were uninjured and mobile. He checked his watch. Only an hour to sunset. Based on the time of the call and how long it had taken his men to arrive, he guessed he was thirty minutes behind the Americans. The moon would be nearly three-quarters full and would provide considerable light, but it would be at least two hours before it rose high enough in the night sky to help.

Rising, he eyed the mountains again. They would almost certainly be heading for the coast. Perhaps for a submarine rendezvous. If he decided to pursue now, it would be a long night and they'd have to take what provisions they had in the truck with them, including water.

He pulled a map from a pocket and unfolded it to the local area. The peaks to the south ran on a line from north-northeast to south-southwest. On the other side was a valley about three miles wide, which then led to another set of peaks that were only ten kilometers from the sea.

Decision made, he called to his men and they ran over to see what he wanted to do.

Nieman gave instructions and the men nodded. Nieman led the way as they began tracking the footsteps. The path the men from the aircraft had taken was clear, leading toward the river bank, then along the river to the bridge.

Crossing the bridge at a full run, the men quickly reacquired the trail on the other side as it led toward the mountain on the south. Nieman was wishing he had some dogs, but he had every confidence that he and his men could stay on the trail of the enemy. Even though the plane was a Lysander, which he knew was used primarily by the British, it didn't mean the men he was chasing weren't American. How he'd love to catch some Americans. He'd punish them for what the bombers were doing to all the great German cities. He would take a great deal of delight in that. Yes, he would.

—

Deep woods, western end of Ligurian Apennines mountain range
2 miles southeast of Lysander landing zone
1 August, 0615 Hours

Rogers and Watson walked carefully, the pilot in the lead this time. The terrain was difficult, but not impossible. Heavy morning mist hung over them, reducing visibility to about a hundred yards. Pine trees surrounded them, spaced as close as a couple of yards from each other, branches interlocked close to the ground. The surface of the old growth forest floor was remarkably clear, with just pine needles and some small scrub brush scattered about.

They'd been forced to stop a little after sunset the night before for safety's sake. Breaking into two of Watson's cans of spam, they'd had an unsatisfying dinner with water to help swallow the salty meat. Keeping watch in two-hour shifts, they'd managed to get a little rest. At first light, they'd struck out again, still in a southeasterly direction. Unable to see far enough ahead to properly plan a line of ascent to the ridge that was somewhere ahead, they'd been only able to react to what they *could* see.

After two hours of grueling climbing, the men finally reached the ridge. They could now descend into the next valley, leaving one more set of mountain peaks to navigate before reaching the sea. They stopped to rest and sat in silence, too tired for conversation.

Rogers realized his situation was not just bad, it was horrible. The invasion of southern France was maybe two weeks away and with the knowledge that was stuck in his head, he simply could not be captured. Too much was at stake. He had known that the flight was critical, the information had to be learned, but now it just looked stupid. He'd heard the stories of the men in the know for D-Day, and how they'd been forbidden to go anywhere near the continent prior to D-Day. Maybe we got complacent, he thought. Cocky, perhaps. It didn't matter. He was here.

Things go wrong in life for the most innocuous reasons. You can't find your car keys in the morning and search for two minutes before finding them exactly where you'd put them the previous night. On the drive to work, you get hit broadside by a moron who's mad at his wife after a morning argument. All because for two minutes your brain froze up. Shit happens.

War is nothing but one big shit ball. Things never go right. Rogers never believed he would be shot down. The thought just never occurred to him. But he had been shot down, and the entire fucking invasion was at risk, thanks to him. On the other hand, by taking a gamble on the reconnaissance flight he'd found a German armored battalion only fifty miles from the French border, hidden in plain sight around and on a serpentine road winding through the western Apennines. He'd estimated about forty tanks plus the support vehicles. Whether the German high command was planning to move them to France was unknown, but if they did, and the Allies didn't know it, things could go very bad on the beaches.

Shit happens. And then it shits on itself some more.

The one precaution Rogers had taken could put him in serious jeopardy: he carried fake identification, which included a new set of ID tags with a new name, Captain Frank Newport, which was how the pilot knew him so he couldn't give away Rogers' real name. His papers stated he was a supply officer for a battalion based south of Rome. He had supposedly been transferred to Cherbourg and was on the way there. He hoped that if he did get captured, the identity switch would lead the Germans astray long enough for the invasion to get underway. If he was found out, they might hand him over to the Gestapo, although they probably would anyway. He might be treated as a spy due to the subterfuge, which would mean eventual execution. Getting back alive was the better choice, and how to do that had just become priority one.

Rogers checked his watch. Ten minutes had already passed. Standing, he asked, "Ready to go?"

"Yes, sir. Want me to take point?"

"Sure, go ahead."

Watson stepped around Rogers and headed for a large gap between some trees, possibly a clearing. The mist had lifted an hour ago, burned off by the morning sun, which shone brightly through the trees.

Walking quickly, Watson made it to the clearing. It turned out to be a rocky outcropping, a natural observation point. The valley opened in front of them in an incredible panoramic vista. Watson shrugged off his rucksack and set it down, then he stepped out onto the outcropping to enjoy the view.

Rogers never fully understood exactly what happened next, but one moment Watson was standing there a few feet in front of him, and the next he was gone. Sounds of loose rocks colliding with others came to him. A scream, followed by a sickening thud. The terrified cry cut off.

Rogers stood there for a moment, not believing his eyes. Then he was spurred into action. He stepped carefully toward the edge, creeping forward a half step at a time. Finally, he realized he should get on all fours. He crawled forward, and looked over the precipice.

At the bottom of what must be a forty-foot drop lay a broken Lieutenant Watson. Even from this distance, Rogers knew his pilot was dead.

Scooting back from the edge and the grisly sight below, Rogers got to a point where he felt he could safely stand. He picked up the rucksack and searched for a few minutes before finding a way down.

When he got to Watson, he knelt beside the pilot and crossed himself. He gently closed Watson's eyes, laid his hand on the younger man's forehead, and said a quick prayer. He mentally apologized to Watson, put his hands in the man's jacket pocket and removed the extra clips for the Colt .45 and slid them into his own pocket. He also pulled Watson's Colt from its holster and made sure the safety switch was in the on position.

Rising, he looked around. There were a few rocks scattered around the base of the cliff, but nowhere near enough to bury Watson. He had no tools to dig a grave. Sick at the thought of leaving the man in the open, he forced himself to set aside the feeling.

He spotted Watson's hat a few feet away. Picking it up, he placed it over Watson's face. "I'm sorry, Doug. Thanks for getting me to the ground safely."

Standing at attention, he gave Watson a salute, then turned and marched off into the forest, thinking, *only six or seven miles to the coast.*

Sunlight shone on Watson's still form. Light reflected from the lens on the compass lying face up a few feet from the pilot.

Chapter 2

Colonel Kenton's Office – Camp Barton Stacey
Andover, England
2 August, 0730 Hours

The commander of U.S. Army Rangers special mission squads, Colonel Mark Kenton, was accustomed to having worried people gathered around his big oak desk.

Alan Finch, who worked directly for Prime Minister Churchill, sat on Kenton's left. In his early thirties, he was tall and slender, and wearing a perfectly pressed dark blue suit, white shirt and blue tie. He'd once appeared in a meeting with the Prime Minister and others in a rumpled suit that he'd slept in the night before. He vowed never to look that way again.

He was a co-author of Operation Devil's Fire. The end result of that hugely successful mission was the destruction of the Nazis' atomic bomb facility and the eventual theft of the Germans' jet bomber intended to carry the bomb to the United States. Following the mission's success, Churchill had pulled Finch out of MI5, promoted him, and put him to work on his staff.

To Finch's left sat Howard Lawson, the other co-author, from the Office of Strategic Services, the OSS. Lawson seemed to spend considerable time either in London or Barton Stacey. He reported directly to the head of the OSS, General William "Wild Bill" Donovan.

The newly promoted Sergeant First Class Tom Dunn was to Lawson's left. Dunn, who at six-two and a hundred eighty-three pounds, was a lean and fit U.S. Army Ranger. Dunn had brown hair, and dark brown eyes that could light up in joy or turn black in anger. He was the squad leader responsible for executing Operation Devil's Fire. He had a reputation for quick thinking. He and his men were all graduates from Achnacarry House, the British-run commando school.

Dunn, who'd wed Pamela Hardwicke just four days ago, had been on his honeymoon when Kenton called requesting his presence at the meeting now in progress. Pamela had been disappointed; their stay at Hayling Island had been tranquil and wonderful, but she understood. She knew what she was getting into from the start of their whirlwind relationship.

They'd risen early and driven the thirty-five miles back to Barton Stacey. After a farewell kiss, she went straight to the hospital, where she worked as a nurse, and Dunn drove on to the meeting.

Rounding out the group, Lieutenant Samuel Adams, Colonel Kenton's aide, sat to Dunn's left.

This group was a kind of mission brain trust and worked well together. Everyone present had top secret clearance, and had earned that mantle quite some time ago. Kenton often handed out the mission objectives and sat back while Dunn worked out the details. Today, the mission information would come from Finch and Lawson.

All the niceties had been completed and Finch cleared his throat. All eyes turned to him.

"Gentlemen, we have a potentially critical breach of security for the invasion of southern France."

A few groans swept around the room. Everyone knew the invasion was coming, but no one was privy to the details.

"Colonel Frank Rogers, one of the intelligence officers on General Truscott's planning staff, is overdue from an unauthorized scouting mission. Rogers has complete knowledge of the invasion including strength, locations of landings and the calendar.

"He was in a two-seater Lysander. For twenty-four hours it was unknown as to what happened, whether they'd crashed into the Ligurian Sea or over land, or what. Late yesterday, an Italian partisans group found the wreckage of a Lysander. They reported the plane landed safely, but was destroyed afterwards. We presume it was by the pilot, Lieutenant Doug Watson. Rogers and his pilot were gone and have not been seen.

"The partisans sent two men to track them and found Watson's body at the bottom of a forty-foot cliff."

"Oh, son of a bitch. We've got a colonel on his own in the mountains?" asked Dunn.

"Indeed we do, Sergeant."

"Wait. Are you telling me they were able to track the men through that rough country?"

Finch and Lawson exchanged a glance that Dunn caught.

"What else?" he asked.

"There's a Waffen SS unit in the area."

"Oh, damn."

"The good news is the partisans can tell the Germans are terrible trackers in that kind of country. The unit, about a half-squad size, started out on the trail, then must have lost sight of the evidence of the two men in front of them, and wandered around before apparently reacquiring the trail."

"That's one hell of a lucky colonel," Adams said.

Finch nodded.

Dunn examined Finch's and Lawson's faces, who were both doing their best to keep blank expressions. But Dunn knew how things worked. He knew what his men were good at. Excellent at, to be honest. Tough, impossible jobs. Ones that no one else could pull off. Search and rescue in the Italian mountains, the Apennines, if he remembered his geography correctly. Three to four thousand foot peaks. Dense woods.

Smiling grimly, Dunn looked at Kenton, who'd been his boss since the Anzio debacle in early 1944. Kenton had earned distinction by helping his unit be successful in a disaster. Dunn and he got along extremely well. Their relationship was based on the U. S. Army's natural pecking order at first, then respect for each other's capabilities. Over time, it evolved into a deep friendship. While the requirements of a chain of command were always met, Kenton tried to involve Dunn in decision making when possible. Unusual for the army, but it worked very well for this pair.

Dunn said, "Search and rescue. Got it. When do we leave, and are we going by air or under the sea?"

No one in the room was surprised, although both Finch and Lawson looked relieved.

Kenton answered, "Early morning. We're flying you the long way around to Corsica. From there you'll fly into Italy. We hope that by the time you get to Corsica we'll have more information.

"Lieutenant Adams has a map showing the location of the burned aircraft and where Watson's body was found. I'd suggest that you retire to your barracks and work out a plan. Report back here at 1200 hours."

Chapter 3

Nine-year-old Marie Agostini skipped her way down the main road going through the village. Today she was happy. Yesterday she wasn't. She'd found her mother in the kitchen quietly crying. Again. She'd been doing that a lot lately. Little Marie had put an arm around her mother and kissed her forehead gently. A little while later, Carlotta's sobs ceased and she wiped her eyes with her apron. When Marie asked why she had been crying, all Carlotta would say, as she always did, was, "I'm just sad today. Go and play."

Marie thought her mother was crying because her husband, Marie's father, hadn't returned from the war yet. But maybe it was because of the bad men who sometimes came through the village, the ones in the gray uniforms. The horrible *Germans*. Marie sometimes heard her mother and Aunt Teresa speaking softly, thinking she was asleep on the sofa. They talked about people called Nazis and a man named Hitler. They called him the monster who ruined Italy along with the other cretin, Mussolini. Marie had to ask her oldest brother, Damiano, what that word meant. He made her tell him where she'd heard it and when she told him, his eyes changed, becoming hard, angry. It scared her, the change, and she stepped back, but his eyes changed again, back to soft and loving as she liked him best.

Damiano never picked on her, unlike her cousin, Salvatore, who lived a village away, thank goodness. Salvatore wasn't mean, well maybe he was because he liked to pinch her underneath the upper arm and twist hard enough to make her cry. He seemed to enjoy tormenting her. Damiano always put a stop to it when he saw it, one time knocking the bigger boy to the ground. Damiano was her knight in shining armor. She loved to read and had learned about those special men of the middle ages. How wonderful they must have been.

A medium-sized black dog with a white chest and weighing perhaps twenty kilograms bounded alongside her as she skipped. Marie talked to her dog as she moved. Things like, "Hi Lila," and "Good girl, Lila," and "Pretty day isn't it, Lila." Marie knew Lila couldn't understand her, but she liked to pretend she could.

When Marie reached the edge of town, it wasn't that far, she stopped and Lila sat down, her tongue lolling as she panted. Marie bent down to pet Lila and rub behind her ears. After a little while, Marie started back toward the center of the village.

Ville di Murlo lay in the valley between two sets of peaks and ridges that were part of the Apennine Mountains. The town was laid out along the main road, which followed a mountain river. At the western edge of the village, the road curved southwest to cross the river, which continued in a westerly direction.

Marie and her faithful companion reached the center of town, where Marie told Lila to stay. Marie opened the door and entered the store, which smelled old to her, like it always had. The shelves lining the walls were empty. She sometimes tried to imagine them being full with many choices of things she didn't remember having.

"Hello? Mr. Gavino?"

"Hello, *Signorina* Marie." Gavino's eyes lit up at the sight of the sweet Marie. A small girl with long raven black hair and dark eyes, she so reminded him of his own daughter, now married and living Rome. Somehow, she had managed to survive the German occupation as had her husband, an older man, exempt from that idiot Mussolini's army. When they'd first married, having a son-in-law only ten years his younger was maddening, but when the war came he was glad of his daughter's choice.

Gavino, at seventy years old, was an active man with surprising strength. He had gray hair combed straight back, although some of it stuck out in thin wisps. He bent down and pulled three objects from underneath the heavy wooden counter. He laid them on top and pushed them toward Marie, who gave a huge smile and her eyes brightened.

"Three! We can have potato soup now!"

"You can make wonderful soup with your mother, no?"

"Yes!" She ran around the counter to give Gavino a hug. He wrapped his arms around her and squeezed.

She stepped back and looked up at his kind face. She opened a small coin purse she'd carried in a dress pocket and asked, "How much, Mr. Gavino?"

Gavino smiled broadly. "We'll take care of that some other time." He always said the same thing.

"Thank you."

Marie gathered up the potatoes in her small hands.

Gavino walked her to the door and opened it. She ran out onto the road and immediately began skipping. Lila ran alongside her favorite human.

The shopkeeper watched her until she disappeared from view.

Such a happy child, he thought. Then his smile disappeared.

A single tear overflowed and ran down his cheek.

RONN MUNSTERMAN

Chapter 4

Colonel Kenton's Office – Camp Barton Stacey
2 miles northeast of Andover, England
2 August, 1200 Hours

The same group met at the expected time, plus Sergeant Dave Cross, Dunn's second in command. They had worked together back at the barracks throwing ideas out there until some started to stick.

Dunn carefully explained the plan. Kenton and Adams asked a few clarification questions, which Dunn answered smoothly.

"I'm planning on an evening jump, the location to be updated if we get any new intelligence in Corsica. It's going to be weird jumping in near daylight."

The two civilians, Finch and Lawson, chuckled, perhaps nervously.

"We do have a sticking point," Dunn said.

"What's that?" asked Kenton.

"We may need to contact partisans once we're on the ground, but they might not speak any English. We need a translator, just in case."

This brought a moment of gloom as everyone thought about the untold numbers of Italian partisans killed trying to save their own country from the Nazis.

Dunn continued, "I double-checked and Bob Schneider can speak French and German, but not Italian."

Corporal Schneider had joined the squad at Dunn's request after he'd learned from Operation Devil's Fire that he needed a translator. It had proven extremely valuable, especially when Schneider had been able to read some top secret documents that Dunn and squad had stolen from a German headquarters in La Havre, France. Which, of course, they'd then promptly blown up.

Kenton nodded, then said, "I planned ahead, I have someone in mind. He's on Andy Bagley's squad. I talked to Bagley and he's been made available. Al Martelli. A Bronx kid. Sharp."

"Thank you, sir. I'll check in with Bagley and make the arrangements. Do we need to make a temporary trade?"

Kenton shook his head. "Take him as an extra. Bagley and his men are on some post-mission downtime."

Dunn raised an eyebrow. If Bagley's men were recuperating, Martelli might not be thrilled to go back out. Well, too bad. He was needed.

"Yes, sir."

"Anything else you need?"

"No, sir. We'll get our gear ready tonight, by 2300 hours."

Kenton stood up and stuck a hand out to Dunn. "Good luck, Tom."

Dunn rose and shook hands. "Thank you, sir."

The sergeants saluted and Kenton returned them.

A few minutes later, Dunn and Cross were outside walking back to the barracks. The two men, Rangers and best friends—Cross had been best man at Dunn's wedding—walked in silence.

Cross finally spoke first, "Hard to believe you just got married a few days ago. How'd Pamela take the news of a mission?"

"Pretty well. She understands. Although she kept telling me to be careful on the drive back."

"Wise woman."

The men glanced at each other and shrugged. They knew they'd do their best, but plenty of men giving their best never came home. It could happen to them, too.

They reached their own barracks and Cross peeled off to head inside. Dunn walked on down to Bagley's barracks, which were the third one down. Clouds had moved in during the morning hours and it started to rain, a slow drizzle. Dunn sped up and got to the door just as the rain began falling harder.

Bagley was standing just inside the door putting a piece of paper up on a cork bulletin board.

"Hey, Andy," Dunn said.

Bagley turned to face Dunn and smiled. "Hi, Tom."

The men shook hands.

Bagley was twenty-four, the same age as Dunn, but much shorter. His face was wide, as was the rest of him. A former high school wrestler, the cartilage in both his ears was mashed and misshapen, and his nose was permanently bent in two directions.

"You here for Martelli?"

"I am. The colonel said he'd talked to you already."

"He did. When I told Martelli he was going to Italy he about jumped sky high."

"Bronx Italian kid, right?"

"Yes. Parents own a deli and live upstairs. They came over just before he was born, I think. He's our age and a hell of soldier."

"Good to hear."

"Sure you don't need us along?"

"No, I hear you're doing post-mission wind down."

"Best of luck, buddy." Bagley smiled, then said, "Let me introduce you." Turning to face the open room, he called out, "Martelli!"

A young man with black, swept back hair, who had been lying on the bunk with his hands folded behind his head, jumped to his feet. "Coming, Sarge."

Martelli loped to the front of the large room and stopped just short of the two sergeants.

"Martelli, meet Sergeant Dunn. Dunn, Martelli."

The men shook hands and eyed each other for a moment.

"Pleased to meet you, Martelli."

"You, too, Sergeant Dunn."

"I hear you're excited to go with us to Italy."

Martelli's face lit up. "I sure am!"

"Where's your family from originally?"

"Oh, it's just a small place no one's heard of; Sant'anna Avagnina."

"Hm, sure, that's right by Mondovi."

Martelli's expression turned to one of wonderment. "How could you possibly know that?"

Bagley answered for Dunn, "He's a sergeant, Martelli, he knows everything."

Dunn grinned. "I'll give away my secret when we walk back to my barracks. Grab your gear."

"Will do, Sergeant Dunn." Martelli ran off, shaking his head.

Bagley edged closer and asked, "How *did* you know?"

Dunn smiled. "Just reading the map of where we're going. Checking everything, you know, just in case."

"Huh. Yes, okay. But what are the odds his family would be from around where you're going?"

"Let's just say the colonel is very thorough while searching for a translator."

"Ah. Of course he is."

Dunn turned to leave, but stopped and asked, "Hey, Bags, have you seen Saunders today?"

"No. I heard he left for Corsica yesterday. Don't know anything else."

"Sure, okay. Thanks." Dunn would have liked to say hello to his British Commando friend, Malcolm Saunders, but it would have to wait until they all got back to Barton Stacey after their respective missions.

Chapter 5

The Hardwicke Farm
5 miles south of Andover, England
2 August, 1850 Hours

Dunn kissed Pamela. Drawing back, he stared into his wife's blue eyes. She hadn't cried at the news, but her eyes were wet. To be honest, so were his. All the way to her parents' house south of Andover, he'd had one recurring thought: married for only four days and he had to ship out.

They were sitting in her parents' living room, on a sofa that had seen better days, but which was still comfortable. Across the room was an upright piano. To their left was the window looking out onto the barnyard. Her parents had discreetly gone for a walk while their daughter, their only surviving child, had to say farewell to her new husband.

Pamela touched Dunn's right cheek and he closed his eyes at the cool caress.

"I'm glad we stayed home, instead of going to the Star & Garter," she said.

"Yeah, me too. Don't think I could have faced another boiled chicken dinner. Your mom's lamb stew was outstanding."

"You do realize I can't cook as well as she does?"

"I doubt we'll starve."

"Hmm. Time will tell. I'll do what I can to learn more than making tea."

"Sounds like a good plan. Of course, I have simple tastes. Meat and tators are my favorite."

"Yes, you are simple," Pamela said. Then she shrieked as he dug his fingers into her side and tickled.

Laughing together felt so good to Dunn. Just being with her made him feel alive.

He'd sent his family some snapshots taken after the wedding, but it was too soon to hear back from them. His last letter from them contained a twenty dollar bill and a homemade wedding card—by his younger sister, Gertrude—and a note to have dinner somewhere. The letter said Gertrude was doing well and had decided to go to work at the Rock Island Arsenal near Davenport, Iowa. Their parents had misgivings about her being so far away, almost ninety miles, but she was eighteen and needed to make up her own mind. Other news was that the eldest sister, Hazel, had finally gotten a letter from her husband, a sailor in the Pacific, saying he was fine, he missed her, and loved her, but not much else, since he couldn't say where he was.

Dunn leaned back, draping an arm over Pamela's shoulder and drew her near. He closed his eyes. Pamela rested her right hand on his chest, content to feeling his chest rise and fall.

"What are you thinking about?" she asked, after a few minutes.

"Baseball and hot dogs."

"Sounds like an American thing."

"Oh, for sure. Summer, baseball, hot dogs. Yep, I'm sorely missing all that. The Cubs are probably playing a game right now."

"Do you think they'll win?"

"Not really. They usually win less than half their games. Finished in fourth place last year, out of eight teams. But there's nothing like a game at Wrigley Field. It has brick walls in the outfield that are covered by ivy. Beautiful park. Named after the gum family."

"So you've been there?"

"One game every summer. Whole family. I guess you'd say we're baseball nuts. Nothing like a baseball park hot dog and Cracker Jacks."

"Cracker Jacks?"

"Carmel popcorn with some peanuts thrown in and a surprise toy."

"Sounds good."

"It is." Dunn placed his hand under Pamela's chin and lifted it for a kiss. Afterward, he said, "I'd love to take you to a game at Wrigley."

"Well, then, I'd love to go."

"Good. You'd like Chicago."

"Would I?"

"Lake Michigan is so beautiful. The water is more green than blue. And the beaches are great."

"Is that some place you'd like us to live?"

Dunn didn't say anything for a moment. In all of their conversations, they hadn't talked about any details of where they would live after the war.

"You're still okay with moving to the States?"

"Of course, silly. That's not even a question."

"Huh. Okay. I haven't thought about Chicago. Maybe. Although it is huge. Over three million people. There's a lot to be said for a smaller city like Cedar Rapids."

"I imagine so. Where else could we go visit? Can we see the Grand Canyon?"

"Yes, we sure can, although that's quite a road trip."

They talked about other places to see in the United States and when conversation dwindled, kissed some more.

Dunn pulled back at last and brought his left wrist up to his eyes to check the time. "Damn it. I have to go."

"Must you?"

"Yes. I'm sorry. We have to pack our gear later tonight."

Pamela poked Dunn in the chest with a forefinger. "You come back to me, Mr. Dunn. That's an order."

"Yes, Ma'am."

They got up and said farewell at the front door with another long kiss. Then Dunn was out the door. He said his goodbyes to Pamela's parents, getting a hug from her mom and a handshake from the dad.

As Dunn climbed into his jeep, he looked at his wife in the doorway, and waved. She raised a hand, then turned away and shut the door. Dunn knew she was crying. And damn if he didn't feel like doing the same.

Chapter 6

Landing zone
1/4 mile Northwest of Cà di Landino, Italy
2 August, 2230 Hours, Rome time

Sergeants Malcolm Saunders and Steve Barltrop knelt close to each other, while the rest of the squad of Commandos formed a kneeling semi-circle around them. After counting heads right after landing and getting the right number of ten, including himself, Saunders had sent a couple of men to round up the two paracrates that had been dropped with them. The flight from Corsica had been mercifully short, especially compared to the one from England, which had lasted eight hours.

Saunders, the squad leader, was a Londoner, although he called himself a Cockney as a point of pride. A six-footer, Saunders was heavily muscled, yet moved with the fluid grace of an athlete. Under the Brodie helmet, Saunders' noggin was covered by thick red hair, as was his upper lip where a handlebar moustache rested.

He'd been a commando since the year before when he, Barltrop, and some of the current squad members were first trained at Achnacarry House in Scotland. They happened to be there at the same time as Dunn and his squad. Saunders had made it his life's ambition to torment Dunn and the rest of the Americans while there. He'd been remarkably successful.

He and Dunn were forced to work together on a mission to Calais, France, and ended up being, to their surprise, good friends, and capable of working extremely well together. While Dunn reported to Colonel Kenton, who Saunders thought was a fair-minded officer, Saunders had the misfortune of being under the command of Colonel Rupert Jenkins. Jenkins' biggest problem, as far as Saunders could tell, was that he just didn't like anyone, maybe not even himself. But like family, you couldn't choose your leaders, and had to live with them.

The metal paracrates, each one supported by two tires, were sitting a few yards away from the men. The things looked more like a corrugated tin trash can on its side with wheels, than anything fancy. This was the first time the men had dropped with these types of containers and they were understandably concerned about the seven hundred fifty pounds of plastic explosives packed in fifty pound satchels and cocooned within the shock absorbing paracrates. It was one thing to understand intellectually that the explosives wouldn't go off without an electrical charge by way of a detonator, and quite another to hit the ground hard five yards from a bomb that had been falling alongside oneself, relatively speaking, of course. Nothing had happened, and everyone was grateful for that without saying it out loud.

The total of fifteen hundred pounds was supposed to be enough. The combat engineer who had worked with them assured them that it was more than enough to knock out a main bridge support. He had given them exact instructions on where to place each fifty pound satchel, and what to do if they lost some of the explosives.

"Glad to see everyone is in good shape," Saunders said. He glanced at his men, individually making eye contact, and they each nodded in turn.

Geoffrey Kopp and James Pickering had joined the squad to fill the empty slots left behind when Casey Padgett and Wesley Merriweather had been killed. The two men had been setting charges in buildings along the Wilhelmshaven submarine dock, when bad luck had struck them. By chance, a German had stepped out of the barracks at that moment and spotted the British soldiers. Although they'd killed him, a second German right behind him had shot and killed Padgett. Merriweather died when a charge he'd just placed by the building went off while he was trying to carry Padgett's body away. It sent a piece of a window frame through his back, dead center.

Kopp was a true Cockney, like Saunders, but there the similarity ended. Kopp was thin, topping out at a hundred forty pounds. Pickering had an easy smile and a round pleasant face that made people want to be around him. The remaining men had been with Saunders and Barltrop since commando training. Neville Owens was the resident expert on demolitions. William Endicott was from Liverpool, George Mills from Manchester, and Edward Redington's father was a pastor. Tim Chadwick had boating skills learned from his father, who like Cross's dad was a fisherman. Christopher Dickinson was the card shark and magician of the group.

Barltrop was Saunders' right-hand man and best friend. When Saunders' girlfriend, Sadie—who was now his fiancée—had been almost killed by a buzz bomb in London, Barltrop had made sure Saunders made it to the hospital in one piece. He'd literally forced Saunders to allow him to do the driving in spite of Saunders' anger. Barltrop had known it was the fear talking.

The cooling night air held a southerly breeze that seemed to carry animal sounds from across the various peaks and valleys: cattle lowing, a dog barking, birds chattering. No human sounds were present, most of whom must surely have been indoors while it was dark.

From the intelligence they'd received during their briefing the day before, Saunders knew there was little German activity other than men and equipment moving toward the front miles to the south. The rail line they were planning to disrupt ran through Bologna and acted as a major supply artery direct from Germany.

Saunders had a map spread out on the ground and he examined it in the light of a nearly full moon. He had the area memorized and on the way down from the aircraft, he'd been able to find the three sleeping villages that formed a right triangle, with Cà di Landino at the point where the two perpendicular lines met at the bottom. The landing zone was along the longer vertical line going northwest toward Castiglione dei Pepoli, and was made up of several fairly large fields that formed an overall square measuring five hundred yards each way.

They were on the downside of a moderate slope that led to Cà di Landino. Going southwest lay a valley two miles long that opened up at La Storaia, a town twice the size of Cà di Landino, which only meant that instead of being two-tenths of a mile long, it was four-tenths. Following the steep contours of the valley, each town was only one-tenth of a mile wide.

The single-track rail line naturally followed the bottom of the valley, which rose about three hundred feet over the two miles. The target bridge was a quarter-mile from Cà di Landino.

"Anyone lose any equipment or weapons?" asked Saunders.

The weapons for the night were the 9mm Sten submachine guns. The weapons were longer than usual due to the attached suppressors. Night operations were so dependent on stealth, not carrying the suppressed version had seemed reckless to Saunders.

The men shook their heads.

"Let's get going. Pickering, Redington, you take one of the crates. Endicott, Owens, the other one. We'll see how we're doing half way and maybe switch off."

"Yes, Sarge," replied the four men. If they were unhappy at having to manhandle the seven hundred fifty pound rolling bomb, they showed nothing of it. They put the sling of their Sten submachine guns over their shoulders and moved in their assigned pairs to the paracrates. Each pair took up the simple handles, which were attached to a five-foot-long swiveling tow bar. With a collective grunt, they got the crates rolling. The rest of the squad led the way, weapons at the ready. Barltrop had point and Saunders walked right behind him.

As expected, the terrain was rough, but they were able to find a path through the woods. After fifteen minutes, Saunders reckoned they had made it about half way. He called a halt and went back to the men laboring with the crates.

He put a hand on Pickering's shoulder and asked the group, "You guys doing okay?"

"We are, Sarge."

"Good. It's downhill from here. You need to attach the safety ropes and turn the blasted things around."

"Yes, Sarge," replied Owens, who then started to do as directed.

Saunders turned away to return to his position behind his second-in-command Barltrop. He suddenly froze in mid step as a faint sound filtered through the forest trees, coming from the north. After a few more seconds, the source became clear. Trucks. Big ones and a lot of them.

"Down," he said, motioning with his hands. He grabbed the nearest commando, Chadwick, by the arm and pulled him along with him.

As the rest of the men got low to the ground, Saunders led Chadwick up the hill toward the paved road he'd seen on the map. They made their way carefully to a point just inside the tree line and knelt behind a clump of trees. They had a clear view of the road and the sounds were getting louder.

A few minutes more passed, then the first truck's grille appeared around a bend in the road to their right. The driver had the lights off, relying on the brilliant moonlight to guide him. As soon as the truck completed the curve and hit the west-bound straight away, the driver upshifted and the truck gained speed rapidly. Following about fifty yards behind, a second truck nosed around the bend.

Chapter 7

Ville di Murlo, Italy
2 August, 2245 Hours

Three men sat huddled together, as if trying to keep their words close, which they were. Knowledge of their conversation was restricted. If the Germans discovered them, they would die, as would their families as both punishment and example.

Umberto Gavino, the seventy-year-old shopkeeper, said, "We received word that Damiano's mission is set to go."

"How many Germans can we kill?" asked Renato Frontino. At twenty-seven, he was the youngest of the group and was a school teacher.

"The target may have up to fifty men."

"Reprisals are going to be horrific, Umberto," complained Antonio Pastore, the village druggist.

"Yes, I know." Gavino shrugged. "We have no choice, Antonio."

"But couldn't we pick smaller targets? Perhaps just a soldier here or there?"

"We must truly damage the Germans. If we can kill those fifty men, then the replacements will have to go there instead of the front line north of Rome."

"I agree," Frontino said. "The more we can hurt them the better."

"But at what cost?"

Frontino threw up his hands with an exasperated expression on his face. "Look, Antonio, what price have we already paid to the bastards?"

Frontino's voice began to rise and Gavino put a hand gently on the man's shoulder.

The younger man nodded and lowered his voice, "It will not stop until they are driven from Italy completely. Many Italians have died and will die, whether we do this or not. So let's do it and kill more of them."

"But what of Damiano's mother? What do we tell her if he's killed?" asked Pastore.

Gavino answered with his own question. "What of Carlotta's husband? She cries often. Marie has told me so. What do we tell her? Will her husband ever come home? We don't know. But there is no other way."

"Very well, Umberto," Pastore said. "Don't worry, I was just playing the devil's advocate. I vote 'yes.' "

Gavino nodded. He wasn't upset with Pastore. The operation's risk was enormous and someone had to make sure they were thinking things through fully. However, if Damiano didn't return, it was he, Gavino, who would have to tell an already grieving woman that her son was dead.

"I'll contact Turin right away."

Chapter 8

Saunders and Chadwick waited patiently, watching truck after truck drive past. Each one was the standard German six-wheeled canvas-topped vehicle. When the last one rolled away, a total of fifteen had gone by in the span of a few minutes. The only thing that mattered to Saunders was that they kept on moving. He listened for several more minutes until the last of the sounds disappeared into the night. It grated against everything he knew to allow the trucks to go on their merry way. However, staying on mission was critical, so the trucks lived.

After making his way back to the squad, Saunders stood with his hands on his hips. "Bloody hell. Look at that thing."

"That's a massive bugger," replied Barltrop.

The bridge in question spread out below them. The Italian construction engineers had clearly made the most of the situation they'd faced in building a two-hundred-foot-long bridge across what was not a valley at all, but a deep gorge. Constructed of stone, the bridge spanned the north-south gorge that probably dated back to the glacial age. The bridge was connected at each end to the natural rock and supporting the rest were three massive stone pillars designed in a typical Roman-style arch. The center pillar was the target.

According to the army engineer who'd worked with them, the fifteen hundred pounds of plastic explosives had to be wrapped around the pillar on a line that was one-fourth the way up from the bottom. The satchels would behave like shaped charges, directing nearly one hundred percent of the energy inward. This would shear off the pillar from its base, and the weight of the stones above would collapse the entire pillar, taking a one-hundred-foot span with it. Enough to make repair terribly difficult, if not impossible, for the Germans.

Saunders had questioned the man several times about the quantity. He didn't want to get there and after blowing the charges have the bridge still be standing.

The engineer had replied, "Remember, Sergeant, the fifteen hundred pounds of explosives you will have is much more powerful than an equivalent weight in a standard aerial bomb. About two and a half times more. If you set the charges properly, you'll be satisfied with the end result."

Saunders had seen no alternative but to accept the man at his word. But he still worried.

"Well, I see why the bombers couldn't take it out," Barltrop said. "That outcropping above the bridge on the other side must be a hundred meters thick. Be like bombing the submarine pens at Wilhelmshaven."

"Aye. I've never seen anything quite like that." Saunders turned to his men. "Okay lads, let's get down there and start working. Steve, take charge of that. I'm heading up top to scout it out." To Chadwick, he said, "You come with me."

Saunders and Chadwick headed north to make their way to the outcropping where the bridge started its journey across the gorge. The rest of the squad worked out how to get the paracrates down the remaining slope.

It still took about fifteen minutes to wind their way to the bottom of gorge. The brush around them was thick, sometimes as tall as their thighs, but enough open spaces were present to make it all the way down.

The four men who had played the part of mules were happy

to finally drop the handles of the paracrates and step away. Each pair, Pickering and Redington, and Endicott and Owens, set to work opening the crates. This took a few minutes, and they finished about the same time. When they lifted up the top half and laid it all the way open, men who worked with explosives all the time took an involuntary step back.

"Shite," muttered Pickering.

The men glanced at each other with sheepish expressions, and a few chuckles bubbled up. After that, they were fine and everyone set to work in removing the prepared satchels weighing fifty pounds each. In addition to the explosives, each paracrate contained a roll of wire to be used to wrap around the pillar and support the explosives. Several timers were included to provide extras.

Up above, Saunders, who had the lead, and Chadwick were almost to the top of the bridge. The ground was rough, mostly rocky, and Saunders had to pick his way carefully, using one hand to steady himself and one to carry his weapon. Chadwick followed Saunders' footsteps. The men moved silently.

Just before reaching the top, Saunders stopped and held out a hand, palm facing toward his partner. Chadwick stopped immediately. Saunders crept forward slowly, almost in a duck walk. He looked north in the direction opposite the bridge. Moonlight glinted off the rails as they disappeared in the distance and night.

Saunders swiveled his head and looked down the rails going over the bridge. His gaze carefully followed the tracks, searching for movement and any other tell-tale signs of a sentry. He didn't fully expect to find sentries guarding a bridge that seemed to be in the middle of nowhere, but if Allied intelligence had determined this bridge to be a strategic failure point for the Germans, so had they.

After Saunders signaled to Chadwick, the commandos stepped up onto the bridge. There was room on both sides for an extremely narrow walkway. It would be almost like walking the plank. Saunders motioned for Chadwick to take the east side. Once there, Chadwick started off across the bridge, Saunders keeping pace on the west side.

Chadwick glanced straight up and was amazed at the size of

the overhang pressing down over his head. It was at least thirty feet above him, but he felt like he was in a cave and needed to duck.

As Saunders walked along, continually checking ahead and behind, he came to admire the workmanship. He wasn't sure how old the bridge was, but he guessed it was built sometime in the 1880s or 90s. He'd always enjoyed looking at wonderful construction, and had considered it as a career, that is until 1939, when he'd joined the army after Germany invaded Poland. His favorite structure in London was the Houses of Parliament, simply because of its sheer size at first, then at its intricate detail when viewed up close and with an appreciative eye.

When he reached the midpoint of the bridge, he called out softly to Chadwick, "Hold up, mate. Going to check on the lads."

Chadwick nodded and turned around to face his sergeant. His head was in continual motion right and left to keep watch on things.

Saunders put a hand on the waist-high wall, and leaned over. Forty feet below, he could see movement as the men were rapidly stringing the fifty-pound satchels around the pillar at a height of about ten feet, using the paracrates as step ladders. Satisfied that they were making progress, he scanned the valley floor in all directions and found nothing to worry about.

Pulling back from the stone wall, he waved at Chadwick to join him. Chadwick jogged across and peered over.

"Blimey. Good thing we're not scared of heights."

"Aye."

The men stood for a moment, caught up in the view, then Saunders tapped Chadwick's arm.

"Back you go."

Chadwick walked back across the tracks and paused with a boot on one rail.

Saunders called out, "What's wrong?"

Chadwick didn't reply and Saunders was about to ask again when Chadwick knelt and put a hand on the rail.

"Sarge! The rail is vibrating. I think a train is coming."

"Oh bloody hell, you must be joking."

Chadwick shook his head.

Saunders looked south, but saw nothing. When he looked the

other way, what he saw nearly made his knees go weak. Coming up the grade from Cà di Landino, smoke pouring from its stack, was a train.

"Oh, sod it. Run," shouted Saunders, as he grabbed Chadwick by the arm and pushed him toward the south end of the bridge.

The men sprinted.

The train's sound grew louder.

Chapter 9

Somewhere in the Apennine Mountains, Italy
2 August, sometime after dark

Colonel Rogers woke up suddenly. He lay frozen, fear rising like ice through his chest. Had some noise awakened him? He found himself holding his breath as he listened intently, wondering whether the Germans had tracked him down. Maybe with dogs? He resumed breathing and minutes passed, but he heard nothing other than the wind blowing through the trees. He willed his muscles to relax, but fight or flight adrenaline was still coursing through his body. His arms felt shaky, as though he'd carried something too heavy too far.

Fear of being caught had forced him to find a place to hide for the majority of the day. He had found a pine tree with branches touching the ground and crawled in underneath the thick, welcoming boughs.

Working his way out from under the tree, he stretched his muscles.

He wondered, rather worried, *how had he fallen asleep?* The last thing he remembered was sitting back against the pine tree's trunk to rest. Exhaustion must have set in. He raised his watch near his face, but it was too dark to read. Still deep in the woods, he could barely make out the shapes of the trees he knew were there. On top of that, he'd discovered during the afternoon that he didn't have a compass, having forgotten to retrieve it from Lieutenant Watson's body. He'd had to rely on the sun, and keep in mind that it wasn't stationary, to stay on a southerly path. At some point, he'd broken off a pine tree branch and stripped it to make a decent walking stick.

Knowing the nearly-full moon would be coming up eventually, he wondered whether to wait for it and eat or try to make his way. His stomach gave a great rumble and made his decision for him.

He pulled out a can of Spam and by feel got it open, no easy feat he discovered. He forced himself to eat slowly, but even then, the can was wiped clean in a few minutes. After washing down the Spam with a drink from the canteen he shoved everything back in his pack, including the empty can. He leaned against a tree, afraid to lie down for fear of falling asleep again. Now to wait for moonrise.

He chastised himself for the hundredth time for even taking the flight by asking, again, what the hell had he learned of value. Yes, he'd seen the German tanks, but perhaps what he hadn't seen was valuable, too: no troops preparing for mobilization or in transit toward the French coast. All of this was information he needed to get to headquarters on Corsica. But how?

As he pondered these difficulties, time passed and the moon rose over the eastern peaks and shone through the trees. Rising, Rogers looked at his watch: 2322 hours. He slipped the pack on, grabbed his walking stick, and headed in the direction of what he hoped was south. He walked slowly, placing his feet carefully to reduce noise.

Suddenly a whooshing, flapping noise startled him and he froze in mid-step. Not ten feet away, what he thought must have been an owl slammed its razor-sharp claws into something small on the ground. The owl didn't even break flight, grabbing the meal off the ground the way an infielder fluidly scoops up a groundball. As it flapped away, it screeched a victory yell.

Rogers let out a little laugh, shaking his head at his fright. He took a couple of steps and suddenly realized he'd been wandering around the Italian countryside, the Nazi occupied countryside, with his weapon still in its holster. He undid the flap on the holster and drew the weapon. He debated flipping off the safety. He was sure he'd chambered a round sometime shortly after he and Watson had left the flaming aircraft. He finally decided to leave the safety on because he reasoned he'd be far more likely to shoot himself the next time he was surprised. Carrying the .45 in his right hand and the stick in the other, he started off again.

He checked the moon's position every few minutes and was surprised by how quickly it seemed to be shooting to the top of the sky. He checked his watch, now easily visible. He could hardly believe how much time had already passed. He was breathing hard and his legs felt wooden.

After crossing a clearing of about fifty yards wide, he stopped to rest and take a drink, sitting on a large stone. While screwing the canteen's cap back on, he heard a muffled sound somewhere behind him. He quietly slid off the rock and knelt beside it, watching to the north.

He waited several minutes, but saw nothing moving and heard nothing else. Perhaps he'd imagined it. Finally, he decided to move ahead. Soon, the moon was directly overhead. He reached the peak, but didn't pause to congratulate himself. He stared off to the south and was dismayed. There was yet another valley and beyond it more peaks. He must have miscounted when examining the map earlier. How could he have made a mistake like that that? His body was demanding a rest already and desperation was setting in. He wanted to give up and just lie down. He almost knelt, but at the last moment realized if he did, he wouldn't get up again.

He leaned against an outcropping and examined the valley in the moonlight. A small river snaked through the low area, winding alongside a town, before heading off to the west.

Feeling marginally rested he took a deep breath, and moved forward. At least it was downhill, he thought. He walked carefully; the surface seemed loose underfoot.

The bullet struck a rock next to his left foot, whining as it ricocheted off into the dark night. A split second later, the shot's sound came from behind him.

Instead of wasting time turning around to see where the shooter was, Rogers dropped his walking stick and raced down the hill, zigzagging his way.

Another shot flew by his head, its supersonic wake snapping, making him involuntarily duck.

Sounds of boots striking the earth came to him, but he couldn't tell how many were in pursuit.

The tree line was ahead, perhaps fifty yards. If he could just make it.

More shots pierced the air near him. It seemed as though there were three or four shooters.

Twenty yards to the trees.

A soundless hammer struck his left hand. It burned. The pain traveled up his arm, then the arm and hand went numb.

Rogers stumbled and nearly fell to his knees, but just in time, caught his balance. He zagged once more and sprinted into the cover of the trees. In spite of the shock his system was suffering from the bullet wound, his head was clear and so was his thinking. He stopped behind the second pine tree he passed and knelt. He raised the Colt .45, switched off the safety, and sighted down the barrel into the open area. At the top of the clearing, he made out four shapes walking fast in line abreast about five yards apart. They were still a good seventy-five yards away, too far for the Colt to be effective.

He pulled back and took a moment to look at his hand. The hole was between his thumb and forefinger, through the webbing. It was bleeding heavily. He quickly safed and holstered the .45, then yanked a handkerchief from his back pocket. He wrapped his hand and tied it in place, using his teeth to help tighten it. He groaned from the pain, which burst up his arm again.

Pulling the Colt back out, he then rubbed the back of his left hand in the dirt to darken the white handkerchief. He edged to the side of the tree. The men were now about fifty yards out, rifles at their hips, pointed in his general direction, though Rogers was sure they couldn't actually see him yet. The problem with firing at them was going to be the muzzle flash, which would be a beacon to his position. A memory of a western where the good guy shoots at the bad ones with two Colt .45 revolvers came into his head. He doubted he could do that even if his left hand didn't have a hole in it.

When the men reached the thirty yard mark, Rogers raised the Colt, flipped off the safety, and aimed at the man on his right. He remembered to squeeze the trigger and was slightly surprised when the gun went off. He immediately sighted on the second man from the right. In his peripheral vision, he saw that the first man dropped straight down. Firing a second time, he was thrilled when that man also collapsed. The remaining two Germans dove to the ground for cover.

Time to move.

Rogers backed away from the tree in a straight line. Two rounds thudded into the opposite side of the tree. He pivoted to his left and ran several yards to take up station kneeling behind another tree. More enemy rounds hit the area where he'd been.

He peeked around the side of the tree. The Germans were up and running at an angle away from him obviously trying to get to the trees for cover. Deciding that giving away his position was worse than was the possibility of hitting a man running at full speed, he refrained from shooting.

He forgot and put his left hand on the tree to help himself stand up and pain shrieked through his hand. He dropped back to his knees, sucking his breath through clenched teeth. He couldn't say it out loud, but he was thinking *fuck, fuck, fuck*. He raised his hand above his heart and the pain subsided slightly. Then he felt blood running down his wrist and he wondered when the blood loss would become a problem.

He could hear the men moving through the forest as they had obviously given up on any thought of stealth. They seemed to be attempting to circle around behind him, forcing him back out into the open ground.

Rising to a crouch, he moved off deeper into the forest to the southwest. Every ten yards or so he stopped to listen, but heard nothing. He was either too far away or the soldiers had reverted to their training and were treading more carefully.

After about five more minutes, Rogers found himself on the edge of another clearing, much smaller than the first one, perhaps only twenty yards across. Where were the damn Germans? He strained to listen, but still nothing. Knowing he'd have to circumvent the open space, he chose the west side to put the clearing between him and, he hoped, the Germans. As he maneuvered around to the southwest staying about two yards inside the trees, he took another look at the clearing and spotted a dark opening off to his left. He stepped closer to the edge of the clearing and took up a position behind a tree. The opening was under a small outcropping, which he figured must have blended in with the rest of the down slope making the opening invisible from the upper side.

It was about five yards away and closer to the west side of the clearing. Rogers debated whether to continue running through forest or to stand and fight. Neither seemed appealing. Running could increase the chances of being run down and shot, and killed, or captured. Then there was the wound and blood loss. He would eventually weaken and slow down. Holing up might help him evade the soldiers. Perhaps they would continue on down the mountainside. Then he could at least do more effective first aid by stuffing the wound with medicine and bandaging it better.

His decision made, he got down on his belly, the backpack weighing him down, and started crawling toward the opening. It was slow going, especially since it was uphill, but he didn't stop until he made it to the dark hole. It was about four feet high and perhaps twice that in width. Not until he'd crawled part way through the opening did he wonder about wild animals seeking refuge, too. Were there bears here in the Apennine Mountains? Or vipers? He didn't know. Too late, he decided, and kept on going until he was inside. The cave's dirt floor was smooth and cool to the touch. A few loose stones peppered the ground.

Getting to his knees, he crawled on all fours back to the edge of the opening. The clearing seemed exceedingly bright to his eyes, which had dilated fully in the cave. Nothing moved except the tree branches in the light summer breeze.

Still on his knees, he leaned against the cool rock on his left. He ejected the partially spent magazine from his Colt, keeping one round in the chamber, and reloaded the weapon. Now he had eight rounds.

His hand throbbed, sapping his energy. Time passed and he began to have trouble concentrating as his mind wandered to thoughts of family and home. He felt like he should slap himself to stay alert. The sound of footfalls finally reached his ears. They were coming, as he expected from his left. He focused intently on the trees fifteen yards to the east. Another sound. Unintelligible whispers. Were they giving up and going back? Roger's heart raced and his nostrils widened, all in preparation of fight or flight, although there was nowhere to run. He turned his head left and right trying to pinpoint the location.

There. Movement.

Two shadows separated from the trees. The men were just inside the tree line at the edge of the clearing. He suddenly realized that if he just sat quietly in the cave they would go around just like he had. He also understood that he couldn't simply let them leave. If he did, they would be between himself and the coast, and he wouldn't know where they were.

The men were to his southeast, less than twenty yards away. While struggling to come up with an idea, he shifted his position, and his right boot clunked into something.

Chapter 10

3/4 mile southwest of Cà di Landino, Italy
2 August, 2341 Hours

The train roared onto the bridge at thirty miles an hour. Covering forty-four feet per second, it would take four and a half seconds to reach the far end.

Chadwick was the faster runner and was pulling away from his sergeant. Still twenty yards away from the bridge's end, the commandos were running for their lives unaware they were fighting physics; distance as a function of speed and time.

The bridge shook under the weight and motion of the thundering train.

Saunders' boots felt heavier than usual, but he kept pumping his legs. Chadwick looked over his shoulder and realized Saunders had fallen behind. He stutter stepped, as if about to stop and help Saunders.

Over the growl of the train, Saunders yelled, "Don't stop. Get your arse off the bridge!"

Chadwick regained his pace.

The train's bright headlight suddenly came on and illuminated the British soldiers. Neither man looked back. They could almost feel the front of the engine crushing their backs.

Saunders saw Chadwick reach the end of the bridge and dive off to the right. It was getting harder to stay on his feet as the bridge's shaking got worse.

Two more steps.

A train whistle pierced the night air.

Saunders dove.

The train's front edge flew past his rear foot, missing it by inches.

Saunders' world turned topsy-turvy as he rolled and tumbled down the slope, his arms and legs flailing. After what seemed liked hours, he finally slid to a stop on his back. He lay there for a moment, his head lower than his legs, and his right shoulder wedged tight into some sort of barbed shrub.

Above, the train rumbled past.

When Saunders extracted himself from the shrub's grip, he discovered it had sliced his neck and cheek. Getting to knees, he called out, "Chadwick? Where are you?"

From somewhere to the south Chadwick replied, "This way, Sarge."

Standing up, Saunders asked, "You okay?"

"I think so. You?"

"Met a nasty bush. Might need a bandage."

"I'm coming your way." Chadwick's voice was already closer.

Suddenly, from above them and to the south, came the squealing sounds of the train's brakes.

A moment later, a rustling sound indicated Chadwick was quite close. Soon, he appeared to pop out of nowhere. He stepped closer and grabbed Saunders by the arm, turning his face more toward the moon. "You look a right mess."

"Thought as much."

"May need er, a few stitches there on your cheek. Otherwise, Sadie might change her mind."

"Smart arse."

Chadwick grinned. "You're bleeding quite a lot. Let me do something right here. Better sit down. Your neck is all right, just a bunch of scratches we can take care of later, but I'll put some gunk on it for now."

"Did you hear the train stopping?" asked Saunders.

"Yeah."

"We should get down below first."

"This'll just take a minute. You really need this."

"Hurry, then."

Saunders sat down, crisscrossing his legs. Miraculously, he still had his weapon in his hand. It had helped to have the extra long sling over his head and opposite shoulder. As he thought about it, he realized with a bit of belated worry that if his luck had been worse, the sling could have caught on something, a rock, a tree stump, and he'd probably have hanged himself with a broken neck.

"Here. Turn your head." Chadwick knelt and quickly opened his personal first aid kit. He first cleaned the cheek wound by pouring antiseptic powder on it. Then he pulled the skin together using two small strips of tape like a butterfly bandage. Next came the bandage itself, held on by two longer strips of tape. He daubed the blood off Saunders' neck and watched to see what would happen. A little more blood welled to the surface of the skin, but didn't drip. Chadwick applied some of the gunk, a medicinal salve, on it. The bandage could wait.

"You're good for now. Let's get back down there. We can check on the boys' work. Yeah?"

"Right, then." Saunders got his feet.

The train engine revved up and it started moving.

Saunders looked up the hill, but could see nothing. A moment later though, the sounds were coming closer and it was obvious the train was coming back. "Must be coming back to see if they hit us."

"Who?"

"The engineer. He just missed me, so maybe he thinks I'm lying up there near the track."

"Like a prize, then?"

"Summat like that, yeah. Let's go."

With a quick peek, Chadwick made sure his sergeant was steady. Satisfied, he started downhill at a careful pace. Every now and again, Chadwick glanced over his shoulder, clearly worried about Saunders.

After about the fourth time, Saunders growled, "I'm not a

young pup, Chadwick." Saunders got a chuckle in return and the big redheaded sergeant smiled to himself.

Eventually, they made it back to the rest of the squad. The charges were all in place and the men were inserting the detonators and hooking them into the wire that would pass the electrical charge from the timer.

Saunders found Barltrop directing the work.

When Barltrop looked at his sergeant, he raised an eyebrow. "What the bloody hell happened to you?"

"Mean bush attacked me."

Barltrop blinked and shook his head at Saunders' cavalier attitude. "Right. Well, we're nearly done. Timer is set for midnight."

"Good."

"We heard the train. What happened there?"

"Ah. Sort of had to run for our lives."

"Close?"

"Whisker for me. Too bloody slow these days. The train backed up. Must be looking for us."

Barltrop nodded and called up to the men working on the detonators, "A little more speed is in order, gentlemen."

"I'm doing the last one now, Sergeant Barltrop," replied Owens.

The rest of the men climbed back down and ran over to join the two sergeants. A minute later, Owens jumped down and did the same.

Saunders checked his watch. "Seven minutes. Grab your gear and weapons, and let's go."

The men gathered up their rucksacks and Sten guns, which had all been stacked carefully together.

"Pickering, take point," directed Saunders.

Pickering took off to the southwest to climb the same side of the valley they'd come down. The rest of the men followed, Saunders in the lead, with Barltrop next.

As they departed, Saunders looked up at the top of the bridge, but the angle was wrong and he couldn't see if the train was there. The engine sounds had stopped soon after he and Chadwick had reached the men. *Maybe it'll be on the bridge when the explosives go off,* he thought, hopefully. That would be something to see.

After five minutes of hard walking and climbing, Saunders called a halt. They were far enough away to be safe. He checked his watch. Two minutes. He could see the top of the bridge and was excited to see that at least two-thirds of the cars were strung out across the bridge. "Everyone down."

Once his men got into a prone position, Saunders did the same. He had his left wrist near his face and the watch was clear in the moonlight. One minute.

The second hand moved so slowly, Saunders thought for sure the watch had stopped, then it would tick over. Muttering to himself, he counted down, "Ten seconds . . . three, two, one."

The second hand swept past the twelve and it seemed to pick up speed. Thirty seconds. Forty-five. One minute past due. Nothing.

Chapter 11

Gestapo Headquarters
Turin, Italy
2 August, 2355 Hours

Hotel Nazionale was less than a mile west of the river Fiume Po, which ran roughly northeast to southwest through the heart of Turin. A grand old hotel, the Nazionale was made famous in the late 1890s through 1910 by the Western Europeans, especially the British, flocking to Turin in search of a beautiful holiday spot. Following the Great War, the hotel suffered a collapse of interest for a few years until the excesses of the 1920s drew people again. Raising prices and providing outstanding service had become the hotel's trademark and it worked. Things had gone exceedingly well until the war came.

The German forces arrived in mid-September, 1943, after Italy capitulated to the Allies. They needed to ensure the continuation of war production at the Italian factories. A week later, on the 21st, the Gestapo arrived under the leadership of Colonel Dieter Colbeck.

A tall, thin man, Colbeck face bore a weak chin with an overbite. Colbeck was also a member of the SS. His route to

Turin had started at the age of twenty-four in 1931, when he'd joined the Nazi party in his home town of Stuttgart. He'd become a fervent, fanatical believer soon after, and witnessed close at hand Hitler's meteoric rise to chancellor in 1933. By 1939, when the war broke out, Colbeck was already an SS captain working in the main Stuttgart Gestapo office. Promoted to major in 1941, Colbeck was assigned as an advisor to the Turin fascist police. Fluent in Italian, he'd provided excellent results and in 1943 was promoted again, to colonel, and awarded the new Gestapo command in Turin.

The Hotel Nazionale's opulent Grand Ballroom was now the colonel's office. Seated behind a massive oak desk, he took a last bite of his late dinner and wiped his lips with a cloth napkin. Pushing the plate aside he picked up his black phone. When the person on the other end answered on the first ring, the colonel gave a crisp order and hung up without waiting for a reply.

One of the doors leading to the kitchen opened and a round, middle-aged Italian burst into the ballroom. He quickly cleared everything from Colbeck's desk and left as fast as he'd come in. He said nothing. Talking to the head of the Gestapo was never a good idea.

A door opposite the kitchen and leading into the hotel's main lobby opened. A Waffen SS captain entered, followed by an Italian with his hands tied in front, and two SS sergeants who flanked the prisoner.

"*Heil* Hitler!" the approaching captain said, giving the stiff, raised-arm salute.

"*Heil* Hitler," replied Colbeck. He eyed the prisoner carefully. The man hung his head, his long, unkempt dark hair shielding his eyes from the German's scrutiny. He wore a once-white shirt and brown pants with suspenders.

"Is this the one?" asked Colbeck.

"Yes, sir. We found him with the explosives and timers. He had a hand-made drawing of the truck factory's floor plan."

In Italian, Colbeck asked, "What's your name?"

The man raised his head and looked at the German for the first time. "Damiano Agostini."

Colbeck was surprised when he saw Damiano's eyes. He'd expected to see terror in them. Instead, he found intelligence and calm. He seemed to be young, perhaps seventeen or eighteen. Just a bit too young to have been conscripted into the idiot blackshirt's army. Old enough to be dangerous.

"Do you admit to planning to plant explosives in the *Reich's* Italian truck factory?" Colbeck gave the man a stern look.

Damiano stared back, defiant and hatred rising in his own glare. "I admit nothing."

"Of course you don't." Colbeck waved at the guards to move the partisan out of earshot.

Colbeck turned his attention to the captain and asked in German, "How did you find this man?"

"We used a reliable collaborator who worked his way into the partisan group. It took months of patience, but it paid off." The captain smiled, pleased with himself.

"How did you find the collaborator?"

"We watched him for weeks. He worked at a cafe. We made note of all of his activities, learned that his mother was seriously ill and needed medicine, father killed in Africa, no other family. We offered medical help for his mother, which he gladly took. After that, we simply threatened to withdraw the drugs. We gave him specific instructions to follow, easy ones at first to see if he could pull them off.

"Next we arranged for him to receive some information by 'overhearing' a conversation at the cafe. He made contact with a partisan and then we gave him more information to pass on. It all went perfectly."

"No chance he was caught out by the partisans and turned?"

The captain looked surprised. "No, Colonel, no chance."

Colbeck waved the sergeants back. They marched Damiano back in front of the colonel.

Colbeck rose and walked around the desk to stand right in front of Damiano, his face inches away from the young man's.

In a soft voice, Colbeck said, "I'm going to have you tortured for days. Do you think you can stand up to it?" Before Damiano could answer, Colbeck answered his own question, "No one stands up to it. Every man has a breaking point. Then he tells me everything I want to know.

"After that, I'm going to have you shot. But not until I find every single one of your family members and kill them in front of you."

Colbeck expected this to frighten the Italian beyond words and he watched the young man's face closely. There was no change in expression. Wait, is that a smile, wondered Colbeck. Yes, it was.

With sudden rage, Colbeck slapped Damiano, then shouted, "What are smiling at, you worthless piece of shit?"

The force of the strike had turned Damiano's head. He slowly turned it back to face the Nazi. The small smile never left his lips.

At last he spoke in a voice terribly old for such a young body, "I have no family. You bastards already killed them. As for what I know, it's too late to help you."

Colbeck thought about this for a moment, then asked the captain, "The explosives. Where are they now?"

"I sent them to the armory by the river."

"They were disarmed?"

"Yes, sir, by my men right away."

Colbeck frowned, thinking. What had the boy just told him? A thought ran through his mind and he asked quickly, "How many men were with you?"

"We went in force. I had fifty men."

"Are they back in their quarters?"

The captain looked at his watch and replied, "I'm sure they are."

The building housing the men was right across the street, a former furniture store. The men all lived on the first floor.

Colbeck glanced at Damiano and got a definite boyish smirk in return.

A decoy! The boy was a damn decoy.

Pivoting, Colbeck grabbed the phone on his desk.

Damiano took a small sidestep, placing Colbeck between himself and the large window behind the Nazi's desk.

Just as Colbeck raised the phone to his ear, he was slammed backward into Damiano, who was ready for the blast, covering his face and head with his hands, still tied together. The partisan smoothly slid the short-barreled Walther PPK out of Colbeck's holster and flicked the safety off. He shot the two stunned sergeants in the face, the captain in the heart, then Colbeck in the center of the back. Five seconds had passed.

Still carrying the pistol, Damiano turned and ran to the ballroom door, where he stopped long enough to peer out into the lobby. Germans, office workers and guards, were running toward the hotel's front door, but none to the ballroom. Closing the door quietly, he turned and ran across the ballroom, then slowed down at the kitchen door. He went through the door at a walk. He spotted the round man who'd cleared the colonel's lunch. The man grinned widely and thumped his chest. Damiano stepped over to him quickly, laying the weapon on a work table. The man pulled a knife from a drawer and carefully cut away the ropes binding Damiano's hands. Damiano rubbed his wrists.

"All as planned, Damiano?"

"Yes." He picked up the pistol and said, "It paid off practicing with my hands tied. Thanks for suggesting it."

"You're welcome." The man patted the young man's shoulder.

Damiano smiled, then stuck the PPK in his belt under the once-white shirt.

"*Ciao*."

"*Ciao*, young one."

Damiano departed through a door leading to an alley. Making his way to the end of the alley, he strolled out into the dark Italian night. Time to head home to see his family, after first stopping to change his appearance and clothing. Home. He especially missed his beautiful, wonderful little sister, Marie.

He glanced over his shoulder at the flames roaring in the building housing the German soldiers. The boyish smirk returned as he walked away.

Chapter 12

3/4 mile southwest of Cà di Landino, Italy
3 August, 0001 Hours

Saunders turned toward Owens and asked, "You set a redundant timer?

"Yes, Sarge."

"Bloody hell." This was a demolition man's worse scenario. Live explosives tied to a faulty timer or detonator or both. Rare, but not impossible. He was wishing for a wired trigger, the kind where you pushed down a plunger to send the spark of electricity down the line. But they couldn't bring that in the space they had. Maybe he should have insisted on another paracrate. Nothing for it now, but to go back.

"Owens, you have the extras?"

"Yes, the timers and detonators."

"Come with me. The rest, follow behind, but stop at a hundred fifty yards out."

Saunders got up, feeling a bit woozy, which made him wonder if he'd concussed himself on the jump off the bridge. He shook it off and started to run. Owens joined him, running side-by-side with his sergeant.

When they were about fifty yards away from the center pillar, Saunders thought he saw movement under the bridge. He stuck his arm out to stop Owens. Coming to a halt, Saunders let his gaze roam around the base of the pillar. There. Three, four, six soldiers. Four attempting to take down the explosives. Two men had their rifles in their hands, standing guard, while the other four worked, their rifles nowhere to be seen, but which were presumably stacked nearby.

Saunders realized the obvious: they had disconnected the timers; they descended from the train while he and his men were climbing up the same side of the valley. They had passed each other in the night, literally.

Saunders appraised the situation. By getting closer, he and Owens could handle them. Signaling to Owens, they dropped prone and began crawling forward, heading for a five-foot-tall boulder to their right about five yards away.

It was slow going over the rough ground, but they made it and set up behind the boulder. Rising with his Sten gun ready, Saunders peeked over the rock. The Germans were still in about the same position. He tapped Owens, who was on his left, on the helmet. Owens stood up, also ready to fire.

Softly, Saunders said, "On three. One—"

The crack of multiple rifles firing shattered the night's silence. The sounds came from behind the pair of commandos.

Just as Saunders skipped the countdown and snapped, "Fire," the two German sentries dove for cover and the four men on the pillar jumped down and scattered, bending over as they ran to scoop up their weapons.

Saunders' and Owens' bullets struck empty space, thudding into the pillar and the rocky valley floor, spraying rock chips everywhere.

The sentries raised their heads and weapons, and fired. The commandos ducked and moved farther to the right.

Saunders glanced over his shoulder. He could hear the German Mausers going off, but they drowned out the sounds of the suppressed Sten guns. Knowing he could rely on Barltrop to lead the counterattack there, he returned his focus to the problem at hand. Two against six. Not the best odds now that surprise had disappeared.

He glanced around carefully, taking in everything. The ground between the enemy and himself was essentially bare. Saunders and Owens needed to separate to create an overlapping field of fire before the Germans moved. Directly to his right was the southernmost pillar. He eyed the distance, calculating. The bridge's shadow darkened the gap. Maybe.

He tapped Owens on the shoulder and pointed to himself, then at the pillar. He explained quickly what he wanted and got a nod in return. Saunders bolted, relying on the darkness to keep the enemy unaware. When he reached the south pillar, he ran around the back side and then moved along the pillar to take up a position at the northeast corner. He knelt and peered around the edge. Crouching behind several rocks were three Germans. Saunders could only make out their helmets and he didn't have a decent shot. Their attention was focused on the rock where he and Owens had been at first. Saunders raised his Sten and took aim.

He'd been doing a mental countdown, and when he reached the number of seconds he'd given Owens, the other commando's Sten gun erupted, the muzzle flash bright and twinkling.

The silhouettes rose and began firing.

Saunders fired a short burst. Bullets struck the rock in front of the men, spiting sparks into the night. He adjusted his aim and, before the Germans could react, raked them with 9mm rounds. They collapsed on themselves.

Saunders fired another burst at no one in particular, then reloaded. He was rewarded by twinkling muzzles and the cracks of Mausers off to his left, perhaps twenty-five yards away. The Germans were trying to flank the position Saunders and Owens had just abandoned.

Owens opened fire. Thuds sounded clearly in the distance and two enemy soldiers fell.

From a spot ten yards farther south, a lone muzzle flash. A bullet hit the valley floor at Saunders' feet and he dove head first back behind the pillar. Another round pinged off the pillar, the ricochet screaming away.

Owens fired a short burst.

Saunders looked out around the pillar's edge.

Another shot rang out from the Mauser toward Owens'

position.

Saunders fired just to the right of the muzzle flash. A grunt told him he'd hit the mark, and the last German fell dead.

To the south, intermittent rifle fire continued.

Saunders glanced in Owens' direction expecting to see his partner lean out from behind the boulder. Saunders gave a short whistle. No response. Getting worried now, he called out, "Neville? Answer me, Neville!"

Saunders burst into a full run. When he reached the boulder, he found Owens lying on his side. Saunders knelt and rolled his partner onto his back. "Neville?" he asked softly, knowing it was too late. The Mauser's round had pierced Owens' chest. "Oh, laddie."

Saunders folded Owens' hands on his chest and gently closed the man's eyes. Taking a deep breath, Saunders looked around for the satchel Owens had been carrying with the timers and detonators. He found it a few feet away, where Owens had put it before firing his weapon. Grabbing it, he ran toward the center pillar.

Once there, he circled it carefully and was relieved to see the charges still in place. The Germans had been removing the detonators before taking down the explosive satchels, the smart thing to do.

Behind him, the firefight seemed to be winding down; the volume of Mauser fire was dwindling. At least something good was happening.

Saunders rolled one of the empty paracrates over close to the pillar and, using it like a step stool, set about the daunting job of reinserting ten detonators and connecting the two timers.

Barltrop had immediately realized his goal was to prevent the Germans from gaining access to the base of the bridge. He divided his men into two groups of four, separated by about fifty yards, with his own group taking the lead and getting ahead of the Germans on the valley floor. Chadwick led the second group, maneuvering them up the slope in an attempt to flank the enemy, creating an L shape, with his team on the short leg and Barltrop's on the long one.

At first, the firefight was fierce with many rounds expended, creating a peculiar cacophony of the Mausers' sharp cracks and the suppressed Stens' chuffing. The opposing numbers seemed to be about equal, based on the muzzle flashes. The difficulty both sides encountered was the steep angle of the slope and the density of the trees.

Now the firing was intermittent as it became more difficult to find a worthy target. In front of Barltrop was a small open space surrounded by trees. The Germans were on the far side, trying to make a hole in the defense.

Barltrop slapped in a new magazine, activated the bolt, then fired at a shiny spot he thought was a helmet about twenty yards away up the hill from his position. Sparks flew when the round glanced off the helmet, which disappeared from view.

Firing seemed to dwindle to a stop for a moment, then resumed. Barltrop slid down behind a tree and glanced over at Redington a few yards away. Barltrop gave a low whistle and Redington looked his way. Barltrop grabbed a grenade and held it so the other man could see it. Then he held up three fingers and got a nod in return.

On the countdown, the two men pulled the pins, then threw the grenades in unison as hard as they could up the hill.

The blasts were blinding in the night, but the commandos had turned away making sure they were behind a tree looking away to preserve their night vision.

Barltrop peeked out from behind the tree. The grenades' smoke was swirling upwards. He fired a short burst and there was no return fire. He glanced toward the bridge wondering when Saunders and Owens would be back. Before they arrived, he wanted to clear the area of the remaining Germans.

Taking a moment to reassess the tactical situation, he realized that even though the Germans had the high ground, they couldn't advance because of the L-shaped defense. It would force them to turn their backs on Chadwick's men to move north. He thought about how he'd try to break the L and decided the German leader would want to get back up the hill, move west, and come down on Chadwick's right flank.

As he stared out at the German position, he realized he had read the German commander's mind because there were five soldiers making a break for a yet higher position, angling to get west of Chadwick.

Whistling sharply, Barltrop raced out from behind the tree, heading toward the retreating Germans.

Chapter 13

Somewhere in the Apennine Mountains, Italy
3 August, 0009 hours

Rogers grasped the stone his boot had kicked aside and picked a spot he estimated to be behind the two soldiers.

The stone, about the size of a large potato, flew through the air and crashed into the woods, bouncing off a tree before rolling through the brush. He was counting on their being spooked by his killing two already and was relieved when they started firing at the noise. Still on his knees, he raised the Colt and fired at the muzzle flashes until the magazine was empty. He heard two grunts and then the sound of bodies hitting the earth.

Jumping to his feet, he jammed the empty Colt into the holster and pulled Watson's from behind his back. He ran straight toward the point where he'd seen the muzzle flashes. Bursting into the woods, he immediately found the two soldiers lying in crumpled heaps on the ground, rifles near where they'd collapsed. He'd hit them both! More surprised than anything, he quickly checked them for a pulse. Finding none, he sat down abruptly feeling a strange elation, which he realized was a mix of relief and excitement. He'd taken on four German soldiers alone and had beaten them.

He calmed himself and the analytical part of his mind took over. He rolled the soldier nearest him onto his back and was momentarily shocked to see that the man's lower jaw was missing, shreds of bone and red stuff was all that remained. The next shock came when he tore his gaze from the gore. The man's bloody collar displayed the silver-on-black double-lightning S's. These weren't just German soldiers, they'd been Waffen SS. His next thought was what could he find? He began rummaging through the man's pockets, and found an identification wallet. He filed the name away in his mind: *Oberscharführer* Otto Nieman. There were a few bills of Italian currency in one pocket. He found nothing in the others. He quickly repeated the actions on the other dead man finding the same sort of things. He dropped everything on the ground.

Turned into a scavenger by necessity, Rogers took the men's canteens and added them to his pack, as well as a couple of tins of some kind of meat. Picking up one of the German Mausers, he also took the men's extra 8mm ammunition pouches. Slipping the rifle sling over his shoulder, he looked skyward to find the moon's position, again cursing his not having a compass. He checked his watch—0014 hours—and tried to guess where in the sky the moon would be at this time of the night to get his compass bearings. He was grateful it was almost a full moon, as it helped keep him from stumbling over everything.

He thought he was pretty sure which way was south, so he first sat down to reexamine his left hand. It hurt terribly, throbbing with each beat of his heart, which was still racing from the firefight. The dirt-covered, white bandage was soaked through in places that, in the moonlight, appeared as shiny black splotches. He didn't dare use a syrette of morphine, so he was going to have to buck up and bear it.

Rising, he suddenly felt lightheaded and wobbly. He immediately bent over at the waist, steadying himself with his right hand on a tree, and regained his balance. More slowly this time, he stood upright. All seemed okay, so he took a first step toward the south. He hoped he'd be able to find a village, and someone there unafraid enough to help him with his wound. And also be unafraid enough to connect him with some Italian partisans.

He managed to take two more steps before the world reeled and he collapsed, unconscious.

Chapter 14

3/4 mile south of Cà di Landino, Italy
3 August, 0014 Hours

Saunders set the second timer for three minutes and connected it; the backup timer, which he'd connected first, was set to five minutes. He checked his watch, then jumped down from the paracrate and ran over to Owens' body. Kneeling, he grabbed the dead man's hands and pulled them over his left shoulder. Rising and hoisting his mate, he adjusted Owens for better balance and took off at a jog. His Sten gun flapped against his right hip, hanging from its sling.

As he ran, all he could think about was that only a few weeks ago, he'd had to leave to Casey Padgett and Wesley Merriweather behind at the Wilhelmshaven submarine pens. If it was at all possible, he was going to get Neville back to friendly territory.

In the distance, Saunders noticed that the Germans were firing less frequently. He hoped it was a good sign and that Barltrop had met with success. When he was about two hundred yards from the explosives, he looked up to his left and was thrilled to see the same portion of the train still sitting on the bridge. Would it stay put?

Barltrop got his men in position, trailing the Germans by about twenty-five yards, spitting distance in a firefight.

Chadwick had spotted Barltrop on the move and had ordered his men to stop firing.

Barltrop waved everyone down and opened up with his Sten gun. His men joined in.

Chadwick and his men did, too.

In less than thirty seconds, the German attempt to flank Chadwick had turned into utter and complete failure as each one was gunned down in the murderous crossfire created by Barltrop's and Chadwick's men.

Saunders was close enough to hear the spitting sounds of the Sten guns, which were slightly to the left of his direction of travel. Taking a chance, he gave a low whistle as he changed his angle.

It became much more difficult to advance, but he struggled on. A few seconds later, he saw Barltrop heading his way. Above him, the train's engine started to whine and growl and the big drive wheels began to spin and shriek on the rails.

"Get the men out of here!" Saunders shouted.

Barltrop could plainly see Saunders with Owens over his shoulder. Barltrop gave a quick order to his men and they all took off at a sprint down and south from the bridge. Barltrop ran over to Saunders and when he got close, Saunders' tortured expression told him all he needed to know.

Barltrop swallowed hard, then said, "Let me spell you, Malcolm. You must be exhausted."

"I'm okay. Let's just get the bloody hell out of here before that bridge goes."

"Let me help." Barltrop held out a hand, but Saunders brushed it away.

"I . . . have him."

"Stubborn arse."

"Aye," muttered Saunders, as he got started again.

Barltrop turned and got his hand under Saunders' armpit and shoved, walking alongside his sergeant, bearing some of the weight.

"How much longer?" asked Barltrop.

"What time is it?"

Barltrop checked his watch. "Coming up on seventeen after."

"We need to get down."

Barltrop spotted a deep shadow a bit to their right and said, "Over there."

A car-sized boulder lay half buried in the ground.

The two men made their way there and got down, carefully putting Owens behind the rock. Ducking, they waited.

Saunders raised his head to see how far they were from the blast center and guessed it to be about five hundred yards. Should be okay, he thought. Then he said to Barltrop, "Better cover your ears and open your mouth."

Barltrop complied without a word as his sergeant did the same.

Two seconds passed.

The explosion was massive. Even though the charges had been somewhat shaped, when the concussion wave hit the two men's position, Saunders thought he might be suffocating. After the wave passed by, he could breathe again.

Both men rose and watched.

Smoke and debris were swirling in the air, but the pillar was still in place.

"Bloody hell!" Saunders' heart sank.

"Just a second, Sarge. Give it a moment."

Slowly, excruciatingly slowly, the pillar shifted downward, as if a giant hand had swiped out some of the stones. With a thundering crash it settled on itself, briefly doing a balancing act. The weight above pulverized the bottom ten feet of the pillar. A great plume of dust shot skyward.

The center of the bridge suddenly gave way.

Saunders and Barltrop both grinned in joy.

The last few cars of the train began falling, pulling the rest of the cars along with them as they went. The cars that had made it off the bridge, and the engine, teetered for a few seconds before sliding off the track.

The couplings snapped apart. The cars separated and began tumbling, some rolling over and others going ass over teakettle.

The sound was deafening; the shriek of metal and wood ripping apart created a beautiful symphony for Saunders.

While the two commandos watched the train crash down the hill, a terrific bone-jarring, cracking boom pierced the night.

Both men looked up at the overhang. The one that prevented the bombers from destroying the bridge.

Another crack.

With a roar, the entire overhang fell off the mountain and plunged its way down into the valley floor.

"Cor blimey!" shouted Barltrop, who was practically hopping up and down.

Saunders slapped his friend on the back and shouted, too.

Behind them, above the settling din, they could hear cheers from their squad mates.

Five minutes later, with Barltrop now carrying Owens' body, having forced Saunders to give in, the two men joined the rest of the squad.

When they got within ten yards, Saunders watched as each man's face fell from grinning at their success to shock. Chadwick and Pickering stepped forward and took Owens from Barltrop and laid him gently on the ground.

Saunders gave his men a moment, then said, "Lads, Neville was doing his job. Let's get him back."

This galvanized the men into motion. Chadwick picked up Owens and nodded at Saunders.

"Two miles, lads," Saunders said, as he started the trek to the landing site for their pickup.

Chapter 15

Camp Barton Stacey
2 August, 2330 hours, London time

Dunn spoke quietly to his men, "Italy. We're heading first to Corsica for staging and to await word on whether our missing colonel has been seen by anyone friendly."

Dunn and his men were in their barracks finishing their packing and weapons checks while Dunn talked.

The wooden barracks was just a big open room, with the compact armory and Dunn's private quarters at the rear.

Counting himself, Dunn's squad had ten men, plus Alphonso Martelli from Bagley's squad, who would be the Italian translator. Bob Schneider, Dunn's French and German translator, was closest to where Dunn was standing. A funny man with a hearty laugh, Schneider was a recent and valuable addition. As was David Jones from south Chicago. Jones was *the* sharpshooter in a bunch of sharpshooters and a natural, disciplined sniper. Patrick Ward had graduated from Yale and then promptly enlisted. The squad's Texan, Stanley Wickham, had developed a peculiar Brit-Tex accent, which drove the girls crazy.

Eugene Lindstrom was the western-most member, having grown up in his namesake Eugene, Oregon, the son of unimaginative parents or else they had quite a sense of humor. Eddie Fairbanks looked just like the actor, Douglas Fairbanks, Jr., including the moustache. Jack Hanson, a short, but tough man, had earned himself the nickname "Squeaky" due to his high-pitched voice. A farmer's son from northeast Kansas, Daniel Morris wanted nothing more than to return to work the land he loved.

Dunn's right-hand man, Dave Cross, had been with Dunn since North Africa. Cross was recovering from a gunshot through the left side. Fortunately, it had gone straight through and hadn't damaged anything Cross would need in the future.

The squad had returned from an adventure in France only thirteen days ago. They'd been there on a mission to assassinate General Erwin Rommel. Jones was supposed to have made the shot, but incredibly, a British Spitfire had strafed Rommel's staff car at exactly the same moment Jones was about to pull the trigger. They'd only just learned that Rommel had survived what appeared to be a fatal crash. Dunn was still kicking himself for not checking what he thought was a dead body.

Following up on top secret papers found at the crash site, previously owned by another passenger in the wrecked car, a definitely dead German scientist, Dunn and his men had traveled with the help of Georges, a member of the French Resistance, all the way into Vichy controlled territory. There, they destroyed a factory that was manufacturing an electromagnetic pulse bomb that would have changed the battlefield and given the Germans an advantage for the first time since the Allies had landed on D-Day. However, the bomb was already gone and Dunn and his men had to track it down at a nearby airfield. They destroyed both it and the aircraft that was to have dropped it.

The men would be carrying the Thompson .45 caliber submachine gun, which was everyone's preferred weapon. The Thompson fired 700 rounds per minute and its .45 ACP round had enormous stopping power. The weapon was named after its inventor, retired General John T. Thompson, who had always been interested in developing a machine gun that a soldier could carry. The beast weighed in at eleven pounds, but was worth every single ounce.

In addition to the Thompson, each man would carry a 1911 Colt .45, which also took the .45 ACP round. The third weapon they would take along was the combat knife, a long-bladed nasty-looking affair.

The men finished their packing and looked at Dunn.

Dunn carefully looked each man in the eyes and was satisfied with the strength and determination he saw reflected back to him. The squad saw a man they would give their life for.

"Once we get to Corsica and get you guys situated, Cross and I will meet with General Truscott, the missing colonel's commander, to get the latest intelligence.

"Welcome to the squad, Martelli. You'll be with me wherever we go. Understood?"

"Yes, Sergeant Dunn."

"You can call me 'Sarge' like everyone else."

"Yes, Sarge." Martelli gave a lopsided grin, happy to be included with this particular group. They were famous in the world of U.S. Army Rangers and stories were circulating about their adventures, some of it speculation, some it closer to the truth. It was known that Dunn had been shot during a mission a few months ago, captured and held prisoner by the Gestapo while in the hospital. Thanks to a sympathetic doctor and the French Resistance, Dunn had escaped to rejoin his men just as they were preparing to board a boat northeast of Calais.

"Sarge, do you want me to take my Springfield?" asked Jones, the sniper.

"This will be a standing order for you, Jones. Wherever you go, that rifle goes. Get it?"

"Got it."

"Good."

Dunn was pleased when the room erupted in laughter at the word play. It was a great sign of his men's state of mind. While they were focused on the job at hand, their minds were loose enough to take pleasure in the small things. Dunn had been around combat veterans long enough to know that while each man might fear dying, a perfectly normal thing, they were typically far more afraid of letting their buddies down.

"Any questions?"

No one said anything and a few shook their heads.

"Let's get a good night's rest. We load up at 0500 hours."

Chapter 16

2 miles south of Cà di Landino, Italy
3 August, 0157 Hours, Rome time

The lonely sound of a single aircraft drifted through the night to the men standing on a flat-topped ridge. Saunders struck a match, which flared briefly before settling into a steady, surprisingly bright light, then he lit a campfire-like stack of wood. The signal from Saunders was received at the far end of the half-mile long field by Endicott, who put a match to his own stack.

The men on the ground all looked up, but couldn't quite see the plane. Then it banked into a left turn, coming from the west. Moonlight glinted off the windscreen.

"I see it," Barltrop said, pointing.

Saunders tracked his eyes in the direction of Barltrop's arm. He nodded, mostly to himself, thinking, *almost there*.

The planning for this pickup had been dicey. The risks were high because they might be discovered before the plane could take off due to the fires. Since it was the only way out after the mission, other than slogging their way through enemy lines for many, many miles, the benefits far outweighed the risks as far as he was concerned.

The pickup had been prearranged for this time of the morning. A miss would be backed up by another flight exactly two hours later. After that, no more flights.

Saunders eyed the C-47 as it rolled back to the right to level out. It seemed to just hang in the air, then it slowly began to descend toward them.

A few minutes later, the aircraft was bouncing, then rolling toward Saunders and the men. In the distance, Endicott was running full speed to rejoin the group.

As soon as the pilot had turned the plane to be able to take off in the direction from which it had arrived, the plane stopped moving, but the engines were still running. Saunders and the men headed for the door, which popped open. The crewman got the stairs in place and waved his arms in a big pinwheel to hurry the commandos along. Barltrop and Redington handed Owens' body up to the men already in the plane, who then found a place to put the dead commando.

Saunders waited until Endicott arrived and helped shove him up the stairs, and into the plane. Saunders jumped on the steps and made his way inside. The American crewman pulled in the stairs, then he closed the door and locked it in place. The man looked forward where the copilot was staring intently in his direction. The crewman gave a thumbs up.

Only two minutes had passed.

The engines immediately revved up and the plane started rolling, picking up speed rapidly.

Saunders checked on his men, glad they were already snugged into place and found a spot next to Chadwick, where he sat down and buckled himself in.

A moment later, the plane shot skyward.

Saunders folded his hands in his lap and leaned back, even though he knew sleep wouldn't come. It would be a forty-five or so minute flight back to Corsica, and who knew whether they could make it safely over German territory.

He replayed the bridge's collapse, the train tumbling down, the overhang collapsing. A successful mission. A job well done. With acceptable losses. *Who the hell came up with that phrase?* he wondered. Certainly it had been some bloody bastard who'd never seen a man killed on the battlefield.

He glanced at his men, noting that none of them seemed to be sleeping. They were all staring either at their feet or the wall or black window across from them. No one made eye contact with anyone else.

It was hard, this losing three men in less than a month. He knew that troops on the line could lose that many in just a few minutes, perhaps seconds, of combat. Maybe they got used to it. But in a small unit whose role was in-and-out attacks, hours-long and sustained firefights were unusual.

The bond his men had was extraordinarily strong. Typically, combat veterans grew close together. However, replacements were never a part of that bond because at some point, combat veterans no longer wanted to get close to anyone new. They were going to get killed soon anyway, was the thought. The distancing routine included not even wanting to know their names. This was all a defensive protective act by the veterans. But in Saunders' case, his men all accepted, even embraced, the new men and he knew the same was true of his friend Dunn and his squad of Rangers. Perhaps it was due to knowing that the newcomers had gone through the exact same grueling training at commando school.

Saunders closed his eyes, but that only brought the image of Owens lying there on the ground, so he opened them and stared at his feet instead.

Saunders woke up suddenly, surprised he'd fallen asleep. He looked around quickly and noted that his men had done the same. Must be almost there. He started to unbuckle himself when the crewman who'd met them at the plane's door exited the cockpit. Saunders raised a hand and the man headed toward the commando.

The man leaned close, putting his left hand on Saunders to steady himself against the movement of the aircraft. "Hey, Sergeant, we're almost there. Be landing in a few minutes. You all okay?"

Saunders nodded.

The crewman leaned back and held out his hand to Saunders. "I'm Phillips, the radioman."

Saunders shook his hand, but didn't say anything, glancing away.

"I called ahead. We'll have a truck for you and your men. I thought you might need it to help with your . . . casualty."

Saunders turned his gaze back to Phillips and examined the radioman with a different perspective. Deep concern was etched on Phillips' face and this touched Saunders.

"What's your first name?"

"John."

"Well, John, thank you for your compassion."

Phillips nodded. "You're welcome. Okay, I'm going back up front. Just sit tight until I come back and give you all the all-clear sign. Okay?"

"Sure. See you soon."

Thirty minutes later, Saunders' men were settled in, four men in each of two tents. Saunders had made arrangements for Owens' burial in Corsica, which had been easier than he'd expected. The man he'd spoken with had been understanding, and vowed to personally see to it that the body was handled with respect.

Saunders elected to give his men the entire day to sleep and otherwise recover. They could fly home the next day, maybe the day after. For now, rest was more necessary than getting back to see what else Colonels Jenkins and Kenton might have up their sleeve.

Chapter 17

Hampstead Air Base
3 miles north of Andover, England
3 August, 0502 Hours, London time

Under the morning British sky, Dunn waited with his men for their transport to arrive.

Cross checked his watch, then said, "You guys ready for the longest, most boring flight of your useless lives?"

"I'm afraid of the landing, myself," Squeaky Hanson said, with a moan.

"Yeah, what's the point of flying if you can't jump out?" asked Schneider.

They heard the sounds of airplane engines and turned toward a C-47 Goonie Bird trundling its way along the tarmac. A ground crewman guided the pilot into the right place for the men to load.

"Let's get aboard, gentleman," Dunn said.

The men picked up their gear, slipped their weapons' slings over the shoulders, and headed toward the plane.

Ten minutes later, the plane was airborne, heading south. Its flight path would take it just west of the Cherbourg peninsula, and around the horn of Brittany over the Bay of Biscay. Just short of the Spanish border, it would turn east and fly almost on the tops of the Pyrenees mountain range, then for the last three hundred miles, across the Mediterranean Sea to Corsica.

Just as the C-47 crossed over the English shore, four P-51 Mustangs drew up alongside and waggled their wings. With their external tanks completely full, the famed fighters would be able to escort the Rangers' transport all the way to Corsica.

Chapter 18

Ville di Murlo, Italy
3 August, 0612 Hours, Rome time

The brightening morning light awoke Rogers. It took him a few minutes to determine where he was and had what had happened. His wounded hand screamed at him. Knowing he had at least one more set of mountain peaks to climb, he realized he had to get help. Soon. Maybe in the valley that stretched out below him. It ran east and west, and the sun was going to come up fully over a peak to his left. A small village sat nestled along a river to his southeast.

Two hours later, all Rogers could think was, *one foot after the other.* The light headedness had returned; he couldn't work out when that had happened. The last time he looked at his hand, the entire bandage was red and dripping like a worn faucet. The rifle and rucksack were gone, as were both of the .45s, lost somewhere on the stumbling, downhill journey that he couldn't quite recall.

Rogers was unable to calculate how far it was to the village from where he was standing, but he headed directly toward it, knowing it might be his only chance.

He crossed a field, and turned east. He had to work his way through a grove of trees. At last he stood on a road. Ahead lay some houses with the river flowing past on his right. Exhausted, he took a couple of more steps and collapsed on the road, landing on his left side.

Something wet and cold touched his face. Then something wet and warm. Struggling to open his eyes Rogers finally got one partially open. Four immense teeth were inches from his nose. A long tongue flicked out from between the teeth and licked his cheek again.

Rogers heard a sweet voice say, "Lila," followed by something in Italian.

Rogers knew he was in trouble when it seemed to him that the black and white dog licking his face had spoken to him. This worried him considerably. The voice spoke again from a slightly different direction.

"*Ciao?*"

Rogers rolled his head and looked up. A little girl was kneeling beside him. He raised his right hand toward her, and then passed out.

Marie shook the soldier, but he didn't wake up. There was a lot of blood. She was glad it didn't make her sick like some of her sillier friends. She pushed his shoulder again and was happy when he opened his eyes.

In her own language she said, "Wait here, I'll go get some help."

He must have understood, she thought, because he nodded and closed his eyes.

She rose and sprinted all the way home.

Ville di Murlo, Italy
3 August, 1122 hours

Marie sat on a chair beside the soldier as he lay sleeping on her bed. She now knew he was American and the bright silver bars on his shirt collar meant he was an officer, a captain, according to the doctor. Marie had stayed around the house in the hopes she could talk to this mysterious man who suddenly appeared in her village and had collapsed. He was a handsome man under the dirt her mother had washed away, with light hair and the beginnings of a beard and mustache.

She tried to imagine him living in America, but the only pictures she'd ever seen of that amazing country were from a place called Brooklyn sent home by a friend's uncle. In one, he was standing in front of a vegetable table outside his small store, smiling broadly. The pictures were all older than Marie.

Where was this captain from? She examined his hands, looking for a wedding ring, but there wasn't one on his right hand and the other was completely bandaged. She'd seen the hole in his hand for a fleeting moment before her mother shooed her out of the room. It had fascinated her.

Lila lay on the floor next to Marie, seemingly asleep, but she suddenly raised her head, perked her ears, and stared at the man. He took a deep breath and stirred slightly, as if trying to make himself more comfortable in the bed. Lila got up and made a move to lick his face, but Marie said, "No."

Lila snorted her displeasure at this, but did lie back down.

The man opened his eyes slowly, blinking a few times, and then looked around the room. Marie thought he was trying to work out where he was.

To be helpful she said, "Hi. My name's Marie."

The eyes, which a delighted Marie noted were brown like her own, turned toward her face.

A weak smile crossed the man's lips. He responded with a word that Marie took to be a greeting.

She touched her chest with a forefinger and said, "Marie."

Then she touched him on the chest and shrugged her shoulders.

He smiled again, this time showing his nice teeth. He touched his chest and said, "Frank."

Then he pointed at her without touching and said, "Marie."

Marie giggled and said, "*Buono.*"

Rogers frowned, clearly not understanding. Then he reached into his shirt pocket with his good hand and after unbuttoning it, pulled out a small book. He looked at Marie and gave a "come on" wave with the book.

She repeated the word.

Rogers tried to flip through the book, but it was too much of a challenge with one hand, so he struggled to sit up. Marie immediately helped by grabbing him behind the back and pushing him forward, then fluffing up the pillow against the headboard. He butt-walked toward the pillow and leaned back. Using his damaged hand's thumb, he was able to begin looking up the word in the English-Italian dictionary and useful phrases book. He found it and glanced up Marie.

"*Buono,*" he said. Good.

Marie squealed in delight and clapped her hands.

Rogers gave her a sheepish look, feeling like a schoolboy guessing the right answer.

He looked back at the book and found what he wanted. A phrase. He read it aloud and looked at Marie.

She nodded her understanding and said, "One moment."

Rather than waiting for him to look up that one, she took off at a run toward the kitchen.

While she was gone, Lila took advantage and first put one paw on the bed and when the human didn't say no, proceeded to climb slowly and carefully into bed with Rogers. The way he was positioned in the bed, his good hand was on the outer edge of the bed. Lila pushed her nose up under his hand and looked at him expectantly. He rewarded her with a rub of the head and behind the ears. She closed her eyes and sighed.

When Marie returned, she found them both apparently asleep, but Rogers' nose woke him up. He opened his eyes and his stomach flip-flopped at the smell of potato soup. His mouth started watering.

Marie told Lila to get down and after the dog jumped off the bed, Marie pulled her chair closer and sat down. She handed Rogers a spoon and held the bowl close for him. He fed himself without pause and when he'd eaten all but the remains of the creamy part of the soup, he handed the spoon to her. He grasped the bowl in one hand and drained the bowl in one long and rather ungentlemanly slurp.

Marie laughed.

Roger suddenly thought of his own daughter, who was six. He felt his eyes begin to tear up, so he handed the bowl back to Marie and looked away. But not fast enough.

Marie set the bowl down on the floor. Lila immediately came over and started licking it.

Marie pulled a cloth napkin from her dress pocket and stood up to gently pull Rogers' face back toward her. She dabbed his eyes dry.

Rogers stared into Marie's eyes and saw a kind soul who had already done more than her share of suffering.

She sat down again and asked, "*Familiare?*"

Rogers didn't need the book for this one, but he opened it to the last page and shook. A black-and-white photo fell out. Marie grabbed it and looked at it longingly. Rogers and his wife were seated on the front steps of a brick house. In front of them stood a girl and a boy. The girl, who had the mother's light hair and eyes was directly in front of Rogers and turned just slightly away from the camera, perhaps feeling shy. Rogers' hand was on her shoulder. The boy looked like a small version of the dad. The mother held an infant in her arms, his happy round face pointed at the camera.

Marie glanced up at Rogers, who was smiling. She put her finger on the girl and gave him a questioning look.

"Susie." Rogers held up six fingers and Marie nodded.

"Susie," repeated Marie. Then she touched the boy.

"Frank, Junior." Rogers held up four fingers.

"Frank, Junior." She said and moved her finger back to Susie and repeated, "Susie."

She touched the baby.

"William."

Last, she touched Mrs. Rogers' image.

Rogers said, "Bessie."

She repeated all four names to herself. She nodded and gave the photo back. To his surprise, she leaned over and hugged him briefly. When she released him, she turned and ran out of the room, leaving him to wonder, *what next?*

She soon returned with a photo of her own. She handed it to Rogers.

A beautiful young woman and a handsome man were standing under a large tree. They appeared to be about twenty. In turn, he touched each person's image and she gave him their names: Carlotta and Rocco and added, "Mama, Papa."

Rogers nodded.

She touched her papa's image. Then made a motion indicating "away." She made explosion sounds and shrugged.

Rogers' face fell as it hit him. Her dad had gone to war and not returned.

Tears began to trickle down Marie's cheeks. Rogers took the napkin and returned her kindness by wiping her face gently. She leaned over to hug him and this time didn't let go for a long time.

Marie had been called away to do chores for her mother. Rogers had drifted off to sleep again. A rap on the door woke him and a silver-haired man stepped through.

"Do you remember me?" the man asked.

Rogers stared at the man. "You do seem familiar."

"My name is Dr. Marcucci. I treated your wound." The doctor pointed toward Rogers' bandaged left hand. "You were not very lucid at the time."

"Oh. Thank you."

"How are you feeling?" asked the doctor.

Rogers was temporarily surprised to hear English, but realized the doctor would likely have taken English in college as a matter of course. Although accented, the doctor's pronunciation was excellent.

"Better." He raised his hand. "Still hurts like a bear."

The doctor raised his eyebrows at the colloquialism he'd never heard. It wasn't difficult to infer the meaning, however.

He nodded, then said, "I'm afraid I have little to help with the pain. A few aspirin tablets."

"I'll manage okay." Rogers couldn't help but think about the lost rucksack with the morphine in it.

"What is your name?"

Rogers nearly said his real name, but remembered just in time, "Frank Newport."

Dr. Marcucci held out his hand and Rogers shook it.

"You are U.S. Army?"

"Yes, sir. Captain."

"What happened to you? How did you end up in Ville di Murlo?"

"I'm an army photographer. I was getting some movie film of the Italian countryside. We strayed too close to the Germans and got shot down." Rogers was amazed at how easily the lie rolled off his tongue.

Dr. Marcucci accepted it on face value, but asked, "We?"

"Ah, yes. I'm afraid my pilot met with an accident and died. He fell off a cliff."

"Tragic. I'm sorry to hear that."

"Yes."

"Where did that happen?"

"Somewhere north of here. On the other side of the mountains." Rogers started to feel uneasy about the questions. He didn't know the doctor, after all.

The doctor asked, "Were you able to bury your friend?"

Rogers looked away, feeling ashamed. "No. I didn't have any tools and there weren't enough rocks lying around."

Dr. Marcucci crossed himself and muttered a quick prayer in Italian. He patted Rogers' arm. "Don't feel bad. You had no choice. He's in a better place."

Rogers nodded.

The doctor changed tack and put a palm on Rogers' forehead.

"No fever. That's very good."

"Thanks for patching me up."

"You're welcome." The doctor gently grasped the colonel's injured hand.

Rogers watched as the doctor removed the bandage.

At that moment, a woman stepped into the room. Rogers immediately recognized her from the picture Marie had shown him. She had grown gaunt since the photo and had a haunted look about her. Following right behind her was another woman of about the same age. Their resemblance to each other was clear: sisters.

Marie's mother didn't speak to Rogers as she stepped near the bed to pick up the soup bowl.

"*Grazie*," he said.

She merely nodded and turned away. Rogers thought she might have had an angry expression, but wasn't sure.

Because Rogers' attention was on her, he didn't notice the other woman staring hard at him, as if memorizing his appearance. Her expression was definitely angry.

Chapter 19

Camp Barton Stacey Hospital
3 August, 1048 Hours, London time

Nurse Pamela Dunn leaned over and placed the back of her hand against the forehead of an American patient. She frowned because it was hot; he was still running a fever. The man, who was perhaps nineteen, looked up at her with hazel eyes that held fear. As if waiting for her to tell him something awful.

Turning away, Pamela lifted a dry washcloth from the small table next to the bed and dipped it in a small bowl filled with cool water, and wrung out the excess. She folded it carefully, and began sponging the man's forehead, then wiped the rest of his face and neck. He closed his eyes at the brief respite from the heat. When she was done, Pamela put the cloth on the table.

She retrieved a thermometer and said, "Let's put this under your tongue, shall we?"

He obediently opened his mouth and she slid the silver tip under his tongue.

While he was busy with the thermometer, she took his pulse at the wrist, using the large clock on the wall a few beds down to time it.

"Still beating?" he mumbled through the thermometer.

"Shh. No talking. And yes, you have a pulse."

He grinned a little, which gave him a wacky expression from trying to hold the glass stick in place.

Pamela gently laid his hand back on the bed and went to the end of the bed, where she wrote his pulse and respiration numbers on his chart.

She removed the thermometer and held it up to her eyes. A hundred and one. Not what she wanted to see. He'd had the fever for twenty-four hours and had been given aspirin and a penicillin shot. She shook the device to push the mercury back toward the silver bulb. She put it in a pocket on her nurse's blouse. She'd cleanse it later.

"I'm going to check your wounds now, James."

Pamela always made it a point to call all the enlisted men by their given names. Officers, not so much.

"Okay, ma'am, but please call me 'Jim.' "

" 'Jim' it is."

Pamela gently opened the patient's pajama-style top, which had been left unbuttoned. He had a bandage high up over his right chest and another just below the rib cage on the left side. The results of a German MP42 machinegun. He'd been shot while fighting near St. Lo, France. The field hospital had been able to operate on him within an hour of getting shot, which saved his life. At least, so far.

Lifting the edges of the chest bandage as carefully as possible, Pamela pulled it off and threw it in a trash container nearby. She closely examined the round, purple and puckered wound. There were no red lines radiating from it and it looked okay. She leaned closer and sniffed.

"Like my after shave?"

"Shh." She smelled nothing to indicate an infection here. She quickly replaced the bandage with a clean one.

She removed the other bandage. The wound looked much the same. This puzzled Pamela. She'd expected one or both to show signs of infection. Pulling his top father apart, she began to examine him torso. Finding nothing she said, "Can you sit up if I help you?"

"Yeah, sure."

With her assistance, he managed to get upright in the bed.

"I need to get your shirt off." Pamela began sliding the top off his shoulders and he wriggled his arms out. Soon Pamela was able to view his back, which was her first concern. She removed the bandages on the exit wounds, checked for infection and found none. She quickly treated and bandaged them again.

"Did you cut yourself before you got shot?"

"What? Well, I don't know."

"Does anything hurt besides your gunshots?"

Jim looked surprised. "How could I know if something else hurts? The gunshots hurt enough to cover up anything else."

Pamela shook her head. "No, something has to be hurting you. Lie back down."

Jim complied and gasped as her hands slid to his waist and started to slide his bottoms off his hips. "Wait a minute!"

"Shh. I'm a nurse. Don't get all wound up."

Jim blushed, but didn't say anything.

As soon as she got them past his knees, she saw it. A gash about two inches long ran across his right leg just above the knee. It looked angry and swollen. It was red and purple, and yellow puss was leaking. Red streaks ran up the thigh toward the heart. *How was this missed?* she wondered.

She laid a clean white towel across his waist and thighs, like a sarong for his modesty.

"Lie still. I'll be right back."

Having been watching her, Jim started to rise so he could see what was there.

Pamela put a palm on his forehead, not so gentle this time, and pushed until he laid back down. "I said, 'Lie still,' and I mean it, buster."

"Yes, ma'am."

Not more than a few minutes later, Pamela came rushing back with a rolling table filled with medical supplies. A tall, thin man wearing a doctor's white coat was with her.

Without saying a word, the doctor leaned over and examined the infected, festering cut. Turning to Pamela he said, "Let's clean the wound so I can see whether I need to debride it."

"Yes, doctor."

To the patient, Pamela said, "Jim, this might hurt a little bit, but it's very important that we do it."

Jim nodded, but said nothing. He clasped his hands over his chest, in between the two bandages on his torso.

Standing right next to the doctor, Pamela opened a bottle of alcohol and, while holding a patch of gauze under the wound, slowly poured the liquid over the cut.

Jim sucked in a breath and his eyes watered.

Pamela dabbed the wound, and then moved to the side.

The doctor stepped closer and Pamela handed him some gauze. He worked carefully, but quickly for several minutes.

Pamela checked on Jim, whose face had gone pale. She reached out and touched his hand, and smiled. She was rewarded with a grateful expression.

"Hmm," the doctor said.

Pamela recognized it for what it was. Not good news. The infection must be deep in the skin, possibly into the muscle.

"Nurse, you caught this just in time. Get him ready for surgery right away." The doctor turned and walked off.

Jim's expression darkened with fear. "What does he mean 'surgery?' "

Pamela busied herself with covering the cut with a clean bandage. While she worked she replied, "The cut is infected. Doctor wants to open it up and clean it very thoroughly to get rid of the infection build up. To do that we'll inject a local anesthetic so it won't hurt you."

"What'd he mean 'just in time?' "

"The infection is spreading, but now that we've found it, we hope to prevent it from becoming worse."

"Like what? It's not gangrene, is it? I've seen it on other guys. It looks . . . horrible."

Pamela finished with the bandage and looked at Jim. "No, it's not gangrene. And yes, that is horrible. What you have is a big infection that's spreading, and we want to stop it."

"Will I lose my leg?" Jim's voice cracked at this barely avoided prospect.

Pamela hesitated. Making a patient worry was not what she wanted to do, ever. But she also told the truth when necessary. She reached down and finished pulling off his pajamas bottoms for the upcoming surgery. While folding his pajamas neatly, she replied, "Yes, possibly, if we can't stop the spread of the infection."

Jim closed his eyes. A tear leaked out and ran down the side of his face.

Pamela dabbed the tear away with a paper tissue. "I think you'll be fine, Jim."

"Will I?"

"Yes."

"Do you promise?" He opened his eyes.

Pamela didn't answer right away.

"Do you promise?" he repeated.

"I can't promise what isn't up to me. But Dr. Abbott is excellent. You can trust him."

Jim stared at Pamela for a long while. He had, of course, noticed earlier how beautiful she was, but the pain had prevented him from truly appreciating it. It struck him squarely in the heart. Her blond hair was tied up in a bun under the white nurse's hat, and she wore no makeup, none of the girls did these days, but it was her eyes that held his attention. Not just the blue, but the caring that seemed to flow outward directly at him.

"What's your name, ma'am?"

"Pamela. Pamela Dunn. Mrs. Dunn." Pamela thought it best to add the last bit.

He quickly stole a glance at her left hand and saw the wedding band.

"Ah rats. Okay. Well, I guess I can't very well ask you out for dinner can I?" Before Pamela could reply, he continued quickly, "I'm sorry. Your husband is a lucky man. What does he do?"

Pamela needed to finish getting him ready for surgery, but replied anyway, "Ranger. Tom's a Ranger."

Jim smiled. "You married a yank, huh? That's swell! Are you going to move to the States after the war?"

"We're planning on it. Look, I need to get you ready for surgery so let me work on you. Time is important."

"Okay, sure, I understand."

About an hour later, the orderlies wheeled Jim back into place and got him situated in his bed. Within a minute, Pamela reappeared by his side with a smile. Jim returned the smile.

"What did the doctor say, Mrs. Dunn?"

"He was able to completely clean out the wound and he stitched you up. Twenty stitches, in case you want to brag about it. He said the cut looked like you'd run through some barbed or concertina wire which could have been rusty. So . . ."

She brandished a hypodermic needle, ". . . you need a tetanus booster."

Jim's face grew pale at the sight of the needle.

Pamela laughed lightly, then said in a whisper, "Jim, you survived two gunshots and a little needle scares you?"

He nodded.

"Well, I'll be extra gentle."

"I wish you would."

"Don't get fresh."

"No, ma'am."

"I am the one with the needle, you know."

"Yes, ma'am."

Pamela smiled as she stuck him.

Chapter 20

Ville di Murlo, Italy
3 August, 1155 Hours, Rome time

Frank Rogers was surprised when the doctor returned with an older man who was carrying a small black satchel.

"May I introduce Umberto Gavino?" asked the doctor.

The men shook hands.

"I spoke with Umberto about your . . . situation. He is able to help you make contact with your people."

Rogers looked at the black bag again and Gavino opened it carefully, then tipped it toward the American. Inside lay a Morse code key and a transmitter.

Rogers' chest nearly exploded from excitement. A way to get back and report what he'd discovered! He swung his legs off the bed and stood up, smiling broadly.

To Gavino he said, "*Grazie!*"

Gavino said something in rapid-fire Italian and Dr. Marcucci translated, "We must get you out of this house to somewhere safer. For you and for this family. How do you feel?"

"I feel good. Rested. I'm ready to go wherever you want me."

"Good. Get your things and follow us." Gavino closed and latched the satchel, then he and Dr. Marcucci left the room. Rogers could hear their footsteps on the stairs.

Rogers put on his boots, which had been placed neatly by the bed. He found his hat on a hook by the door, and went out the door.

When he got to the bottom of the stairs, he spotted the men waiting at the back of the house by the kitchen door. Rogers glanced into the living room, hoping to see little Marie again, but the room was empty. In fact, the house felt entirely empty to him.

Walking into the kitchen, he asked, "Where are Marie and her mother? I'd like to say thank you."

Dr. Marcucci said, "It's better that you don't see them again. They have been sent to another house for a few hours. That's all you need know." The silver-haired man's eyes narrowed. "You understand?"

Rogers nodded. "Yes, sir." He hadn't realized how dangerous his presence might be for others. He now knew what kind of risk both of these Italians were taking. "I understand completely."

"Good. We'll leave now. Wait for Mr. Gavino to wave at you. Do you see his truck?"

Rogers stepped a little closer to the door and peered out. He saw an alleyway running across the width of the house. An old, he guessed mid-twenties, panel truck was parked there. "I see it."

With no more talk, the doctor exited the house. He glanced left and right, then apparently satisfied that the coast was clear, put his black hat on and walked away to the left. Gavino hurried out the door and around to the back of the truck, where he opened the back doors. He checked the alley in both directions, then waved to Rogers, who ran out and climbed in the truck. Gavino closed the doors and got in. He immediately started the engine, let out the clutch, and drove away.

Behind them, out of sight, a tall, slim figure was peeking around the corner of a building. After watching Gavino drive away with the American, the person had a secret worth telling.

Light sifted through the two small windows in the doors and Rogers found himself sitting amongst a few wooden crates. He leaned over and peered into one and discovered it was half full of small oranges. Grabbing one, he held it to his nose and took a deep sniff.

He was still sitting with the orange to his nose and his eyes closed when Gavino stopped the truck, the brakes squeaking their displeasure. A moment later, the shopkeeper opened the back doors and motioned for Rogers to get out. He saw Rogers' death grip on the orange and grinned.

"Keep it," he said in his native language, waving toward the American.

Rogers inferred the meaning and grinned back. He got out of the truck and his eyes squinted in the bright sunlight. He wanted to look around at his surroundings, the beautiful old buildings on one side, the rising, tree-covered mountain on the other, but Gavino grasped his left elbow and directed him to the back of a stone, two-story building. There were no windows on this side of the structure, which struck Rogers as odd, given the view. Gavino opened the single door, and went in, pulling on Rogers as he went.

Stepping into the gloom of the darkened first floor, Rogers felt blind as his eyes struggled to react to the darkness. He sensed rather than saw that the space was wide open, perhaps all the way to the front of the building. His nose picked up the smell of motor oil and grease. An auto repair garage, he thought with certainty.

Gavino stopped briefly and let go of Rogers' arm, then a pair of light bulbs came on which were spaced equally from side to side of what Rogers saw was indeed a mechanic's garage. A small, black convertible sat close to the wall on his right, its hood propped open on its metal support bar. To the left was room for another vehicle and toward the front on the left sat a small enclosed office.

The Italian kept moving, turning left, and stopped. Bending at the waist, he grasped a large metal ring and lifted. Opening the heavy wooden door revealed a descending staircase. Gavino led the way down the stairs, flipping on another set of lights for the basement, which was a much smaller space, perhaps half of the main floor.

A cot with some blankets and a pillow on it sat against the opposite wall. A long table and three wooden chairs were along the right-hand wall. Gavino placed his satchel on the table and quickly reconnected the Morse code key and transmitter to a long cord hanging from the ceiling. Rogers assumed it to be a make-shift antenna. Gavino plugged the set into an electrical outlet. He pulled out a chair and nodded for Rogers to sit. The shopkeeper pulled out a chair for himself and joined Rogers.

Rogers sat down and examined the radio set. He could hear a low hum. He found the frequency dial and set it to the one he needed. Putting his right hand on the black key, he wondered whether he'd be able to transmit Morse code properly; it had been a while since training. He practiced tapping out his personal call sign on the table a few times. It felt clumsy, but he knew it would come across clear, if not slow.

Rogers looked at Gavino and wondered how he was going to communicate with him since the doctor hadn't joined them. He needed to know where he was and how far it was to the coast. He had no map, but perhaps the other man did.

"Map? Italy?" he asked, a little louder than he meant to, as if that would help Gavino understand English.

To Rogers' surprise, Gavino nodded and replied, "*Si. Mappa Italia. Uno momento.*" Gavino got up and went to a wooden box to the left of the table. A moment later, he returned with a military topographic map of northwest Italy. He spread it out on the table in front of Rogers, then with a fingertip pointed to a village in a valley. "*Ville di Murlo.*"

Rogers examined the map. He found the map's scale and estimated that he was about seven miles from the coast. If he went on a direct line, he would come out about half way between Genoa, on the east, and the French border east of Nice. Probably the best location, since both would have sizable German forces, especially Genoa.

He pulled a stubby pencil from his shirt pocket, and a small flip-style notebook. He began composing his short message. When he finished, the next step was to transcribe it into code. It was a simple replacement code using the key for the day, which was committed to memory. Completing that took a few minutes.

He placed his forefinger on the key button and began. His first sentence was simple: Rogers alive. Where to meet needed. He included his call sign.

He stopped and waited. He knew the other end was verifying his identification and it could take a few minutes. Headquarters would debate how best to pick him, then run it past General Truscott. Rogers shuddered at the thought of having a conversation with his commander. He could only hope that discovering the German forces where they shouldn't be would save his ass.

His set began receiving and he wrote down the coded message as quickly as it was coming through. He decoded it and it read: Wait 5.

Now the debate was beginning, or maybe they jumped a step and were calling the general.

A noise behind him caused him to turn and look over his shoulder. Dr. Marcucci was coming down the stairs. He spoke to Gavino, then nodded to Rogers who replied in kind.

Rogers turned back to the set. The five minutes took forever, but he was ready when the set began chirping again. The message was terse: Send location.

Have critical info for boss. Rogers sent the information about the German armored battalion he'd spotted.

Several minutes passed as the person on the other end decrypted the message. Then: Understood. Message on way to boss. Send your location.

Rogers keyed in the name of the village, and its coordinates hoping it would be deciphered correctly.

A moment later he received his reply: Location understood. If safe, stay put. Contact in 2.

He reread the message. Stay put? What for? He wrote a short message and transcribed it into code, then sent it: Pickup point needed.

The next reply asked: Are you safe?

He sighed, then replied: Yes.

Stay put. Contact in 2.

He had no choice, so he sent: **Understood. Stay put. Contact in 2. Over and out.**

Out was the reply.

Rogers sat back curious, worried. No pick up on the coast? Maybe they just needed to determine the best way to retrieve him. Surely they wouldn't just leave him. Would they? No, that didn't make any sense. It was contrary to the problem of his knowing too much about the invasion. No, they would have to come get him.

He turned off the set and put away his writing materials. He got up and stretched. He hadn't realized how tense he'd been during the transmission. Now, in typical army style, all he could do was wait. The natural question came to mind and he looked at the doctor.

"I need to stay here so I can contact my headquarters in two hours. Would that be okay?" he hadn't thought to ask the question before sending he understood.

The doctor didn't reply right away, instead he spoke again to Gavino, but Rogers could tell he was asking the question because Gavino looked right at him. Rogers heart dropped thinking Gavino was going to say no. Then the shopkeeper smiled and fired off a response.

"Yes. Mr. Gavino says he can take care of you as long as you need as well as making the transmitter available to you, too."

Relief washed over Rogers. At least he had a place to hole up for the near future! He moved back to the chair and sat down, suddenly feeling exhausted, even after the naps he'd had at Marie's house.

Gavino and Dr. Marcucci sat down near Rogers. The doctor placed the back of his hand against Rogers' forehead for a few seconds.

He removed it and said, "No fever yet, that's very good news. I have only limited amounts of drugs for infection."

Rogers wasn't sure whether that meant he'd be out of luck if his hand did become infected or not and he didn't want to ask. If it came to that, he'd find out then.

"May we get you anything? Are you hungry?"

The colonel realized he was indeed hungry even after the soup, but he felt guilty about taking food from their tables. But he had to keep up his strength, didn't he? "I am getting a little hungry. I have an orange Mr. Gavino gave me. I could sure use some water, though," he added while looking almost embarrassed to ask.

Dr. Marcucci spoke to Gavino, who nodded and said, "*Si*." Then he got up and went up the stairs.

"Where are you from, Captain?" The doctor asked, then gave Rogers a sly expression. "Or can you tell me things like that?"

Rogers grinned. "Yes, I can talk about that. I'm from Norfolk, Virginia, that's on the east coast."

"Yes, I know. I studied United States geography some years ago when I was thinking of emigrating."

"You obviously changed your mind. Why was that?"

"The black-shirted morons took control of our country. I felt that I was needed here more than ever."

"I can only imagine what it must be like to live here. You must love your neighbors very much."

Dr. Marcucci nodded slowly. "I do. We've lost some of our men from the village over the years, so it has been difficult for those left behind."

"Like Marie's father?"

"You're quite perceptive."

"Not really. Marie told me, or sort of told me." Rogers further explained the photo exchange and Marie's charade explanation of where her father was. "I take it he was killed fighting in the war?"

"We don't know for certain. He was in North Africa in 1942, fighting the British, and we think also the Americans after the invasion."

He was referring to *Operation Torch*, the Allied invasion of Africa in early November, 1942.

Rogers nodded, then asked, "So no word at all? Maybe he's a POW?"

"Well, I think if he'd been taken prisoner, we would have learned that through the Red Cross, if nothing else. He would likely have been released after we got rid of Mussolini and surrendered."

"So you believe he's dead?"

"Either that or he's been captured by the Germans and is being held prisoner somewhere."

"Marie must be very frightened."

"She is, but somehow she stays strong for her mother, who is having a harder time with it." The doctor gave a weak smile and said, "I sometimes think that the roles of parent and child have been reversed in their family."

Rogers could think of nothing to say to that and the men sat in silence for a few minutes.

"Are you married, Captain."

"I am."

"Tell me about your family."

"We've been married about eight years . . ." began Rogers.

The two men spent the two hours getting to know each other. When it was time, Rogers got back on the key set and sent his call sign.

The reply came back within seconds: State your condition.

Injured left hand. Treated by Dr. Otherwise healthy.

Instructions. Stay put. Coming to you. Soonest. Who to contact there?

Rogers reread the last sentence. Coming to me? Who?

He must have taken too long thinking because the next message came: Reply, please.

Sighing, he encoded and replied: Wilco. Contact Dr. or Gavino. Who is coming?

The final message said: Dr. and Gavino received. No need to know last. Out.

More than a little confused, he signed off.

Turning to the doctor, he said, "Someone is coming to get me. I don't know who. I told them to find you or Mr. Gavino. I hope that's all right."

If Dr. Marcucci was surprised, he didn't show it. "Yes. That's fine. I take it you don't know when?"

Rogers shook his head.

The doctor stood up and walked over to Rogers. Patting him on the shoulder, he said, "You can stay here. I'll arrange some dinner for you and stop by to check on your wound."

Rogers got up and shook hands. "Thanks, doctor. I appreciate it."

"You're welcome. I'll see you later." The doctor went up the stairs.

Soon after, Rogers could hear the door being dropped into place. He suddenly wondered if he could get out. *Good thing I'm not claustrophobic*, he thought wryly, as he looked around the room.

Chapter 21

Dunn was amazed by how much warmer it was in the Mediterranean. It felt like it was in the lower nineties, just like a hot summer day in Iowa. But as he looked around at his surroundings, the similarity ended. Where Iowa was rolling hills and flatlands, Corsica was mountainous, with the land rising steeply from the sea to the peaks about twenty miles to the southeast of the base.

The flight had been what you'd expect: long, tiring, noisy, and boring. Most everyone slept, following the old army rule of sleeping whenever possible, since you never knew when the next opportunity to sleep would be.

The men were gathering in the Corsican sunshine, waiting for Dunn to give the go-ahead to move out. Dunn had received instructions from Colonel Kenton to go to General Lucien Truscott's headquarters immediately.

Ten minutes later found the squad outside an enormous command tent. It was set in the shade of a couple of even larger trees, oaks of some type, thought Dunn. After telling the men to stand easy—didn't want them sitting around outside a general's headquarters—Dunn approached the two stern-faced MPs stationed outside.

Dunn handed over his ID and the MPs gave it a vigorous scrutiny. The taller of the two referred to a clipboard, running his finger down a list. He found the name, and said, "General Truscott will meet you in his office in ten minutes. Do you need directions to it?"

"Can we see it from here?"

The MP pointed over Dunn's shoulder toward a small stone building whose age was indeterminate. It was about a hundred yards farther down the road. "Right there, Sergeant."

Dunn followed the finger, nodded, then took his ID back and said, "Is the mess nearby? My men are starving after a long flight."

The MP glanced over at the men, who were chatting quietly. "It's another hundred yards or so past the General's office."

"Thanks."

Dunn stepped over to rejoin his squad.

"Men, the mess is down that road," Dunn paused to point, "about two hundred yards. Take your gear and grab a bite. Cross, you're with me. The rest of you be on your best behavior."

Stanley Wickham called out, "When are we not on our best behavior, Sarge?"

Some of the men snorted in appreciation.

Dunn made a show of examining his wristwatch closely, then said, "So what time is it?"

The group all shared a laugh, and each man shouldered his bag. They strode toward, hopefully, a hot meal.

Dunn and Cross watched the men depart, each feeling pride.

After a moment, Dunn said, "Shall we?" He gestured with his hand.

"We shall."

About ten minutes later, a jeep with General Truscott and his driver in the front, and another officer in the back seat, rolled to a stop next to where Dunn and Cross were standing.

The general jumped out of the Willy's as did the other passenger.

Dunn and Cross exchanged salutes with the officers and the Rangers introduced themselves.

"Good to meet you, men. This is Colonel Handley, my aide. He'll be joining us for your briefing."

Dunn was surprised by the general's voice. It seemed much too soft and silky for a commanding officer. Dunn hadn't heard that the general, as a boy, had accidentally ingested acid that altered his larynx.

A Brigadier General, Truscott was a fit man of about five-nine. He wore a white scarf around his neck, even in the Corsican heat, a trademark he'd started in Sicily. His only concession to the heat was to not wear his leather jacket. Known to be exceedingly superstitious about his clothes, he also had on his lucky boots. A tough, direct commander, he had the respect of his men because he respected them.

Truscott passed two MPs standing guard outside, and opened the door to the building before anyone could open it for him. Leading the way down the narrow hallway, he entered his office and went around a standard army desk, and sat down. A window behind him looked out at the sea over the tops of some trees as the ground sloped away to the water.

There were four wooden chairs arranged in a semicircle in front of the desk. Dunn and Cross waited until the colonel selected his chair, the rightmost one, and they sat down leaving an empty chair between themselves and the colonel. Dunn sat closest to Handley.

"This is a very serious problem we have here. Our missing colonel has top secret information stuck in his head and if he's captured by the Germans it'll just be a matter of time before he gives it to them. I cannot tell you what he knows, only that he must be rescued and brought back here as soon as possible.

"From what I've heard about you, I'm hopeful you can pull this off. In fact, from what Colonel Kenton tells me, you may be the only men who could do this. Colonel, would you give the sergeants the latest?"

"Yes, sir." Handley turned in his seat slightly to face the sergeants. "We just got this information in the last half hour.

Rogers has made contact with some Italian partisans. He's wounded, but not seriously, and has been treated by a doctor." Handley got up and walked over to a map hanging on the wall. Finding the spot he wanted, he touched it with his finger.

"He's holed up here, in Ville Di Murlo, a small town lying in the valley between two sets of peaks that run east to west. It's only seven miles from the coast, but he can't escape that way because the Germans patrol the coast so heavily. You'll have to drop in, secure him and get him to a transport, which we'll fly in to take him out," the colonel paused, "and you of course.

"When you arrive, you are to locate either the village doctor, or a man named Gavino. You'll be shipping out tonight at 1900 hours, before sunset. Any questions?"

"No, sir. We're ready."

Truscott said, "That'll be all, gentlemen. Good luck."

Dunn and Cross rose quickly, saluted, and departed.

Chapter 22

Marie's house
Ville di Murlo, Italy
3 August, 1435 Hours

Marie's aunt, Teresa, slammed her fork down on the kitchen table.

"How could you let an American into *your* house?" she shouted. "After what they did to your husband, I'd think you would want to kill him, not feed him!"

Carlottta, the younger of the two sisters, shouted back, "We don't know that they killed Rocco! We have no word from anyone."

To Carlotta's surprise, Teresa didn't reply. She just threw an impatient look her way, something she'd done since they were little girls, got up and left the room. Carlotta could hear the clack of Teresa's shoes on the wooden floor as she went down the hallway. Carlotta thought she was leaving the house. Instead, she heard a drawer being pulled open and the rustling of paper. Too late, she realized what was happening. Oh no!

Carlotta got up, knocking her chair over, and ran down the hall and into the living room. She got there just in time to see

Teresa triumphantly hold up a piece of paper.

"No!" shrieked Carlotta.

Teresa held the paper so she could read it. " *'Dearest Carlotta, I blah blah blah. Tomorrow we go into battle against the Americans for the first time. Blah blah blah. Love, Rocco.'* " Teresa snapped the paper in the air. "The last letter from him. It had to be the Americans!"

"Give me that!" Carlotta screamed and ran across the room. She tried to snatch the letter out of the air. She missed and Teresa waved it around, tormenting her sister with a smirk. Teresa took a step back and rotated to keep the letter away. Carlotta naturally followed and accidentally stepped on her sister's instep. Teresa lost her balance and fell sideways. Carlotta landed on top of her and scrabbled to get the precious letter. Now that Teresa was pinned, she was unable to get the paper far enough out of reach and Carlotta got a grip on it. Then the inevitable happened: the letter tore in two as Carlotta yanked hard and fell back.

She landed on her back and stared at the half of the letter in her hand. She let out a cry then rolled over into a fetal position and sobbed.

Marie, who had been standing at the doorway, ran into the room. She gave Teresa a dirty look as her aunt got to her feet. Teresa tossed the other half of the letter in the direction of her weak sister, then stomped past Marie and out the front door.

Marie knelt by her mother and wrapped her arms around the distraught woman.

"Shh. Shh. It's all right," whispered the nine-year-old girl while thinking, *Dear God, when will this end?*

Teresa Rusconi was thirty-eight, unmarried with no prospects, and sickened by her sister's aiding of the enemy. Just because the Americans had *liberated* Rome didn't automatically make them her friends. She'd been the one to put two and two together and figured out what had happened to Rocco. Her Rocco. Her stolen Rocco. But Carlotta refused to believe her, saying it didn't matter who killed him. Instead she wept and moaned all day.

Walking fast, she traversed the distance to her house, about six blocks away. She got in her small, black 1936 Fiat Toppolino and started it. She rarely drove it, but this circumstance would have to be an exception.

Pulling away from the curb, she drove the car to the east, and left the village behind. She was thinking, *I might not be able to punish the Americans who killed Rocco, but I can punish this one.*

Chapter 23

Ville di Murlo, Italy
3 August, 1842 Hours

Marie played near the river bank, throwing stones into the water, skipping them as her brother, Damiano, had taught her. The day was overcast and there were no shadows. Lila suddenly began to growl and pointed her nose to the east, tail still and ears back. After a moment, Marie could hear the distant sound of big trucks. The sound was getting louder. She ran up to the road and looked eastward. Seeing nothing, she ran across the street into an alleyway between Mr. Gavino's store and a neighboring building. She knelt on one knee and grabbed Lila's collar with one hand, while stroking the dog's head with the other.

"Shh, girl," she whispered.

Four German trucks roared into the village. They had no tops covering the backs and Marie could see they were full of soldiers. As they drove closer, she stood up and edged herself to the corner of the building. *There seems to be a lot*, she thought. She counted the men as the trucks passed her. Each had ten men, then she added four for the men driving to get forty-four. The men looked tired, and were unshaven, making their faces look dirty. Marie imagined they didn't smell very good, either. A soldier in the last truck saw her leaning out. He grinned, then raised his hand giving a gesture that Marie knew was naughty. She looked away, then ran into the store.

Once inside, she called out, "Mr. Gavino?"

No answer. She walked to the back of the store and called his name again. Still no reply. She opened the back door and peered outside. The store's truck was gone. Unsure of where he might be, she ran back to the front of the store and looked out the window. The soldiers were gone, at least. She carefully opened the door and slid back out onto the sidewalk. If she leaned she could just see the trucks. She hoped the mean one wouldn't turn around and see her. Problem was, they were between her and home. She took a tentative step into the street for a better view, readying herself to bolt and run.

While she thought about the problem, the trucks stopped and the soldiers jumped out and formed into lines, standing straight and still. Even from a distance of three blocks she could hear one man, the leader, shouting at them. When he stopped, they all ran in different directions in pairs. They disappeared into houses and buildings. Marie was sure that was bad.

Another sound came from the east. Something smaller, a car, she thought. She ran back into the store and ducked, peeking over the windowsill. Soon a black convertible with its top down drove by with two men in it. The man in the back seat wore all black.

The hair on the nape of Marie's neck bristled.

Gavino estimated he had maybe two minutes before the Germans arrived inside the garage. He'd grabbed Dr. Marcucci on the way to the garage, following the street on the backside of the buildings, out of the German soldiers' view.

He raised the door over the stairwell, then went down to the basement calling out Rogers' assumed name, Newport.

Rogers woke up with a start.

"Yes, I'm here."

When Rogers saw Gavino's face, he knew something was wrong and his knees went weak. His stomach churned.

"What's happened?"

"The Germans are here in the village," reported the shopkeeper.

Dr. Marcucci translated.

Gavino walked over to the table and began packing up the Morse code key and transmitter. When he finished, he turned to face the American.

"I have to move this to another location. It's unlikely that they will find this cellar, but if they do, finding out that we hid you will be bad enough, but that we had a radio will make it worse on the village." He stepped closer and put a hand on Rogers' shoulder. "You understand, don't you?"

Rogers nodded. "Yes, I do. I wouldn't want someone to be hurt on my account."

Gavino nodded in return. "I will park my truck in the garage right over the door. It will improve our chances of this room staying hidden."

"Whatever you need to do."

"I'll come back as soon as it's safe."

"See you then, Mr. Gavino." Rogers smiled, although he didn't feel it.

After Gavino left, Rogers felt the need to exercise having been cooped up for so long. He started with two sets of sit ups, then some leg squats. He tried a pushup, but the weight on his left hand proved to be too much and he gave up. Last, he ran in place for five minutes, until he was huffing, and even in the cool air of the cellar he was sweating. Finally burning off some of the energy and with it perhaps a tiny bit of the anxiety of not knowing what was happening, he sat down on the cot, swung his legs up and fell back. He closed his eyes, but this time sleep was elusive.

Too many things had and could still possibly go wrong. Not for the first time, he was regretting choosing to go on the reconnaissance flight. The thought that Watson's death was his fault hurt him deeply. He couldn't help but picture the young man's parents getting the most feared telegram in America. This thought led to wondering how his wife, kids and parents would feel if they got one for him. He realized for the first time just how big the risk he'd taken actually was. He might not return home. Ever.

He suddenly understood that he wouldn't have been able to live with himself if he hadn't taken the flight. Finding the German armored battalion and sending the information to headquarters made it worthwhile. Knowing the enemy's location was only part of the intelligence game, the other part was to know strength. No, he'd done the right thing. He was sure of it.

Hauptsturmführer Adelsberger, the captain in charge of the SS unit, stood in the street, in front of the village Catholic church. The stone building had heavy wooden double doors at the top of a set of stairs. Century-old stained glass windows rose tall on both sides, and above the doors. The bell tower and steeple were topped by a gold cross, which was at least six stories from the ground.

Adelsberger watched as his men screamed and shouted and pushed old men, women of all ages, and children into the street in front of the church. A slightly built woman of about fifty stumbled and fell to the pavement, landing face first. An old priest, wearing a black frock, quickly helped her to her feet. Blood streamed from her nose and forehead. The priest used his handkerchief to help with her injuries. He looked at the SS captain, his expression clearly showing his disappointment with Germans.

Adelsberger smiled.

Soldiers began the process of lining everyone up in rows along the street, continuing the pushing and shoving and shouting. Soon, the entire village population of just over five hundred people was standing in the street. Their bewildered, frightened faces looked toward the captain.

Adelsberger spoke nearly fluent Italian. The product of two medical doctors, he had grown up in a forward thinking Berlin family. He'd been taught that education was his first and only responsibility while growing up. Born in 1920, he'd been sixteen when his mother had been forced to *retire* from the medical profession under a new Nazi law curtailing women's right to work in certain fields. Dr. Adelsberger, the father, had explained to the young man that sometimes people had to give up certain rights for the betterment of the country. When the young, impressionable youth had asked if country took precedence over family, the father, who had been a young doctor serving near the front lines in World War I, had replied, "Absolutely." The next day, the son had joined the Hitler Youth and never looked back.

The opportunity to join the SS came a few years later, and he'd signed up immediately, and passed the difficult requirements easily. Within in his first year, his apparent ruthlessness was recognized and rewarded with an assignment to officer training school. His first post was to Paris in late 1940, after the Nazis had established rule and control of the French capital. There, he received the tutelage of an older officer, an SS Colonel who, in late '43, recommended Adelsberger for his own command in Italy.

Adelsberger scanned the villagers slowly, but found nothing of interest. He waited patiently as his men finished positioning the terrified people. Four of his men suddenly grabbed two elderly men and marched them toward the captain.

All eyes followed the two men. The captain wondered whether all of the idiots were thinking, *I'm glad it's not me*.

The soldiers stopped the two old men directly in front of the captain. Adelsberger glanced at them, sizing them up. Finally, he spoke.

"Who do we have here?"

The taller of the two replied, "I'm Dr. Marcucci."

One of Adelsberger's eyebrows lifted. "This village has its own doctor?"

"I serve this village and several others, as needed."

"Aren't you wonderful, then?"

Dr. Marcucci looked away at the insult.

The captain laughed. To the other man he asked, "Your name?"

"Umberto Gavino. I own the store."

"A store owner. How nice." Adelsberger opened the flap of a pocket on his black tunic and withdrew a piece of paper. He carefully unfolded it, as if it were priceless. Without looking at the paper, he recited, "Umberto Gavino, aged seventy, shopkeeper. Partisan member. Dr. Marcucci, aged sixty-eight, doctor, probably a partisan member." He shifted his gaze from one man to the other, then asked, "Does this sound about right?"

Neither man replied.

"Come now, gentlemen. Answer the question. You've been caught. Tell me the truth and I might go easier on you."

Silence.

Unperturbed, Adelsberger nodded to one of the soldiers.

A light rain began to fall.

The soldier marched toward the first line of people. The Italians all immediately looked at their feet.

While the solider was busy searching for the perfect victim, Adelsberger looked down the street to the east and waved a hand. An idling truck surged into motion. The back of the truck was uncovered and several men sat along the side benches.

The solider selected a thin old woman who was wearing a light blue scarf over her gray hair. He yanked her out of the line and dragged her toward the captain. She began screaming and tried to pull away, but the soldier was too strong. Just as they neared the captain, her feet tangled up in each other and she fell hard onto the pavement, landing on her side.

The soldier put a foot on her shoulder and pushed her onto her back. She clasped her hands over her chest and began to cry.

Adelsberger unholstered his Luger and pointed it at her.

Dr. Marcucci shouted, "No! Please!"

Adelsberger didn't even look at the doctor. Instead he aimed at a dress button over the woman's stomach, a few centimeters down from her sternum, and pulled the trigger. The impact doubled the woman up as she clawed at her abdomen. A red blossom appeared on her dress.

Dr. Marcucci started to kneel to attend to her, but Adelsberger clouted him on the side of the head with the pistol. The doctor stumbled and fell onto his side holding his bloody head. Two soldiers grabbed him under the arm pits and lifted him back to feet.

Adelsberger stared at the doctor, then at Gavino.

"I asked you both a question."

The old woman's sobbing suddenly ceased. Gavino and Dr. Marcucci exchanged a glance, a sickened expression mirrored on each other's face.

The rain began to pour. Water ran from the old woman's face, washing the tears from her cheeks. Blood swirled in the water underneath her and flowed away following the contour of the street. Both of the Italians' hair was plastered against their skulls.

At that moment, the truck pulled up and stopped just past the group of men and the dead woman. Two men jumped down from the back. Another pair handed down a small wooden ammunition box. They placed the box on the ground next to the captain and then climbed back up in the truck.

Gavino read part of the box's stenciled label: 9mm. It contained rounds for the captain's pistol.

Adelsberger nodded at the soldier who'd selected the old woman for death. The man walked back toward the line of villagers.

Adelsberger made a show of looking at his watch. He raised his pistol to the Italians' eye level. Their eyes focused on the gleaming barrel.

"Gentlemen, it looks like it might be a close one as to whether I'll run out of villagers or daylight first."

Gavino spoke. "Yes, I am a member of the partisans. Please don't hurt anyone else."

The soldier reached the line of people again and turned back to Adelsberger.

The SS captain waved a hand and the soldier started walking back.

Adelsberger put his pistol away and snapped the holster's flap closed. He waved his hand again and the German soldiers pushed and prodded Gavino and Dr. Marcucci into the back of the truck. The soldiers kept the two men separated by seating them between other soldiers, but on the same bench, presumably to prevent them from making eye contact. The last soldier to climb aboard sat down next to Gavino, shoving the Italian hard to make more room for himself.

Gavino leaned forward to look at the doctor, but the same solider elbowed him in the chest and shouted, "*Nein!*"

The shopkeeper slumped back and he closed his eyes. He knew his life was over, but his main worry was that the only two people in the village who knew the American was locked in a cellar with a truck over the door, and who had no radio, were now German prisoners.

Chapter 24

Camp Barton Stacey Hospital
3 August, 1752 Hours, London time

Pamela Dunn started working at the camp's hospital during the winter of 1943-44. She transferred from a hospital north of London to Barton Stacey so she could be at home with her parents. Her brother, Percy, had been killed in 1940 at Dunkirk. He was twenty years old. Three years later, her parents were still having a terrible time with the death of their only son. Of late, it seemed her presence had begun to help them through the awful days and even worse nights.

She'd met and fallen in love with, of all people, an American Army Ranger. But in spite of this shortcoming, Mr. and Mrs. Hardwicke had grown to love him, too, and were delighted to see her get married only last week.

The ward she roamed was on the south side of the wooden building, and the evening sunshine poured through the large windows giving an air of hope to the injured men recuperating there. There were only seven men in various stages of healing, four fighter pilots from a nearby American airbase, and two soldiers. The pilots had all received machine gun wounds, and the two soldiers had both been in the same jeep that left the roadway tossing them like so much trash onto the hard British soil. The American soldier, Jim, whose leg she'd recently saved, was the seventh patient. He was making good progress.

Wearing a white nurse's uniform and peaked hat, she walked slowly by each man, nodding and smiling. The men, for their part, were frozen in place and could only watch the stunningly beautiful blonde walk by them. Pamela was glad she was already smiling because otherwise she would have probably grinned at their open mouths. But she was used to the reaction and had always taken the road of being the comforting nurse who said no when asked out. Her coworkers had often called her the ice queen and were totally surprised by her reaction to Dunn.

Dunn had arrived the previous April after being shot. He'd saved the life of a Ranger recruit during a live-fire exercise, and was rewarded with a .30 caliber round piercing him through the shoulder. He was the ideal patient, never complaining, even though Pamela knew he was suffering. His dark eyes and quick smile were the kickers for Pamela. Over the time he was there, she'd begun hinting, hoping he'd pick up on it. When he didn't, she increased her flirtations. Finally, it must have sunk in and he asked her out.

The first date had gone remarkably badly, with her inadvertently insulting him and he had overreacted by halting the date and not speaking to her when he dropped her back at her flat.

Eventually, they'd gotten back together, and the relationship grew passionate quickly. The romance had been difficult, yet exciting for Pamela. When Dunn was back from a mission they spent as much time together as possible. When Dunn was away on a mission, she worried every waking moment, fearing that he would meet the same fate as her brother. Now he was on another mission and when he would return was unknown, as usual.

She'd given up her flat, which she had shared with another young woman. They'd planned to live on her parents' farm in the small house not too far from the main farmhouse. He wouldn't be able to spend many nights there, what with his duties, but he expected he could on some weekends.

"Mrs. Dunn?"

Pamela heard the words, but they didn't sink in right away and were repeated. Turning around, she found her supervisor, Olive Cohn, with another woman wearing, not the usual nurse's whites, but a khaki uniform, a tie, and a partially brimmed hat that sat back on her dark wavy hair, showing her face. A Queen Alexandra's Imperial Military Nursing Service insignia rested on her jacket collar.

Cohn said, "Mrs. Dunn, I'd like you to meet Miss Jenny Kelly. Miss Kelly, Pamela Dunn."

Kelly stuck out her hand and grinned.

Pamela felt drawn in by the woman's friendliness and shook hands warmly.

Kelly was small, perhaps five-two, and appeared to be thirty-five or so.

"I wonder if I could talk with you for just a bit, Mrs. Dunn?"

Pamela's mind raced for what seemed forever as she wondered if something had happened to Tom, but finally discarded that thought because she knew Colonel Kenton would come himself if something ever did happen.

Calming herself, she managed to reply, "Yes, of course, Miss Kelly." Pamela cast a glance at Cohn, but the nursing supervisor's face was expressionless, although she did say, "You may use my office."

Pamela nodded and led the way out of the ward and down a short, brightly lit hallway. Pamela noticed that Kelly's heels clicked on the tile floor while her own sensible and indispensable soft-soled shoes were silent.

Cohn's office was the first door on the right. Pamela stepped to the side and waved her hand indicating that Kelly should precede her. Kelly nodded and went in the office. A small room, there was only a wooden desk, a file cabinet and two guest chairs. Kelly sat down in one and Pamela in the other.

Kelly seemed to be appraising Pamela, eyeing her uniform, her hands, and finally her shoes. Pamela sat with her feet together and her back perfectly straight. She looked at the lady from the QA, as the Nursing Service was known, and waited.

Kelly then got right to the point. "I am recruiting for nurses who might volunteer to serve on the continent at field hospitals near the front line. You have been highly recommended."

Pamela's confusion was clear on her face and Kelly continued, "Miss Cohn. I stay in touch with many nursing supervisors around the country. I am certain you would be a fine addition to our group."

"I just got married," Pamela said, mostly to herself.

Kelly patted her arm gently. "I know, dear. But your husband is away on missions, often for long periods."

How does she know that, wondered Pamela, but she said, "Yes. That's true, but . . ."

"I understand. You want to be here when he returns. That's only natural. But your country needs your help. We're dreadfully short of qualified people."

"I don't know, Miss Kelly, I'd have to think about it."

"Here's some food for thought: you'll gain experience that you would never get here. You'd learn to become a surgical nurse in addition to normal nursing duties."

"Surgery?" Pamela let some excitement creep into her voice. Surgical nurses were the elite of her profession.

"Yes. Think of where that would put you after the war. Why, any hospital would jump at the chance to snatch you up!"

Pamela looked away, thinking. It seemed to be an incredible opportunity. But how would Tom react? He wasn't even here to talk to. Would he understand her desire to advance her career and make a difference? She thought he would. Hoped he would.

She gazed at Kelly for a moment, then said, "When do you need to know?"

"I can give you forty-eight hours. Then I have to move on. You understand, of course."

Pamela nodded. "Yes, of course. How do I get in touch with you?"

"You just give Miss Cohn your reply and she'll contact me. Please do join us. We need you. Badly."

Pamela suddenly wondered what it was like over there. "Where would I be going?"

"Either France or Belgium, that's all I am able to say."

"What's it really like in a field hospital?"

"It can be terrifying and exhilarating at the same time. Wounded and dying men come in all the time." Kelly looked down at her hands as if seeing blood on them.

"I'll be honest with you. Giving comfort to a wounded man who is certain to survive is easy. Comforting a man who will then die right in front of you is devastating. It hurts deeply, but you won't be able to dwell on that one man because there will be ten more coming who need you.

"The sounds of the battlefield can be horrible, frightening. Everyone is afraid at some time or another, but we persevere because we must."

Pamela nodded, trying to picture it all. "Thank you for being honest. How soon would I . . . leave?"

"Within a fortnight."

"Oh my. That's awfully quick."

"The men continue to arrive."

Kelly stood up and held out her hand, which Pamela shook again as she rose, too.

"Please say 'yes.' "

"I'll let you know as soon as possible. Thank you for coming to talk to me."

"I hope to see you soon."

Kelly left the office and Pamela could hear the heels clicking and echoing, then fading away.

Pamela sat down abruptly, trying to think of how she was going to tell Tom.

It wasn't until ten minutes had passed that she rose slowly and returned to the ward and the seven recuperating men.

Chapter 25

American airfield, Corsica
3 August, 1900 Hours

The setting sun threw long shadows across the dirt and grass airfield. Dunn walked amongst his squad as each man double-checked his equipment.

Dunn stopped in front of Stanley Wickham and patted him on the shoulder. "Doing okay, Wickham?"

"Yes, Sarge, just a gettin' my stuff situated." He pronounced it sitch-ee-ated in his Texas drawl. The British part of his peculiar accent dropped out and Dunn noted it.

"You feeling okay?"

Wickham looked at his sergeant, who he'd been with for over a year. He started to say something, stopped, then said, "I'm fine, Sarge."

Dunn's eyes narrowed. "Better tell me now, before we get in the air, Stan."

Wickham shrugged. "It ain't nothing."

Dunn just waited as he stared into the Ranger's hazel eyes.

"Shit fire, Sarge. I got a 'Dear John' letter from home, is all."

"Well, I'm sorry to hear that. Were you planning on a future with her?"

Wickham shrugged again. "I suppose. Turns out she fell for a 4-F. The guy has flat feet, but he's there and I ain't. I'll be all right."

Dunn nodded, but said, "I need to be able to count on you, Stan. Can you stay focused?"

Wickham gave an affronted look as he spoke in his Brit-Tex accent, "O' course, I can. Besides, the British girls do love me."

Dunn chuckled. "Yes, they do."

Dunn moved on to Dave Jones. Jones had his M1903 A1 Springfield over his shoulder and carried the Thompson. Dunn knew he also had a shooter's bag with a Unertl sight and other sniper tools in his carry bag.

"Jonesy, you all set?"

Jones nodded and grinned at Dunn. He was glad his sergeant had finally started calling him Jonesy, like the rest of the squad.

Next, Dunn checked on Bob Schneider, who as the biggest man in the squad at six-four, was carrying the radio set they would use to contact Corsica when necessary.

"You okay with the extra weight?"

"Yes, Sarge. No big deal. What's fifty pounds?"

"Good man."

Dunn moved casually on down the line just chatting with the men to help keep them loose. He was always rewarded with a grin. The last man, the shortest, Jack Hanson, slipped the sling of his Thompson over his shoulder.

"Hey, Dunny. I'm ready."

Dunn grinned in spite of himself. For reasons he could not fathom, he allowed Hanson to call him 'Dunny.'

"I can see you are, Hanson. See you in Italy."

Fifteen minutes later, the C-47 Goonie Bird lifted into the sky and made a graceful banking turn to the north. To Italy.

Dunn looked out the window across from himself, but the sky was darkening to the east as the sun grew closer to the western horizon. It would be a short flight, maybe thirty minutes, so he didn't bother napping.

Thoughts of the last time he'd been in Italy surfaced. In April, 1944, he'd just lost two men south of Cisterna, but still managed to capture a small fortification anyway. Because Dunn was a survivor of the Kasserine Pass debacle, where he'd earned the Bronze Star for taking leadership of a squad and wiping out a machine gun nest, combat death was not new to him. But as the squad leader, he'd still taken it hard. A few months later in Calais, France, while trying to blow up a German Panzer division's ammunition dump, he'd lost another man. It had broken his heart. If not for Pamela's strength, he hadn't been sure whether he could get past it.

Leading a squad of lethal U.S. Army Rangers brought him unbelievably deep pride, not in himself, but in his men. Time and time again they had proven they could overcome the impossible, taking the mission at hand to a successful completion. Because of them, he was going to receive the Medal of Honor for his actions during Operation Devil's Fire. In his mind, he didn't deserve it, his men did. If it were possible, he'd give it to each of his men instead, but Colonel Kenton had said only one person could receive it. He had obtained approval all the way up to President Roosevelt, who had been kept aware of the mission.

Like many men his age, twenty four, Dunn had signed up the day after Pearl Harbor. He'd never been interested in the navy, so he'd bypassed the long line at that recruiting office and went into the army's instead. He had been a semester short of graduating from the U of I, the University of Iowa. He figured his parents' reactions to his news had been the same as was happening all over the country that night; his mother had run from the room crying and his father looked at him with an expression part fear, part pride.

More thoughts of home started to rise, and Dunn let himself be drawn into the world of memories. His best friend, Paul Thompson, playing baseball together, Dunn at first base, Paul at catcher. Paul always told Dunn he had to play first because his arm wasn't strong enough for anywhere else. Dunn in turn told his friend he had to play catcher because he was too slow to play anything else. Paul was the better player and wanted to make it to the Major Leagues, so he played college ball at the U of I. Paul enlisted in the navy the same day Dunn joined the army and was somewhere in the Pacific on a submarine. Dunn got letters every few months and Paul said he was fine. Dunn hoped it stayed that way.

For years, Dunn had carried guilt over the death of Paul's younger brother, Allen. Dunn and Allen had been taking hay bales off the conveyor belt in the Thompson's barn loft, when Allen suddenly lost his balance. Dunn grabbed his T-shirt, but it ripped and Allen fell to his death. Paul had told Dunn right away that he didn't blame Dunn, but Dunn did. It was only after meeting Pamela that Dunn was finally able to forgive himself.

Dunn had a few girl friends in high school and college, was even going steady with a girl during his college senior year. After he'd signed up, she'd said she couldn't handle his being away and broke it off. Although she'd hurt him, Dunn figured she was just protecting herself and understood.

With Pamela, it was a different story. He worried all the time that he'd end up hurting her. He'd even talked about putting off the wedding until the war was over because he didn't want to make her a war widow. She'd put her foot down and said 'no' to waiting.

"Sergeant Dunn?"

A tap on Dunn's shoulder brought him back to the present. He looked at the man who'd touched him, the jumpmaster.

"Yeah?"

"The pilot says we have a problem. Wants you to come up front."

Dunn nodded, got up, and walked into the cockpit.

"What's going on, sir?" he asked the pilot.

The copilot replied instead. "We're going to have zero visibility over the target." He raised his left hand and pointed directly ahead. Dunn could see what looked to be fog or clouds stretched out in a line across their entire forward field of vision. He recalled hearing that during the airborne drops for D-Day, many paratroopers had jumped into a solid cloud bank over the western half of the Cotentin Peninsula. It had created severe problems.

"How good a navigator are you, sir?"

The copilot stared at Dunn for a moment, surprised that the Ranger hadn't decided to scrub the mission on the spot. "I'm pretty good, but it's easy to be off just a little and that can make a big difference on the ground."

"Well, sir, I trust you to get us as close as possible. We can't go back."

The pilot turned his head briefly to look at the Ranger, then back to the front. "As you wish, Sergeant. May as well get your men up. We're under ten minutes now."

"Yes, sir. Thank you."

"Don't thank me yet."

Dunn went back and told the jumpmaster what was going on, and passed on the information to each of the men so they wouldn't be surprised at the plane's door to see thick clouds.

Not too much later, the red light came on

"Everybody up!" shouted the jumpmaster.

While the men got into position and slapped their hooks onto the wire above them, Dunn had a few worrisome minutes. He knew the numbers from the D-Day jumps. There had been many deaths because paratroopers had landed in water-filled canals and drowned due to the weight of their gear. Others were shot as they drifted earthward. Still others just plummeted to the ground. Many of those who died had jumped in visibility conditions just like his men were about to leap into. Dunn said a quick prayer.

The light above the door turned green and the men did their job. In less than a minute, they were all in the air, falling toward Italy.

Chapter 26

Ville di Murlo, Italy
3 August, 1914 Hours

The one hundred twenty-five-year-old courthouse held the village jail. Constructed of heavy limestone from the quarries near Turin, the courthouse was two stories tall with wide wooden double doors flanked by windows on both sides. Facing south, the windows let natural light illuminate the dark wood panels of the courtroom, creating a warm, enveloping environment.

The jail, on the other hand, was in the basement.

Shopkeeper Umberto Gavino sat on a wooden chair in the middle of the jail cell, his clothes still wet from the rain. Faint light, barely making it through the filthy and tiny window set high on the cold stone wall, cast his shadow on the stone floor in front of him. Manacles held Gavino's hands behind his back, binding him to the bottom of the chair. His forearms were forced painfully around the back of the chair, shoulders pulled tight against the wood.

As soon as the German SS unit had arrived, he'd known his life would be forfeit. He was perfectly aware of the SS and Gestapo interrogation methods. No one could withstand their torture. His only hope was that he wouldn't tell the Germans everything. Perhaps he could deflect them with some truth mixed with lies. When they eventually discovered the lies, perhaps he would already be dead. He could only pray for a quick death. He also knew that the time they'd left him alone was doing what it was supposed to: strike fear into him.

The heavy sound of several men's footsteps coming down the stairs made him recall that the American was trapped in the cellar of the garage with a truck parked over the door in the floor, thanks to him. Perhaps he'd outsmarted himself and the American would die alone in the cellar.

How had the SS Captain known he was partisan? Who had told him? He would probably never know.

Gavino watched helplessly through the bars on his cell for the first sight of his executioner.

The SS captain, Adelsberger, appeared first, marching directly toward the cell door, a set of keys jangling in his right hand.

Gavino could see two other men following the captain, but couldn't make out their faces.

Adelsberger quickly unlocked the door and opened it outward, before stepping through. He stared at Gavino with cold eyes, as if the Italian was worthless. The captain moved aside and Gavino came face-to-face with the Gestapo agent.

The man wore a long black leather coat, a black suit with a black shirt and tie. His head was adorned with a fedora, black. Gavino guessed the man to be at least a hundred and ninety centimeters tall and perhaps a hundred kilograms. His shoulders were wide, his hands large, like a farmer's. But this was no farmer. He moved too quietly and efficiently, more like an elite athlete.

He stopped about a meter from Gavino and stared down.

Gavino's heart felt like it would stop under the gaze of this man's blue eyes. He'd thought the captain's eyes were cold, but these were something entirely different. These were the eyes of a predator, as if Gavino had been hunted down and captured like a wild beast.

A scraping sound came from behind the man, and a chair appeared, which he smoothly settled into it. He continued to regard Gavino, but said nothing. He seemed to be examining everything about Gavino, his face, hair, clothes and work boots. The man was breathing slowly. Calmly. All of this pushed Gavino over the edge and he was about to say something just to get things started, but the Gestapo agent held up a finger for silence. A corner of his lip curled up. Gavino's heart raced. He prayed for it to just stop. Then he wouldn't have to face this . . . creature.

Another minute passed, then the man spoke in perfect Italian. His voice was low, nearly a whisper and Gavino tried to lean forward to hear, but was still attached to the back of the chair.

"My name is Greg Schluter. No doubt you have surmised I am Gestapo, no?"

Gavino nodded.

Schluter nodded in return and favored Gavino with a small smile.

"Are they treating you well, *Herr* Gavino? No, wait, I can see they have not." He raised his left hand and motioned toward Gavino.

The SS captain immediately stepped behind Gavino and unlocked, then removed the manacles.

Gavino slowly pulled his hands back to his front, never taking his eyes off Schluter, and rubbed the chaffed skin. "*Danke.*"

"*Bitte sehr*. No need for you to be uncomfortable. Yet." He paused to let that sink in. "Let me tell you what I already know, so we can save ourselves some time, and perhaps you some pain. What do you say to that?"

Gavino shrugged.

"I will take that as a 'yes.' You are Umberto Gavino, a shopkeeper, although the shop barely has anything worth selling these days. You are seventy years old. A widower. Your only son died in Ethiopia. My goodness, wasn't Mussolini *ein esel?*

"The more important item is that you are a member of the local partisan group, which aligns itself with the Comitato di Liberazione Nazionale. You also helped an American who came into your village earlier today. You and the doctor, that is."

Schluter opened his suit jacket and pulled out a gold cigarette case. The Nazi eagle was engraved on the top. He flipped it open and drew out two. Leaning forward, he handed one to Gavino, putting the other in his own mouth. Then he deftly pocketed the case and from another pocket a lighter appeared. He flicked the flame on and held it out for Gavino, who leaned forward to light the cigarette. The Gestapo agent lit his own cigarette and took a deep drag.

Schluter said in his normal voice, which was deep and powerful, "Good, no?"

Gavino nodded.

"I have but one question for you, *Herr* Gavino. Where's the American?"

Gavino suddenly couldn't speak. It was as if his throat had closed on its own accord. He shrugged. It was the best he could do.

"You don't know where the American is?"

Gavino shook his head.

"Umberto, come. This is very important. You can tell me where he is. I assure you he will be well treated."

Gavino found his voice. "I don't know, *Herr* Schluter."

Schluter blew smoke out through his nose, almost a disappointed sigh. Leaning forward again, he flicked his hand out so fast Gavino only saw a blur, and knocked the cigarette from the shopkeeper's mouth. Adelsberger stepped on it, grinding out the flame.

"I am very good at getting information from people." Schluter looked up at the captain who was standing beside Gavino. "Is this not true, Captain?"

"Yes, it is true." The captain spoke in Italian also.

Schluter held his hands out palm up as if to say, *you see?*

"Where is the American?"

"I don't know, *Herr* Schluter," repeated Gavino.

"A pity we must do this. Tell me, are you familiar with *verschärfte vernehmung?*"

"No."

"Allow me to translate: *verschärfte vernehmung* or enhanced interrogation techniques."

Gavino's bladder released itself.

Schluter looked down at the dripping liquid, and then back at Gavino's face. "I see *that* means something to you." Schluter stood up, carefully removed his leather coat, and hat, handing them to the sergeant who had been behind him. Next, he slipped out of his suit jacket. He removed his Walther PPK from its shoulder holster and handed it to Adelsberger. Lastly, he removed something from one of the coat pockets and turned back to Gavino.

Schluter grinned and a deep terror struck Gavino.

"Shall we begin, *Herr* Gavino?" asked the Gestapo agent as he pulled on leather gloves. Black.

Chapter 27

Colonel Rogers checked his watch. It was getting to be time to reconnect with headquarters. Why hadn't Gavino returned? He got up from the cot and walked around, stretching his legs. He needed that radio. What had Gavino said? Had to park a truck over the door? Shit. Was he trapped in this place? Sudden panic gripped him and he ran up the wooden stairs and pushed on the door above his head. To his surprise, it gave way and lifted. His heart leapt in hope of escape. Then the door hit something solid and stopped moving.

"Shit, shit, shit," he muttered.

The door was heavy and his arms were already getting tired, but he was able to peek out through the six-inch gap. In the dim light inside the garage he could see the garage door, which was closed. The truck's rear tires were a few feet away. Stymied, Rogers lowered the door and knelt on the stairs to think.

There was indeed no way out. He'd already examined the room below and found no exits. He was about to resign himself to his situation when, through the heavy door, he heard screeching sounds. He rose enough to lift the door just a tiny bit, and looked out through an inch-tall gap. The garage door, which was on rollers, had been pushed sideways a few feet. A pair of small, thin legs was walking around. A black dog ran around sniffing the floor.

The sweet voice called out, "*Ciao*? Frank?"

The black dog ran to the end of the truck and lay down facing Rogers. Then Lila did the funniest thing: she began crawling toward the trapped American on her belly, using her front paws to pull herself along while dragging her rear legs. To Rogers it looked like the combat crawl he'd seen and performed himself. In spite of his predicament, he laughed softly.

A scuffling sound came from the side of the truck and he saw Marie on her hands and knees peering at him with her dark eyes. "*Ciao*, Frank!"

Rogers smiled. "*Ciao*, Marie." Even though he knew she didn't speak English, he asked, "Can you move this truck?" He pointed upward and pushed the door against the truck, showing the small gap he had no chance of using.

Marie evidently understood what he wanted, but she shook her head and shrugged. She ran back to the front door and closed it. She got down again and pointed at herself, then said, "*Assistenza*. Mama."

Rogers inferred the meaning and nodded. "Hurry," he said. "Rapid!"

"*Rapido*?"

Rogers nodded.

She held up her hand, palm toward him. "*Aspettare*." With that, Marie left, going out the back door, Lila right behind her.

Rogers understood he was to wait, as if he could do anything else. He lowered the door and sat down on the stairs.

It was four blocks from the garage to Marie's house. She ran quietly down the back streets, stopping at each corner to look for German soldiers. One block from her house, she heard the heavy pounding footsteps of men running. She watched carefully as five Germans ran from her right to the left. She listened intently and when the sounds subsided, she ran to the corner of the building that was on the main road.

Kneeling, she grabbed Lila's collar, and looked out. To her

surprise, the Germans were all getting back into the trucks. Well, not all, a group of six walked into the courthouse and out of her sight.

Rising, she ran back down the street where she'd come from and turned left. Running as fast as she could, she made it to her back door.

"Mama? Where are you, Mama?"

Carlotta ran into the kitchen and hugged Marie tight for a long moment. Then she held her daughter at arms length.

"Where were you? I was so worried!"

"Not now, Mama. We have to rescue the American."

Carlotta looked surprised and asked, "What? What do you mean?"

Marie grabbed her mother's hand and pulled. "Come on. We have to go move a truck, so he can get out of the garage cellar."

Carlotta didn't move, still rather dumbfounded. "Cellar? What cellar?"

"Mama. Trust me. Just come with me. Please?"

Carlotta nodded slowly, then allowed herself to be pulled out the door and down the steps.

With Marie running ahead to check each street before they crossed, they maneuvered their way to the garage's back door.

Once inside, Marie pushed her mother toward the truck and said, "Start the truck. I'll open the door and you back out. I'll tell you when to stop."

Carlotta obeyed her daughter and climbed up into the truck's cab. The key was in the ignition; who would steal a truck here? After starting the engine, she looked over her shoulder and waited until Marie opened the garage door wide enough for the truck. She put the gearshift into reverse and let out the clutch slowly while increasing the gas. The truck moved smoothly. Marie ran along the vehicle until she could see around the hood. When the black bumper cleared the door, she waved her hands.

Carlotta stopped the truck and waited, the engine idling.

Marie knocked on the door and it swung up.

Rogers climbed out while still holding onto the door so it wouldn't slam into the concrete floor. Once out, he slowly lowered the door and turned to Marie.

She rewarded him with a grin. She pushed him out of the way

and gave her mother a *come forward* wave.

Carlotta smiled at her daughter's strength and drove forward until the truck was back where it had been. She shut off the engine and clambered down. Marie ran back to the front door and pulled it closed.

Rogers stuck out his hand and Carlotta shook it. "*Grazie*," the colonel said.

"You're welcome."

Rogers raised his eyebrows. "Oh, you speak English."

"Yes. Some, anyway."

"Mama, not now. Let's go. We have to find a place to hide him."

Rogers looked at Marie as she talked, then at Carlotta. Even though he couldn't understand, he could tell that Marie was clearly in charge here. He wondered how that had happened.

Carlotta gave him a look that was part embarrassment and part pride. "She's my strength."

Rogers nodded.

"We have to leave. The Germans are here."

"I know, Mr. Gavino told me."

Carlotta's expression darkened.

Rogers' heart jumped. "What happened?"

"The Germans took him and the doctor."

"Took them? Where?"

"To the police, er, station."

Rogers felt his face bloom red. "This is all because of me, isn't it?"

With an exasperated sigh, Marie interrupted, grabbing Rogers and her mother by their hands and pulling toward the back door.

To her mother she repeated, "Not now. Let's go."

The adults followed Marie and Lila out the door into the overcast, damp Italian evening.

Chapter 28

Ville di Murlo, Italy
3 August, 1925 Hours

Umberto Gavino's head lolled to the side, blood dripped from his nose and lips. His left eye was swollen shut. His breathing was shallow and rapid.

Adelsberger poured a half bucket of water in Gavino's face and the Italian returned to consciousness. He lifted his head and opened his right eye. Gavino was startled to see the doctor in the cell seated next to him in another chair, bound and bleeding. The doctor's frightened eyes met Gavino's gaze. He shook his head once. Gavino at first thought the doctor meant not to tell the Germans anything, but now he wasn't so sure.

When had he arrived? Gavino realized he'd been knocked out for at some time, but how long was beyond him. He'd never in his life experienced this much pain and didn't know how much longer he could survive.

"Welcome back, Mr. Gavino. Thought we'd lost you there for a little while."

Turning his head, Gavino saw Schluter standing a meter away.

"No more, please."

"Mr. Gavino, I would love to accommodate you. All you need do is tell me where the American is. That's not so much to ask is it?"

"I don't know, *Herr* Schluter. Please."

Schluter nodded, but not to Gavino.

Adelsberger raised his Luger and shot Dr. Marcucci in the forehead. The doctor's head snapped back then fell forward onto his chest. Blood sprayed onto Gavino.

Gavino screamed and tears ran down his cheeks.

Schluter leaned over and put his hands on his knees so he was face to face with Gavino. "Where is the American?"

"I don't know."

Stepping back, Schluter removed his Walther PPK from its shoulder holster. He pointed it at Gavino's right eye.

"Where is the American?"

"I don't know."

Schluter cocked the weapon's hammer, the sound extraordinarily loud in the confines of the stone and metal cell.

"Where is the American?"

"I don't know."

Fifteen seconds passed; the German holding the weapon, the Italian staring at the gigantic hole at the end of the barrel. Gavino's breathing nearly stopped.

Schluter released the hammer. He stepped back and holstered the weapon.

In German, he spoke to his SS captain. "Bring me a villager. The younger the better."

"*Jahowhl, Herr* Schluter."

Adelsberger departed and Schluter retreated to the corner of the cell farthest from Gavino. He got out a cigarette, lit it and started puffing, seemingly oblivious to the dead man a couple of meters from him.

A few minutes passed and the sounds of footsteps and a girl crying filtered down to the cell.

Gavino's heart sank. No, not Marie.

Adelsberger came into Gavino's view. Through the cell bars, the shopkeeper could see a thin girl in the SS man's iron grip. Relief flooded through him. It wasn't Marie. But when

Adelsberger finally got the crying girl into the cell, Gavino saw who it was: the granddaughter of the woman murdered right before his eyes in the street. She was only fourteen.

Adelsberger forced the girl to her knees on the cold stone floor in front of Gavino. The girl gave up and crumbled into herself, sobbing. The SS captain pulled his Luger and pointed it at the back of the girl's head.

"Where is the American?" asked the Gestapo agent from the corner of the cell.

Gavino hesitated.

Adelsberger jammed the barrel into the girl's head. She begin wailing again.

"All right. I will tell you. Please, spare the girl."

Adelsberger looked at Schluter, who nodded. Holstering the Luger, Adelsberger grabbed the girl, dragged her into the back corner and threw her against the wall, where she curled up in a fetal position, still sobbing.

Schluter stepped in front of Gavino with an expectant look on his face.

Gavino told him everything.

Chapter 29

Open field about 2 miles west of Ville di Murlo, Italy
3 August, 1932 hours

It took Dunn only a few minutes to get his men together. Fortunately, no one had ended up in a tree or in the river that wound by the field where they were all hunkered down.

Dunn had a map spread out on the ground as he and Cross knelt side by side.

On the way down, after popping out of the clouds, which were perhaps five hundred feet above the terrain, Dunn had tried to get his bearings. The only thing that had caught his eye was a twinkle of a few lights off to the east. It was nearly impossible to tell how far away they were in the dim light of near sundown, but he guessed about two miles.

"Did you see the lights off that way?" asked Dunn, lifting a hand toward the east.

"Yeah, I did."

Dunn poked the map with his finger and drew a circle. "I'm guessing we're somewhere in this area. The river seems to more or less follow the route on the map. The village should be this one." He pointed to a tiny black dot on the map. "I'm surprised it's even on the map."

"Aren't we lucky," Cross said dryly.

"Hm. Yeah. So let's get started. I'm guessing almost an hour and a half to get close. I bet we'll have to cross the river, too. There's got to be a bridge. I hope."

The men rose and Dunn put the map away. A few minutes later, the squad started across the field, running at double-time to the east in two columns.

About 2 miles west of Ville di Murlo, Italy
Main road to village

Damiano Agostini was excited. He was almost home safe. The nearly one hundred kilometer trip from Turin had been long and arduous, some of it on foot. Fortunately, he had been able to get rides from farmers and passed unchallenged through the Nazi checkpoints with his excellent, but forged papers.

Damiano had changed his appearance to match the papers he carried by cutting his long hair, as well as changing his clothes. He wore a patterned shirt and black slacks, a jacket, and a newer pair of black shoes, all courtesy of a Turin partisan. On his head he wore a black, wide-brimmed fedora. With dark stubble on his jaw and chin, he looked much older than seventeen.

His last ride had dropped him off a few kilometers farther west and given him the pithy warning, "Be careful. The Germans could be around."

Damiano had merely nodded at the understatement and thanked the driver with a wave of his hand, but then he'd touched the pistol in his belt for reassurance. Not that it would do much good if he were outnumbered. Although, he thought, he *had* been outnumbered in the Turin Gestapo commander's office.

Prior to killing the four Germans, he'd been plagued with the fear of whether he'd actually be able to do it when the time came. To overcome this, he'd combed through his memory for every horrible thing he'd learned about the Germans, not the least of which was how they'd turned on the Italians after Italy had surrendered almost a year ago. The Germans forced the Italians to continue to do their bidding, even to helping run their prison camps where the American and British airmen were held in captivity.

He had been relieved that he'd been able to do it, but had been surprised by the sheer speed and violence of it.

Altogether, he'd been away from home for several weeks, training with the Turin partisans, learning to shoot, fight hand-to-hand, to assemble bombs, and how to use tradecraft to follow someone or to determine whether he was being followed. He'd employed the latter and was certain he hadn't been followed. Out on the open road, it was abundantly clear he'd been correct. No German was behind him.

The Rangers' speed had dropped to a careful walking pace as they neared the village. Their direction of travel had taken them near the road that Dunn was sure led across a bridge and into the village. They were about ten yards south of the road, advancing through knee-high grass. Alongside the road were intermittent low shrubs and a few trees. Cross, who was on point, raised his hand. The men stopped and dropped to one knee, each man on the alert. Cross made his way back to Dunn.

"Got a male civilian ahead about fifty yards, walking on the road away from us." He pointed with his Thompson's barrel.

Dunn took a look. The dim light made it difficult, but he spotted motion and could make out the form walking slowly along the road. Farther ahead and to the right were a few lights from the village. Dunn estimated they were only a quarter-mile away.

The man's presence presented a problem. If he learned they were closing in on the village, he could alert the village, and if any Germans were there, them, too. If they waited for a short time and let him proceed into the town, he'd likely go directly to his destination.

While Dunn was deciding, still watching the man, the form suddenly dropped to the ground and disappeared from sight.

Dunn immediately gave hand signals and the squad quickly and silently rearranged themselves into one skirmish line. Dunn moved close to the road with four men, Cross followed, completing the line with the other four men. All were on one knee, their weapons up and pointed toward the spot where the man was last seen. Martelli, the interpreter, was next to Dunn.

Suddenly, the man burst through one of the shrubs and came face-to-face with the barrels of several Thompsons. He skidded to a halt and dipped his hand toward the gun in his belt.

"Don't!" Martelli shouted in Italian. Hearing his own language surprised the man and his hand froze. He wisely raised both hands. Martelli told him to come closer.

Dunn stepped forward and the man's eyes widened in recognition. Now that he was close, Dunn could see that this was just an older teenager.

"What are Americans doing here?" the Italian asked, clearly happy.

Martelli began the translating.

Instead of answering, Dunn held out his hand and said, "Give me your gun."

The man complied. Dunn looked at the weapon, recognizing it before handing it off to Cross, who had joined the group.

"What are you doing with a Gestapo pistol?" Dunn's eyes narrowed in suspicion.

Instead of being alarmed at the question, the Italian smiled. "I took it from a Gestapo agent in Turin. I killed him with it, plus three other damn Nazis. My name is Damiano Agostini. I am partisan." He stood taller, shoulders back.

"How old are you?"

"Seventeen."

Dunn shook his head. Only a little younger than some of his own men.

"Why were you running away from the village?"

"I saw Germans on the main street."

Dunn looked at Cross with an *uh oh* expression. Cross nodded. Their orders had been specific: do not engage the enemy unless forced into it. Allied presence in this part of Italy could cause the Germans to react with reinforcements along the southern coast, including France, at the wrong time.

Turning back to the teen, Dunn asked, "Do you live in this village?"

"I do, yes, with my mother and sister."

Dunn found himself in a quandary. Instead of sneaking into town under darkness, a villager knew they were there, plus he didn't know whether he could trust this kid. On the other hand, maybe the kid would prove to be useful. If not, Dunn could subdue and silence the kid. Hopefully, without killing him.

Dunn had few details about where the missing colonel was being kept safely, but he decided to lay one out there and see what happened.

"Tell me the names of other partisans in the village."

"How do I know I can trust you?"

Dunn smiled at the question since he'd had the exact same thoughts. Then he pointed to the forty-eight star American flag sewn on his right sleeve.

"We aren't German," Dunn simply said.

Damiano nodded. "An excellent point. Umberto Gavino is the only one I'm allowed to know."

Dunn's ears picked up Gavino's name, which was one of the two identified in Rogers' message, which Truscott's aide had passed on to Dunn.

"Stay here," commanded Dunn.

Dunn looked at Cross and tipped his head indicating to step away with him. Cross followed Dunn a short distance from the Italian, just in case he understood English.

"What do you think, Dave? Do we trust him?"

Cross gave a shrug. "I don't know. We only have his word that he's one of the good guys. He might just be bragging to us."

"My thoughts exactly. On the other hand, he could help us find the missing colonel more quickly. I'm thinking we give it a go and see what develops. That's assuming the Germans leave soon."

"Let's try it," replied Cross. "We can take him out, if we have to."

"Right."

Dunn walked back over to stand in front of Damiano. He handed his Thompson to Cross, then said to the Italian, "Take off your jacket and turn around."

After Martelli's translation, Damiano complied without a word. He held his arms out straight from the shoulder. He knew what Dunn wanted to do.

Dunn quickly frisked the teen and was satisfied that there were no hidden weapons. He took the jacket from him and checked it, too, before handing it back. Dunn lifted the fedora off and looked inside. You never knew. He replaced the hat.

"Okay."

Damiano put the jacket back on and looked at Dunn expectantly.

"We might be able to use your help. You up to it?"

"Yes."

Dunn put his hand on Martelli's shoulder. "This is Alphonso Martelli. You will stay with him and do exactly what he says. Do you understand?"

Damiano stuck out his hand for Martelli to shake. "An honor, Mr. Martelli."

Martelli shook Damiano's hand and nodded once.

"Okay, gentlemen. Let's go."

Chapter 30

Ville di Murlo, Italy
3 August, 1950 Hours

A squad of SS soldiers poured into the garage. After ensuring no one was there to ambush them, one jumped into the truck and got it moved out of the way. The squad leader, Sergeant Clauer, bent over and lifted the door, letting it fall open against the floor with a thud. Light from below filtered up. He raised his MP40 submachine gun and went down the stairs. When Clauer got to a point just before where his feet would be exposed to anyone in the cellar room, he stopped and turned sideways, then knelt on one knee. With his weapon in front of him, he slowly leaned farther and farther down until he could see the rest of the room. A cot and a table sat against the far wall.

Satisfied that no one was there, he rose and ran down the rest of the steps. Some of his men had followed right behind him and they thundered down the stairs, too.

"Tear it apart," Clauer said. He grabbed one man by the arm. "Report back that the American is not here. Go. Now." He shoved the man toward the stairs.

"Get in here." Carlotta pushed Rogers into her kitchen through the back door. She ran in behind him and Marie followed.

"Wait here," ordered Carlotta. She ran into the pantry.

Rogers heard her rummaging around, and when she came out she had a small bag in her hand. Holding it out toward him she said, "Take this. It's not much, but it will help you get by. We'll wait here until it's dark, then you must leave. You can't stay here. Head for the coast."

Rogers nodded, but his stomach was churning. How was he going to get back to Corsica now?

Gestapo Agent Greg Schluter sat in the mayor's chair with his feet on the polished walnut desk. Cigarette smoke trailed above him toward the light hanging from the high ceiling.

A Berlin native, Schluter was a sixteen-year-old boy when Hitler was named Chancellor in 1933. That same year, young Schluter joined the *Hitler Jugend* with incredible enthusiasm and energy. He studiously and carefully updated his performance booklet with all of his achievements in athletics and Nazi indoctrination, excelling at both.

In 1934, Schluter participated in the annual Nuremberg rally. He still recalled Hitler's words of encouragement, saying Germany would live on in the Hitler Youth. Following the rally, he joined the *HJ-Streifendienst*, the Hitler Youth-Patrol Force, which was a political police unit. It was in this role that he first began working with the Gestapo, providing information on disloyal citizens. One of his favorite activities was roughing up members of the Catholic Youth League. At one time a member himself, he had nothing but contempt for the church, and the league members, some of whom were former friends.

In the summer of 1935, the fiercely loyal eighteen year old denounced his own father for calling the *Führer* deluded. The man had repeatedly refused to join the Nazi party. That was his own choice, so he went to a concentration camp, where he died of a heart attack. Schluter's mother never spoke to him again after telling him to move out. She died a month later. Schluter didn't attend her funeral.

The next year, too old for the Hitler Youth, Schluter joined the Gestapo and proved to be an effective interrogator. His size helped intimidate people, and he refined his technique over the years to a combination of soft talk and hard fists that always yielded results. His reputation grew and so did his responsibilities, and eventually he ended up in Genoa. It was the happiest time of his life.

He was lost in thought imagining his conversation with the American when the sound of pounding boots on the street outside caught his attention. He quickly dropped his feet to the floor and leaned forward onto the desk.

The SS soldier dispatched by the squad leader knocked on the door, opened it after hearing "come in," and stepped through. He marched up to the desk and stopped at attention, his eyes focused on Schluter's. He raised his hand and said, "*Heil* Hitler!"

"*Heil* Hitler!" Schluter gave the Hitler salute, then looked over the man's shoulder. "Where's the American?"

"Sir, Sergeant Clauer said to report that he was not in the garage cellar."

Schluter's jaw muscles clenched and his eyes grew dark. "You are certain?"

The soldier thought he might wither under the man's intense gaze, but was able to say, "Yes, sir. We are sure."

Schluter jumped to his feet and shouted, "Go get Sergeant Clauer!"

Before the man could even reply, Schluter was out of the office and running down to the jail cell.

Schluter burst into Gavino's cell and grabbed the smaller man by the throat. He squeezed hard. Gavino's good eye began to bulge and his face turned red. Still Schluter squeezed. Just before Gavino fell into unconsciousness, the Gestapo agent released his grip. Instead of stepping back, he put a palm on Gavino's forehead and shoved. Gavino toppled over backward and his head hit the stone floor with a resounding crack. He appeared to lose consciousness, so Schluter grabbed a pail of water and dumped it on the Italian.

Gavino sputtered awake and looked up at his tormentor.

Gavino had terror in his eyes, Schluter, fury in his.

"You lied to me!" shouted Schluter, spittle flying from his

lips.

Gavino shook his head side to side. "No. I told you the truth. I told you all I know."

"The American was not there."

Gavino looked perplexed. Schluter saw it, but was too enraged to let the truth guide his actions. Schluter drew his Walther and cocked the hammer. He bent over and pressed it against Gavino's forehead. He slowly, agonizingly pulled the weapon back. Then in a fluid and frighteningly fast motion, turned and pointed it at the still sobbing girl.

Gavino stared in shock, then burst into tears. He'd known this girl since her infancy. He looked back at Schluter and wondered, what kind of monster is this? If he was willing to shoot the girl, what else could he do?

"Please! Don't hurt her. No more. If the American wasn't there, I don't know where he is. Please don't hurt anyone else."

Schluter had calmed down. Perhaps the threat of killing the girl had vented all his rage. He holstered the weapon and turned to Adelsberger, who had been standing watch outside the cell, and said, "Help me lift him back up."

Adelsberger stepped into the cell and the two men lifted Gavino back into the seated position.

"Get the doctor's body out of here," ordered Schluter.

Adelsberger glanced at the doctor's still form and judged he'd only need two men.

"*Jawohl.*" The SS captain left to go get some men for the task. He wasn't about to get himself bloody.

"If the American is not in the cellar, the one whose door was under a truck, where is he?"

Gavino could only shake his head.

"Think, Mr. Gavino. Someone helped him. Was it another partisan? Who else is a member of your group?"

"The doctor and I were the last. There is no one else," lied Gavino.

"You'll forgive me if I say I don't believe you."

"It's true."

Schluter shook his head, and turned away from the blood-and-water soaked Italian. He stood in thought for some time. In the meantime, Adelsberger's two men came in and carried the body out. Going up the stairs the soldier carrying the torso lost his grip in the slick blood and the poor doctor's head thumped against the step. The men laughed and resumed their task.

"Stand up," Schluter said.

With difficulty, the Italian got to his feet. He swayed, but remained upright.

"Walk. We're going outside."

On the way up the stairs, Gavino saw the doctor's blood on the step. He paused and crossed himself. Schluter saw the motion and slapped Gavino in the back of the head.

"Move."

Once outside, Gavino realized how bad the cell had smelled. The rain had stopped and the fresh air seemed so wonderful. How much longer would he get to breathe it in?

Schluter guided the man to the open-topped Mercedes staff car parked by the curb and opened the back door.

"Get in."

Gavino complied and Schluter slammed the door shut.

Schluter's driver, who had been standing at attention the whole time, opened Schluter's door in the front.

As Schluter got in the car, he gave a brisk order. The driver ran to the back of the car, opened the trunk, grabbed something, then handed it to the Gestapo agent after closing the trunk. He got in the driver's seat.

"Where to, sir?"

Schluter looked in the dimming light down the street ahead of them. He turned and looked back the other way. They were closer to the west edge of the village.

"Straight, to the end of the village slowly, then turn and come back."

"Yes, sir." The engine started and the car began moving forward.

Schluter brought the megaphone to his lips. In English he shouted, "Captain Newport! You have five minutes to surrender or I will kill a villager every five minutes until you do."

As the car continued to move, Schluter repeated his threat again and again.

Inside Carlotta's house, the mother and daughter heard the man yelling. Carlotta strained to hear at first, but it grew louder. She went to the window and peeked out, standing to the side. The car was right in front of her house when the German shouted again. She suddenly realized the words weren't German. When she translated in her head, she moaned, then said, "Oh no."

She ran back to the kitchen where Rogers was getting to his feet. From his expression, she knew he'd heard and she knew what he was going to do.

Marie stood next to her mother, fear in her eyes. She didn't understand the words, but knew from her mother's and the American's body language that it was bad.

"I have to turn myself in. I cannot allow someone to die for me."

Carlotta stepped closer and put a hand on Rogers' shoulder. She nodded and turned away to take Marie's hand. Carlotta bent over and whispered to her little girl. Marie's reaction was so swift neither adult could stop her. She ran to Rogers and put her arms around his waist and hugged tight. He nearly stumbled, but regained his balance just in time. He put a hand on Marie's head and stroked the dark hair. "It's okay, Marie. Let me go, please."

Carlotta translated and Marie burst into tears and hugged tighter, if that was even possible.

Rogers was stumped. He didn't want to pry the little girl's hands off, but was about to when a thought came to him. He pulled his family's picture from his shirt pocket and said, "Could you keep this safe for me, Marie?"

At first, Marie wouldn't look when her mother translated, but after a moment she glanced up and saw what it was. She let go and grabbed the photo. Rogers bent to hug her, but she scampered away. Soon they heard the pounding of her feet on the stairs. She soon ran back into the room and handed Rogers her parents' picture.

"If you keep mine safe."

Rogers took the picture solemnly and put it in his shirt pocket. He hugged Marie and looked at Carlotta, who gave him a small smile.

Rogers opened his other shirt pocket and pulled out the small notebook he'd used to code and decode his Morse code conversation with Corsica. Along with it, he handed her his identity papers, hoping to further obfuscate the facts for the Gestapo.

"Please burn this. No one can see it."

Carlotta took the items, and opened the front door of the wood burning stove, whose fire was still going from dinner. She tossed them in and they watched as they caught fire. The notebook and papers quickly curled into black wisps, then collapsed into ash.

With that, Rogers walked out the back door and turned left to the west in the small alleyway. He ran a block to put distance between himself and Carlotta's house; no need to draw the Nazis' attention to her or Marie.

He found an opening between houses and ran through its narrow width to the main road. He stepped into the street, his hands over his head.

Taking a deep breath, he shouted, "Here I am!"

The Mercedes was about fifty yards away, having reached the edge of town and turned around. Rogers saw a man in the passenger front seat speak to the driver. The car immediately sped up. When it reached a point across the street from him it stopped, its tires screeching on the pavement. The man in the front seat got out, pulled his weapon and walked toward Rogers.

Rogers' eyes were focused on the unwavering barrel of the handgun. He recognized it as a favored weapon of the Gestapo and his heart dropped. He raised his gaze. A satisfied smile was on the man's face.

The Gestapo agent could have been the Nazi poster boy for the Aryan race, thought Rogers.

Chapter 31

Just west of Ville di Murlo, Italy
3 August, 2001 Hours

Dunn and Cross knelt on the west side of the bridge, behind its metal framework. Dunn had a pair of binoculars to his eyes.

"You won't fucking believe this, Dave."

"What?"

"I think Rogers just surrendered to the Germans." He examined the officer; he matched the picture he'd been given by someone on General Truscott's staff. He wore an officer's hat and had officer's insignia on his lapel. The fading light glinted off silver, train-track captain's bars. Dunn handed the field glasses over to Cross.

At a distance of one hundred yards, Cross watched an American get into a black German car with a man wearing a dark suit.

"Fuck. Gestapo," Cross said.

"Yes. I think so."

Cross gave the binoculars back to Dunn, who was thinking fast. There were four trucks strung out farther along the street, facing the opposite direction, east. Dunn and his men were terribly out of position. With no way or time to get in front of the trucks to form an ambush, it seemed the colonel was doomed to whatever the Gestapo agent had in store for him.

The only hope might be an all-out attack. The street appeared to be vacant except for the Germans, so the villagers must have been able to go inside their homes. As Dunn turned toward his men to wave them forward, the German staff car's engine suddenly roared and the black car tore down the street at high speed, weaving past the trucks, which were also starting to move, albeit more slowly. Less than a minute later, the car and trucks were out of sight and their engines' sounds faded.

"Damn it. We're fucked and so is the colonel."

"How long do you think he can stand up to the Gestapo?" asked Cross.

"I've heard a couple of days or so is all most men can take."

"Wait a minute." Dunn snapped his fingers. "I knew something was out of place: he's wearing captain's insignia," Dunn said. "I wonder if he worked up a false identity."

Cross glanced at Dunn. He knew his friend was sharp, had proven it time and again, but this was just pretty damn observant. "Nice job."

Dunn shrugged it off and said, "If I'd done a nice job he wouldn't be having his ass hauled off to who knows where by the fucking Gestapo."

"Point taken."

"We've got to get in that town and find the partisans, if any are still living, and find out where they would be taking him. They're bound to know."

Dunn got up and gave the sign for the men to come forward. The men gathered in a small circle around the sergeant.

Dunn motioned for Damiano to join him. The teenager stepped through the circle to stand near Dunn, Martelli by his side.

"There was a Gestapo agent in your village."

Damiano groaned. This was always bad news.

"Where would his headquarters be located?"

"It's in Genoa."

This surprised Dunn. "Why not Turin? That's where you said you'd killed a Gestapo agent."

"That was where the assignment was. This area is definitely under Genoa. I know the building."

"You know exactly where the headquarters are located?"

"I do."

"How?"

"It's my next target. When you do well on an important assignment, you get another important one."

"Sounds just like the fucking army," murmured Hanson.

Dunn ignored him and spoke to Damiano, "We need to get into your village unseen. Is there a place we can stay without attracting attention?"

"Yes, there's a vacant building near my mother's house. I can take you there."

"It's on the south side of the main street, close to the river. We can cross the bridge, then move off the road and nearer to the river, coming up on the back side. You understand this?"

"We do."

Dunn gave the order and the men formed a single file. Dunn led the way with Damiano and Martelli right behind him.

Once inside the darkened wooden building, Dunn told the men to rest, which they gladly did, flopping down anywhere there was enough space. They were situated in the basement, having entered through a door that led out to the river. The building had been a restaurant and above the back door was a wooden deck, presumably for outdoor dining.

Dunn and Cross sat cross-legged on the floor. Damiano and Martelli joined them.

"I want to see my mother."

"You understand, I can't let you out of my sight while we're here?"

"But she is on our side. Maybe she can help."

"I'm sorry. No."

"She's a good cook. Wouldn't you like a good meal?"

Dunn smiled. "We would, but we can't stop for that. What I need for you to do is describe the exact location of the Genoa Gestapo headquarters."

"I could draw you a map. Would that help?"

"That would be helpful, Damiano. Why don't you work on it with Martelli?"

Damiano nodded enthusiastically. Just before Martelli and the Italian moved off to find a space of their own, Dunn asked, "How far from here to Genoa?"

"A little under seventy kilometers," Damiano replied immediately.

Dunn's eyebrows lifted at Damiano's quick reply and the teenager said, "I like maps."

Dunn nodded, then calculated the conversion. "About forty miles. Okay, thanks."

Dunn was lost in thought for a few minutes, then he said, "I'm wondering whether the Gestapo would really take him to Genoa."

"Where else would he go?" Cross asked.

"He's an officer, maybe they'll think he belongs to a bomber crew. Maybe that was his plan for the subterfuge all along in case he did get picked up. He may have a complete history built up. Where would they take a bomber pilot?"

"A POW camp," Cross suggested.

"Yes, that's what I'm wondering. *We* know how important the colonel is, but they think he's a captain. If they don't know who he really is, they would have no reason to thoroughly interrogate him beyond mission information, unit strength and so on. Nothing about his real purpose."

"What if he holds out, then collapses and gives them the truth anyway?" asked a dubious Cross.

"Could happen exactly like that. But the bigger question is still where would they go?"

"Martelli, Damiano, come here," called out Dunn.

When the two joined the sergeants, Dunn asked, "Where's the nearest prisoner of war camp? One where American and British bomber crews would be taken?"

For this, Damiano had to think a bit. "There's a big one across the river from San Giuseppe. That would be only about thirteen kilometers."

"What's the name of the camp?"

"Prigione di Guerra 135."

"Do you know what the layout of that place is?"

"No. We could contact the partisans around San Giuseppe. They would almost certainly have a few men working on the inside, cooks, servants."

Dunn nodded, then got up and started pacing as he thought out loud. "So if they do have men inside, they would be aware of the arrival of new prisoners. We could find out if anyone matching our captain's description comes in." Dunn purposely didn't give away Rogers' true rank to Damiano. "The problem becomes how to get him out of the POW camp."

"You want to break *into* a POW camp?" asked Cross. His expression was part aghast at the idea and part excited by the prospect.

"It can't be any harder than breaking *into* an atomic bomb lab, Dave." Dunn was referring to Operation Devil's Fire.

Cross shrugged. "Good point."

To Damiano, Dunn asked, "What's the best route to San Giuseppe?" Dunn pulled out his map and laid it on the floor, kneeling. "Show me."

Damiano got down one knee, also, and examined the map. He quickly found San Giuseppe and pointed at it.

"See that large bend in the river?"

To Dunn, it looked like a wide letter U, with the upper tips flaring to the outside.

"Yes."

"The camp sits there."

"Damn. The river guards it on the three sides."

"The road from our village goes mostly north to Millesimo. From there, it's east to San Giuseppe."

Dunn took stock of their armament and realized they would be vastly underpowered. With only small arms fire, and no weaponry like a mortar, or explosives, breaching the prison would be next to impossible.

"How many partisans are here in your village?"

"I don't know for sure. We limit the number each man knows in case he's captured. I know only the one I mentioned before."

"We need you to contact Mr. Gavino and bring him here. His name was given to us as a contact."

"What happened to keeping me in your sight?" Damiano smirked.

"Martelli will be going with you and things changed. Can you do it, or not?"

"Of course I can do it."

"Quick as you can. And quietly."

"I will return soon."

"Martelli, escort our new friend outside. Get him past Hanson and Lindstrom, then stay with him, but you stay out of sight of the public."

"Okay, Sarge."

Damiano and Martelli left through the back door.

Chapter 32

Damiano couldn't find Mr. Gavino anywhere. He first checked the store and the apartment above, but no one was there. No one was out of doors in the village. He believed they were hiding out of fear of the Germans in case they returned.

Martelli was trying to figure out how to stay out of sight, but could come up with nothing, so he stuck close to the youth as they ran down the street to the garage. They found the doors open and a truck parked half way out of the garage.

Puzzled by this, but not wanting to waste any time, Damiano ran to the door in the floor. To his shock, it was open. No one ever left it open. He looked around the garage in sudden fright. What if the Germans left someone to watch over it? And he'd fallen right into the trap? He willed himself to calm down and focus.

He went part way down the exposed stairs. A quick inspection showed no one was there, but the cot and table had been thrown as if they'd been searched and angrily cast aside.

Running up the stairs and turning out the light, he ran back into the street and sprinted for home. He stopped at the bottom of the steps to the front door and turned to Martelli who'd been by his side the whole way.

"You should stay here. Hide by the bushes," he told Martelli.

Martelli shook his head. "I'm supposed to stay with you."

"Please. I don't want my family to know there are more Americans here. They'll be in danger."

Martelli saw the pleading in Damiano's eyes. Dunn would kill him if he let the boy escape, but the kid was right, it was dangerous to know about more Americans being here, and Dunn had given him instructions to stay out of sight.

"Fine. Two minutes. That's all."

"*Grazie!*"

Dashing up the steps two at a time, Damiano burst into the house.

"Mama? Marie?"

From the bedrooms upstairs, he heard, "Up here, Damiano."

He also heard a squeal of delight and he smiled. The light sounds of his sister running down the hall came next.

They met just as Damiano got to the second floor. Marie launched herself into his waiting arms and hugged him so tight he thought he'd stop breathing. He stroked her hair and said, "Hi, little one. I missed you."

"I missed you too. I was so worried."

Damiano suddenly found he couldn't speak for fear of crying. He hadn't thought that a nine-year-old girl could worry about him.

When he finally got his voice, he said, "I am fine. Let's go see mama."

He let go of Marie, and she grabbed his hand, pulling him down the hall. "Mr. Gavino is here."

Damiano felt relief at this news. Although he wondered why the man would be upstairs.

"The Germans hurt him. Bad."

Damiano's relief washed away. Gavino meant so much to his family, and to the partisans.

The siblings entered Marie's room where Gavino was lying on her bed, where Rogers had been not so long ago. Carlotta was seated on a chair next to the bed, gently dabbing his swollen face with a cool wash cloth.

Carlotta had watched the Gestapo agent force Gavino out of the car, before the American got in. By the time the car was safely out of sight, Gavino had managed to walk to the curb outside her house, where he collapsed. Carlotta enlisted the help of the man next door and, between them, slowly got Gavino back to his feet and into the house.

Damiano gasped. Gavino's kind face was yellow and purple, and blood oozed from cuts above his closed eyes, and his lips, which were swollen to twice normal size.

Carlotta turned and stood up, tears welling. She hugged her son. "I thought I would never see you again," she whispered.

"I'm fine, mama. Is he awake?"

"He was sleeping until you came in."

Gavino opened his good eye. It was bloodshot.

"I have to talk to him."

"I think you should wait until morning."

"Er, mama, it can't wait." Damiano was in an awkward position. So far, he'd hidden his membership in the partisans group from her. She'd thought he'd been traveling to get store supplies for Mr. Gavino, which in and of itself could be a dangerous task due to not only the Germans, but other Italians who would want to rob and perhaps kill the bearer.

"I can't explain right now, you must believe me, but I must talk to him now."

"Carlotta, it is all right. Please go downstairs. Take little Marie with you," Gavino said, his voice barely audible.

Carlotta looked from Gavino to her son and back to the shopkeeper. Understanding hit her hard. Her lips compressed into a thin line. She started to say something when Gavino mouthed the word, "Please."

She nodded. Grabbing Marie's hand, they departed.

Damiano sat down on the chair and put his hand on the older man's shoulder.

"What happened?"

"Gestapo beat me." Tears leaked from the damaged eyes. "I told them where an American was. They were going to kill poor Anna."

Damiano sucked in a breath. He liked Anna. Very much. "Is

she all right?"

"Yes. She's suffered such a fright, though."

"I'll talk to her sometime. When I can."

"What do you need to say to me, Damiano?"

Damiano leaned close enough to whisper in Gavino's ears, "American soldiers are here."

"But too late to rescue the American."

"You knew they were coming?"

"Yes, I was to be their contact. Alas, I can't really move right now."

"I understand. I need someone to work with so we can help the Americans. Who else can I talk to?"

"You know the rules."

"You said it yourself, you're out of commission. We need to help these men. So you must tell me who else I can call on."

Gavino closed his eyes and Damiano immediately touched him on the shoulder, fearful the older man had fallen asleep or worse, passed out.

"Mr. Gavino, please."

"Very well. Antonio Pastore."

"You're kidding. The druggist?"

"Yes, it is he."

"I never would have thought he'd get mixed up with the partisans."

Gavino chuckled lightly. "Would you have suspected an old shopkeeper?"

"No. I guess not. Do you know where he is?"

"Probably at home."

Damiano nodded. The druggist lived two blocks away, conveniently closer to the building housing the Allied troops. "What's the code word?"

Each group of three had a code word to use when one member needed access to another group. Some members were part of several groups and Gavino was one of those trusted few, acting as an intersection with his groups.

"Alesia."

Damiano knew his Roman history and smiled. The Battle of Alesia took place in 52 B.C. and pitted Julius Caesar against the Gallic tribes led by Vercingetorix of the Arverni. By defeating the Gallic army, Caesar ended the Celtic domination in France, Belgium, Switzerland and Northern Italy.

"But he already knows you're involved."

"Okay. I must go now. Please get well soon." The young man patted the older one's shoulder.

Gavino grasped the hand. "Be careful. Be very careful."

"I will."

Outside, Ranger Martelli was checking his watch. Thirty more seconds and he would go in.

Damiano ran down the stairs and found his mother and sister in the living room. Marie was curled up, already asleep next to her mother, who draped an arm over the little girl's shoulder. Carlotta looked up expectantly.

"Mama, I have to leave again."

"Why? You've only just returned. We have to talk about what you're doing."

Damiano crossed the room and knelt in front of his mother. He looked into her frightened eyes and said, "Please trust me. I must go. I don't know when I'll be back."

"No. You can't be a part of this. It's too dangerous."

"It's too dangerous not to help, Mama."

Carlotta began to cry and Damiano rose to lean over and hug her. When she wouldn't let go, he gently grasped her hands. "It will be all right."

He let go and stood upright. "Tell Marie I love her."

Carlotta could only nod.

Damiano dashed out the door, forgetting about Martelli. When the American jumped in front of him, Damiano flinched, then recognized who it was.

"You scared me to death."

"Yeah, well, I was getting pretty scared there myself. Now what?"

"Follow me." Damiano led the way directly to Pastore's house.

Chapter 33

Prigione di Guerra 135
San Giuseppe, Italy
3 August, 2045 Hours

Colonel Eberhard Dentz, the commandant of Camp 135, hung up the phone. The front gate guard had called to say a Gestapo agent named Schluter was bringing in an American prisoner. While it wasn't completely unusual for this to happen, he'd never met Schluter, although he'd certainly heard of him. Everyone had. Dentz's skin suddenly crawled.

He rose slowly, the back injury from trench warfare in France still haunted him daily. He put on his uniform jacket, which had been hanging on his office door. Next, he placed his brimmed hat on his head, then he stepped over in front of a small mirror on the wall. Injured did not mean unprofessional, and if anything, Dentz believed himself to be professional. He knew many officers, especially combat veterans, looked down upon him and all prisoner of war commandants, but he was good at his job. It was the best way for him to contribute to the German war effort.

Camp 135 currently housed only about sixty prisoners, most of which were enlisted, but there were a dozen officers. The nationalities were split between American and British. Dentz far preferred the Americans to the British, whose officers were snobbish and class conscious even in captivity. The Americans barely paid attention to rank amongst themselves. Dentz was sorry that the ranking officer was British, a smug colonel who'd been captured at Tobruk. It had been about the last good thing to happen for Rommel in North Africa.

As the commandant stepped through the outer office, he stopped by his secretary's desk, where a beautiful blonde sat typing.

"Abriana, I need you to stay very late tonight."

Abriana Lachmann was of German-Italian heritage, and spoke both languages fluently, which was how she got the job as secretary to the commandant.

"Is anything wrong, sir?"

"No. Nothing is wrong. We have a new prisoner coming in with the Gestapo. I don't know exactly what they might want."

"Of course, sir, whatever you need."

Dentz nodded his thanks and walked away. He stepped out onto the small porch of the headquarters building. The air was still warm from the day, but a cool breeze came down from the mountains to the north. He imagined it being like home. All he needed was a cigar and a brandy. He sighed deeply, wondering whether his wife missed him and if she was safe. She was in Berlin with his small son, Fredrich, a wonderful late-in-life surprise.

His attention was drawn to the motion of a car heading toward him. The big staff car, which had the top down, pulled to a stop almost at his feet. There were four men sitting in the car, an SS soldier acting as the driver, the Gestapo agent, and in the back seat an SS captain and the prisoner. Before the driver could get out to open the door for him, the passenger in the front seat jumped out and moved to stand at the foot of the three-step staircase. Dentz noted the man's height and sharp dress. The Gestapo agent was a large, powerfully built man.

"*Heil* Hitler!" snapped Schluter with the matching salute.

"*Heil* Hitler," returned Dentz.

The Gestapo agent climbed the steps and said, "Greg Schluter."

"Colonel Dentz."

Schluter didn't offer his hand. This suited Dentz just fine.

"Where can I take the prisoner for questioning?"

"You haven't questioned him yet?" This was a surprise. Typically, the Gestapo only handed over prisoners after interrogation.

"We were just a few kilometers away when we captured him. This is much closer than my office in Genoa. When I'm done with him, you can have him. Unless of course things take a turn for the worse." Schluter's smile raised the hair on the back of Dentz's neck.

"Of course, *Herr* Schluter."

Captain Adelsberger got out of the car and walked around the vehicle to stand outside Rogers' door. He drew his Luger and motioned for Rogers to get out. Rogers, whose hands were shackled behind his back, making the trip from Ville di Murlo to the POW camp miserable, scooted over and got his feet out on the dirt. By leaning forward to get his center of gravity over his feet, he was finally able to stand. Adelsberger waggled his pistol, indicating that Rogers should move to the bottom of the steps.

Rogers looked up at the two men on the porch. The Gestapo agent had said surprisingly little to him on the drive, but Rogers was under no misapprehensions that this would continue. He fully expected a forceful interrogation.

The man with the Gestapo agent, Rogers assumed, was the camp commandant. He was older, with gray hair showing under his officer's cap. The way he stood seemed to indicate favoring his left leg, as if avoiding putting too much weight on it.

A poke in the back prodded Rogers and he walked up the steps. The commandant glanced his way briefly, then turned away saying something to the Gestapo agent in German. Rogers inferred it was something like, "this way."

The Gestapo agent followed the commandant, and the SS captain guided Rogers into the building. They entered an outer office where a drop-dead gorgeous blonde rose from behind a desk. The commandant introduced her to the Gestapo agent. The Gestapo agent nodded to her, but said nothing. He followed the commandant into another room off to the right.

When he stepped through the door portal, Rogers knew this would be the place. A table and three chairs were in the center of the room. Two chairs were on the same side, facing the third. The chairs were already pulled away to make room for someone to be seated. There were no windows. A bare bulb hung from the ceiling. It swayed in the air movement caused by the door opening.

Adelsberger pointed to the chair facing the door.

Rogers took the hint and sat down. He took a few deep breaths while not appearing to do so. He wanted to calm himself, but not alert the interrogator.

The Gestapo agent said something and Adelsberger holstered his weapon, walked over behind Rogers and removed the shackles. Rogers immediately rubbed both wrists. Adelsberger moved over by the door, closed it and drew his weapon again. He glared at Rogers. The American returned the gaze briefly, then looked at the commandant standing behind the agent.

The older man appraised Rogers briefly, then grabbed one of the chairs and moved away before dropping the chair in the corner and seating himself.

The Gestapo agent spoke to Adelsberger, who nodded, then left the room.

The agent sat down at last and said in English, "My name is Greg Schluter. I am Gestapo."

He smiled. "But then I imagine you know that."

Chapter 34

Ville di Murlo, Italy
3 August, 2100 hours

Hanson and Lindstrom heard the soft footsteps at the same time. Their weapons snapped up, ready.

A low voice called out from the darkened west side of the building, "It's me, Martelli."

"Come ahead," ordered Hanson.

Martelli and Damiano stepped around the corner and stopped in front of the two Rangers.

"We have two more men with us," Martelli said, tipping his head back toward the direction he'd just come from.

"Have them come around slowly with their hands up," replied Hanson.

Martelli translated.

Damiano smiled. "You don't trust us?"

"Cut the crap, kid. Bring 'em around, hands up."

As Martelli translated, Damiano lost the smile and said something crisp in Italian that Martelli didn't bother to translate.

The two men rounded the corner, their hands held high.

Damiano said, "May I introduce—"

"Not to us. Tell them to stand still while we frisk them."

Martelli translated and the men nodded.

Lindstrom stepped behind the first man, the oldest, and with one hand holding his Thompson, frisked the man with his other hand. Finding nothing he said, "Clean." Then he moved on to the younger man. When Lindstrom put his hand on the man's right side, the Italian flinched. Lindstrom raised his weapon and poked the man in the back.

"Stand still."

Martelli translated and the man said something quickly, then chuckled lightly.

"What's so fucking funny," demanded Hanson.

"Renato regrets that he is quite ticklish."

"Swell. Tell him to hold still."

Another quick word from Martelli.

This time, Lindstrom was able to complete the task without interruption.

"Clean," he said again.

"Come on, let's get you inside." Hanson opened the door and stepped back, holding it open with a boot.

Damiano was puzzled by Hanson's unfriendly attitude and as the other two Italians walked through the door, he stopped beside Hanson.

"Why don't you like me? I'm helping."

Martelli translated.

Hanson just glared at the young Italian.

Damiano shrugged and walked though the door.

Most of the men were sprawled on the floor, relaxing, while Dunn and Cross sat cross-legged next to each other, chatting. At the sight of the Italians, they both stood up and moved toward the newcomers.

Damiano was amazed by the way they walked: with strength, barely constrained power, and yet somehow graceful. He wanted to be like that.

Once again he said, "May I introduce Renato Frontino," he turned his hand toward the younger man with his palm up, then pointed at the other, "and Antonio Pastore. Mr. Frontino is one of my teachers. Was. Mr. Pastore is our druggist."

Everyone shook hands and sat down on the floor in a circle.

Pastore spoke first. Martelli translated for him. "Damiano explained to us your problem; that you need to rescue the man the Gestapo took away earlier. We can help you, are glad to help you."

A crash of thunder boomed. Soon after, rain began to fall. The wind picked up and splattered the heavy drops against the door. Another boom of thunder rolled across the countryside, followed quickly by yet a third.

Unfazed by nature's fire and brimstone, Dunn nodded. "Thank you." He slid a pack of Lucky Strikes out of his shirt pocket and shook a few part way out. He offered them to his guests. Both men smiled widely at the American cigarettes and each took one, lighting up. Damiano reached in to grab one and Pastore admonished him.

Damiano blushed.

Martelli said, "Mr. Pastore asked 'what would his mother would say?' "

Dunn and Cross chuckled, and Dunn patted Damiano's arm. "My mother is the same way and I'm twenty-four."

Damiano gave a small smile.

Dunn turned back to the other two partisans. "We aren't sure whether we need to get to Genoa, to the Gestapo headquarters, or to the POW camp at . . ." He looked at Damiano for help.

"San Giuseppe."

Pastore nodded energetically. "He is there. We have a reliable witness who saw him arrive with the Gestapo. He was seen entering the commandant's office."

The younger man, Frontino, interrupted, "You cannot rescue someone from inside that POW camp." He shook his head. "No. Impossible."

Dunn shrugged. "We have to try."

"Why is this man so important?"

Dunn shook his head. "Can't tell you that. We just have our orders."

"There are just over sixty prisoners there. How are you going to find just one man?"

Dunn raised his eyebrows in surprise. "Only sixty?"

"They've been shipping them to Germany for the past month."

"I see. Well, this is where you come in. You get us there as quickly as possible and we might have a chance to get our man out. What time was he seen?"

"Perhaps fifteen minutes ago."

Dunn looked at Cross. "He might still be in that building. Maybe we can work out a way to get him before they move him."

Turning back to Pastore, he said, "Can you get us to the camp right away?"

"How many are you?"

"Eleven."

"A tight squeeze, but we have a small truck; it's critical that we use only one so we don't attract the Germans' attention."

"How soon?"

"Five minutes, if you are ready to go."

"Let's go. We're ready."

True to their word, Pastore and Frontino were back in five minutes. Dunn and the squad had moved out of the building, around to the east side, close to the street. The rain was still coming down hard, making visibility difficult. The men had broken out their army-green ponchos and had tucked their Thompsons under the waterproof covering. Hanson and Lindstrom were already wearing their ponchos, having been stuck outside on guard duty.

Dunn leaned out, checking the street in both directions. Then he spotted the truck at the curb.

'Small' did not quite cover it. It was some sort of van, similar to the one Georges, the French Resistance man, had used to cart them around France on the last mission, but smaller. He thought getting all the men inside it might be like getting people into a clown car. Without the laughter.

Frontino got out of the truck from the driver's side and walked up to Dunn, a pleased smile on his face.

Frontino rattled off something in Italian.

Martelli, who had stayed close to Dunn, translated: "Works perfect, no?"

Dunn sighed quietly, then smiled. "Sure. Thanks."

A few minutes later, Dunn managed to get all but one man

squeezed into the back of the truck. Squeaky Hanson, the smallest of the crowd was left. He leaned in and turned back to Dunn.

"Dunny, don't make me do it. I'll never live it down."

Dunn put a hand on Hanson's shoulder. "No choice, Squeaky. Climb up there and find someone's lap."

"I'm not a kid!"

"If I could just strap you on the roof, I would, but then the Germans might realize we're here." He said this with a deadpan expression.

Hanson picked up on Dunn's sarcasm and gave in with a little smile.

"Fine. But you owe me for this."

"Agreed, I'm indebted to you. Up you go."

All the men were sitting cross-legged, and Hanson climbed in and a found a spot on Morris's lap. Unmerciful wolf whistling started right away.

Dunn leaned in and said, "Cut the bullshit." The whistles stopped.

Dunn closed the door, but as he turned away, one more wolf whistle came from the truck. Shaking his head, he went around to the front of the truck and got in the passenger side. He scooted over, waiting for Pastore to join him.

Pastore and Damiano were standing close to each other arguing.

"Why can't I go? Haven't I proven myself?"

"You can see there's no room."

"I can sit on your lap, like the little American did."

"That's not the only reason, and you know it. You're mother needs you and so does Mr. Gavino. I need for you to stay here and keep an eye on things. Stay close to the radio in case we call. We don't know what the Americans are really going to do."

This angered Damiano so much his face turned red, much like a kid throwing a tantrum. Exasperated, Damiano said, "As you wish, Mr. Pastore." Then he bowed. "Master."

"Get going, Damiano, before you get in trouble."

"I'm going."

Dunn watched the argument, not understanding any of it, but the tones were clear. So he wasn't surprised when Damiano turned away and stomped off into the night, waving his hands in the air, talking to himself.

When Pastore got in, Dunn said, "Damiano's quite unhappy."

Martelli, from right behind Dunn, translated for the Italian.

Frontino started the truck, slid it into first gear, and pulled away from the curb.

"He's young and can be petulant, but in the end he obeys," replied Pastore.

Dunn nodded. Then he removed his helmet and put it in his lap trying to be as inconspicuous as possible while wearing a U.S. Army uniform.

The windshield wipers scraped across the glass, making it possible to see, at least for a few seconds at a time.

"How long to get close to the camp?"

Frontino answered this question. "Possibly an hour. We shouldn't run into any checkpoints. The Germans are too busy fighting you farther to the south, but the road is winding and dangerous, especially with the rain."

"It'll be best if you can drive by the camp without stopping so I can get a feel for it, then drop us off somewhere out of sight of the camp, maybe a half-mile away."

"I will do that."

"Do you know anything about the Gestapo agent who took our man?"

Pastore answered the question. "He's vicious and loves to hurt people. He's been in Genoa a long time, was even there in 1942, when Himmler came to visit. He works well with the SS captain who was with him today. They have tortured and killed many Italians, not all of them partisans. They're known for rounding up people and taking them away; probably they were sent to death camps.

"There's a rumor that he's done even worse things. Possibly the worst ever."

"What things?"

It took Pastore five minutes to tell him. Martelli asked him to repeat himself several times and seemed to have trouble taking in what was said. He managed, though, but looked sick at the end.

"Dear God," Dunn said. He closed his eyes, but then opened them right away because the images Pastore's narrative created wouldn't go away. He stared out the windshield seeing nothing, his thoughts as dark as the Italian night.

Chapter 35

Prigione di Guerra 135
San Giuseppe, Italy
3 August, 2110 Hours

Rogers remained impassive to Schluter's announcement. Of course he knew he was Gestapo.

"What is your name?"

"Frank Newport, Captain."

"Yes, I see your insignia. Please stand and empty your pockets onto the table."

Rogers hesitated, if only to indicate he wouldn't comply with requests immediately. Passive- aggressive. He emptied his trouser pockets onto the table: a penknife, a few American dollar bills, a 1902 Morgan silver dollar from his grandpa, and a piece of gum. When he finished, he put his hands in his lap. Rogers was exceedingly glad he'd asked Carlotta to burn his code book and papers.

Schluter eyed the stuff without curiosity. "Your shirt pockets."

There was only one thing in Rogers' shirt pocket and he didn't want to give it up. Knowing he had no choice, he pulled the photo out and laid it gently on the table. He was sick at the thought of the Gestapo agent learning about Carlotta and Marie. He started thinking fast.

Schluter leaned forward and slid the picture closer.

"These people look Italian."

"Aunt and uncle on my mother's side."

"What part of Italy?"

"Near Salerno."

The German smiled. "I've been there!"

"No kidding?"

"A beautiful place, isn't it?"

"I don't know. I was never able to visit. Then the war, you know."

Schluter nodded. "Of course." He laid the photo back on the desk, but closer to himself. "I do apologize, but I'm required to keep this for a short time."

Rogers noticed a little uptick on the corner of the Gestapo man's lips making the colonel wonder what the man knew.

"Well, there's nothing I can do about that, is there?"

"No. There isn't." The man folded his hands in front him on the desk. "Tell me about your unit."

"All I'm required to tell you is my name, rank and serial number."

"Are you sure that's how you want to do this?"

"It's the way I've been ordered to do this."

A knock on the door interrupted them and the SS captain came back in, carrying a camera.

"Stand up, Captain."

Rogers stood up, eyeing the man with the camera.

In quick succession, the man took several photos from the front, then ordered Rogers to turn his head to the right and left for profile pictures. As soon as he was done, he stepped back and resumed standing behind Schluter.

"Sit."

Rogers complied.

Evidently Schluter decided to take another tack. "Where were you born?"

Rogers remained silent.

"What can it hurt?"

"Virginia. Norfolk."

"A southerner."

Rogers shrugged.

"We found the remains of your aircraft."

"What aircraft?"

"The one you crashed in a few days ago. North, a couple of valleys from Ville di Murlo."

Rogers wasn't surprised that Schluter knew about the plane. He might even know about Watson and the running gunfight.

"I believe you were flying reconnaissance for your bombers based here in Italy. Or perhaps trying to determine damage done to Turin. This suggests to me that you are based somewhere near Rome to give you the range you need.

"Why not just tell me which unit you belong to? Then I can get you checked in to the camp, so to speak." Schluter chuckled at his own little joke. Rogers didn't join in. "Then you can get to bed and get some long needed rest."

Rogers couldn't believe his good fortune. The Gestapo agent had drawn the wrong conclusion from the facts. The primary question was whether Rogers could accede to the conclusion. Or did the German have other facts at his disposal that might create trouble for Rogers?

Schluter changed directions. "Who else besides the shopkeeper and the doctor helped you?"

Caught by surprise, Rogers almost reacted, but stopped himself just in time. "There was no one else." He stared right into the German's eyes hoping that would be convincing.

Schluter tapped his fingers on the table top. "Captain . . . come now, you can do better."

Rogers shrugged. "There was no one else."

"I know you were in the cellar of the garage. I also know you were blocked in by a truck. Who moved that truck for you?"

Little Marie's and her mother's faces flew into Rogers' mind. He quickly shoved them aside. "Yes, I was in that cellar, but I don't know anything about a truck. When I started to get worried, I just went up the stairs and opened the door." Rogers stopped.

He'd been taught to answer questions when necessary, but never to reveal more information than was asked. His instructors had said the interrogators were not stupid, even when they might appear to be a bit dense. They would leave dead air hanging and rely on the prisoner's human nature to want to fill the vacuum. That would be when seemingly innocuous information would get out.

"You got worried? What was troubling you?"

"What you might expect: how was I going to get back home?"

"Where was it that you wanted to get to?"

Rogers said nothing.

"After you left the cellar, what happened?"

Rogers was grateful for the time it'd taken to travel to the POW camp. He'd used the ample time to create a new set of events.

"What does it matter? I'm here now, isn't that enough for you?"

"Who were you protecting?"

"No one."

Schluter picked up the photo and tapped it against the table, as if absentmindedly.

"Are you married, Captain?"

"No," lied Rogers.

"Here's what I think: this isn't your family. It's someone in the village. I'll wager that if I send my SS troops back there and show this around, I will find this family. When I do, I will order them all to a concentration camp. They'll never return home." He laid the photo flat and turned it so Rogers could see it and tapped a forefinger on it. "Tell me who these people are."

"I already told you: my aunt and uncle on my mother's side, from near Salerno."

"What were you doing in the aircraft?"

"What you said earlier."

"Which part?"

"Assessing bomb damage."

"Where did you take flight instruction?"

"Can't say."

"But you are a pilot?"

Again, Rogers shrugged.

Schluter stood up abruptly, the chair screeching across the floor out of the way. He leaned forward, placed his palms flat on the table. "Perhaps being nice to you is not the best way to extract information."

"I appreciate you being *nice* to me, but I can't help it if you don't like the answers."

"You are not being truthful with me."

"I am being truthful, as much as I believe I can be."

"So you are holding back."

"Of course I am. I told you the minimum requirements for a prisoner. I've already exceeded that. Because you've been so nice to me."

Schluter stood upright and ran his hands down his suit jacket, smoothing the material. He turned and pulled his gloves from an overcoat pocket and put them on using exaggerated motions for Rogers' benefit.

Rogers knew this was going to be bad. He hoped he could withstand it before giving up anything important.

"Torture doesn't really work."

Schluter smiled. "Is that what your experts tell you? You'll be quite surprised by how well it works."

"I just don't have anything worth telling."

"Where are you stationed?"

"If I tell you, will you take off your gloves?"

"Let's see where we end up, shall we?"

It wasn't that Rogers was afraid of getting hurt, although he was, but more that if he could 'give up' some useless information and avoid telling Schluter the valuable stuff, then fine. Excellent even.

"Why were you in the village?"

Rogers held up his injured hand. "I got hurt. Needed some help."

"So the doctor patched you up?"

"Yes."

"The doctor is dead."

Rogers' face paled. *Oh no*, he thought.

"The doctor was less forthcoming than you."

Rogers wanted to leap across the table and throttle the Gestapo agent.

"I see this affects you. All you Americans form attachments to the locals." Schluter shrugged. "I don't understand it. What do you care about these people? They don't deserve your affection. This is your weakness."

"We have different philosophies."

"Indeed we do. You care about people as individuals. All I care about is how they can serve the Fatherland."

Rogers said nothing.

Schluter put his gloved forefinger on the photo. He was touching Carlotta's image. "We Gestapo know lots of things because we have reliable sources. This is Carlotta Agostini. She has a little girl." Schluter paused to examine the ceiling, then focused his blue eyes on Rogers. "Marie. I imagine she's quite a little sweetheart? Is that the right term? Sweetheart?"

Rogers' heart jumped. *No, please.*

Schluter leaned back in his chair, triumphant. "Answer my questions and I might let them live."

Rogers closed his eyes for moment, then opened them to see Schluter's smiling face. Oh, how he wanted to wipe that grin off the man's face.

"Where are you stationed?"

"I'm attached to the Fifteenth Air Force out of Bari. I fly out of a little dirt air strip a few miles south of Rome."

"Where did you train for piloting?"

"Near Los Angeles."

"California?"

"Yes."

"Where's the film with the pictures you took?"

"It burned when I set the plane on fire."

"How many good German soldiers did you kill in the mountains?"

Rogers figured Schluter would know the answer already. The one thing that Schluter had said that was apparently true was that Gestapo agents did know a lot.

"All the ones I found."

"You're quite resourceful in a ground-based firefight for a pilot."

"Training."

"I see."

"Who was the other man?"

"What other man?"

"The one at the bottom of the cliff. What did you do? Did you push him off so you could have all the food?"

Rogers stifled a groan. The damned German network of information was wide.

"He fell. An accident."

"So you're not the pilot are you?"

"Yes, I was."

Schluter sighed and got up. He picked up his chair and moved it over by the door. He said something to the SS captain brusquely, clearly an order.

Both men gripped the table, one at each end and moved it aside.

Rogers looked at the commandant, who'd remained quiet during the entire proceeding. The man just stared back, perhaps a bit sympathetically, thought Rogers. The man turned away, got up and left the room.

The SS captain grabbed Rogers' hands and pulled them behind the chair, and shackled them again. He moved off to the side.

Schluter stood in front of Rogers and held up his gloved hands, which he'd balled into massive fists. "A pity you lied to me."

Rogers had a second to think, *I hope Bessie and the kids will be all right without me.*

The first blow broke Rogers' nose.

Chapter 36

Only partially due to the downpour that seemed to follow their every move, it had indeed taken close to an hour to reach the POW camp. Although it was about nine miles as the crow flies, it was much farther to travel across the winding, switch-backed roads between Ville di Murlo and the camp. The road had been completely deserted, to Dunn's relief. Contrary to popular belief, the Germans weren't everywhere in every country. They'd far overextended themselves and were also too busy fighting for their lives on the front line to man every inch of Italian soil.

As they came around the last curve, the camp spread out in front of them. The road they were on formed a T-intersection with another that followed the winding river, which did indeed surround the camp on three sides. Frontino turned right, driving as slowly as he dared without attracting the Germans' attention. The camp was on the opposite side of the river and it was difficult to make out its shape in the rain.

The curving river formed a large U with the open side facing roughly northeast. As they traveled farther down the road, Dunn spotted a bridge about a hundred yards from the T-intersection. Driving past it, he could just make out that it was a rough wooden structure, probably rather hastily constructed.

"Are there any other bridges?" he asked, as Martelli translated.

"No," replied Pastore. "That's the only way in. On the other side of the camp is a dense woods that sits on a sizable hill."

Passing the southern edge of the camp, Dunn was able to determine that it was about three hundred yards deep.

"Can you turn around and go back? Take us to the point where we came around that last curve?"

"*Sì*," answered Frontino.

The young man found a dirt side road, which was muddy from the rain, turned the truck around and started back. The rain began to let up and visibility improved significantly with the clouds thinning enough for some moonlight to filter through. As Dunn expected, the road crossing the bridge led to a main front gate. It was wide enough for one vehicle to pass through. A guard shack stood to the northern side where presumably a bored, tired German soldier was standing to get out of the rain.

The buildings were easier to make out. Rows of prisoner barracks stretched across the entire camp northwest to southeast. A large building sat forward of the lines of barracks, closer to the bridge. Dunn thought it was the headquarters building. That would be where Rogers would be, if he was indeed here at all.

"Would that be the commandant's building?"

Pastore nodded. "*Sì*."

"Where are the German barracks?"

"It's right behind the commandant's building."

"So all the guards are in the same place?"

"*Sì*."

Tall, dark towers seemed to stand guard over the compound. Dunn knew he had to assume each of them was manned by one or two soldiers. He also had to believe the Germans might have dogs at their disposal, too.

Frontino turned left at the T-intersection and pulled over when Dunn told him to stop.

"You think sixty prisoners are being held at the camp?" asked Dunn.

"*Sì*." Pastore replied.

"How about guards?"

"About fifty."

"How do you know this?"

"We keep an eye on the camp, watching the daily activity."

Dunn nodded. That made sense to him. "Anyone ever escape?"

"We've heard of prisoners being recaptured, so yes. Whether any really get away to safety we don't know. We also don't know how they get out, which I assume is your next question."

"It was. Are the fences electrified?"

"No, they aren't. I don't know if you could see when we went by in the dark and rain, but it is a double set of fences about ten feet apart, with concertina wire over both fences."

Dunn nodded and tapped his thumb absently against the top of his helmet, which was still in his lap. He stared out the windshield. After a moment, a rough idea formed. He needed to get out of the truck and move around. To Martelli he said, "Tell the guys to exit the truck and get out of sight over there." He pointed out the right window to the brush and bramble on the north side of the road, the closest cover. "You stay here a little longer."

"Right, Sarge."

Martelli passed on the order and the hurried, rustling sounds coming from the back of the truck told Dunn his men wanted to get out as much as he did.

"Thanks for getting us here, Mr. Frontino, Mr. Pastore."

Frontino answered, "You're welcome. What can we do to help?"

"Do you have a radio set we can call you on?"

"We do."

"What's the frequency?"

Frontino gave Dunn the frequency, and asked, "You have your own radio? I didn't notice it."

"Yep, one of the guys has it with him." Dunn glanced out the window for a moment, checking on his men. Satisfied they were all in the right place, he donned his helmet and shook hands with both Italians.

"I guess you should head on back to your village. We're going to try and come up with a plan here."

Pastore unlatched the door and Dunn asked one more

question.

"Would you be able to get your hands on explosives?"

Pastore released the door handle. "Yes. We can do that. How much would you need?"

Dunn shook his head. "I'm not really sure. How much could you get?"

"We have access to regular dynamite, but none of the good plastic stuff. About ten kilograms, perhaps."

Dunn mentally converted that: twenty-two pounds.

"Timers and detonators?"

"Yes, we can get those."

"How quickly?"

Pastore grinned. "We are like the, er . . . Boy Scouts? Always prepared. We can go get it and could be back in a couple of hours. If the rain lets up more, maybe sooner. Anything else?"

Dunn smiled. "Well, actually, yes, perhaps two more things." He told the Italian, who nodded and said that would be no problem.

"And one last thing."

When Martelli heard the last thing Dunn wanted, his eyebrows shot up. As soon as he translated, so did Pastore's.

The Italian said, "That may prove a challenge, but . . . we will do as you ask!"

Dunn tipped his head in thanks.

Dunn waved at the two men in the truck as they drove west into the wet night.

Martelli's expression was still a bit wide-eyed.

Dunn noticed and grinned at the young man.

"All part of the job."

"I see why your reputation is what it is."

Dunn shrugged. "Let's go."

He led the way as they scrambled across the wet grass and made their way over to the men, who were all hunkered down in the forest of shrubs and trees.

Finding a spot next to Cross, Dunn crouched, cradling his Thompson with the barrel down because of the rain.

"This looks like a tough nut to crack," Cross said, looking at his friend and boss. "I've been searching my brain and nothing's there."

"Well, I could have told you that and saved you the trouble."

"Oh, ha ha. You're swell. Thanks."

"What are friends for?"

"Yeah, well, I'm still waiting to find out."

Dunn chuckled and patted Cross on the shoulder. "Okay. Enough bullshit. I have some ideas."

"Really? You do?"

"Yep. I do." Dunn looked out at the men and called a name softly.

A moment later, Jones shuffled up beside the two sergeants. "Yes, Sarge?"

"In these conditions, what would you say your max range is?"

Jones held his finger up, as if checking the wind, then opened his hand palm up. He studied it for a moment, then deadpanned, "Point-blank, Sarge."

In spite of the circumstances, Cross laughed out loud. Dunn rolled his eyes, looking up at the heavens.

"Dear Lord, save me from the comedians."

Jones tried to look contrite, but didn't quite get there, although he did say, "Sorry, Sarge. It would probably be three hundred give or take a bit."

"A hundred would be no problem?"

"Yeah, no problem."

Dunn winked at Cross in a way that Jones couldn't see. "How about in this lighting?"

"Lighting? What lighting? No, Sarge, I have to be able to see my target." Jones paused, suddenly realizing he'd been had. "Ah. Okay. I guess we're even."

Dunn laughed. "Okay. We're done with the bullshit."

"So what'd you come up with?" asked Cross.

Dunn gathered all the men as close as possible so they could hear. Then he spent over five minutes outlining his idea. No one said anything the whole time, although several exchanged glances.

At the end, Cross shook his head.

"You are fucking kidding us, right?"

"Nope."

Cross took in a breath and blew it out. "Could work," he said at last.

Chapter 37

Carlotta Agostini's house
Ville di Murlo, Italy
3 August, 2215 Hours

Carlotta patted Umberto Gavino on the upper arm after wiping his face with a cold washcloth.

"Is that better?" she asked gently.

"Yes, my dear. Thank you."

"I'm going to let you rest now. Close your eyes and sleep."

Gavino obeyed.

Carlotta made her way downstairs and checked on Marie, who was still on the sofa sleeping. She pulled the blanket up to cover her daughter's shoulders and leaned over to kiss her on the forehead. Marie stirred lightly, but didn't awaken. Carlotta turned off the lamp near the sofa and in the near darkness moved toward the kitchen, where she'd left a small light on. She was almost through the door when she smelled cigarette smoke. Had she left one burning in there? No, she didn't remember doing that. Wary, she stopped at the door and leaned forward to see if someone was there.

"Hello, Carlotta."

Carlotta scowled and strode the rest of the way into the room. "Teresa. What are you doing here?"

Instead of answering, Teresa Rusconi took a deep drag and blew it out toward the ceiling, staring at her sister through the curling smoke.

Carlotta's lips compressed into a thin line and her eyes narrowed. She put her hands on her hips. "I asked you a simple question."

"I thought I'd come by and say 'hello.' "

"Damn you, Teresa, you have no right to barge into my house after the way you behaved. Get out."

"We should talk."

"I don't want to."

"It's important."

"Where have you been?"

"Doing something I had to do." Teresa smirked at her sister.

"Do you have any idea what happened here in our village today?"

"No. I drove straight here."

"You haven't talked to anyone?"

"No."

"Something terrible."

Teresa shrugged.

Carlotta blinked her eyes in disbelief. "You don't even care. Dr. Marcucci is dead. So is poor old Mrs. Paretti."

"That is sad."

"Mr. Gavino was beaten so badly he almost died. He's upstairs resting now, but we have no doctor to help him."

"He has you, doesn't he?" Teresa flicked her cigarette ashes into an ashtray.

"I don't understand you. What happened to you? Why are you so hateful?"

"You deserve it."

Carlotta's mouth dropped open for a moment, then she snapped, "I *deserve* it? You are crazy. Are you still angry that Rocco chose me? After the way you treated him?" Carlotta's voice rose.

"He deserved it, too. This entire village deserved what happened today."

"What? *What?*" Carlotta screamed the last. Then it fell together. Teresa's insistence that the Americans had killed Rocco in North Africa. Her fight with Teresa. The sudden arrival of the SS and the Gestapo.

"*You!* You turned in the American. You traitor! You caused the death of two people for spite?"

Teresa stood up, crushed her cigarette out, and shouted, "Yes! I turned the American in! I don't care about the others! I did what had to be done!" She ran to the kitchen door, turned, and looked at her sister.

Carlotta felt like she'd been hit in the face. Never had she seen such vehemence and hatred in anyone's eyes. She involuntarily took a step backward.

Teresa pivoted back to the door and ran out, letting the door slam.

Behind her, Carlotta heard a frightened voice call out, "Mama?"

Upstairs in Marie's small bed, Gavino, who was supposed to be asleep, got up and put on his shoes. A bit unsteadily, he made his way to the door. There was suddenly the matter of vengeance on a collaborator.

Chapter 38

Prigione di Guerra 135
San Giuseppe, Italy
3 August, 2230 Hours

Rogers' chin rested on his chest. Blood dripped from his broken nose, and lips.

A splash of cold water from a metal cup brought him back to consciousness. He was barely able to raise his head to see where the water had come from.

A grinning specter seemed to float in front of his eyes. Then it resolved into the face of Schluter.

"Welcome back, Captain." The face retreated as the Gestapo agent stood up. He slapped the cup on the table with a clang.

Rogers jumped at the sound. His eyes focused on the cup. "Thirsty," he croaked through his busted lips.

Schluter picked up the cup and held it out to his side. The SS Captain took it, filled it from a canteen, then handed it back.

Schluter held it up so Rogers could see it, then moved it around in the air. Rogers' eyes tracked it everywhere it went. Putting it down on the table right in front of Rogers, taunting him with it, Schluter said, "You may have the entire cup. Just as soon as you begin telling me the truth."

"I have been."

"No. I'm certain you have not."

In the other room, a phone rang a few times before stopping. A moment later, the door opened, and the commandant stuck his head in. "*Herr* Schluter? A word, please? It's urgent."

Schluter sighed, exasperated at the interruption. He walked into the other room.

"What is it?"

"A phone call, sir. I'm to give you a message: 'explosion at Genoa Gestapo headquarters.' "

Schluter rubbed his face with both hands, grinding the heels of his hands into his eyes until he saw stars. When he lowered them, he shouted, "Fuck! Damn partisans. I'm going to kill every last one of them. Shit. Damn it."

The commandant had wisely retreated behind his desk.

Schluter turned his attention to Colonel Dentz. "Obviously, I have to leave. Captain Adelsberger is going with me. Get a guard in here. Keep that American exactly where he is. No food. No water. Nothing."

"As you wish, sir."

Schluter ignored the man and went back in the interrogation room to stand in front of Rogers.

"I have to leave. I will be back. I hope for your sake you're ready to tell me the truth."

Schluter stomped out of the room. The SS captain followed and slammed the door shut.

Rogers could hear fading footsteps, then came the muted sounds of a conversation, followed by the clunk of a phone being hung up. Another door slammed shut.

Struggling hard against his bindings, he found he still could not loosen them. Instead, he discovered he could grip the back of the chair. Getting a solid hold on the chair, he maneuvered himself until he could rise to a stooped-over position with the chair sticking out behind him like a misshapen caboose. Leaning over as carefully as possible, he positioned his mouth then lowered it. Lapping and slurping sounds came as he sated his thirst. He sat back down, a satisfied expression on his bloody face.

Chapter 39

Gavino's store
Ville di Murlo, Italy
3 August, 2245 Hours

Umberto Gavino made it through the light rain to his shop. He'd had to stop several times on the trek because he thought he was about to pass out. He opened the door and turned on the light. The bare shelves seemed to mock him as he shuffled past them to the back room. He sat down in front of an old wooden desk set against the far wall. The chair creaked as he bent over to slide open the bottom drawer. Instead of rummaging around in the drawer with his hand, he felt the bottom of the drawer above it, the one that couldn't be opened, and found what he needed. He pulled and the tape came loose. When his hand reappeared, it had a Beretta Model 1934 in it.

He ejected the seven-round clip, examined it, and slapped it back in place. He worked the slide to seat a 9mm round in the chamber. It was an older weapon, one he'd had for many years, but he knew it would do the upcoming task efficiently. Setting the gun down on the desk, he picked up the phone and dialed a number. After a dozen rings, he depressed the disconnect button and dialed another number. There was no answer there either. He hung up the phone and sat back.

Pastore and Frontino were both gone. He assumed that Damiano had found Pastore and then they'd pulled in Frontino to help with the Americans.

Rising slowly, Gavino switched on the weapon's safety and tucked it into his belt. He thought briefly about going upstairs to his apartment to clean himself up, but decided against it. He might need the energy for the deed he was about to embark on. And also, perhaps his bloody clothes would show the evil witch what she'd done. Although, what he'd heard her screaming at poor Carlotta indicated she didn't care about the pain and suffering she'd caused.

He went to the store's back door. He put on a coat and hat that were on hooks nearby. Switching off the light, he stepped out into the rain. His truck was parked just outside and he climbed in with some difficulty. Once he started it, he pulled out and headed toward the only place he could think of where Teresa might be, her house a few blocks away.

When he pulled up outside her house, his was the only vehicle on the block. There were no lights on in the house. Not encouraged by this, he shut off the engine and got out. He stood there a moment, examining the house closely. Like most houses in the village, it was a two-story structure. Walking around to the side of the house, he craned his neck upward. Through a second floor window, he detected faint light.

Moving as rapidly as his damaged body would allow, he went to the back of the house where he saw her car. It was not running. Opening the driver's side door, he reached in and felt around for the ignition switch. Something dangled there and he snatched the key out, and then shoved it into a pants pocket.

Gavino pulled the gun out and thumbed off the safety. He went up the back steps slowly, as quietly as possible, gun at the ready. Turning the doorknob, he pushed on the door gently, afraid it would squeak. When he got it open just wide enough, he slid through.

Going through the kitchen into the hallway, he found himself at the foot of the stairs leading to the top floor. He put a foot on the first step and stopped again to take in everything. Light shone against the wall at the top of the stairs, coming from one of the bedrooms. Suddenly, a shadow slithered over the wall and then was washed out when a light in the hallway flashed on.

Teresa came into view carrying a suitcase and while looking over her shoulder, perhaps as a final goodbye, took the first step down.

Gavino raised the Beretta.

Teresa turned her head to look where she was going. And saw Gavino.

The shopkeeper fired three times, each striking the traitor between her breasts. Her mouth opened for a scream that would never come.

Gavino backed out of the way as the body plummeted down the stairs, the suitcase bouncing along with her. She ended up face down, arms akimbo.

Gavino raised the pistol once more and fired into the back of her head.

He switched the safety back on, tucked the gun in his belt and walked out the front door. He'd get help later and dispose of the traitor's body. Ordinarily, he would have dragged her into the street and put a sign on the body saying something like 'death to collaborators,' but out of consideration for Carlotta, Marie, and Damiano, he'd chosen not to.

Chapter 40

Gestapo Headquarters
Genoa, Italy
3 August, 2355 Hours

Gestapo Agent Greg Schluter's office was in ruins. Parts of the ceiling lay shattered across the floor where they had fallen, with glass shards from the windows and light fixtures everywhere. He made a mental note not to fall down, but he threw his hat to the floor, where it lay like a forlorn puppy. Dust was everywhere. The bomb had gone off just inside the building's front door. The stone around the door was only so much rubble now.

Schluter and SS Captain Adelsberger had been forced to gain entrance through the building's back door. Their only light was from flashlights, which cast cones of light filled with swirling dust particles.

Before leaving the POW camp at San Giuseppe, he'd stopped to call the SS barracks where he'd sent his men earlier. He ordered them to seal off the building and the streets around it. Once that was done, a door-to-door search would begin. Next, he called his chief of staff and told him to call in all of the agents.

"Go check on the records room downstairs," Schluter said to

Adelsberger. "I want to know if there's any damage there. Check the dark room, make sure it's in working order."

"Yes, sir." Adelsberger scrambled over the rubble into the hallway, where he found the stairs to the lower floor nearly completely blocked by stones. He picked his way carefully through and went down the stairs.

Schluter made his way over behind his desk and was pleased to see it was still usable; all the drawers worked, although he decided against sitting in the glass-covered chair.

The lights in the hallway came back on. Schluter assumed Adelsberger had checked on the fuses and fixed whatever the problem had been. His office was still dim, since all the light fixtures had shattered, and he kept his flashlight on.

He thought about what he knew. Fortunately, no one had been injured in the explosion, unlike the one in Turin a few days ago, which had killed almost fifty German soldiers. He'd known Colbeck well and was sorry that he'd been killed. How someone had pulled off murdering him, and three others in the man's office was unknown, and seemed to be a feat of the impossible. The only thing Schluter was sure of was that it had been Italian partisans, whether it was the damn communists or some others, he didn't know and didn't care. At some point, someone was going to pay for that attack and for this bombing.

"*Herr* Schluter?" Adelsberger had made his way back to the door of Schluter's office.

"What is it?"

"Everything is in fine shape downstairs, including the dark room."

Schluter nodded. "Start examining the files for American pilots in Italy. Start with those around Rome. Wait. No, wait a minute."

"Yes, sir."

Something about the American captain didn't add up. He'd spotted it right away but chalked it up to the man being afraid. No, while he did seem afraid, it almost was closer to an act of being afraid. But it wasn't fear of injury or death. No, he was hiding something he valued more than he did his own life. What?

Schluter closed his eyes, picturing the man staring back at him after he'd been struck several times in quick succession.

Something in the man's eyes. What was it? Not fear. Anger? No . . . well, perhaps partly. Schluter knew he was almost there. It just wouldn't come out.

He changed his mental focus to finding who had bombed his office. Would it really have been the usual group of partisans? The city had been under a sort of truce for a few months. No attacks on German soldiers or agents in exchange for no reprisals on the civilians. Who would have broken the truce? A new group? Or a new commander? Suddenly, an inkling surfaced. Exactly what he'd been waiting for.

Schluter let his brain follow the logic: commander, command, command staff. His lips curled into a wry, satisfied grin. Command staff. That was it.

"Adelsberger, start digging out files on Allied command staff members. Italy, Sicily, and Corsica. How long for you to develop those pictures of the American?"

"Call it an hour, sir."

"I'm going to get you some help on looking for the captain in those files you gather. You take care of developing the photos first."

"Yes, sir."

True to his word, Adelsberger got the pictures developed in just under an hour.

Schluter stepped into the large, well-lit room in the basement. File folders were arranged on two tables, first by geography, then by command. The four agents and Adelsberger were seated around the tables with open files in front of them, each with a picture of Rogers near the folders they were examining.

Schluter sat down at the end of a table and picked up a folder from the Sicily group. He opened it and disregarded the information sheets, instead focusing solely on the pictures. The information in the files was thorough and in many cases included pictures of the subjects around whatever town they were near, and some included what appeared to be a high school senior photo. The latter came by way of spies in the United States working for the Gestapo. If the subject was married and had kids in America, their names were included, photos if possible. Know your enemy.

Hours passed, but the men stayed on task and focused. Looking for one man.

The break finally occurred at fifteen past four in the morning.

"Sir!" one of the agents stood up, excitedly waving a folder. "I think this is him." He practically ran around the table to hand the folder to an expectant Schluter.

The chief Gestapo agent opened the folder and found Rogers' face staring back at him, a little smile on it. He was wearing his uniform. Schluter noted the silver eagle insignia.

Schluter read the information out loud. "Rogers, Frank, Senior. Colonel under the command of Major General Lucien Truscott, posted to Corsica, May, 1944. Army Intelligence. Operations Planning." Schluter looked at Adelsberger. "I knew it!"

Then he finished up reading the facts, "From Norfolk, Virginia. Married, Elizabeth, Bessie. Three kids. Frank, Junior, Susan, William." Schluter's heart jumped in excitement. Family. Weakness. Which meant answers would be forthcoming. He'd learned early in his career that threatening a man's family was the most productive form of torture. Fear of pain being inflicted on loved ones could drive a man insane.

Schluter folded the file in half, then tucked it into the inside pocket of his suit jacket.

He nodded at the agent, "Good work."

"Thank you, sir." The man beamed. Attaboys were rare coming from Schluter.

"Thank you, everyone. Return the files, and get back on the streets. We still need to find the bastards who bombed us. Adelsberger, with me."

The agents all stood and said, "Yes, sir," to a departing Schluter.

The only working phone was in an office down the hall from his own. Schluter picked it up and gave connection instructions brusquely to the operator.

A few rings later, Commandant Dentz answered.

"Schluter here, Colonel Dentz."

"Yes, *Herr* Schluter?"

"Keep our American exactly where he is. Different

instructions now. Give him water. Have someone take care of his wounds. Untie his hands and let him stretch. Keep a guard in the room. *Verstehen?*"

"*Jawohl, Herr* Schluter. I understand."

"One last thing: absolutely no one is to engage him in any form of conversation. I have an important phone call to make, then I'll be leaving for your *Stalag* within the hour."

"I look forward to your arrival."

Schluter hung up, smiling at the man's bullshit. No one ever looked forward to a visit from a Gestapo agent.

Schluter made his call. It was to Gestapo headquarters in Berlin. He instructed that a short message be given immediately to the chief of the Gestapo, Heinrich Müller: Potential information on invasion of southern France.

Chapter 41

West river bank across from Prigione di Guerra 135
San Giuseppe, Italy
4 August, 0428 Hours

The small skiff slid soundlessly into the water carrying Stanley Wickham, Squeaky Hanson, and Eddie Fairbanks, along with their equipment. The water craft had been Dunn's first request of Pastore.

The Rangers benefitted from the overcast sky, but it was beginning to lighten in the east. They kept as low a profile as possible, and at least it was still black behind them. Wickham and Fairbanks each pulled on an oar, being careful not to make any splashing noises when raising or lowering it. Hanson knelt in the bow, acting as a silent coxswain.

The river was only ten yards wide, making it seem more of a moat than river. The water moved slowly, so they had been able to enter the water only a short distance upstream to account for the southbound push of the river. The land on the east side rose only slightly from the river and near the water, reeds stood like sentinels.

When they reached the far bank, Hanson climbed out,

carefully, to make sure his boots hit solid ground quietly. He carried the bowline and when his feet got purchase on the wet sloping ground, he pulled. The skiff dutifully followed until its shallow, flat bottom slid up onto the slope.

Wickham made his way to the bow and got out. Fairbanks started grabbing satchels and handing them off to Hanson and Wickham. Soon, the men were ready. Each picked up a satchel and shrugged it onto his back. With their Thompson .45s ready, they started through the waist-high reeds, the only sound the slight rustle of their uniforms against the vegetation.

Hanson had point. When he reached the edge of the reeds, he stopped and took a knee. The men behind him did the same. They were effectively invisible with only their helmets above the reed tops. Hanson turned his head to the south. In the distance, perhaps fifty yards, he could make out the low dark shape of the simple bridge they'd passed hours earlier. Looking straight ahead were shadows that would be the buildings within the POW camp. The nearest was about a hundred yards away. That meant the first fence would be nearby. Hanson scanned left and right. No movement. "Let's go," he whispered over his shoulder.

The ground in front was mostly bare, with weeds or grass growing in sparse patches. The men cradled their Thompsons in the crooks of their arms and started crawling. It was slow going, but after a few minutes they reached the fence and Hanson stopped his forward motion. While still lying prone, he shucked off his satchel, set it to one side, then rolled over onto his back. He could easily see the fence, constructed of barbed wire with a few inches between strands. The wooden posts were about three feet apart, making a solid frame. Wooden braces ran horizontally at five feet and at the top, which was about ten feet off the ground. Coiled, razor-sharp, concertina wire sat on top of the upper frame.

Hanson carefully examined the wire fence for a couple of minutes, then whispered, "Not electric." It wasn't that he didn't believe the Italian. He just wasn't about to risk his life on one of them.

"Okay," replied Wickham in a low voice, sounding relieved.

Rolling over onto his stomach, Hanson said, "Okay, let's get this thing on the road."

Wickham and Fairbanks split apart, one going left and the other right. When they got to a point about ten yards away, they set to work, as did Hanson.

Their goal was twofold: quick entry into the camp, and a diversion.

Ten minutes later, Frontino checked his watch. Time. He put the truck into gear and pulled back onto the river road. He was driving a different, and much larger truck on this trip. Twenty yards down, he turned left onto the wooden bridge, the truck's tires thumping on the wood slats. He drove forward slowly. As expected, the guard at the main gate stepped out of his one-person shack and stared at the truck, his weapon at the ready.

When Frontino neared the gate, the German soldier held up his hand. Frontino obediently stopped the truck. The soldier eyed the truck carefully before moving closer. He approached the driver's side. Scanning the inside of the truck, he stepped closer, the barrel of his Mauser drooping. He made a winding motion indicating that Frontino should roll down his window. Frontino put his hand on the handle and jiggled it. He held up a finger asking for a moment.

Irritated, the soldier took a step backward to make room to raise his weapon.

Frontino stared at the man and shrugged apologetically.

From the north came the sounds and bright light of explosions from the first set of charges set by Hanson and crew.

The soldier started to turn toward the noise.

Blood spattered the window as the soldier's face disappeared. His body thumped to the ground. The crack of a long weapon being fired reached Frontino's ears over the rumbling of the explosions.

Frontino stomped his foot on the accelerator and let out the clutch. The front end of the truck ran through the gate, splintering the wood and sending shards in all directions.

Two hundred yards away, across the river and the road, and in a hidey-hole on the downslope of the hill running to the river,

Jones swung his rifle to the south. He sighted on the lone soldier in the guard tower near the fence, perfectly silhouetted against the brightening sky. He gently pulled on the trigger and the 1903 Springfield A1 roared. A split second later, the man's head snapped back, then he collapsed.

Jones sighted on the shape in the north tower and fired. Task complete. On to the next.

Scanning the prison yard, he spotted the southern guard tower on the far eastern side of the camp. Just before settling his cheek against the loving caress of the weapon's beautiful wood stock, he saw motion on the road. Four more large trucks tuned right onto the river road and drove across the bridge into the POW camp—Dunn's second request of Pastore. Jones smiled to himself. *Only Dunn could pull this off,* he thought, pride welling in his chest. Then he focused through the sight.

Frontino slammed on the brakes and stopped the truck right in front of the commandant's building, at the foot of the stairs. The back doors of the truck burst open. Three men jumped down and someone slammed the doors shut. Frontino drove around the right side of the building to advance to the main target, the guards' barracks, with the remainder of the Ranger squad.

Dunn, Ward and the Italian partisan, Pastore, ran up the steps. Dunn stopped at the door, stepping to the right side. Ward immediately took up position on the left. Pastore stood behind Dunn, a Beretta in his hand, aimed at the floor. Dunn nodded, then kicked open the door. A round from a Mauser screamed past Dunn's ear and lodged in one of the wood posts holding up the small porch.

Dunn fired a burst into the enemy soldier, who dropped to the floor in a heap. A German officer was to Dunn's left, but he immediately raised his hands. Dunn motioned for him to lie down. The German complied.

"Clear on the right, Sarge," Ward said.

"Roger," replied Dunn. He stepped into the building.

The dead German and living officer were in what appeared to be an outer office. A large desk with a typewriter on it sat to the left. To the right was a door and straight ahead another. Dunn moved slowly to his left to see behind the desk. He took one more sliding step to the left, weapon at the shoulder.

At that moment, a beautiful young blonde woman came into view as she stood up from behind the desk, fear etched on her face. She raised her empty hands at the sight of the weapon in the American's hands. Her eyes were focused on the barrel of the Thompson.

Ward went into the room and took a spot to the right.

Pastore came into the office, standing behind the two Americans. The woman made eye contact and Pastore tipped his head toward the German officer whose eyes were transfixed on Ward's Thompson just a few feet from himself. Pastore shook his head ever so little. The woman smoothly slid her gaze from him to Dunn.

Dunn gestured for her to come out from behind the desk and lie down next to the German officer. After she had done that, Dunn knelt down close to the officer's face.

"Do you speak English?"

"Yes."

"What's your name?"

"Colonel Dentz."

"Okay, good. Colonel, where's the American who came in tonight?"

Dentz raised his head slightly and shrugged.

Dunn hit him in the side of the face with a quick jab. The man's head bounced off the floor and for a moment Dunn thought he'd hit him too hard when the man's eyes went a little haywire. When the man's eyes regained their focus Dunn repeated, "Where's the American who came in tonight?"

With a tip of his head, the man pointed to the door on the right side of the room.

Dunn patted him on the head. "Good boy." He rose and said to Ward, "Keep an eye on them."

He quickly stepped over to the door, but when he tried to turn the knob it was locked. Dunn sighed and was about to turn around when he spotted a key hanging to the left of the door. To the officer, Dunn asked, "Anyone else in there? Another guard?"

He got a nod in return.

Dunn looked at Pastore and pointed at the woman and the

officer. Pastore nodded and stepped to the far left of the office where he pointed his weapon at the two people on the floor. Dunn waved Ward to the left of the door, which would swing open from the right to the left, going into the other room. Dunn grabbed the key off the wall and unlocked the door in one fluid motion. Grasping the knob, he twisted it and pushed as hard as possible, then raised his Thompson.

"*Halt!*" came a shout from the guard, who was standing with the barrel of his Mauser pointed at a bloody mess of an American.

Dunn ignored the guard and said, "Rogers?"

From the bloody face came a croaking reply, "Yes." Rogers only had one eye open, the blood had flowed so heavily into his right eye it was a gummy mess.

"We're going to get you out of here, sir."

"Well, I would certainly appreciate that."

Dunn looked back at the guard whose blue eyes were wide with fright. Raising the Thompson and aiming square between the eyes, Dunn said, "Colonel Dentz, tell your man I'm an expert shot. I will shoot him and he will not be able to shoot my man. After I shoot him, I will kill you and the young woman."

All the while, Dunn was watching the guard's trigger finger. It was inside the trigger guard, which made his threat a partial lie. It would be possible for the finger to jerk at the moment of impact.

"Colonel? Now!"

Colonel Dentz said something in rapid German. If it was possible, the guard's face became more terrified than it had been, but the Mauser stayed in place.

Dunn's jaw muscles clenched and unclenched for a few seconds. Then he said, "Colonel Rogers, on the count of three. Do you understand?" Dunn wanted the colonel to be ready to move his head out of line with the Mauser.

"Yes, I understand."

"One."

"Two."

From the office came some more rapid German.

The guard lowered his weapon, placing it on the table.

Dunn rushed into the room and knocked the guard to the

floor. He put a foot on the man's back and held him there.

Ward ran in right behind his sergeant. He knelt by the guard and with items stored in one of his own jacket pockets, tied the guard's hands behind him, bound his feet, and gagged him.

While Ward was attending to the guard, Dunn was busy releasing Colonel Rogers. Using supplies from his own first aid kit carried on his belt, Dunn quickly bandaged the worst of the cuts in the forehead to stem the flow of blood. He wiped the colonel's right eye clean.

"Thanks, Sergeant. Who are you guys, anyway?"

"I'm Dunn. We're the bus out of here."

"Excellent, let's go."

"We will be getting you out posthaste, sir. But I have men working on something else, too."

Rogers got to his feet with Dunn's help. As they started past the table to get to the door, Rogers, stopped and grabbed his belongings off the table. He was grateful they were still there.

A sudden ruckus came from the outer office, shouting and scuffling sounds followed by a shot and a groan.

Dunn put a hand on Rogers' shoulder and said, "Stay here, sir."

Dunn ran into the outer office. Colonel Dentz was on the floor writhing in pain, his hands over his stomach.

"What happened?" asked Dunn, looking at Pastore.

Pastore appeared to be shaken and rattled off something. Dunn had no idea what the man had said.

Dunn looked at the German officer, whose face was pale and scrunched up in pain. Raising his hand, he pointed at the woman, then at the German. "Help him."

She got the idea and nodded, and ran to a cupboard on the wall. She retrieved some first aid items and started working on the officer.

The sounds of another explosion from the second set of charges, for the second, interior fence, echoed across the river valley.

Chapter 42

Prigione di Guerra 135
San Giuseppe, Italy
4 August, 0440 Hours

Jones lined up on the guard in the tower who had his weapon aimed at the truck parked behind the commandant's headquarters. Jones' shot was half again as long as the first one, about three hundred yards. The bullet exited the muzzle at 2800 feet per second. A third of a second later, the German's rifle left his lifeless grasp and tumbled to the ground below. One more critical shot to go. Jones swung the fierce muzzle to the north, acquired the last guard in the northeast tower, and removed that threat.

It was time for the next phase.

He found the barracks housing the German guards. He gauged the distance, then quickly adjusted his scope. To his left, Jones saw his three squad mates, Hanson, Wickham, and Fairbanks rushing toward the barracks. Straight ahead, the rest of the squad was setting up a position in a line facing the barracks. Sighting through the scope, Jones saw the door to the German barracks open slowly.

While Dunn and his men were handling the prison headquarters, Cross and his men were jumping out of the truck thirty yards south of the German barracks. Cross dispersed his men in a line facing the barracks. As each man got to one knee and brought up his Thompson, Cross looked left, to the northwest. There he clearly saw Hanson, Wickham, and Fairbanks running in a combat crouch toward the left, as they looked at it, of the same barracks.

Taking a knee himself, Cross saw the barracks door open. The first two Germans coming out collapsed on each other, the sounds of two rifle shots crisp in the morning air.

"Fire!" shouted Cross. Their Thompsons launched the heavy .45 caliber rounds through the thin wooden walls and shattered the glass of the three windows on their side. From the left, Hanson and his buddies ground to a stop, knelt and fired into the structure, raking the entire front from left to right.

Cross called out, "Cease fire!" Then he tapped Morris on the shoulder. As one, the two soldiers rose and sprinted to the barracks. As they ran, each unclipped a grenade from his shirt. Cross went to the window on the left and Morris to the one on the right, skidding to a halt, then kneeling quickly. Facing each other, Cross pointed at Morris. Prior to the attack, Cross had told Morris that his grenade should go in a short distance, while his own would go farther inside. Morris nodded, then they pulled the pins together, waited for a count of three and tossed the pineapples through the windows. They took off running away from the barracks, and after about ten yards dove to the ground.

The twin explosions sent debris flying through the busted windows. Smoke swirled in the air. Cross got up and waved his men forward. Advancing himself, when he made it to the corner of the building front, he took a quick peek. Nothing moved. Morris and Schneider shoved the barrels of their weapons through the windows while standing to one side. They fired several long bursts into the interior. Cross held up his hand for quiet.

Hanson, Wickham, and Fairbanks were still kneeling about forty yards away, weapons trained on the barracks. The door to another building opened and a British solider stepped out.

Hanson made eye contact with the man, who appeared to be an officer, and made a shooing movement with his hand. The man nodded and turned around, stepping smartly back into the building.

Cross ran to the barracks door, Schneider right behind him. At the door, which was still open, the hinges on the left, Cross leaned in and surveyed the open layout. It was a scene of carnage like any battlefield after a fierce firefight. It looked like there might be as many as forty dead Germans lying all over the room. Some had fallen to the floor, others never even made it out of their bunks. One set of bunks to his right, which had been close to a grenade, was in flames.

Cross guessed it wouldn't be long before the fire spread to the rest of the building, which suited him just fine. He didn't want to have to send any men in and check for survivors, whose only final outcome would have been a .45 caliber bullet in the head. However, to his right he could see the rifle racks containing all the Mausers for the guards. He wasn't willing to take any chances of getting his men shot later as they rounded up the camp's prisoners for the escape trucks.

"Schneider, get Morris and help me check for survivors."

"Yes, Sarge."

A moment later, the three men moved inside the building. They quickly determined none of the Germans had escaped the onslaught of bullets and grenades. By the end, they were all coughing up a storm as the smoke from the flames spread. Running out the door, they bent over and coughed some more. After drawing in some clean air, they gathered themselves, and Cross gave the order for the next phase.

Jones maintained his position, scanning the camp for threats with his naked eyes and also through the scope. Doors to prisoner barracks were popping open, and thin, worn men were looking out to see what the hell was going on, now that the shooting had stopped. Soon, men were milling about all over the camp. The four trucks he'd seen earlier drove into the camp and stopped near the commandant's headquarters. The drivers hopped out and opened the back doors.

Cross ran over to the building where Hanson had seen the British officer, since it was the closest one. Wickham joined him. The officer had stepped back outside, and his men were standing around, mouths agape at the sight of American soldiers.

Cross stopped in front of the officer, a man of about forty-five with graying hair and dark brown eyes. Cross saluted and the man returned it in British fashion, open palm facing Cross.

"Sergeant Cross, sir. And this is Corporal Wickham."

Wickham saluted.

"Colonel Carlisle," replied the ramrod straight Brit as he offered his hand. The three men shook.

"I'm the ranking officer here. I trust you chaps are here to rescue us?"

Cross smiled. "We are, sir. How many are you?"

"Only sixty-two, I'm afraid."

"That's about what we expected. The Germans have been transporting men out of here?"

"Over the past month, yes. Nearly two hundred have been shipped to camps in Germany." The man's face briefly showed the pain that had caused him. Then he steeled himself and called out, "Sergeant Yates!"

A short, wiry sergeant separated from the group standing around. He marched up to a point just to Colonel Carlisle's right. The colonel right-turned to meet him since Cross was in the way. The two Englishmen saluted.

"Prepare the sick and wounded first for transport. Ensure their comfort."

"Straight away, Colonel!" Another salute and the sergeant departed, grabbing three men from the group. They ran on a beeline for a barracks in the next row.

Colonel Carlisle turned to face Cross again. For the first time he smiled, only a small one, but a smile nevertheless.

"How many are there of *you*?"

"Eleven, sir, plus a few partisans."

Colonel Carlisle's mouth dropped open.

"You accomplished this with so few?"

"Correct, sir."

"I would love to chat with you about your attack, Sergeant Cross, it was a beautifully executed plan." He paused a moment to look around at the camp. "Later, of course."

"Certainly, sir. But you'll be wanting to speak to my boss, Sergeant Dunn. He put this all together."

"Wonderful. Did he plan this in England a few days ago? Or somewhere closer?"

"Oh, uh, well he came up with it last night, sir." Cross turned slightly to point in the direction of the road leading back to Ville di Murlo. "Somewhere over there."

The colonel's brown eyes moved to follow Cross's pointing finger.

"You say he put this together in one night?"

"Um, more like about ten minutes."

Colonel Carlisle examined Cross's face closely, as if to determine whether Cross was having him on. It was then he noticed the Ranger patch on Cross's shoulder.

"Rangers. Of course. I've always heard you lads were quite marvelous, but this is too incredible. Yes, indeed, I would like to have a sit down with your Sergeant Dunn."

Chapter 43

Ville di Murlo, Italy
4 August, 0502 Hours

Carlotta Agostini opened her eyes and found Umberto Gavino gently shaking her shoulder. His expression was a mixture of sadness and hardness that alarmed her immediately. She looked around and sighed with relief at the sight of little Marie curled up in a ball at the other end of the sofa.

Rising onto her left arm, she whispered, "Mr. Gavino, what is it? What's happened?"

The shopkeeper rose and held out his hand.

"Come with me, Carlotta. I have something to tell you."

Carlotta grasped the hand and followed Gavino. Instead of turning right at the hallway to go to the kitchen, he went the opposite way, pulling the woman along toward the front door. Once outside, he motioned for her to sit on the steps. When she did, he joined her.

Still holding her hand, he laid his other hand atop it.

"Carlotta, something bad has happened to Teresa and I wanted you to hear it from me."

Carlotta's heart jumped, even though she had been so angry

with her sister.

"She's dead, isn't she?"

"Yes. I'm sorry."

Carlotta began to sob quietly and Gavino put his arm around her shoulder, pulling her close. She dropped her head against his chest and wept.

After a few minutes, she pulled back and wiped her eyes with the back of her hand. Gavino gave her a handkerchief and she finished cleaning her face.

"What happened?" Carlotta looked at Gavino and noticed he had swallowed heavily. He wouldn't meet her eyes. "Please tell me."

In a soft voice he replied, "It would be better for you not to know."

"What on earth does that even mean?" Carlotta's voice rose.

Gavino shushed her and said, "Don't wake Marie."

"I want to know."

"Please, Carlotta."

"No. You tell me right now."

Gavino looked away, down the street. Even though the sun's disc was not visible yet over the mountain peaks, light was diffusing into the village. It seemed so terribly normal and hid the cruelty of the last day.

"Carlotta, I heard Teresa tell you she had told the Germans that the American was here. She brought the Gestapo and the Nazi SS troops into our village."

"What did you do?"

"You know I am partisan and I have certain responsibilities."

Carlotta swooned and fell back on the stairs. Gavino's quick reaction saved her from cracking her head on the riser's edge. After a moment, her eyes fluttered, then opened. She jumped to her feet and started pummeling Gavino's head. He fought off the blows and managed to get to his feet, and embraced her in a bear hug, pinning her hands between their bodies. He held her tight until she stopped struggling.

Her strength left her and she sagged against the old man. He gently lowered her to the steps, then sat down beside her again.

In a barely audible whisper, she said, "You killed her. You murdered my sister. How could you? Explain that to me."

"I had no choice. You know what happens to collaborators. I did what had to be done."

Carlotta's head was spinning. What had Teresa's last words to her been? She struggled to remember. In a memory burst it came back to her: *Yes! I turned the American in! I don't care about the others! I did what had to be done!*

Carlotta gulped at the irony of it all. *I did what had to be done.*

"That's what she said to me, Mr. Gavino. 'I did what had to be done.' Exactly as you said it." She raised her head and looked at Gavino, who was finally able to return her gaze.

"I called her a traitor. She caused the death of two innocent people out of spite. Toward me. Do you know how guilty that makes me?"

"You are not responsible. She was."

"I think I was angry enough to kill her myself." Carlotta shrugged. "Though, I doubt I could really have done it." She paused to wipe her face again with the cloth. "But I think she could have killed me. She hated me for marrying Rocco. She thought he was hers. Now he's no one's." Another bout of crying hit her and Gavino continued to hold her.

"He may still return someday," offered the shopkeeper.

Carlotta shook her head. "I feel it. He's dead. He'll never come home. Poor Marie will grow up without ever truly knowing her father. As she grows older, the few memories she has will disappear." She paused to sigh deeply. "I've always known he wasn't coming back, but I guess I just tried to keep hope going. I've been grieving too long. I haven't been strong for Damiano and Marie. Perhaps it's time to live life again."

Gavino took the handkerchief from Carlotta's yielding hands and wiped her eyes. Then he put a finger under her chin and turned her face toward himself. "If that is true, Carlotta, that Rocco is not coming home, then your responsibility is to make sure Marie doesn't forget. Remember, you are not alone. I am here to help if you need it. I know we aren't related, but to me you are like a daughter and Marie and Damiano are like my grandchildren. Please know you are loved. If you are ready to live again, you have people who can help."

Carlotta nodded and leaned her head against his shoulder.

They sat like that for a long time, unmoving, each comforted by the other's presence in the aftermath of everything that had happened in the past day. Unspoken was the common thought that it was all over and everything would be okay if the villagers just all helped each other.

Unknown to either was a central, harsh truth: in war, nothing is ever completely over.

Chapter 44

Inside Prigione di Guerra 135
San Giuseppe, Italy
4 August, 0519 Hours

The four rescue trucks were lined up in a column. Dunn and Colonel Carlisle stood beside the truck last in line, which was the last to be loaded with the prisoners. Dunn had ordered a sweep of the entire camp, all of the barracks and the tiny building used for solitary confinement punishment, but no one had been inadvertently left behind. Earlier, the colonel, an infantry commander, had tried to engage Dunn in conversation about the attack, seemingly enthralled by the sheer audacity of it, but the Ranger had politely demurred quoting the need for continuing speed of action to rescue the men. Dunn did, however, agree to sit with the colonel on the ride out.

The sixty-two men had been evenly distributed in groups of fifteen to a truck except the first one which contained seventeen. To those numbers, Dunn added one of his own men to each truck to explain what would be expected of the men as soon as they reached their destination. This group included Schneider, Ward, Morris, and Wickham, who Dunn put in with a bunch of British flyers so they could enjoy his peculiar Brit-Tex accent.

"Cross!"

Cross looked at his sergeant from his spot by the first truck. "Yes?"

"Get our men loaded."

Cross nodded and gathered up the remaining Rangers, then got them into their truck, which was parked next to the first in line. They would cross the bridge, then pick up Jones on the river road.

SS barracks
Genoa, Italy
5 August, 0525 Hours

Greg Schluter was anxious to get going. Müller had called him a few minutes ago. The conversation had been brief, but Müller had expressed high interest in the outcome of the upcoming interrogation. He told Schluter to be quick about it.

"Hurry up!" Schluter shouted at the men as they climbed into their trucks.

SS Captain Adelsberger, standing next to the Gestapo agent, asked quietly, "Why are we taking an entire platoon to an interrogation, sir?"

Schluter gave Adelsberger an amused grin. "I have plans for after the interrogation and they include the need for an *entire* platoon of elite SS troops. That is all you need to know, Captain."

"Yes, sir," replied the mystified Adelsberger.

"I want these trucks on the move in five minutes. Not a minute later."

"Yes, sir."

Adelsberger left Schluter's side and ran to each truck exhorting and physically pushing men into the trucks.

When the five minutes were up, Adelsberger joined Schluter in his staff car, sitting behind the driver. The moment the SS captain closed the door, the driver gave it the gas. Behind them, all of the trucks were pouring black smoke as the drivers floored their gas pedals in an attempt to keep up with the faster car.

Leaning forward, Schluter drummed his fingers on the back of the front seat.

"How long to get to the camp?" he asked the driver. He hadn't paid attention on the reverse trip from the camp to Genoa.

"A little more than an hour, *Herr* Schluter. The roads are slick."

"*Verdammt! Nein!*" Schluter slapped the top of the seat back. "You will make it in less than an hour."

"*Jawohl*, Herr Schluter."

Satisfied, the Gestapo agent sat back in his seat and closed his eyes. Thoughts of the upcoming resumed interrogation of *Colonel Rogers* flew through his head. He imagined what the man's expression would be when Schluter told him his real rank and name, and when he threatened the man's family all the way back in supposedly safe America. A cruel smile touched his lips. A moment later he drifted off to a sound sleep.

River road near Prigione di Guerra 135
San Giuseppe, Italy
5 August, 0527 Hours

Dunn was in the lead truck, the one his men had arrived in. Next to him was Colonel Carlisle. Frontino was driving. Dunn spotted Jones on the left side of the road. Just as he was about to reach across in front of the colonel to tap Frontino on the arm, the Italian put on the brakes, having seen Jones already. The truck rolled to a stop.

Jones ran to the back and handed up his rifle. Lindstrom pulled in the weapon, then offered a hand to Jones, who grasped it to climb aboard.

"Nice shooting, Jonesy," Lindstrom said, patting Jones on the shoulder. "Really nice."

Jones nodded and said, "Thanks."

Jones exchanged nods with Martelli and Cross who sat on the truck's floor close to the small open window going into the truck's cab. Next to Cross, Colonel Rogers lay on his back with a folded jacket as a pillow and his eyes closed. Cross had worked on the facial injuries as much as possible, and changed the bandage on Rogers' hand.

"How's he doing, Sarge?" asked the sniper.

"Pretty good, considering," replied Cross.

Jones nodded again and pulled his satchel off his back, setting it on the floor in front of him. He retrieved his rifle from Lindstrom and set to work breaking it down for cleaning.

Dunn had turned in his seat to look into the back of the panel truck. Jones was in. To Frontino he said, "Go!" pointing.

Frontino understood the gesture, if not the word, and stomped on the gas. The truck shot forward. Behind them, the four trucks filled with former prisoners of war followed.

Dunn said to Martelli, "Ask him how long it will take to get to the village."

Martelli asked the question and repeated the reply for Dunn, "Should be there in about an hour."

Dunn checked his watch. The aircraft he'd requested by radio a few minutes ago should be making their landings within the hour. He'd had to talk to General Truscott himself to get approval. Dunn explained the situation: the sixty-two prisoners' lives at stake, given that the Germans were transporting them into Germany, not to mention securing the military-intelligence-filled head of Colonel Rogers. Truscott had grilled Dunn on the plan and asked twice what the chances were for failure. Dunn had replied that there is always a chance for failure, but he thought the plan was solid and more importantly that his men would execute it flawlessly. Additionally, the aspect of surprise would help them win the day.

The planes were to land in a field southwest of the village. Dunn was concerned that the rains during the night would have softened the ground too much for the heavy C-47s, but when he asked Pastore about it, the Italian said the ground had been dry for quite some time and the rain shouldn't make a difference.

"Colonel Carlisle, it's imperative your men disembark from the trucks and load into the aircraft as fast as humanly possible."

"Indeed. We will do exactly that. I can't thank you enough."

"How long have you been there, sir?"

"Late June."

"Not too long, then, sir. I'm glad."

"Nineteen forty-two."

Dunn's face said it all.

Carlisle grinned at catching Dunn. "Sorry, Sergeant. Couldn't resist. Eighth Army, near Tobruk."

Dunn gave the colonel a wry grin. "Score one for the officer, sir."

"Indeed."

Dunn looked through the window to the back and said, "Martelli, ask him about German activity along the road to the village. Whether they've been there lately."

Martelli relayed the question and listened carefully to Frontino's long reply.

"He says they almost never use this road. Of course that doesn't include the arrival of the SS unit yesterday. But he thinks the only reason they were there is that they were tipped off about Colonel Rogers' presence.

"The road isn't the best way to or from anywhere, unlike the coast road that runs all the way to Genoa on one side and to Nice on the other. So the Germans tend to use that one."

"Tell him 'thank you.' " To Cross, Dunn asked, "How's the colonel?"

"I'm fine, sergeant," came a strong voice from below the window. "And thanks for the rescue."

"Our pleasure, sir."

Dunn leaned against the door, but kept his eyes open and he watched the road ahead, alert for anything out of place.

Chapter 45

Outside Prigione di Guerra 135
San Giuseppe, Italy
4 August, 0625 Hours

Schluter's driver had roared through the mountain passes from
Genoa almost maniacally and made it in less than an hour.

Schluter's first indication of trouble at the POW camp was
when he noticed there were no guards in the towers. Then when
the driver turned the staff car onto the bridge, he saw the guard's
body lying off to the side and the gate wide open, hanging from
its hinges in shatters of wood and wire.

"Hurry!" he shouted.

The driver sped up and roared through the gate. He slammed
on the brakes in front of the commandant's headquarters building
and the car skidded to a halt. Schluter bolted from the car and
took the steps two at a time.

Adelsberger started to yell for the Gestapo agent to wait, but
it was too late.

Schluter sprinted into the office and found the commandant
dead on the floor, shot in the stomach. A German soldier lay dead
to Schluter's left. Schluter pulled his sidearm from its holster. A

whimpering sound came from behind a desk. He ran over and the blond secretary cringed into a ball at the fury in his face. He ignored her and spun to the right. He hurried into the interrogation room and his heart dropped. The American was gone!

Adelsberger ran into the office and immediately drew his weapon, taking in everything in a glance.

Schluter looked down to the left of the table and was shocked to see a German solider lying there, bound and gagged. He spotted heavy blood on the man's tunic and the floor, and he leaned closer. The throat had been cut. Had Rogers somehow gotten the best of the guard? But how did that explain the missing tower guards and the dead guard at the gate? That was too much for one man. What the hell?

Schluter walked back out of the interrogation room and to the woman. Pointing his pistol at her, he asked, "What happened to the American? What happened here?"

She cried out in fear and hid her face in her hands.

Schluter recognized he'd get farther by calming down. He holstered his weapon and, speaking softly, said, "I'm sorry. Here, let me help you up." He offered his hand.

The woman uncovered her eyes and looked at his hand cautiously, then at his face. He seemed suddenly calm. She lifted her hand and he helped her up.

"Are you hurt?" asked Schluter, nodding in the direction of the front of her dress, which was covered in blood.

"No, sir. This is Colonel Dentz's. He's . . . he's dead."

"Yes, I know. Here, why don't you sit down?" Schluter led her to a nearby chair. "Wait here a minute."

To Adelsberger, he said, "When the trucks get here, do a sweep of the camp and bring anyone found directly to me." Due to the breakneck speed the driver had taken, the trucks were likely at least five minutes behind.

"Yes, sir."

Adelsberger departed and Schluter turned back to the woman. "What happened? Take your time."

"Some partisans burst into the office and killed the commandant, and the two soldiers," she lied.

Abriana had been a member of the partisans for the last two

years. She'd known Antonio Pastore for several years and had been recruited by him. While Dunn and his men had been getting the prisoners rounded up and loaded into the trucks, she and Pastore had been working on her story, since she would be the only survivor. Pastore had sliced open the guard's throat. Next, he had covered the colonel's nose and mouth with his hands. After a feeble attempt to save himself, the colonel had expired.

"You say partisans did all this?"

"Yes, sir. I was so afraid they'd kill me, too." Abriana began to cry.

Schluter patted her on the shoulder and said, "It's all right, you're safe now."

She nodded, but said nothing.

Schluter made as if to leave her, but she quickly grasped his arm. "Please don't leave me," she nodded toward the colonel's body, "with him." Her blue eyes pleaded with him for comfort.

Schluter smiled and patted her hand. Then he gripped and removed it from his arm.

"Did you see where they took the prisoner?"

"No. I just hid behind the desk where you found me."

The sound of heavy vehicles arriving came from the compound outside the office.

Schluter glanced out the still-open door, then turned back. He gave her a hard stare, checking her face for signs of lies, then said, "I'm sorry, but I need you to stay here. I have some work to do."

She started to say something, then changed her mind.

As the Gestapo agent started to turn away, Abriana spoke up anyway. "*Herr* Schluter, would it be all right if I go clean myself up? There's a bathroom down the hall."

He nodded absently, then turned and walked back to the front door, being careful not to step over the body. Not that he was superstitious.

Adelsberger was organizing the search ordered by Schluter as the men climbed down from the trucks. In moments, some of the SS troops were fanning out to various parts of the camp.

Standing on the office's small porch, Schluter glanced around. The morning sun was growing in strength and long shadows began to appear on the dirt compound. He took a deep breath, enjoying the air, which smelled fresh and clean due to the nighttime rain. Not ordinarily a reflective man, a childhood memory suddenly came to him.

It was a sunny day. His father held his eight-year-old hand as they hiked along an animal trail in the Black Forest. They both wore knee-length lederhosen. The father was walking at a pace that was slower than his own natural gait, but fast enough to challenge his son. Each carried a rifle slung over the shoulder, Greg's fit for his smaller size. The father suddenly stopped and put his hand up for silence. Greg stopped, too. Mr. Schluter dropped to one knee quietly and raised a hand. Greg followed the pointing finger but didn't see anything. There! Slight movement. Something gray and white. Excitement coursed through Greg's body. A rabbit. Only fifteen meters away facing away from them.

Carefully and quietly, just as his father had taught him, Greg slipped the rifle off his shoulder and dropped to one knee. He raised the rifle and sighted along the child-sized barrel at the rabbit. With his thumb, he flipped off the safety. Breathing as he'd been taught he waited a moment, then when the breath was correct, he pulled the trigger. The sharp crack of the round broke the forest silence. The rabbit fell over, twitched once, then died.

Greg grinned wide and stood up. Before he took a step to retrieve his prize, he worked the bolt and from a pouch on his belt drew out another round, which he slipped into the breach. He closed the bolt and flipped on the safety. Then he looked at his father.

Mr. Schluter smiled at his son, proud that he'd remembered everything.

"Excellent, my boy. Very well done. That's our dinner tonight. You have scored your first kill."

He reached out and patted young Greg on the back.

Schluter smiled at the memory. *Yes, that was my first kill. Of many as it has turned out. Almost all of them human*, thought the proud Gestapo agent.

For a split second, he missed his father, but no longer than that.

He turned and looked back into the office. His face turned red and he scowled. Someone was going to pay for this. And he knew who it would be.

Turning back to the compound, he shouted at his SS captain, "Adelsberger! Come here! Bring two men."

Adelsberger waved at him in reply and spoke rapidly to the last group of men, who, except for two, departed with their instructions.

A moment later, three-black-uniformed men stood before Schluter.

"Yes, *Herr* Schluter?" Adelsberger said.

"Come with me."

The men all stomped back into the office. Schluter waved at the dead colonel and spoke to the two SS soldiers.

"Get this body out of here. Put it behind the building."

"*Jawohl, Herr* Schluter." The men bent down and, with one man at each end, picked up the colonel and carried him outside.

Schluter motioned for his captain to be seated in the same chair the forgotten secretary had been sitting in. Schluter sat down in the chair behind the late commandant's desk. He leaned forward, hands folded in front of him.

"We are going to punish the village for this."

Adelsberger looked back at Schluter calmly. "Yes, sir."

Schluter sat back in the chair and put his hands behind his head. "Where do people go when they are afraid?"

The SS officer was perplexed by the question and raised his eyebrows. After a moment, thinking of the Allied bombings, he offered, "The basement?"

Schluter chuckled. "No. Where do people gather to offer up prayer?"

"Oh, I see. Church."

"You ever see a church burn?"

"I honestly can't say I have."

"There's a particularly beautiful church in Ville di Murlo."

"Ah, yes, sir, I remember it. Toward the west edge."

"Correct. You are no doubt familiar with the story of Lidice, are you not?"

Adelsberger's eyes widened. "Yes, sir, I am. The destruction of the entire village. Its inhabitants were either killed or sent to camps in retaliation for the gutless assassination of our great Reinhard Heydrich, back in '42."

Schluter leaned forward again. "We are going to have our

own Lidice today."

Adelsberger nodded enthusiastically. "Very good, sir. I look forward to it."

"As do I, Adelsberger, as do I." Schluter rose from his chair. "Come. I'm certain the men will find nothing worthwhile. Let's get ready for our historic day, shall we?"

"By all means, sir."

Abriana's face paled. She, too, knew the story of Lidice. And now a monstrous atrocity was being planned for Ville di Murlo? How could she contact Pastore? He was probably still on the road to the village with the Americans. She opened the door to the bathroom and peeked out. She was just in time to see the backs of the two Nazis as they stepped off the porch. Apparently, in their horrifying excitement, they'd completely forgotten about her.

She stepped out of the bathroom and instead of running to the front room, walked across the hall to another small office. There she picked up a phone and relief washed over her when she got a dial tone. She quickly dialed a number from memory. Three rings later a voice answered, "*Ciao?*"

Quickly and succinctly, Abriana gave her message.

For a long several seconds there was no reply and just she was about to ask 'are you still there?' she heard, "Dear God. Message understood. Get somewhere safe, my child. Consider your mission complete."

"I will as soon as possible."

She hung up the phone, and prepared herself to leave.

At the other end of the call, Umberto Gavino hung up the phone. His heart raced upon hearing Abriana's message.

Chapter 46

Main street
Ville di Murlo, Italy
4 August, 0640 Hours

Dunn turned in his seat to look into the back of the truck. Everyone there was asleep, but Dunn called out, "Colonel Rogers?"

"Yes, Sergeant?"

"We're back in the village now, sir."

"Thanks. Can we make that stop I asked about?"

"We can only risk a few minutes. The planes should be on the ground waiting. I can get the men started on the loading and stay with you, but only a few minutes."

"That's all I need."

"Very good, sir."

Rogers had asked Dunn about the stop and, with Martelli's help, nailed down the request with Frontino, who naturally knew where the house was.

Frontino stopped the truck with a squeak of the brakes.

Dunn opened the door, but turned to the British officer next to him. "Colonel, might I ask you to switch to the truck behind us?

Then all of your men will be taken to the field across the river, there." The Ranger pointed through the windshield. "The C-47s should be on the ground and waiting for you. I will catch you before take-off for a proper goodbye."

Colonel Carlisle, who had indeed discussed at length Dunn's plan and execution of the rescue, replied, "Righto."

"Thanks."

Dunn got out and held the door open for the British officer. As the colonel marched toward the next truck in line, which was stopped only a few yards away, Dunn moved to the back of the panel truck and opened the doors. The men all got out, with Cross helping Rogers.

Rogers nodded his thanks and walked unaided toward Carlotta's house.

Dunn waved at the driver of the truck behind him to move out. He watched as the trucks roared by, waving at each one. When the last one passed, he said to Cross, "What a night, huh?"

"Indeed."

Dunn laughed at Cross's impertinence. Colonel Carlisle must have used that word fifty times on the drive to the village while commenting on Dunn's attack on the POW Camp.

Dunn and Cross shared a look that said mostly, *yeah we did good, but we're not out of here yet.*

The door opened and Carlotta raised her hand to her mouth. A squeal of delight came from down the hall. The sounds of light, but running footsteps thudded and a moment later Marie launched herself past her mother into the waiting arms of Colonel Rogers.

Martelli had followed Rogers and stood behind him waiting patiently on the porch, looking around the street. He was thinking about his family's history and what it had been like for his parents to grow up in a village much like this one. He thought it would have been nice. Except for the Nazi part.

Rogers hugged Marie tight, thinking of his own kids back home. He set her down and knelt in front of her.

She reached out and touched his battered and bruised face gently.

"Are you okay?"

Martelli quickly stepped closer so he could hear for the

translating process. In doing so, he laid eyes on Carlotta for the first time. His eyes widened and his mouth dropped open at her beauty. She looked up at him, taking her eyes off Rogers and Marie, meeting Martelli's gaze.

She smiled.

Martelli blushed. He totally forgot what he was supposed to be doing and instead offered his hand by reaching around Rogers. He spoke to Carlotta.

"Hello. I'm Alphonso Martelli."

Something buried stirred in Carlotta and her smile widened as she took his hand. He started to lift it to his lips for a European kiss, but lost his nerve at the last moment and just stood there holding it.

From the street, Dunn saw what was happening and hollered, "Martelli! Do your job."

Martelli snapped out of it and let go of Carlotta's hand. For just a moment, she tightened her grip and he couldn't pull his hand away.

"Carlotta Agostini, Alphonso. I'm very pleased to meet you. Very." Carlotta chose to speak in Italian.

To Martelli's surprise, she winked at him. He blushed again and she grinned. Finally, she let go of his hand and stepped back.

"Martelli!" Dunn yelled again.

Martelli tore his eyes from Carlotta's gaze and focused on Marie. "What did you say, little one?" he asked, which caused Carlotta to smile again because that was what Damiano called his sister.

Marie wasn't quite sure what to make of what had just happened. She couldn't remember the last time her mother had grinned that wide. And on top of that, she thought she'd seen a wink. When Marie looked at the dark-haired American, all she saw was a nice-looking boy hardly older than her brother Damiano. Deciding it must be nothing, she said, "I asked if he was okay."

Martelli translated quickly.

"Yes, I'm okay. It doesn't hurt as much as it looks like."

Marie nodded, then wrinkled her nose. "Sure it doesn't," she chided.

Rogers shrugged and gave her a *you caught me look*. "Well,

maybe it does. But these guys rescued me, so I'm getting ready to leave, but I wanted to come by and thank you and your mom for helping me. I also wanted to tell you what my real name is."

"It's not Frank?"

Rogers laughed. "Oh, I mean my last name. Rogers. I'm Frank Rogers, a Colonel."

Marie laughed in return, then said, "It's nice to meet you, Colonel Rogers."

"And you, Marie."

Marie's eyes suddenly started to trickle tears and Rogers wiped them away.

He stuck a hand in his shirt pocket and slid out the family picture Marie had given him. He held it out for her, but she shook her head.

"No. I want you to keep it to remember me by."

"Do you still have mine?"

"Yes."

"Good, you keep it then. You be a good girl, okay? Be strong."

"I will."

At that moment, Gavino's truck screeched to a halt at the curb near Dunn. Gavino climbed out of the truck and ran as fast as his beaten seventy-year-old body would allow over to Dunn. He grabbed Dunn's left upper arm in a surprisingly tight grip. Damiano jumped out of the passenger side and ran over, too.

Gavino started rattling off something in Italian.

Dunn held his free hand up for the man to wait.

"Martelli! I need you."

Martelli excused himself and sprinted down the stairs, then over to Dunn.

"Ask him to repeat himself."

Martelli complied.

"Are you in charge?" asked the shopkeeper.

"Yes. My name's Dunn."

"Gavino. Partisan."

Gavino let go of Dunn's arm, and seemed to steel himself.

"Sir, we desperately need your help. I just got word from a woman at the POW camp who's a secretary to the commandant. She overheard that terrible Gestapo man. He said they are coming back here to punish us for what happened at the camp. He has four trucks full of SS troops. They are planning to kill everyone, burn the church, and destroy the rest of the village."

Dunn's heart fell at the news. Good Lord, he hadn't even considered this. Nazi reprisals were known to happen, but to be the cause of one was too horrific to even imagine. Dunn looked at Damiano, the young man he'd met only last night, and saw deep fear etched all over his face.

Dunn checked his watch, then asked, "What time did they leave?"

"They haven't yet. She called me about five minutes ago."

Dunn checked his watch: 0645 hours. If the Nazis left in the next few minutes, they could arrive at about 0750 hours.

"Four trucks?"

Gavino nodded.

That meant a platoon was headed their way and all he had available was a squad plus one, Martelli. Dunn glanced at Gavino and Damiano. They would certainly want to help, as would Pastore and Frontino. The problem was, a firefight with elite SS troops would be far different from some of the other activities conducted by the partisans. Dunn focused his attention on the east side of the village and a tidbit of information came to mind, something he'd noted on the drive. He stood silent for thirty seconds then, not being one to waste time bemoaning his circumstances, decided what needed to be done. As was often the case with him, the plan came nearly fully formed.

"Wait here, sir," he said to Gavino. Then he called out, "Colonel Rogers. We have to leave. Right now."

Rogers turned to look at Dunn and nodded. He touched Marie's cheek and said, "*Ciao*, Marie. *Grazie*."

Marie grabbed him in another hug, then let go and backed up, eyes streaming tears now. Rogers smiled at Carlotta and waved his good hand. She waved back and put an arm around her daughter.

Rogers joined Dunn and asked, "What's going on?"

"The Gestapo and an elite SS unit are headed here and will arrive in about an hour. We've got to get you out of here, sir."

"Oh, dear God, no."

"Yes, sir. Let's go, sir." Dunn raised his hand in the direction of the truck's back doors. Rogers climbed in.

To Gavino, Dunn said, "How many armed men can you muster with rifles?"

Gavino shook his head, "Very few. Most men only have shotguns. We only have a handful of rifles."

Dunn put his hand on the older man's arm. "We can help you, but first I have to get that man on an airplane."

By the time Dunn's panel van reached the open field, the trucks had unloaded their passengers. The former prisoners were moving around under the direction of Dunn's men, who were trying to get them into a semblance of order to prepare for boarding the planes.

Which were nowhere in sight.

Chapter 47

Once everyone poured out of the panel truck and into the open field, Dunn gathered his men. He turned to Colonel Carlisle, who stood nearby, and said, "Sir, can you and your sergeant finish getting your men organized for the flights?"

"Absolutely."

Dunn exchanged salutes with the colonel, who immediately marched off at quick time pace, arms swinging high, as if he was on a parade grounds.

The Ranger whistled twice and when his four men corralling the former prisoners looked his way, pin-wheeled his right arm the way a third base coach does to send the runner home. The men all broke into a run and shortly were standing with the rest of the squad. They formed a semicircle in front of Dunn, and had expectant looks on their faces. Schneider, who had the responsibility of handling the radio, got it off his back and set it on the ground.

Colonel Rogers stood a little behind Dunn and off to one side. He was interested in seeing how this man handled things. Rogers had tried to engage, first Martelli in the back of the truck, then Dunn through the window to the front seat, but neither soldier would answer any of his questions.

"Men, Martelli already heard this, but we've got a terrible problem. There's an SS unit and Gestapo on the way back to the village. Their intent is to kill everyone and destroy the village entirely."

"Holy shit, Dunny!" shouted Hanson.

Most of the others muttered some four-letter word or another.

The men's posture suddenly straightened. Their weapons came to the ready and their eyes grew hard and focused.

Rogers was astonished by the transformation and understood more fully just what kind of men these were and how they had managed to pull off a rescue of sixty-two prisoners. *Plus an errant officer*, he thought at the end.

The change was nothing new to Dunn. He was positive he had the best Ranger squad in the world, for that matter, the best anything squad in the world. They excelled at the impossible and that was just what he was about to ask of them. Again.

"First things first, as you can see, the rescue aircraft for the prisoners haven't arrived. Schneider, get on the horn and let me know when you have Corsica on the line."

"Yes, Sarge," replied the big, multi-lingual corporal. Just as he fired up the device, the droning sound of distant airplane engines drifted down from the western sky.

Everyone turned to look.

As the sounds grew louder, Dunn was able to make out four distinct dots. *Thank God*, he thought. As he watched, he noted four other smaller specks were visible. The escorts he'd asked for?

The first C-47 started its approach. Dunn was able to clearly see that the additional specks were indeed escorts, four powerful, huge, and dangerous P-47 Thunderbolts, their bulbous noses leading the way. Soon they were flying above the field in a race track pattern.

Dunn turned to Rogers, who was watching the Thunderbolts with his mouth open. He lowered his gaze and fixed his eyes on Dunn.

"How in the world?"

"Friends in rather particular places, sir."

Dunn had been able to get his request sent all the way up to Truscott. His fallback would have been to go through Colonel Kenton back at Barton Stacey and then up the ladder as far as needed, even to Eisenhower, who owned the top rung.

Rogers smiled. "Good friends, I'd say."

"Yep."

The first C-47 touched down, ran down the length of the field and turned off the "runway." The pilot reversed direction, but kept the engines running. The rest of the transports lined up and drifted closer and closer to earth.

Cheers went up from the prisoners. Dunn thought they were as loud as any University of Iowa football game crowd.

Colonel Carlisle issued an order and the prisoners all formed into four squad-like groups of fifteen men each. They snapped to attention facing away from Dunn and his men. The colonel and his sergeant were at the front of the formation, facing Dunn.

After the last of the aircraft landed, the colonel gave another order and the men began marching, one group to each plane. The rear doors of the aircraft all opened, and a crewman lowered the ladder-like stairs.

Schneider said, "Sarge, the radio is ready. I have Corsica headquarters on the line."

"I want you guys to do an equipment check, and prepare for battle," Dunn said.

While the men set about double checking their weapons and ammunition, Dunn took the handset and gave a few words of instructions.

"That might take a bit, Sergeant Dunn," replied the man on the other end of the radio call.

"I'll wait right here, but this is critically urgent."

With the handset to his ear, Dunn looked at Colonel Rogers.

"Sir, it's time for you to go. I'm going to have Sergeant Cross here help you over to the airplane."

"I'm not exactly thrilled with the idea of getting back on an airplane after being shot down. I think I'd prefer to stay with you and lend a hand."

"Sir, I have orders, this is not your choice. You will get on that aircraft and get the hell out of here."

"No," replied the colonel, standing up straighter, trying to exert command authority.

Dunn brushed it all aside. Lowering his voice, he said, "Colonel, your only two choices are getting onto that plane under your own power, or getting put in the plane under our power. You need to choose now. Sir."

The colonel stared for a moment, then chuckled, shaking his head ruefully. "As you wish, Sergeant. I'll go. And thanks again for the rescue." He stepped back and saluted Dunn, who perfectly returned it.

"Have a good flight, sir."

"Will do."

Rogers offered a hand, which Dunn shook.

"Sergeant, what's your first name?"

"Tom, sir."

"Thanks, Tom. Good luck."

Dunn started to turn away, but the colonel still had a grip on his hand.

"Tom? Promise me you'll keep the village safe."

"I'll do my best, sir."

Rogers' expression turned dark. "And you kill that son of a bitch Gestapo agent."

Dunn understood completely, but simply repeated himself, "I'll do my best, sir."

"Okay. Okay then."

Rogers released Dunn's hand and turned to head off to one of the airplanes, but Dunn said, "Sir? Was it worth it? Your being here? Did you find anything?"

"I did. I'm hoping that when I get back, I'll find out whether it was taken care of."

Satisfied, Dunn nodded.

Rogers left, with Cross lending a hand.

A voice came over the handset and Dunn replied, "Malcolm?"

"Aye. This better be good. I was sound asleep."

"I need your help. I already set up a flight for you. It can depart any moment."

"We just got here, you know. We've been busy, too."

Dunn noticed the rebuke, unusual for Saunders since Operation Devil's Fire when they had come to a kind of truce with each other, then developed a strong friendship. "Something wrong?"

A deep sigh came across the radio. "I lost Owens."

Dunn was silent a moment. "Sorry to hear that."

"Yeah." Another moment of silence passed, then Saunders said, "Right. So what's your problem?"

Dunn explained the situation and gave Saunders the map coordinates.

Saunders immediately replied, "We're on the way, mate."

"Thanks. Once you're in the air, the pilot is going to hit max speed. You should be here within thirty-five minutes of takeoff, so make it forty-five or fifty minutes from now. I'll have a truck waiting for you. Oh, and you won't have to jump."

"Good to know. See you soon."

"Oh, Malcolm. By the way, I arranged for some stuff to be loaded on your plane. You'll want to break it out and get it ready."

"Righto, mate. I'm ringing off now."

The radio went dead and Dunn gave the handset back to Schneider.

By this time, Cross had jogged back to join the men.

The first C-47, which was carrying the precious cargo in the shape of one Frank Rogers, was speeding down the field in the ungainly way only a Goonie Bird could. Suddenly, it lifted and changed from the clumsy ground vehicle into a graceful flying machine with a beauty all its own. Soon the others were following. The moment they were all up, the P-47 Thunderbolts finished off a lap and zeroed in on the group of transports. Within seconds, the aerial shield of P-47s was high above the transports. The fighter pilots would protect them to the death. A few minutes passed, and the eight American airplanes disappeared from sight over the Apennine Mountains.

"We did it, Tom."

"I know, Dave. I wish we could celebrate. Did you get all the chocolate distributed to the men from the camp?"

"Yeah, I did. To be honest, it was quite like a shark feeding frenzy. I was glad to get out with all my body parts." Cross grinned.

Dunn grinned back. "I saved one small piece. I want to give it to that little girl Colonel Rogers was talking to. Martelli said her name is Marie."

Cross smiled. Of course Dunn would think of something like that. Just like he did every time they were on a mission. All the bases were covered.

"Schneider, you can pack up the radio."

Schneider nodded and set to work on that task.

Chapter 48

Main street
Ville di Murlo, Italy
4 August, 0710 Hours

Dunn stood in front of Gavino's shop talking with the partisan leader. Martelli and the remainder of the squad were gathered close to their sergeant.

Dunn had been surprised to learn that a man of seventy years was the head of the resistance group. Frontino had told him on the drive back into the village. Dunn had left Ward and one of the larger trucks to wait for Saunders' arrival.

Dunn checked his watch for the millionth time. He prayed that Saunders would arrive in time. Dunn had guessed that the Gestapo agent and his platoon of SS troops would arrive between seven forty-five and eight o'clock. Which was why he'd sent Pastore and Frontino on their mission several miles east of the village to buy time. He just hoped the price wasn't too high.

"Mr. Gavino, how many people are in this village?"

"About five hundred, mostly old people and children. We have very few young men like this." He patted Damiano on the shoulder. "Mussolini sent our young men to their deaths or to capture in Africa, Greece, and Russia."

Before saying anything, Dunn debated with himself about getting the people to evacuate, perhaps up into the mountain, but decided that the makeup of the villagers would create difficulties in accomplishing it with any success. Since his goal was to protect them from the SS troops, the best way to safeguard them during the firefight was to get them into one controlled location. He knew that if he and his men, along with a few partisans and Saunders' men, couldn't completely stop the SS, the enemy would take so many casualties they would then become an ineffective unit. Perhaps the old men with shotguns might be able to fend them off. However, even though Dunn realized this was a remote possibility, the only way he could think about his attack was to believe it would succeed in completely destroying the SS unit.

"Is there a place big enough for everyone to go for safety? Or perhaps two buildings close to each other?"

"The church has room for that many. Most in the sanctuary, and the rest in the basement. You saw it at the west end of the village?"

Dunn was nodding. Yes, he'd seen it, you couldn't miss it. It was a huge stone Catholic church.

"Please start moving your people into the church. You have to be barricaded inside within the hour. Have some men take their shotguns inside with them. I know they won't want to take them inside the church, but they must. They can pray for forgiveness later. Set up a perimeter a block from the church with a many men as you can."

"And what of your men?"

Dunn pointed in the direction of the bridge that was about one and a half miles to the east. "That's going to be our defensive position."

Gavino then spoke to Damiano. Martelli continued translating for Dunn.

"You have to be my legs. Start spreading the word from this end of the village. I will begin using the phone and calling those at the other end."

Damiano stood still, a scowl on his face.

"I want to fight!"

Gavino patted him on the arm. "I know you do. Your mother will kill me if anything happened to you—" He held up a finger to silence the young man, who'd started to argue.

"But you have earned the right. After you complete your task, you come back here."

Damiano grinned. "*Grazie!*" he said, then he sprinted off down the street.

Chapter 49

Dunn's upcoming battlefield lay before him.

The river, swollen from the night rain, came rushing down the steep mountainside, and was heavily wooded on both sides. A bridge ran northwest to southeast for just under fifty feet, to cross the river, which was moving fast as it went under the bridge, with white-water points that frothed and churned over both hidden and visible rocks lying in its path. The road coming across the bridge took a sharp turn to the west, a ninety degree angle, then continued on the mile and a half to the eastern edge of the village and beyond.

Dunn stood at the north end of the bridge. Directly north of the river was a stone ledge about thirty feet up. He selected that as the spot for his sniper, Dave Jones. From there, Jones would have an unobstructed view of the bridge and the perfectly straight road for a distance of about three hundred yards, where the road disappeared around a curve.

To the east of the roadway, the heavily wooded mountain continued along its southeast path. To the west, the land spread out in the widening valley that was home to the village. Between the road and the trees was a narrow grassy strip about thirty yards wide, like a right of way. It ran all the way from the bridge to the road's curve. At the far end where the road curved away, the terrain began its ascent to the mountain on the west.

These details were central to Dunn's ambush plan. Ideally, he would have been able to use the woods on the east side of the road, which would be much closer and create a better killing box. The problem with that was any Germans who escaped the initial attack could continue moving across the land on the south side of the river all the way to the west of the village, where they could cross over that bridge to enter the town.

The German SS troops were undoubtedly combat veterans, who would react incredibly fast to the ambush and would begin to return fire within seconds. Dunn's men would have to wipe out almost half of the German force in the first few seconds.

Certain of his choice, he mentally worked out where exactly to position the rest of his men, and the three partisans, Pastore, Frontino, and Damiano, when they arrived.

Chapter 50

Main Street
Potanza, Italy
4 August, 0722 Hours

Potanza was the first town Schluter's SS convoy passed through. They'd been on the road a little more than twenty minutes. Neither man in the open-topped staff car had spoken the entire time.

Adelsberger broke the silence by clearing his throat.

"Sir?"

Schluter turned his cold, blue eyes toward his SS captain, but didn't say anything.

"Sir, the men haven't taken in any sustenance since this time yesterday morning. Perhaps we could stop briefly and take food from the village?"

Schluter's eyes narrowed. "You want to stop and eat, Captain?"

"I am responsible for the men, sir."

Schluter's eyes continued to bore into Adelsberger's, who wanted to look away, but felt frozen by the intense gaze.

"You may be responsible for the men, but you report to me.

No, Captain. We will not stop. The men will eat when we have completed our duty."

"But, sir—"

"I said 'no,' Captain." Schluter finally looked away, but said in a quiet voice, "Do not make me repeat myself again."

"Yes, sir," replied Adelsberger. He kept his eyes straight ahead on the road, but he was thinking dark thoughts about his boss. He imagined a conversation between himself and Himmler, although he'd never met the SS leader, and getting Himmler's approval to remove Schluter from existence. Turning his head away from Schluter to gaze into the forest flashing by, he imagined pulling the trigger himself. A small smile appeared.

But fate would place his hand on the captain's shoulder this morning. He wouldn't be pulling any triggers in his imagined world or today in the real one.

Chapter 51

5 miles southeast of the Ville di Murlo bridge
4 August, 0737 Hours

Frontino drove the lead truck in the two-vehicle convoy. He spotted the left-hand curve and began to slow. The Italian partisan noted that it was exactly as the American, Sergeant Dunn, had described it. The curve was more than ninety degrees, more like a hundred and ten and it was a natural pinch point on the road from Ville di Murlo. Frontino thought it was amazing that the Ranger noticed it on the way back from the POW camp *and* filed it away in his memory.

Frontino came to a complete stop on the far right edge of the road. On both sides, the mountain went up at a steep angle away from the roadbed. The trees were, in some places, as close as a meter from the pavement. He maneuvered the truck into a position that completely blocked the road and he shut off the motor, and pulled the key from the ignition.

He got out and looked at his handiwork. Perfect. He glanced over at the car sitting twenty meters to his north, where Pastore was sitting. The car was running. They didn't want to risk turning it off, fearful it wouldn't start again. Frontino waved at his friend, who responded with a nervous smile and a wave.

Frontino ran around to the back of the truck and opened the rear door. He reached in and grabbed a two-foot-long piece of a rag that had been wound around itself to make a wick. He put the rag on the ground. Next, he lifted out a four-liter fuel can that was about half full. As he worked, he could hear Pastore turning the car around. They would need a quick getaway.

The fuel can had a little metal funnel attached, which he unscrewed and tossed away. He tipped the can over and poured some gas onto the rag. Moving back to the cab, he reached in to pour the rest of the gas onto the seat and floorboard by shaking the can around upside down. Tossing the can on the seat, he ran to the back, where he picked up the gas-soaked rag. He opened the gas tank lid, threw it on the ground, and then fed the rag into the fuel tank filler tube until about two-thirds was inside. He was careful to use one hand so he wouldn't get any gasoline on the other hand, which he would use on the lighter.

He stepped back and admired his work. It would take the Germans a long time to move the truck out of the way. Dunn had said how critical this task was and that he was counting on Frontino and Pastore to accomplish it. He had patted them both on the back and wished them good luck, all through his interpreter, Martelli. Frontino was proud to be included. To know he was trusted gave him strength and courage.

Glancing over his shoulder, he saw that Pastore had completed turning the car around and had pulled to the right side of the road, where he would wait.

Frontino checked his watch. It shouldn't be long now.

5 August, 0748 Hours

Frontino had a sudden fear jump into his head: what if an Italian family was on the road ahead of the Germans? They'd be trapped between his truck and the Germans. He sweated for a long moment, then engine sounds came his way. He recognized that they were big. Relief washed over him, which was definitely a first: he'd never been relieved to know Germans were coming.

Standing next to the closed driver's door, he could see through the interior, out the passenger window. He had positioned his truck so it wouldn't be visible to the convoy's first driver until the German truck was already into the curve.

Frontino's right hand was in his pants pocket fiddling with the lighter. He could clearly tell the trucks were getting closer. Then the sound he was waiting for came: a downshift as the first truck slowed for the curve. With his right hand, kept untainted by gasoline, he pulled the lighter from his pocket carefully and flipped open the lid, holding it at eye level.

The German truck's nose edged around the curve.

Frontino waited.

The windshield came into view and Frontino made eye contact with the driver, who slammed on the brakes as his eyes went wide at the sight of the roadblock. The truck roared to a stop a mere three meters from the roadblock.

Frontino rolled his thumb across the wheel and the lighter flared to life.

The driver's mouth opened in a shout.

Frontino lowered the lighter and held the flame against the rag.

The rag burst into flame.

He tossed the lighter into the cab and as fire *whooshed* throughout the interior, Frontino turned and ran to the waiting car.

A soldier in the back of the truck got up to see what was happening.

Frontino got the car door open.

The soldier spotted Frontino and, possessing excellent reflexes, raised his MP40. At the same moment, the driver put the truck in reverse and floored it. The truck shot backwards and the soldier's barrel dipped as he pulled the trigger. His 9mm rounds stitched an ugly pattern in the hood of Frontino's truck.

Frontino jumped in the car and Pastore stomped on the accelerator while his partner was still closing the door. The car leapt forward, tires screeching and leaving twin tails of rubber on the pavement.

With a great *whumping* sound, Frontino's truck exploded. The fireball went twenty feet straight up and pieces of shrapnel flew into the German truck, shredding the radiator. Water gushed out onto the ground. Several shards zipped through the windshield, just missing the driver's face, and then out the back of the roof.

Frontino's truck burned fiercely, melting the tires onto the pavement.

German soldiers bailed out of the damaged vehicle by going over the sides as it continued to roll backwards. It came to a stop just before striking the second truck in line.

Clear back at the rear of the German column, Schluter's car stopped suddenly. Then came the sound of the explosion. The Gestapo agent stood up in the car, but he couldn't see anything because of the road's curvature. He opened the door, and got out, and Adelsberger joined him. Together they ran to see what had happened.

When they reached the front of the line they ground to a halt, staring at the roaring remnants of a truck.

The first German truck in line was empty, the driver and passengers had jumped clear.

"*Scheisse! Verdammt!*" Schluter started to take off his hat to throw it to the ground, thought better of it and instead clenched his fists and grit his teeth. He gathered himself and turned to face the soldiers from the first truck who were milling about, worried expressions on their faces as they watched Schluter.

They'd seen Schluter's anger before and had been subjected to his rage-filled rants several times in the past few months. Amongst themselves, and very carefully lest there be a stooge in their midst, they'd discussed his antics. Several of the men had suggested Schluter was merely emulating the *Führer*.

"Who was the driver of that truck?"

A man standing at the back of the group raised his hand. "I was, sir."

"Come here."

The soldier stepped up in front of Schluter.

"Tell me exactly what happened."

As the driver explained, Schluter's expression grew more and more angry.

"Partisans, you say?"

"Yes, sir. I'm sure of it."

Schluter turned to Adelsberger. "One more reason to destroy that village. Get this road cleared, Captain. Now."

"Yes, sir."

Schluter walked off the road and found a rock to sit on. He turned his head and stared in the direction he expected the village to be. He pictured the church in flames.

"You cannot stop me," he whispered.

Chapter 52

Just south of the bridge
1 ½ miles east of Ville di Murlo, Italy
4 August, 0753 Hours

When Saunders got out of the truck it seemed to give a sigh of relief and returned itself to its normal distance off the ground.

Dunn started to grin at his friend, but stopped, concern on his face he asked, "What the fuck happened?"

"Had to jump off a train bridge to keep me arse from getting squashed."

Dunn pictured that and grunted. Shaking his head, "Well, glad you were quick enough. I am damn glad to see you, Malcolm, even if you're uglier than usual."

Saunders grinned, his red moustache twitching. "You too."

The two men shook hands.

"Got yourself in a pickle, it seems?" asked the commando.

"Yeah, well we may have been. It was probably five-to-one odds, but now, with your arrival, just in time, I might add, that's cut in half to two-point-five to one. I'll accept that any day."

Saunders nodded. "We brought the stuff you wanted. Or to be more precise, we unloaded what was already on the plane. By the fooking way, where did you get that weirdo plane?"

"The Flamingo?" Dunn shrugged. "I just asked for whatever could be ready yesterday. The guy offered that one."

"Right. Well, it's gonna be a tight squeeze getting all of us back in there. Yeah?"

"I know. We'll manage. We always do."

"I suppose."

While the two sergeants were talking, the men gathered around and nodded and shook hands with their counterparts, Dunn's giving the Brits their condolences; they'd all met Owens and liked him very much. They'd last seen him at Dunn's wedding, just a week ago.

"Hey, Cross, Barltrop!" Dunn waved at the two second-in-command sergeants who'd stepped aside to visit with each other. They looked up and joined Dunn and Saunders.

Dunn motioned for them to follow him to the front of the truck that had borne the British to the bridge from the landing field. Dunn spread a map out on the warm hood. There were pencil marks along the road and the bridge and a few names in tiny, but legible writing.

"I see you've been busy," Saunders said. "This is what your feeble brain came up with?"

"Ha ha," replied Dunn dryly. "Aren't you the funny one? Yep." Dunn explained what Frontino and Pastore were up to and that they should be back soon. He hoped.

Saunders nodded his appreciation of the roadblock delaying action. "You gained maybe fifteen minutes by doing that. Just enough for me and my lads to get here."

"Just between us, I was sweating it until I heard your aircraft coming in."

Saunders dipped his chin in agreement. "This Gestapo guy. He's planning to kill everyone?"

"Yeah. He mentioned that and then completely destroying the village. I assume he means by fire. He also specifically said he couldn't wait to burn the church down. What kind of man wants to do that?"

"A crazy Nazi fooker, that's who."

"He's taking a lesson from whoever destroyed Lidice after Heydrich was killed. If my memory serves me right, they shot almost two hundred men in one day. Then they shipped the women and children off to concentration camps never to be heard from again. They even slaughtered the village's pets."

The men stopped talking, imagining that horrific day.

"This bastard is not getting anywhere near this village." Dunn glanced at the three men around him and saw a determination he knew was on his own face. "No matter what."

"No matter what," replied all three soldiers. They all knew what that meant.

"Down to business, men." Dunn poked the map with a forefinger. "Here's what I think we should do."

Saunders, Barltrop, and Cross occasionally nodded, and also asked a few questions. When Dunn finished, everyone was in agreement. This was the right plan. On paper it looked like the *only* possible solution.

But they all knew that no plan survives first contact with the enemy.

Dunn spotted Pastore and Frontino's car as it screamed around the curve leading to the bridge.

Dunn called for Martelli to join him.

The speeding car didn't slow until it was almost on Dunn and the men around him, then it skidded to a stop just short of the rear bumper of the truck.

Frontino was first out of the car and on the same side as Dunn and the men. He ran up to Dunn and saluted. Dunn smiled at the slight mistake, but gave a salute in return.

"It worked, Sergeant Dunn! The truck blew up right in their faces. They were very close to it when it went off. But we had to leave in a hurry, and I didn't see if it damaged their truck."

"The road is blocked?"

"Completely."

"Did they see you?"

"Oh, yes. I made eye contact with the first driver. They know it was an Italian blocking their way!"

"Exactly what time was this?"

"Seven forty-eight."

Dunn checked his watch. He estimated it would take the Germans perhaps ten minutes to push the burning hulk out of the way, plus eight or so to get to the curve to his south.

"Thank you, Frontino." Dunn patted him on the back and the man grinned wide.

To the soldiers around him, Dunn said, "Eighteen minutes. That's all we have to get everyone in their places. I want it done in ten. Let's go!"

Saunders assembled his men, and Dunn did the same with his and the partisans who were going to fight for their village alongside the Americans: Frontino, Pastore, and Damiano. Gavino was overseeing the gathering of the villagers in the church. Dunn started to second guess himself about that location, since the Gestapo agent clearly had it cemented in his head as being the prime target, but it was the only place large enough for everyone. He prayed he wouldn't regret the decision.

Chapter 53

5 miles southeast of the Ville di Murlo bridge
4 August, 0757 Hours

The flames that had engulfed the Italian's truck had finally died down. Adelsberger decided it was safe enough to try moving it.

The driver of the truck with a sieve for a radiator had another soldier pour water in the radiator and replace the cap. He estimated he could run the engine for four or five minutes.

The driver started his truck and slipped the gear shift into first, then rolled the truck forward, steering to the left. He wanted to hit the burnt hulk toward the rear, which would be the lighter end. The German truck's metal bumper struck the burned-out truck's rear quarter. The truck's rear end swung around to the right with a grinding of metal on metal, and metal on the pavement. The driver turned his wheel to the right and shoved the other truck all the way around so it was resting on the right edge of the road, facing to the south.

The driver heard cheers behind him and he smiled. He backed away successfully, then drove forward past the former roadblock. As soon as he was far enough down the road, he swung the truck over to the right and carefully guided it so it was parallel to the roadway and as far over as possible. Stopping the truck, he glanced out the window, judging the distance. It would be close, but the other trucks would be able make it by. He shut off the engine and got out. He ran to the rear of the next truck in line and, with a helping hand from someone in the back, climbed up. Getting a few pats on the back, he found a spot on one of the side benches and squeezed in between a couple of other soldiers. Down one truck, each one had to carry thirteen or fourteen instead of ten, plus the drivers.

With engines roaring, the three remaining trucks lumbered away. Adelsberger and Schluter followed in the black staff car.

South of the bridge
1 ½ miles east of Ville di Murlo
0803 Hours

There was no breeze now that the storm had passed, and the morning air was crisp and fresh to the smell. Above, the sky was spotted with puffy white clouds. The only sounds were from nature: birds and insects, and an occasional small critter, a squirrel perhaps.

Squeaky Hanson was on the team of six with Dunn. They were positioned in the woods to the west of the road, one hundred yards south of the bridge. The tree line was thirty yards from the edge of the road. Their line formation ran parallel to the road so their weapons would be firing either perpendicularly or obliquely at the enemy's flank and or rear. They were about two yards deep and, thanks to the heavy vegetation, completely invisible to anyone on the road; Dunn had checked himself only minutes before.

The first Ranger on the left was Ward. Then going down the line to his right were Frontino, Dunn, Hanson, Damiano, and last, Martelli. The men were close to each other with about a yard between them. The Americans were armed with their Thompsons, the Italians with a couple of M1s that Saunders had brought with him on the Flamingo. Dunn had given the men a quick overview of how to load and fire the weapon. They were excellent students.

Through the trees Hanson could see the curve about two hundred yards to the south. Directly across the road, the mountainside seemed to rear up into a solid wall extending to the sky. *Dunny chose the perfect ambush spot.*

Suddenly, Damiano said something in a near whisper. Hanson turned toward the Italian assuming he was speaking to Martelli. But instead, the young man was looking directly at Hanson with a quizzical expression.

Hanson looked at Martelli, who said, "He wants to know why you don't like him."

Hanson shrugged and looked away. A moment later he felt a hand on his shoulder.

Hanson flung his arm up to swipe away Damiano's hand. "Don't you touch me." Hanson stared at the Italian with angry eyes.

"Sorry," Martelli translated. "What have I done to you?"

Hanson didn't say anything for a moment, then replied, "Okay, kid. It's not you. I grew up in a tough neighborhood. I was the little guy. All the Italians picked on me. All the time. Ganged up on me. Not my favorite people."

"I'm sorry for your troubles."

Surprised, Hanson looked at the young man and started to say something sharp, but when he saw the kindness in Damiano's eyes, he changed his mind. "Not your fault, kid. Let's forget it."

Damiano smiled. "Okay," he said in English.

In spite of himself, Hanson smiled back. Then he nodded. "Time to be quiet, kid."

Damiano nodded in return and began to examine his new rifle. Again.

Chapter 54

Just north of the bridge
1 ½ miles east of Ville di Murlo, Italy
4 August, 0807 Hours

David Jones knelt on a rocky ledge about ten feet wide and twelve deep. Behind him, the mountain rose steeply, covered by forest. Getting up to the thirty-foot-high ledge had been a challenge. Starting at about half way up, he'd been forced to pull himself up by using small trees as hand holds along the way.

Earlier, when he scouted out the location selected by Dunn, he'd stood on the bridge and was barely able to make out the small opening in the foliage, perhaps five feet wide that gave away the ledge's position. After reaching the ledge, he had stripped some leaves and small branches and affixed them to his helmet and shirt. Jones had taken a kneeling position and whistled. He could clearly see Dunn on the bridge looking right at him, or so it seemed. He could tell his sergeant was straining to find him. After about thirty seconds Dunn waved and shrugged. He was invisible. Jones smiled and waved back.

While Jones had been climbing, Saunders and his men were also getting into their position ten feet below him. They spanned a lateral distance of about ten yards and were perpendicular to a line extending from the bridge. Once the British commandos got into place, all noise ceased, and Jones couldn't see them.

Comfortably in position, Jones peered through his 8-power Unertl sight. The bridge, which seemed to be right under him, but was forty yards away, stretched across the river, then gave way to a ribbon of black that ran off perfectly straight for another three hundred and twenty yards before curving to the left, the east.

Dunn had given the sniper specific instructions, and Jones pictured what the unfolding events might look like, as a way of rehearsing his shots.

As he continued looking through the scope, engine and large tire sounds came from the south. He aimed at the farthest point, at the curve, and waited.

Nothing appeared.

The engine sounds grew softer and the tire sounds disappeared. The Germans had stopped somewhere just out of sight. Blessed with an enormous capacity for waiting, Jones did just that.

A minute passed. Four German soldiers walked into view. They were moving in pairs, with a two-man team on each side of the road. They carried the Schmeisser MP40 submachine gun. Jones knew that the effective range for that weapon was about a hundred yards and it could fire five hundred rounds a minute. That gave it a greater range, but a slower rate of fire than the Thompson.

The Germans advanced slowly, looking everywhere. Obviously their commander had wanted to find anyone setting up an ambush. Jones had thought Dunn had been quite smart to have the partisans set the roadblock and blow up the truck instead of sending a couple of Rangers. It was a nice bit of disinformation. The Germans would be expecting more partisans, not Rangers and Commandos, and this would likely cause them to be arrogant with their apparent superiority.

0808 Hours

The leader, a sergeant on the east side of the road, held up his hand in the universal stop sign. He lifted a pair of field glasses to his eyes and examined the road ahead. He estimated they were just over three hundred meters from the bridge. Holding the glasses steady he relaxed his eyes, waiting for telltale movement. It was similar to how at night your peripheral vision is sharper. He let nearly a minute pass before lowering the glasses and returning them to their case on his belt.

He gave a little wave and the men advanced slowly, heads swiveling.

On the right side of the road, the terrain went sharply uphill, almost but not quite a cliff. Exposed rock showed itself through the grass and trees. To the left, about thirty meters from the road, a tree line stretched nearly to the bridge. The forest was dense and the trees tall, which created a claustrophobic tunnel effect for those walking on the road.

The entire area was still in the shadow of the mountain peaks on the east casting an almost eerie pall over everything. The leader did not like anything he had seen so far. Adelsberger had warned him specifically to watch for likely ambush sites. From where he was walking, the entire damn place was screaming *ambush*, even if he hadn't spotted anything.

When the SS troops hit a point about a hundred meters from the bridge, the leader stopped everyone again. He could clearly see the far side of the bridge and noted that the road bore away to the west after a sharp turn just past the bridge. The bridge itself was about one and a half lanes wide, about five or six meters. Constructed of ironworks, the side rails were just under two meters high, adding yet again to the tunnel effect. The whole time the men were walking, they kept their eyes on the woods on both sides, but saw nothing dangerous.

The leader waved again and the men advanced. At fifty meters from the bridge, he stopped again and turned to look to the west. A forty-meter-wide corridor of grass ran between the south river bank and the north tree line, which had curved to the west. Farther to the west, in the distance, he could make out the village. Turning back to the north, he scanned the far side of the bridge again, then allowed his eyes to rise. Here too, the trees were thick and he saw nothing of concern.

Moving forward, the men approached the bridge. The leader gave a quick order and two men broke into a run, then came to a stop about ten meters onto the bridge. Slinging their weapons over their backs crossways, with the barrel pointing right and the butt under the left elbow, the men climbed up and over the rail, then using the bridge's steel support structure, climbed down far enough to see the underside of the bridge. Finding no wires or explosives, they climbed back up to the roadway. They ran down almost to the other end and repeated the process. When they finished, they ran back to the leader and one of the men held up a thumb.

The leader nodded and waved the men back into pairs. He gave a sharp order and the men took off at double-time away from the bridge.

0816 Hours

When the Germans reached a point half way from the bridge to the road's curve, Jones sighted his Springfield and put the crosshairs on the back of the sergeant's helmet. An easy-peasy shot. With his forefinger outside the trigger guard, he watched the men as they ran away from him. He discovered that letting them go wasn't as hard to do as he'd first thought it would be. He figured his boot camp training would get in the way, but it was his time at Achnacarry House, the school for Rangers and Commandos, that came through for him. That and Dunn grabbing him by the shoulders earlier and saying, "No noise, no movement, and absolutely no shooting until I say."

A hundred yards down the road, hidden a few yards inside the tree line, Dunn watched—without binoculars—the Germans run past. He didn't need visual help; the German soldiers unknowingly passed within thirty yards of ten American soldiers plus two partisans.

When the Germans made it to the curve in the road and went around the bend, the leader stopped the group. A few seconds later, he ran off on his own back toward the trucks. The other three men walked carefully off the road into the woods on the west side and edged themselves back around the curve. They had a direct line of sight on the bridge and the entire road in between.

Chapter 55

1 ½ miles east of Ville di Murlo
4 August, 0820 Hours

Dunn ran everything around in his mind: who was where and when they would do what. Cross and his team of Fairbanks, Wickham, Schneider, Lindstrom, and Morris were about twenty yards to the north of Dunn and his team. Dunn had gone over the plan of attack several times with everyone to ensure they understood their roles. Dunn's and Cross's teams would make up the long leg of the L ambush on the west side of the road, with Jones, and Saunders' crew forming the short leg to the north, above and past the bridge.

Fighting would start in just a few minutes, he knew, and he could feel the adrenaline flowing through his body. The world seemed sharper to his eyes, and the sounds crisp and ultra-clear. His muscles seemed to ripple like a race horse waiting for the starting gate.

Dunn was kneeling behind a tree about a yard deep in the woods, as were all the men. He focused his attention on the south end of the road where it curved away to the southeast. The snout of a German truck nosed into view, moving slowly. So slowly

262   RONN MUNSTERMAN

that Dunn knew what had happened, and so he wasn't surprised at all when, after the truck came fully into view, its cargo area was empty.

Dunn had expected this. It's what he would have done. From the German commander's perspective, the road and bridge wore a neon sign saying *ambush*. Therefore, he'd dismounted his troops placing them on foot behind the trucks. This would save precious seconds if an ambush actually started, and would allow his men to react properly to the attack; they wouldn't have to jump off the truck in the middle of being fired upon to find cover and fight back.

Sure enough, as soon as the truck moved a little closer, Dunn spotted the SS troops marching behind it in two columns. They were in the middle of the road, instead of the edge, as if trying to stay as far away as possible from the trees on the left and the mountainside on the right. When two more trucks came into view, the other SS troops were walking behind their respective trucks, making it an alternating vehicle - soldiers pattern. Eventually, a black convertible staff car acting as the caboose came into view. Dunn could make out that there was a driver, and at least one other person in the car, who was sitting in the back; the Gestapo agent, Dunn surmised.

They were too far away to discern any details and Dunn was not about to raise a pair of reflective-surface binoculars to his eyes. Everything depended on stealth. A protracted battle could have dire consequences for the Allied soldiers, and escape could become impossible, assuming anyone even survived it.

0823 Hours

The lead truck passed Dunn's position and continued toward the bridge. The first squad of SS troops, wearing their black uniforms with the lightning bolt insignias on their collars, marched by. They carried the deadly 9mm Schmeisser MP40 submachine guns. Their eyes were roving the woods on both sides.

On the far side of the lead squad, Dunn spotted a black peaked officer's hat. Dunn had been unsure whether the SS leader would be with the men on the ground or in a vehicle. Regardless, the officer was Jonesy's primary target. Dunn also noted that the German squad was walking about five yards behind the truck. When the firing began that could become a fatal mistake for several of the enemy soldiers, putting them too far from the temporary protection of the truck.

Dunn checked his men. They were ready.

0824 Hours

When the lead truck reached the southern end of the bridge, the trailing end of the convoy passed Dunn's position. The Gestapo agent's details were clear as he sat stiffly upright in the back of the staff car. Dunn was close enough to see that the man hadn't shaved in a day or two; a dark shadow rested on his jaw line. Dunn's own jaws clenched at the sight of the man intent on destroying five hundred people.

Antonio Pastore put the truck in gear and let out the clutch gently, while giving the engine a little more gas. The vehicle moved smoothly down the slope. Emerging from its hiding spot just to the east of the northern end of the bridge, tucked in behind some thick trees, the truck sped up and shot toward the bridge.

Pastore cranked the wheel left and the truck hurtled onto the bridge. He traveled a few yards onto the bridge and stomped on the brake, turning the wheel sharply left again. He stopped when the truck was at a forty-five degree angle to the bridge, its nose almost touching the ironwork railing. Keeping his foot on the brake pedal, he let the engine die by not pressing on the clutch pedal.

Grabbing the two grenades on the seat next to him, he jumped out of the truck, leaving the door open. He pulled the ring on each grenade and tossed them in through the open door. Turning on his heel, he sprinted for the safety of the woods. He wondered whether he would feel anything if a German bullet hit him.

No bullet came, but just as he got to the end of the bridge, the grenades exploded. He dove to the ground, and crabbed his way into the woods on all fours. The truck's gas tank exploded with a giant *whumping* sound.

0825 Hours

Dunn raised his Thompson and fired at the last squad of German soldiers, who were right in front of him. Everyone else on his team began firing. Ten of the fifteen SS soldiers collapsed, their weapons falling from their lifeless hands and clattering on the pavement, although no one could hear over the deep chattering of the Thompsons, and sharp cracks of Damiano's M1. The other five dropped to the ground and began returning fire.

Jones pulled the trigger. The Springfield roared. Adelsberger's head exploded, drenching the man closest to him in blood and brain matter. The corpse folded in on itself and fell to the ground. As fate had already determined, Adelsberger never fired a shot.

Jones shifted his aim, found his target and squeezed off his next round. The bullet pierced the windshield of the truck that was last in line and hit the driver in the throat just below the Adam's apple, in the soft indentation of the neck. On the way out, the round severed the spinal cord. The German fell over. The truck, still in gear, rolled forward as the paralyzed and dying man's foot slipped of the brake pedal.

An SS soldier lying prone on the road and firing into the woods, was closest to the rolling truck. He didn't hear it coming over the sounds of battle. The front left tire hit him in the midsection and continued on over his body, crushing the life out of him. The soldier next to him heard the blood-curdling scream, saw what had just happened, and rose to his feet to escape. Damiano fired off a shot at the standing figure, and then he smirked as the soldier fell dead on his side. When the truck tire hit him, it stopped. This obstruction was too tall to overcome. Damiano let out a chuckle.

Schluter's driver stopped the car. Schluter reacted immediately to the sounds of the explosion and the weapons fire by crouching down in the back seat and crawling out of the car's back passenger door. The men marching directly in front of him had either fallen dead or had dived to the ground, and started firing into the woods to the west. Plinking metal sounds from rounds striking the car were followed by a grunt from the front seat as the driver got hit. He slumped forward, his head resting against the steering wheel.

Schluter advanced alongside the car, staying hidden from the partisans he thought were firing at his men. One of the surviving SS soldiers was only about a meter from him. Schluter whistled sharply and the man rotated his head to look at the Gestapo agent. Schluter gave a *come here* wave. The soldier's expression showed a fleeting moment of *you're kidding, I'm busy here,* but he rose into a low crouch to join Schluter. A couple of rounds struck him and he fell right in front of Schluter.

Schluter crawled forward and unclipped four potato masher grenades from the man's tunic, then shoved them into his jacket pockets.

The Gestapo agent peeked out at the woods. Muzzle flashes seemed to be everywhere along a forty-meter-wide line. Schluter made his way to the rear of the car. No bullets seemed to be hitting the vehicle now, so he duck-walked behind the car. He slowly raised his head to peer over the trunk. He could still see the muzzle flashes from this angle. The sheer number surprised him. It seemed like an awful lot of partisans were involved in the attack.

Carlottta Agostini held her daughter, Marie, tight as the little girl sat on her lap. They both flinched at the sounds of explosions coming from the east. Gunfire sounds came, too, and Marie squeezed her mother tight.

"Mama, I'm scared."

"Shh, now. It'll be all right." Carlotta stroked Marie's black hair and looked at the mass of people huddled in the church. She wondered if it really would be all right. They were entrusting their lives to the American and British soldiers. What if they failed? Tears began to flow down her cheeks. She didn't wipe them away. Instead, she clutched Marie tighter. Looking up at the altar where Jesus hung nailed to a cross, she prayed.

0826 Hours

As soon as the SS commander's body crumpled to the ground, Saunders picked out a target through the M1's rear and front sights, and fired. His men immediately fired. Half of the first squad of Germans fell.

The surviving, but leaderless SS troops all moved to the east side of the trucks, thinking that would be safer. They all eyed the wall of stone in front of them as the mountain rose straight up. Seeing no escape there, they dropped to a prone position behind the truck and began returning fire at the woods on the west side of the road.

Jones spotted movement. A group of five Germans rose and charged toward Dunn's position. Smoke from all of the weapons firing began to obscure the battlefield. When the five soldiers got to the west edge of the road, they all went prone. As one, they grabbed potato masher grenades, untwisted the cap on the bottom of the wooden handle and pulled the porcelain ball. With long overhand arm motions, they threw the weapons toward the woods, which were well within their range.

Jones fired at one of the grenade-throwing SS soldiers as he released the weapon, killing the Nazi soldier.

All five grenades flew into the tree line. Everyone on Dunn's team dove for cover behind trees. Except Damiano, who didn't see the grenade land at his feet.

Chapter 56

1 ½ miles east of Ville di Murlo
4 August, 0827 Hours

Squeaky Hanson saw the grenade land at Damiano's feet.

"Damiano!"

Instead of diving behind a tree for himself, Hanson dove into the bigger, younger Italian, knocking him away from the potato masher.

The grenade exploded.

Hanson screamed and collapsed on top of Damiano.

The other four grenades exploded, showering the forest with deadly shrapnel, but hitting no one.

After the explosions, Dunn immediately recovered. He fired at the soldiers who had thrown the grenades. Jones shot two more of the soldiers and the other two dropped dead from Dunn's long burst.

Saunders and his men began to pick off the German soldiers trying to take cover on the east side of the trucks. One after another fell as they scurried around trying desperately to find cover.

Damiano was on his stomach with a weight on his back. A second later, the weight lifted and Damiano rolled over. The sight that greeted him made him retch and throw up.

Hanson was on his back, blood shooting from what was left of his lower right leg. He was groaning.

Damiano got on his knees, wiped his mouth with his sleeve, and yanked his belt out of his pants. He slipped the belt back through the buckle, making a loop. He lifted Hanson's leg by grabbing the remnants of the trousers at the knee. Carefully, he slid the loop over Hanson's stump and then after finding a long stick nearby, placed it through the loop and began twisting.

Hanson's groaning changed to a scream, but Damiano kept tightening the loop until the blood stopped spraying the grass around them.

Dunn's men resumed their position and began firing.

Frontino was firing as fast as possible with his M1. Wet thumping sounds came from Frontino's left and he glanced that way. Ward had been hit several times in the chest and crumpled, dead. Frontino dropped his M1, reached over, and picked up Ward's Thompson. When Frontino aimed and fired the heavy weapon, the barrel rose with each round. He took his finger off the trigger to re-aim. This time he was ready and hit a German who was no more than twenty yards away.

When the grenades exploded in the trees, Schluter rose and sprinted toward the tree line farther south, his pockets clattering from the grenades he was carrying. He hoped they wouldn't somehow go off in his pockets. He could still get to the church. He was sure of it.

Dunn directed his men to fire into the third truck's gas tanks. Out of the corner of his eye, he saw movement. Someone in black running across the road. Dunn continued firing at the truck. Suddenly, it erupted into a fireball that soared high into the air. The few Germans left near the truck were killed from the force of the explosion and the pieces of truck metal tearing through their bodies.

In front of Cross and his men, seven Germans remained. The men rose and charged toward Cross's position, firing as they ran, screaming at the top of their lungs. Several 9mm rounds hit the tree Cross was standing next to. He ducked back and was looking right at Eddie Fairbanks when a round caught the twenty-one year old dead center in the chest, killing him. Farther down, Daniel Morris took a hit in the face and died before his body hit the ground.

Cross whipped back around to face the charging Germans and fired an entire clip of twenty rounds, raking the seven men, killing them all.

0828 Hours

Dunn realized that Hanson was down and that Damiano seemed to taking care of him. Looking back at the road he tried to find the all-black figure, but couldn't see him anywhere.

Only nine German soldiers, scattered along the hundred yard long kill zone, were still alive. After another torrential deluge of bullets from two sides, three remained. One raised his hands and got to his knees slowly, letting his Schmeisser hang from his shoulder on its long sling.

Cross saw that resistance had stopped and ordered, "Cease fire!"

Dunn ran over to Hanson and knelt down. Hanson was conscious, but still groaning.
    "Martelli!" Dunn waved at his translator.
    Martelli joined Dunn.
    "Give Hanson morphine. Help out here."
    "Yes, Sarge."
    Dunn rose, his Thompson in one hand, and took off running into the woods. Dunn was positive the black figure was the Gestapo agent, and he had a damn good head start. Dunn hoped he could cut the man off at an angle.

0829 Hours

Saunders called cease fire about the same time as Cross. He signaled to his men to head down the hill. They climbed down as fast as they could, and across the road onto the bridge. They advanced until they reached the still hot hulk of the truck Pastore had blown up. Weaving their way around the vehicle, the British Commandos continued on across the bridge.

Saunders kept his men split, half on each side as they walked forward, M1s ready, eyes roving the location of the German trucks and soldiers.

Jones stayed put, as previously instructed by Dunn, keeping a wary eye on the road.

0830 Hours

Cross stared, unbelieving, at the lifeless forms of Fairbanks and Morris. Shaking his head, he motioned to the three remaining men, Schneider, Wickham, and Lindstrom, to join him as he advanced toward the Germans on the road.

When they got within a few yards of the three surviving SS soldiers, who were all on their feet with their hands in the air, Cross stopped. The Germans had moved a little closer to the burning truck as the Americans had approached them. Instead of fear in their eyes, Cross saw something else, something he didn't like: cold appraisal. They had the eyes of killers, which he knew they were. They were SS after all, the most fanatical of all Nazis.

"Schneider, order them to drop their weapons and lie down. Give them three seconds."

Schneider immediately did just that, in a commanding tone.

The SS troops sneered at the Americans and dove behind the truck.

The sharp crack of Jones' Springfield shattered the recent calm of the battlefield. The middle Nazi of the three died and fell.

Cross ran toward the front of the truck after waving Schneider and Lindstrom to the rear.

A burst of Schmeisser rounds hit the pavement at Cross's feet. The rounds had come from *underneath* the truck. Cross bent over and lowered his Thompson without getting his face or body too low, and squeezed off a long return burst. He heard a loud gasp from the other side of the truck.

Jones' Springfield roared once more.

Cross edged around the charred front of the truck and took a quick peek.

All three Germans were down, unmoving.

Now for the cleanup. They would have to check all the Germans to make sure they were dead.

Cross turned to look at Dunn's team to get some help. He was surprised not to see Dunn there. He gave a whistle and a kneeling Martelli looked his way.

"Where's Sarge?"

Martelli jerked his head to the right, "Took off."

Cross finally realized that Martelli was working on someone lying in the grass, but he couldn't see who.

"What happened?" he shouted.

"Hanson's down."

"Shit."

"And Sarge? Ward's dead. I checked him."

Cross's face fell at the additional news.

Just then, Saunders arrived. He and his men had already been checking on the Germans as they advanced.

"Cross, they're all dead back there. Do you need help checking the rest over there?" Saunders pointed south.

Cross gave Saunders a grateful look. "Yes. Please. I've got three men dead and another down."

Saunders grimaced, then said, "Go take care of them."

Cross ran off toward Martelli.

0831 Hours

Dunn ran as fast as possible, dodging tree limbs and occasionally high jumping a few logs. Every fifty yards or so, he would come to a complete stop and listen, although with a pounding heart it was a bit difficult to hear all that well.

After about a half mile, he altered his course, angling more toward the river. He was pretty sure of what the maniac had in mind, with his comments about the church, but it wasn't clear how the Gestapo agent was planning to get to the village. He only had two choices, swim the river, which was moving pretty fast due to the rain last night, or go all the way to the west end bridge and come back that way.

Dunn was deeply regretting agreeing to Gavino's suggestion to use the church as a safe haven, especially since they'd all known it was the main target.

"Fuck," muttered Dunn, partially at his exasperation at himself and partially because he'd nearly fallen after tripping on a tree branch hidden under some leaves that rolled under his boot.

Cross skidded to a halt when he reached Martelli. Kneeling, Cross examined Hanson's wound. Martelli had done a terrific job of getting a workable bandage on it to keep it as clean as possible.

Hanson looked up at Cross, pain in his eyes, but there were signs that the morphine was starting to work. "I fucked up, Sarge."

Damiano said, "He saved my life."

Martelli translated and Cross patted Hanson on the shoulder. "You'll be okay, kid."

Hanson started to nod, but passed out.

"Where exactly did Sarge go?" Cross asked of Martelli.

"He took off at full speed to the west-southwest. I didn't see who he's after."

Cross stood up and looked in that direction, but saw no movement.

"Okay. You have the rank, so you're in charge until we get back. Got that?"

"Yes, Sarge."

Cross started running, worried sick about his friend.

0832 Hours

Schluter knew he was getting close and veered to his right. He had a bloody knot on his forehead from a low branch he hadn't seen in time. His hat was somewhere behind him.

"The church," he said to himself. He would at least take care of that. He figured he had run a kilometer and a half, and was starting to get winded. He was in good shape, but he'd had no rest and, like Adelsberger's men, he hadn't eaten since sometime yesterday. It was taking its toll. He stopped for a breath, leaning against a one meter-thick oak tree.

In the relative silence of the forest, he took a few deep breaths. Just as he was about to start running again, he thought he heard something behind him. He turned to look, but didn't see anything.

More alert now, he listened intently and he heard it again. Someone was running toward him. He quickly stepped around to the other side of the tree. He peered around the edge and spotted an American soldier about fifty meters away.

Temporarily flummoxed by the sudden appearance of an American, Schluter hesitated. Everything came together at once, though, the attack on the POW camp, the road block, and this last ambush, were all the work of American soldiers, not the partisans as he'd been tricked into believing. He would kill this one and get on his way to the village and the church.

The man was running hard, clearly fit and strong. Schluter pulled his Walther PPK and pointed it at the American. Due to the exertion, his arm trembled, and he couldn't get the damn gun to stay on target at all. Disgusted with himself, he holstered it. Looking around at his feet, he found what he needed, and got ready.

0833 Hours

Dunn stopped again to check for sounds, and was about to take off again when he noticed a scuffed area where the leaves had been scattered away. In the middle of the cleared spot was a shoe print. Dunn tracked ahead with his eyes and saw a few more. They were slightly to his left. He changed course and took off again, more slowly, a fast walk, his attention focused on the ground.

He passed a large oak, going by with it on his left.

A great clanging sound burst through his head and he fell back, dropping his Thompson. Dunn's eyes crossed for a moment, and he thought he was about to pass out.

Chapter 57

In the woods across the river from Ville di Murlo
4 August, 0834 Hours

Dunn put his hand to his forehead and it came back bloody. Lying on his back, his helmet off and his Thompson somewhere, he looked up and saw the black figure step closer. Dunn blinked his eyes, trying to clear them, and strained to get his body to react to his commands, but it seemed terribly slow.

With two hands, the Gestapo agent gripped the log like a two-handed sword. He lifted the yard long club over his head to finish off Dunn. He took another step closer and with a scream from deep in his gut he swung the weapon toward Dunn's head.

Dunn kicked out with his left boot and struck Schluter's left shinbone, evoking a scream of pain from the Nazi. Dunn rolled to his right. Schluter lost his balance and the oak club crashed into the spot just vacated by Dunn's head. Dunn rolled over once more and jumped to his feet, arriving at a place about a yard from Schluter.

Schluter regained his balance and, with fury in his eyes, swung the club again. Dunn jerked to his right and the wood

RONN MUNSTERMAN

glanced off his left shoulder, causing his arm to go numb for a second.

As Schluter's swing rotated him past Dunn, the Ranger punched him in the right kidney with his left fist, but the punch was weak from the arm being hit. Schluter grunted but didn't go down.

Instead, Schluter tried to strike Dunn in the face with a vicious backswing. Dunn stepped in and dropped his head out of the way. He punched Schluter just below the solar plexus. This time, the punch scored a victory and Schluter let out a huge *oof* as the air went out of his lungs. He wobbled backwards and Dunn pounced by throwing a haymaker roundhouse that got Schluter on the left cheekbone. Schluter's head snapped to the right and the club tumbled from his hands.

Schluter took two quick steps backwards to get some distance from the enemy. He eyed the club on the ground a little distance away and gauged whether he could reach it time. Dunn saw what he was up to and prepared to charge, ready to tackle the man in black. At the last second, he stopped himself. This wasn't a street fight, this was war.

He started to pull his Colt .45 from its holster, but Schluter reacted surprisingly fast and charged.

Dunn's weapon was partially out of the holster when the Gestapo agent crashed into him. Dunn lost his grip on the .45 and it spun away, landing in a pile of fallen leaves.

Schluter drove his legs and the two men went down, Schluter on top. He pushed off Dunn's chest with his left hand and landed a right jab on Dunn's left cheek, cutting it. As Schluter drew his fist back for another blow, Dunn shot his right hand up and grabbed Schluter's wrist just as it started toward Dunn's face. With a twisting motion, Dunn guided the fist past his own shoulder and with a hip roll got Schluter off balance enough to get him to slide toward the ground. Using his right elbow for leverage, Dunn shoved the German off.

Schluter reacted by getting to his feet and running toward the river.

Dunn jumped up and took up the chase. The German had a five-yard head start. He darted around trees like he was on an obstacle course and was increasing the gap.

Dunn dug deep inside himself and, with a renewed surge of strength, he sped up. Only three yards separated the men.

Suddenly, they burst into the clearing next to the river, which surged by only a few yards away. Dunn saw the water rushing by and he realized they were only a hundred yards from the west end bridge. Schluter veered toward it. His head turned toward the village just across the flowing water.

There it was, the damn church with its forsaken cross reaching toward the so-called heavens.

Schluter patted his pockets and felt the comforting bulges of the grenades. He felt something else under the jacket and a gruesome smile stretched his lips into a thin line. He drew his Walther PPK and looked over his shoulder.

He was shocked to see that the American was only steps away. He turned awkwardly and thrust the pistol toward Dunn. The men locked eyes. Dunn saw hate-filled, cold blue eyes staring at him over the pistol.

Dunn leapt to his left, trying to get outside the swinging arc of the big black hole aimed at his face.

Schluter's finger yanked on the trigger three times. The shots were incredibly loud, but the bullets were nowhere near Dunn.

Dunn was one yard away. His right hand dipped to his belt.

Schluter tried rotating his torso to the left to reacquire his target.

Dunn dove like a linebacker, leading with the raised combat knife.

Schluter completed his rotation and fired again.

The bullet snapped by Dunn's left ear with its own miniature sonic boom.

The knife struck Schluter in the back just under the shoulder blade, piercing the right lung. He screamed and dropped the pistol, and collapsed under the weight of the tackle and the shock of the knife wound.

The two men landed in a heap of arms and legs.

Dunn yanked the knife blade out.

Schluter managed to roll over, then coughed. Blood and bubbles frothed on his lips, looking like some kind of horrendous lipstick. Schluter wiped the blood off with the back of his hand. He looked for a split second at the church steeple and thought of all the greatness he would no longer be able to achieve by destroying it, the village, and the villagers.

With nearly the last of his strength, Schluter jerked his body back and forth.

An exhausted Dunn slipped off.

Schluter tried to sit up, but his damaged body refused to cooperate. Still on his back, he jammed his left hand into his jacket pocket and gripped a grenade. He pulled it out. Barely able to move his right hand, he tried to unscrew the igniter cap, but his bloody fingers slipped. He coughed again and blood sprayed into the air, then settled back on his face making him look like he had the measles.

Still on his knees, Dunn crawled back on top of the German, straddling the man in black. He grabbed the Gestapo agent's throat with his left hand and pulled his right hand back, the combat knife pointed toward Schluter's chest. Dunn stared into the Nazi's blue eyes. The worst of the worst.

Schluter pulled the igniter cap off and yanked the porcelain ball.

"Go to hell, you Nazi bastard!" shouted Dunn.

Dunn slammed the knife in under the breastbone. The evil light went out of the Gestapo agent's eyes. Dunn grabbed the grenade by the wood handle and threw as hard as he could.

It exploded just as it entered the rushing river. A geyser shot into the blue sky and water fell onto Dunn as he lay on his side.

Shaking from the close combat and enormous fatigue, Dunn got to his feet feeling unsteady. He looked down at the dead body of Schluter.

"Fuck you, you son of a bitch." Enraged at what the despicable man before him had wanted to do, Dunn wanted to kick the enemy, but found he couldn't get his legs to move. He collapsed to his knees, panting, then he flopped onto his back.

From somewhere nearby, Dunn heard, "Tom! Are you all right?"

Cross ran up to stand over him.

"God almighty, Tom. What the hell?"

"That's the Gestapo agent. The one who wanted to destroy the village."

"Yeah, well, I kind of figured that out. You're a mess. Are you hurt?"

"Just my face."

"Yeah, I can see that too, you dimwit. What were you thinking?"

"Had to."

Cross tipped his head acknowledging that. "I know. I know you did. He had grenades, huh?"

"Oh, um, yeah."

"Nice throw. Kind of close there, buddy."

"Yep." Dunn closed his eyes for a moment. "Best not mention this to Pamela, okay?"

"For sure. She'd kill you herself."

Cross extended a hand to Dunn, who grabbed it and managed to get to his feet.

"Hm, yeah. Everything all right back there?" Dunn jerked his head toward the east.

"Yeah, Saunders is double-checking, but it looks like all the Germans are dead." Cross gave Dunn a brief narrative of what had happened with the last three SS soldiers. Cross then put a hand on Dunn's right arm.

"I'm afraid I have bad news."

"Who?" asked Dunn, reading his friend's expression.

"Ward. Fairbanks. Morris. All dead. And you must already know about Hanson."

Dunn rubbed his face with a shaking hand. "Ah, fuck." Three lives lost, another with a permanently damaged body.

Dunn looked at the church across the river. A lump caught in his throat. Outside God's house he saw Gavino and a few other men. They were staring at Dunn. Suddenly, a lone figure hurried up to the men on the church steps. Dunn recognized Damiano and the young man waved his arms excitedly and pointed to the east.

"He ran all the way back from the battle to give them the good news," muttered Cross.

"Wouldn't you?"

"Yeah. Yeah, I sure as hell would."

The men all pounded Damiano on the back, and one of them opened the doors to the church. A moment later the villagers, old men, women, and children, streamed out of the church, making their way down into the street. Gavino pointed at the Americans and was obviously telling everyone he'd seen Dunn and the Gestapo agent fighting to the death. Everyone started waving.

Dunn raised his hand and waved. The church bells began to ring and cheers drifted across the water.

Cross looked at his best friend with deep affection and respect. "You pulled it off, Tom. That was one hell of a plan."

Dunn glanced at his friend. "No, *we* pulled it off, Dave."

"Fine. Are you okay?"

Dunn lifted a hand toward the cheering crowd. "Yeah, now I am."

Chapter 58

Southwest of Ville di Murlo, Italy
4 August, 0940 Hours

Dunn, Saunders, and their men made it back to the landing field by way of a couple of trucks furnished by the villagers. The entire village had followed them across the bridge and were milling about talking and gesturing happily. Every once in a while one would break away from the group and grab the nearest soldier, American or British, and plant kisses on the bristly cheeks and hug the man.

The sun was up fully and shone down, warming the morning air. A westerly breeze rustled through the leaves of the trees nearby. The silver Flamingo sat waiting for the men to board, the twin engines off.

Dunn and Saunders stood next to each other, both with a slightly bemused expression as they watched the villagers.

Dunn spotted Gavino, Frontino, Pastore, and Damiano all walking in his direction. Trailing right behind Damiano was black-haired Marie, and next to her, her mother, Carlotta. A medium-sized black-and-white dog loped along behind Marie.

"Martelli!" Dunn called out.

Martelli looked up from where he was kneeling by Hanson's side. He hadn't left the little guy since he'd first patched up the stump. He'd carefully timed releasing the tourniquet to prevent it from causing more damage.

Dunn waggled his fingers and Martelli nodded. He patted Hanson on the shoulder even though the injured man's eyes were closed and he may have been out from the morphine.

The Italians and Martelli arrived in front of Dunn at the same time.

Gavino spoke for the group, who were all smiling ear to ear.

"We can never pay you back for what you've done for the village, but please know you have our lifelong gratitude." Gavino stuck out his hand and Dunn shook it.

"You're welcome, Mr. Gavino. I'm just glad we were here to help out."

"I'm so sorry about your men. We will say prayers for them and their families."

Dunn glanced toward the village where he could just make out the church steeple through the trees. He imagined Ward, Fairbanks, and Morris nodding their heads as if to say it was worth it. They knew what they'd signed up for.

"Thank you. You'll be able to handle cleaning up after the battle? We don't want the Germans to find out exactly what happened."

"Yes. We have a cave for the bodies and we'll find a way to make the trucks disappear, including the one farther out that Frontino blew up. We'll gather all the weapons and supplies and distribute it amongst the partisan groups. It will be nice haul."

"Okay, sounds like you have a great plan."

"There's someone who wants to give you something."

Marie stepped out from behind Damiano and held up some flowers for Dunn.

She spoke solemnly to Dunn and Martelli translated.

"Thank you for saving us. You are my knight in shining armor."

Then she curtsied.

The big Ranger got down on one knee to put himself at the little girl's eye level. He took the flowers and grinned. *"Grazie."*

Marie giggled and leaned close to wrap her arms around Dunn, who reciprocated, patting her back. Marie let go and backed up a step.

Dunn opened the flap on a shirt pocket and dug in. He salvaged the Hershey's bar that was smashed and mangled from the fight with the Gestapo agent. Marie's eyes went wide and she let out a little shriek. Dunn handed it over to her. She said, "*Grazie!*" and ran off toward the village, her long hair flowing behind her. The dog ran at her side.

Damiano shook his head and grinned. "That's my sister."

Carlotta stepped over in front of Martelli.

Martelli stared at the older woman, completely enthralled by her beauty.

She grasped him by the shirt lapels and kissed him on the cheeks. With her gaze firmly on his dark eyes, she kissed him squarely on the mouth. She let go, patted him on the chest and stepped back.

"Perhaps someday, after the war, you'll come visit us."

Leaving a speechless Martelli behind, she walked away.

"Well, and that's my mother," Damiano said dryly, shaking his head in wonder.

Dunn rose and offered his hand to Damiano.

As he was shaking Dunn's hand, Damiano said, "May I go speak to Hanson?"

Martelli slowly came back to reality and translated.

"Sure. Go ahead."

The rest of the partisans did a round of hand shaking with Dunn and Saunders.

Dunn followed Damiano and Martelli over to Hanson wanting to see how he was doing.

Damiano knelt down beside Hanson and touched the American's shoulder. Hanson opened his eyes and found the young Italian's dark eyes staring at him.

"Hey. Are you okay, kid?" Hanson's speech was slow, but clear and Martelli translated.

"I'm fine. I'm sorry I caused this." Damiano's eyes filled with tears.

"Not your fault."

"Again, I want to thank you for saving my life."

Hanson reached up slowly with his left hand and patted Damiano on the side of the neck. "You're a good Eye-talian. You're okay."

Damiano pulled a silver crucifix from around his neck and slipped it over Hanson's head. "This was my grandfather's. I want you to have it."

Hanson looked alarmed, and said, "I'm not Catholic."

Damiano grinned. "God still loves you."

Hanson chuckled. "Okay. Thanks."

"I hope you recover quickly."

"Yeah. Me too."

Damiano got up and with a wave, left.

Dunn took his place and Martelli knelt to examine the bandage and tourniquet.

"How you doing, kid?"

"Ah, I think I fucked up, Dunny."

Shaking his head, Dunn replied, "No, you didn't. You saved that boy's life. I'm just sorry about your foot. You'll be heading home, Squeaky."

"Million dollar wound, huh?"

"Yep. You rest now. We'll be underway soon. Get you to the hospital in Corsica."

"It's going to be hard working with one leg, Dunny."

Dunn put his hand on Hanson shoulder. "Look, Jack, you are a fucking U.S. Army Ranger. Think of all you've accomplished. You're just gonna have to work a little harder now, is all."

Hanson's eyes brightened. "You think so?"

"I do."

"Thanks for everything, Dunny." Hanson's eyelids were getting heavy again and he finally gave in and closed them. Soon his breathing deepened.

Heavy footsteps interrupted the quiet.

"Sergeant?"

Dunn looked up to see the Flamingo pilot standing there.

"Yes, sir?"

"We're going to be overweight. You'll have to leave a few men behind."

Chapter 59

Camp Barton Stacey Hospital
4 August, 0845 Hours, London time

Pamela Dunn smiled at Jim, the nineteen-year-old American soldier under her care.

"We're going to release you back to your unit this afternoon. You'll be on light duty for three weeks, then your battalion's medical staff can reevaluate you."

"Okay, that's good, right?" Jim had been bugging Pamela every day asking when he could get back to the 'boys.'

"It's very good."

"I want to thank you for saving my life."

Pamela had helped diagnose him with an acute infection above his right knee, and the doctor had said it was just in time to save the leg.

"That's what I'm here for."

"Any word from Mr. Dunn?"

"No, not yet. I never know when he might turn up again." She glanced away, looking out the window, where a light rain was falling. She'd told Dunn it was better that they go ahead and get married while they could and enjoy whatever time they were given to be together. This had been in response to him saying maybe they should wait, just in case, you know. But that didn't mean the waiting was easy. Not by any measure was it.

"Tomorrow's our first week anniversary."

"Well, let me be the first to congratulate you!"

Pamela looked at Jim in surprise. She had spoken under her breath, more to herself than to the American.

"Thank you."

Pamela stepped toward the head of the bed and patted Jim on the arm. "Best of luck to you. Listen to your doctors."

"I will."

Pamela turned and walked away. She made her way down the ward toward the hallway. Once there, she turned right, and at the first door on the right, which was open, knocked on the door jam.

Olive Cohn, Pamela's supervisor, looked up from her desk, which was piled high with folders and reports. When she saw Pamela, she smiled and waved her on in.

"Have a seat, dear."

Even though Cohn was only about ten years older, she often called her nurses 'dear.'

Pamela sat down and made herself as comfortable as possible, considering how she felt. Her stomach churned and she felt hot under her white nursing uniform, and was certain her face was red. She folded and unfolded her hands in her lap. She bit her lip, something Dunn had caught on to early in their relationship as a sign something was bothering her.

Cohn, ever the nurse and still observant, asked, "What's troubling you?"

"If I say 'yes' to the offer from Miss Kelly, when would I have to leave?"

"I'd say it would be within two weeks."

Pamela nibbled her lip again, before speaking, "I think I want to go."

Cohn caught the hesitation and asked, "Tell me why you *do* want to go."

"I want to contribute, more than I am now. I mean, I know the work here is important and all, but if I'm over there it'll seem . . . more important. Does that make any sense at all?"

"It does to me, Pamela. What about your husband? Have you talked with him about this?"

"Oh, um, no. He's away right now. I . . . don't know when he'll be back. I sure do hope it's before I leave."

Cohn leaned forward and said, "You're needed. I think you've already decided. Whether it's here or over there you'll be making a huge contribution. But know that there is a nursing shortage over there. Every extra hand helps."

Pamela nodded. "Yes, I know. Please tell Miss Kelly I will go. Whenever she's ready for me."

"I'll call her right now." Cohn stood up and offered her hand. The two women shook and Pamela left the office.

True to her word, Cohn picked up the phone and dialed a number. It was answered on the first ring.

"Cohn here. Pamela Dunn will go."

"That's great news. Thanks. What did you say to convince her?"

Cohn smiled to herself. "I didn't have to say anything. She came to the right conclusion all on her own."

"Did she, now?"

"She did."

"Hm. That is very interesting, don't you think?"

"I do think that. She is a special woman."

"I can't wait for her to get over there. The place I have in mind truly needs a strong woman."

"You've already decided where she's going?"

"Olive, my friend, I knew where she was going before I even arrived at your hospital."

Cohn laughed. "Why am I not surprised? Where are you sending her?"

"You can't tell her, you know."

"Of course not."

"Caen, France. I imagine she'll eventually make it to Paris."

"I'm envious."

"Yes, me too."

The two nurses said their goodbyes and rang off.

Chapter 60

Southwest of Ville di Murlo, Italy
4 August, 0946 Hours, Rome time

Dunn stared at the pilot, a captain. "We're not leaving any men behind."

The pilot stared back at Dunn. "We only have capacity for seventeen people. You have twenty. Why don't you just leave the dead guys? That'll get us to the right number and weight."

Dunn's eyes grew dark. The captain took an involuntary step backwards.

"Captain, we . . . are . . . not . . . fucking . . . leaving . . . men behind. Dead or otherwise. You find a fucking way to get rid of the fucking weight. Tear out the seats. I don't give a shit if we have sit on the floor. Drain some fuel. I . . . don't . . . care!"

The captain was definitely not accustomed to sergeants speaking to him this way. He made the mistake of opting for pulling rank.

"Sergeant, I'm the pilot of this aircraft. What I say goes. If I say we have to get back to the right weight, you'll do as you're told. Leave the dead men behind." He jerked his head toward the villagers who were still standing around, those closest taking an interest in the two Americans arguing, even if they didn't understand a word of it. "Let them bury the men."

Then the pilot made a nearly fatal mistake. He raised a hand and poked Dunn in the chest.

Dunn grabbed the finger so fast the captain wasn't sure he'd seen Dunn's hand even move. Dunn started the motion to snap it, but stopped himself and let go.

The captain started to say something, but Dunn held up a hand. The captain wisely shut his mouth.

"Captain. Let's not get into a pissing contest." He waved a hand in the direction of Hanson. He lowered his voice to say, "He needs surgery. Right away. Let's get him to a hospital. As for the dead men, they helped save every civilian you see here from a Gestapo and SS death unit. If not for the dead men, my friends, the entire village would be gone, the villagers dead. *All* of them. Let's work this out, okay, captain?"

The captain looked around at the villagers. He saw the old men, women, and especially noted the children who, were staring at him as if instinctively understanding. He swallowed heavily. Then he nodded. "Yes, sergeant. We can rip out the seats and toss some equipment overboard. That should get us down to where we need to be. We're going to need some help and tools to speed things up. I don't want to be here much longer. We are literally a sitting duck if the Luftwaffe happens by."

Dunn smiled. "I think we have all the help we need, sir."

1035 Hours

The British de Havilland Flamingo troop carrier was designed by Ronald Bishop and first saw service in 1939. A high-wing monoplane with two engines and twin tail rudders, it roughly resembled the American B-25 Mitchell used by Doolittle on his raid over Tokyo in 1942. This particular aircraft had been in the Mediterranean for a few years, serving in various transport roles for the British. It had eventually ended up in Corsica, where it had been handed over to the invasion planners. The captain had drawn the short straw and was assigned to fly it. The Flamingo's reputation was tarnished by several accidents, one of which was fatal, so the pilot had been less than enthusiastic, but as he and his copilot grew more familiar with the plane, they'd come to appreciate it, and so far, knock on wood, it hadn't failed them.

The captain walked through the long narrow passenger compartment, examining the interior space for anything that didn't belong there. The Italians had provided both the manpower and the tools and had made short work of removing all of the seats, which sat outside on the grass.

Satisfied that all was ready, the captain stuck his head out the rear door. He searched for and found Dunn standing with some of his men about ten yards from the plane. All of them were smoking cigarettes.

"Sergeant Dunn!"

Dunn turned toward the sound of his name.

"Let's load up."

"Right away, sir."

Dunn and Saunders said one more goodbye to Gavino and the other partisans, then gathered their men. In minutes, the men were all aboard and the engines fired up.

Martelli tended to Hanson, making him as comfortable as possible. He got some jackets from the men and rolled them up to make a pillow, and some bumpers to help steady the injured man, tucking him in like a little boy. Hanson was out again. Martelli put his hand to Hanson's forehead.

Frowning, Martelli rose and made his way forward.

"Sarge? We need to get going. Hanson's got a fever already. It's low grade, but it won't get better on its own, I can tell you." Martelli leaned closer and whispered, afraid that somehow Hanson could hear from ten feet away through his stupor. "His leg is getting worse by the minute. I'm afraid they might have to go above the knee to save him."

"Ah, shit. Okay, thanks."

Martelli went back to sit next to Hanson.

Dunn stuck his head into the plane's cockpit. "Sir, how long before we get to Corsica?"

"Forty-five minutes, sergeant."

"Can we radio ahead? Get an ambulance for my man? He's getting worse."

The copilot supplied the answer, "I'll do it once we're in the air."

"I'm grateful."

"You're welcome."

Dunn found a spot on the metal floor and squeezed in between Saunders and Cross. Barltrop sat across from them. No one felt like talking. The day's events had been tough on everyone and fatigue, physical, mental, and emotional set in. The letdown that always followed combat hit them hard and their eyes drooped. By the time the plane was airborne, all four were asleep.

The silver Flamingo soared over the Apennine Mountain peaks into the clear Italian sky.

Chapter 61

Colonel Kenton's Office – Camp Barton Stacey
Andover, England
6 August, 1242 Hours – 2 days later

Colonel Kenton closed the after action report Dunn had written. Lieutenant Samuel Adams was the only other person in the office, sitting to Dunn's left. Both men were across the desk from the colonel.

"Incredible job, Tom."

"Thanks."

"How's Hanson?"

"He'll pull through. The docs said it was touch and go there for a bit due to the infection already setting in. They took his leg off just below the knee. Thanks to the Italian kid, Damiano, and Martelli's quick work, the docs could save the knee. We had to leave him at the hospital there, so we said our goodbyes."

"Did Graves Registration say where your men would be buried?"

Dunn gave a bleak nod. "There's a place for them on Corsica. I said okay."

"I'm sorry."

"Yeah, me too."

"What was the story on this Gestapo guy?"

"It all started because he was looking for Colonel Rogers, although he didn't know who Rogers was at the time, just thought he was a pilot." Dunn pointed at the report. "As I mentioned in there, we saw Rogers get captured. Happened right in front of us. I have to tell you that was an awful moment."

"I'm sure," Adams said.

"Did he say anything to you during the fight?"

"No, not a damn thing. No bluster, nothing. He seemed to be focused on getting to the church. He was a tough fighter, but even before I caught up to him I knew he would be a brutal enemy."

"Did he know the villagers were there?"

Dunn shook his head. "Don't know. Maybe. Maybe not. When I checked his body, he had three more grenades on him. I guess when he saw the ambush, he decided he would still try to kill as many as possible. I think he just hated the Italians for helping Rogers, even though it was only a few people who actually did."

"Typical Nazi retribution."

"Yeah, Cross and I thought of Lidice when we heard what the guy was planning."

"I did, too, when I read this."

"I'm surprised the villagers didn't give you the key to the city." Kenton smiled.

"Ah, yes, sir. No, I got something much better: flowers, a hug, and kisses from a little girl."

"Wonderful. I heard from the British about their POWs. You have been officially thanked by the British army. And another for the few Americans who were there. I can't believe you pulled that off. I'd promote you again, but I'll run out if I do. Have to save them for down the road."

"Oh, ah, well you know I don't care too much about all that."

"Yes, I know."

Kenton opened a drawer and pulled out a box. He held it out toward Dunn and Adams. He lifted the lid, revealing cigars. "Have a couple."

Dunn and Adams each took two, thanking the colonel.

Dunn held one to his nose and breathed in the wonderful smell of an expensive cigar. He stuck them in his shirt pocket.

"For later."

"Of course."

"Before Colonel Rogers got on the airplane to head back to Corsica, I asked him whether it had all been worth it and he said he hoped to find out when he got back. Have you heard anything?"

"I have. What he found was a German armored battalion about fifty miles east of the French border. They were heavily camouflaged by the time thirty-two P-47 Thunderbolts arrived with bomb loads, but they reported at least fifty percent of the tanks were destroyed along with virtually all of the fuel trucks. Yes, it was definitely worth it."

"That is good news. What, might I ask, happened to the colonel when he got back?"

"Word is he's still on General Truscott's staff, so I'd say all was forgiven."

"Glad to hear that."

Kenton looked down for a second, then back at Dunn. "You're down four men. When I first heard, I was worried that it might take a while to get you back to full strength, but something's happened here."

Dunn raised an eyebrow. "What's that, sir?"

"Bagley broke his leg in an exercise the other day. He's out for a long time. I have to reassign his men; his second in command is too new to take over the squad. You can have your pick of his men."

"Martelli, for one," Dunn replied immediately.

"Done."

Dunn crossed one leg over the other, then put his hands in his lap.

"Any thoughts about our next assignment, sir?"

Kenton shook his head. "Not right now. Let's get you back to full strength and allow the men to get to know each other. Then I'm sure I'll find something for you to do." Kenton smiled, the proud commander. "What are your men up to?"

"They're pretty physically banged up and also hurting from the loss of three men plus Hanson. They should be on the way to London in a short while, sir. Gave them a few days R and R."

"What about yourself? Are you taking a few? To be with Pamela?"

"Yes, sir. We're having dinner at her parents' farm tonight."

"I am sorry about your honeymoon."

Dunn shrugged. "We'll manage." Dunn glanced away, thinking for a moment, then looked back at his commanding officer. "Perhaps we could go back to Hayling Island for a few more days?"

"You do that. And give my regards to Mrs. Dunn."

"Will do, sir."

Dunn stared at the paper on his desk. He'd walked straight to his barracks from Colonel Kenton's office. He wanted to complete this task before seeing Pamela. He knew the parents would receive the horrifying telegram long before they got his letter. At least he didn't have to be the first one to tell them.

He spent quite a long time on each letter, making it as personal as possible, and got through the first two able to hold it together. When he got to Daniel Morris's, the nineteen year-old boy from Kansas, it became impossible. All Daniel had wanted to do was go home and farm with his dad after the war.

Dunn put his face in his hands and turned away from the letter so tears wouldn't fall on the paper.

Chapter 62

The Hardwicke Farm
5 miles south of Andover, England
6 August, 1530 Hours

Dunn kissed Pamela long and deep, holding her tight. Her two dogs, as usual, were prancing around them barking happily at the sight of Dunn. They'd quickly grown attached to him.

Dunn pulled back to take a breath and Pamela opened her eyes, revealing the blue irises that Dunn loved to look at. Another kiss followed.

"I missed you, Tom," Pamela said.

"You, too." Dunn looked around the farm yard. It was unchanged; it'd been only a little more than a week since he'd seen it last.

The dogs settled down next to Dunn's boots. Waiting. He knelt to give them both head scratches and ear rubs, and got a few licks in return.

"Shall we go for a little walk?" Pamela asked. "We have time before dinner's ready."

Dunn stood up, groaning as he stretched his muscles, still aching from the intense fight with the Gestapo agent. "Sure."

Pamela gently touched his face, which was a tableau of colors, mostly reds, purples, and yellows. The club on the forehead by Gestapo Agent Schluter had left a lump the size of a large marble; only the helmet had saved him from worse. His left cheek was bandaged where Schluter's massive fist had struck him and cut the skin open.

"How bad was it this time, Tom?"

"I have three dead: Eddie Fairbanks, Patrick Ward, and Daniel Morris, and one who lost his right leg below the knee, Squeaky Hanson."

Pamela's eyes grew wet. All four had been at her wedding the week before. "I'm so sorry, Tom. Are you okay?'

"I guess so. I wrote the letters a while ago. Told them their sons were heroes, which is what everybody says in those letters, but this time it's really true."

"Can you tell me what happened?"

Dunn frowned. "I want to, but I can't. I'll just say we saved a lot of people from a horrible death." He looked away briefly. "God, I hate the Nazis."

"Me, too." Pamela grabbed Dunn's hand. "Come on, let's go. Make you feel better."

They took off hand in hand toward their favorite path, one that wound past the barn and up the hill to the west. The day was overcast, and it felt like it could rain at any moment, but neither cared if it did.

"Would you be interested in going back to Hayling Island?" Dunn asked.

Pamela perked up at this. "Could we? Really?"

"Yes, for a few days anyway. Colonel Kenton gave me the okay this afternoon."

"Could we go tonight?"

"Yep. I'm all packed. Got a duffle bag in the jeep."

Pamela gave a little girl squeal of delight and Dunn laughed, enjoying her happiness.

They walked for a few minutes, just enjoying the scenery and each other's presence.

Pamela said, "There's something I need to tell you."

Dunn looked at her, concerned by something in her tone. "Everything all right?"

"Well, yes" She stopped walking and turned to face Dunn, who came to an abrupt halt so he wouldn't run her over. Pamela took both of his hands in hers.

"I've been offered another assignment."

"You have? Where?"

"Please don't be upset with me."

Dunn's brow crinkled. "I won't."

"Have you heard of the Queen Alexandra's Imperial Military Nursing Service?"

His voice sounding leery, Dunn replied, "Uh, no, I don't think so."

"They serve at field hospitals."

"Field hospitals? You mean on the continent?"

"Yes. I've decided to accept it."

"You mean you'll be over there?" the pitch of Dunn's voice went up in alarm.

"Yes. I don't know where yet. But yes, somewhere over there."

"Ah, Pamela. Do you have to?"

"I believe I do. I feel an obligation to do more than I am."

"Why can't you just stay here where it's safe?"

"Would you?"

"What?"

"Would you? Would you stay where it was safe? Knowing you were needed over there?"

"No. Of course not. But that's different."

Pamela let go of Dunn's hands and stepped back. Her face grew bright red. "Why is that different? Hm? Tell me that."

Dunn was surprised by her anger and stammered, "It, it . . . just is different."

"Explain it to me."

"I . . ." Dunn scrambled to find the right words. "I signed up for this. You signed up to be a nurse."

"I would be a nurse over there."

Dunn suddenly had what he thought was a good argument. "You transferred to Barton Stacey to be near your parents. To help them through Percy's death. What do they say?" Dunn was certain this argument would win the debate.

"Yes, you're right, I did move here for that reason. But things have changed. I'm needed. Really, truly needed. I can make a difference every day for someone in terrible pain and fear. I can help them survive."

She drew herself up tall. "I'm twenty-two. I can make my own decisions. And for the record, Mum and Dad are supportive. You should be, too."

Dunn was completely taken aback. But as he thought about it for a little longer, he realized he shouldn't have been. Pamela had shown herself to be strong and he knew it was part of what he loved about her. But to be within reach of Hitler's army. Hospitals weren't immune to bombing attacks, even if they might be accidental, the bombs didn't care.

He knew how hard it was on her when he was gone on a mission. The worry, the fear. She had willingly signed up for that by insisting they marry now and not after the war. The least he could do was do the same for her.

"You're right. I should support you the way you do me. I'm sorry I didn't react better."

Pamela let out a little sob of relief and leaned in. Dunn grabbed her tight and she murmured into his shoulder, "Thank you. Thank you."

Seaside Resort – Hayling Island
Near Portsmouth, England
6 August, 2012 Hours

Dunn and his bride stood on the beach with their arms around the other's waist. The clouds had dispersed a few hours earlier, and they watched the sun as it dipped closer to the horizon.

Mr. Mitchell, the proprietor, had gladly welcomed them back to resume their honeymoon giving them the key to the same bungalow. Instead of going straight there, they'd chosen to walk along the beach, having taken off their shoes.

Dunn rolled up his trousers and pulled Pamela with him into

the water. They splashed and played for a while, then Pamela grabbed Dunn and kissed him,

"Take me home, Tom."

Dunn knew the code words for what they were and, taking her hand, took off toward the bungalow.

He carried her over the doorstep and set her down. The room was dim as no lights were on and only a little light filtered in around the curtains covering the single window. Dunn kicked the door shut and they stood looking at each other.

Pamela grinned.

"Did you remember to get the shillings for the electric meter?"

"I did."

Pamela giggled and jumped into the bed. Lying flat on her back, she stared at her husband. "Perhaps this time we'll feed the meter afterwards."

"You are so smart," replied Dunn.

Not being entirely stupid himself, he jumped in bed with her.

This time, there was no phone call from Colonel Kenton.

Epilogue

Outside Gavino's General Store
Ville di Murlo, Italy
August 10, 1955, 4:15 PM – 11 years later

The American family of five stood in the warm Italian sun taking in the beauty of the small village. The dad let his family enjoy the view for a little longer, then feeling rather impatient to get things going, asked, "Can we go in?"

His wife put a hand on his upper arm. She knew this meant a lot to him. "Of course, darling."

He crooked his elbow and she slid her hand through. Together they walked up to the door of the little store, the children following, their faces showing curiosity.

The dad opened the door and a little bell rang above him. He held the door open for the rest of his family, then after everyone was in, closed the door, and walked toward the counter. An elderly man with wisps of wild gray hair looked their way. He gave a wide smile. As he walked around the counter, he held his arms up for a hug.

He grabbed the dad, and kissed him on both cheeks. "Colonel Rogers. At last! I'm so delighted to see you." He dropped his arms and stepped back, looking first at the wife.

"Mr. Gavino, may I introduce my wife, Bessie?" Rogers asked.

Gavino hugged and kissed Bessie.

"An honor to meet you, Bessie."

"You, too, Mr. Gavino."

"My eldest, Susan."

Susan, a seventeen-year-old slender, blonde, blue-eyed beauty stepped forward and curtsied. "Pleased to meet you, sir."

Gavino nodded. "Susan."

"My oldest son, Frank, Junior. He's fifteen today."

"My goodness. He looks just you." Gavino shook hands with the teenager, who smiled, apparently not annoyed by the comparison. "Happy Birthday, young Frank!"

Frank, Junior grinned at Gavino's exuberance. "Thanks."

"This is William, who's thirteen."

After another handshake, Gavino said, "You have a wonderful family, Colonel Rogers."

"Thank you. You seem to be doing fine."

"For an old man, eh?" Gavino's eyes twinkled.

"I didn't say it." Rogers smiled. He glanced around the store, noting the shelves full of canned foods and the bread section brimming with loaves of many types of bread. "Your store looks terrific."

"Ah, yes. Far better than it would have been when you were last in the village. Tell me, how was your trip?"

"It was fun!" this from William who was grinning. "The train from Rome was great."

"And the drive from Genoa was all right?"

"It was gorgeous," Bessie said.

"That's wonderful," Gavino said. Looking at the boys, he asked, "What kind of airplane did you fly in?"

Frank, Junior answered right away, "It was a Boeing 377 Stratocruiser. Gosh, it was a beautiful plane. And huge! I want to be a pilot some day. Dad's taken me up in a Cessna 140 a bunch of times. I'm going to get my pilot's license soon."

Rogers beamed at his son's accomplishment to come.

Gavino patted Junior's arm, then turned to William. "And what do you want to be?"

"I want to play major league baseball."

Rogers winked at Gavino, who smiled and ruffled William's hair. "Be sure to practice hard."

"I sure will!"

Gavino smiled at Susan. "And you, young lady?"

"I'm going to college next year, after this one. I love science, especially biology."

"Perhaps you'll be a nurse?"

"Oh no, not me. A doctorate, then research work."

"The world has changed a lot, has it not?"

Susan grinned. "Yes."

Caught up with the children, Gavino asked Rogers, "How do you spend your time?"

"I own a construction business, specializing in new houses. We do all right."

"I believe you are. Congratulations."

"Thanks. Say, how are Pastore and Frontino?" Rogers asked.

Gavino smiled. "They are well. Pastore is still our druggist and Frontino went back to teaching. Both married after the war and have young children."

Rogers nodded, happy to hear the news.

Gavino asked, "Did you ever run across that Ranger, Dunn, again? I've always wanted to thank him again."

Rogers shook his head. "No, I never saw him again. I heard, through the general I worked for, that the SS unit had been destroyed and the village was safe. I did get a short note from Dunn, though, maybe a month later. He said he'd taken care of the son of a bitch Gestapo agent." Rogers looked at his wife. "Sorry."

Bessie just nodded.

Gavino nodded, too. "Yes, I actually saw what happened." The shopkeeper glanced at the children. "Perhaps we can pass on discussing that."

"Yes." Rogers replied. "Were you . . ." he felt a lump rocket into his throat. He was suddenly apprehensive. He managed to swallow the lump and continued, ". . . were you able to arrange everything with Marie?" Tears suddenly welled in his eyes.

Gavino reached out and patted him on the shoulder. "Never fear. All is set. Just as you asked in your last letter."

The men had been writing to each other over the past year. Both men had decided to take a crash course in the other's language.

"She doesn't know we're here?"

"No. This was one secret I was able to keep. No torture, this time." Gavino smiled to lessen the sting of the memories of Gestapo Agent Schluter's treatment of himself, Rogers, and the villagers, including the murders of the doctor and an old woman. He glanced at the children and all three of them were wide-eyed. As one they looked at their dad. Gavino thought their expressions showed that they were viewing their dad in a different light. A good light, he thought.

"Come, let us go now. She is home expecting a visit from me."

A few minutes later, they pulled up outside Marie's house. As planned, the family stayed in the car. Gavino parked just behind them, got out and went up to the front door. He knocked lightly and went on in, as was expected.

Rogers' gaze traveled from the door to the street in front of them. He leaned over and whispered to his wife. He lifted a hand, so only she could see it, and pointed. "It was down there, a couple of hundred yards."

Bessie followed his fingers and nodded. A single tear trickled down her cheek. Rogers used the back of his forefinger to wipe it away.

"What was down there, Dad?"

Rogers glanced into the rear-view mirror hanging from the inside of the windshield at his daughter, who was sitting behind him. "Nothing, Susan."

"Dad . . . you need to tell us. We deserve to know. Something bad happened, didn't it?"

Rogers and his wife had decided not to tell the children the entire story, only that he wanted to revisit the places he'd been during the war. He realized they were just being overprotective. He glanced at Bessie, who nodded encouragement.

Rogers turned in his seat, draping his right arm across the top of the seat. He looked each of his kids in the eye.

"Look. The war is never far from me, even all these years later. When I was here, I was in that house right there." He pointed at Marie's house. "I had hoped to escape through the mountains to the coast. But the Gestapo agent was driving up and down the street yelling that if I didn't come out, he'd kill a villager every five minutes until I surrendered."

Susan gasped and the boys' eyes were huge.

Rogers put his hand over his eyes and couldn't speak for a moment.

Susan put her hand on his shoulder and the boys leaned forward.

"It's okay, Daddy," William said, who was sitting between his older siblings.

Rogers found his voice and said, "Well, I couldn't let that happen, so I walked out of the house and down the street, that way." He nodded to the west, in front of them.

"And that was that. I was captured and taken to a prisoner of war camp for questioning."

"They hurt you, didn't they?" asked Frank, Junior.

"Yes, son." Rogers touched his crooked nose, which Gestapo Agent Schluter had broken with his first blow. "That's how I got this."

Rogers smiled. "But a brave bunch of soldiers, Rangers actually, rescued me." He reached back and ruffled William's hair. Then the entire group got close together in a compact version of a family hug.

A tap on the window broke it up.

"*Mi scusi*, Colonel Rogers," Gavino said, an apologetic look on his face.

Rogers smiled and said, "It's all right."

"You can come in now. All of you. She is waiting for a surprise with her eyes closed. Not an easy feat for a twenty-year-old girl."

Gavino led the way into the house, to the living room. Rogers was right behind Gavino, trying to see around him. Gavino suddenly stepped to the side and Rogers saw Marie.

He gasped at the sight of the young beauty. Her black hair was long, draping her shoulders and framing her face. Her hands were folded in her lap. At her feet lay a black dog with a white chest, and quite a lot of white around the muzzle. Lila. The dog wagged her tail and got up slowly.

"*Ciao*, Marie."

Marie's eyes flew open and zeroed in on Rogers. She leapt to her feet and ran into his waiting arms. She was tall, perhaps five-eight, and she buried her face in Rogers' shoulder. The embrace lasted a long while, then Rogers said in Italian, "It's so wonderful to see you again, Marie."

Marie pulled back and looked at Rogers, eyes brimming.

"You look wonderful, Frank," she replied in perfect English. She turned her attention to his family and she smiled wide.

"Mrs. Rogers, you have a beautiful family."

"Thank you, Marie."

In turn, Marie greeted each of the Rogers children by name, and with a hug and a kiss on the cheek. Frank, Junior blushed at the kiss.

Rogers was dumbfounded. "You remember their names?"

"Well, of course I do, silly." She spun on her heels, the hem of her knee-length blue dress twirling at the motion, and glided over to the mantle. She grabbed a wooden picture frame and returned to Rogers. She held it out for him to see.

Rogers laughed at the sight of the picture of his family he'd given to the nine-year-old Marie. He took it from her and showed his family. Then he held his hand out to his wife, who opened her purse and drew out a small picture frame. She handed it to her husband, who gave it to Marie.

Marie held the picture of her mother and father, and smiled at the memory.

Switching to English, Rogers asked, "How is your mother?" He had been careful enough to ask Gavino in one of his first letters and knew both Mrs. Agostini and Marie's older brother, Damiano were still alive.

"She is fine. Did you know she remarried?"

"No. That's terrific."

Marie glanced around at everyone. "Oh dear. Where are my manners? Please, sit down."

As her guests made themselves comfortable on chairs and the two sofas, Marie stopped Susan from sitting on a chair.

"Please, Susie, sit with me." She took Susan by the hand and led her to the sofa where Rogers and Bessie had settled in. Marie sat between Rogers and Susan.

"Mother remarried in nineteen forty-six. She was finally able to move on from father's death, although to be honest, something happened right after you left. Do you remember the American boy who translated for you out there?" She pointed toward the front door. "When you came to say goodbye?"

Rogers stared off at the ceiling for a moment. It was a long time ago. Finally, the name came to him. "Martelli?"

"Yes, that's the one."

Rogers blinked at her. "What about him?"

"Mother invited him to come visit after the war. I remember because Damiano told me about it later."

"And?"

"He came and never left." Marie smiled. "He's my stepfather."

"You're kidding!"

"Nope. He's ten years younger than mother, but I think they fell in love right there on the porch. You know, love at first sight."

"Well, I'll be."

"I've never seen her so happy. You see, we got an official letter in late forty-five confirming father's death, which had been in forty-two, but the records got lost or destroyed somehow."

"I'm so sorry."

Marie shrugged and Rogers saw the strong little girl who had helped him.

"Well, anyway, after you all left, mother never cried again like she did before, which was almost every day. I just had no understanding of what triggered it. Until he arrived, that is! They live in Genoa, where Alphonso runs a warehouse business. She gave me this house." Anticipating Rogers' next question, Marie said, "Damiano works in Genoa on the docks. It's hard work, but pays well and he got married. Has two girls. Mother is so happy these days to have the grandchildren so close." Marie beamed.

"Be sure to say hello to everyone for us."

"I will, of course."

"And you, Marie? Are you happy?"

"I believe I am. I'm in college now. I start my third year next month. I'm going to be a doctor."

Rogers felt enormous pride for Marie. "Congratulations!"

"It's difficult. So few women in medicine in Italy."

"I admire you for doing this, Marie," Bessie said.

"Thank you. Frank, Do you remember Dr. Marcucci?"

Rogers nodded. "Yes, of course." He held up his left hand and pointed to a round, puckered scar between his thumb and forefinger. "I was able to retain full use of the hand, thanks to his care."

Marie nodded. She took his hand and examined it closely. "Yes, I see he did a great job." She let go and said, "He left college money for me in his will. It's enough to cover everything."

"I am not surprised. He was a good man."

"Yes."

The conversation continued with comfortable meandering, the way good conversation does, for a couple of hours. Susan peppered Marie with questions about college, biology, and medicine. At one point, the boys got bored and asked if they could go out and walk around the village. By the time they got back, it was time to go.

Rogers stood, and everyone else rose with him.

Marie asked again, "Are you sure you won't stay for supper?"

"No, we need to get a move on. I have one more stop today before we head back to Genoa for the night."

"Where is that?"

"San Giuseppe."

Marie's face grew dark. "The POW camp. Are you sure you want to go there?"

Rogers nodded. "I have to."

Marie examined Rogers' face for a moment. "Of course. To put it to rest."

Rogers nodded.

Bessie stepped forward to hug Marie. "You're a lovely young woman, Marie. If you ever decide to come to America, you come see us, okay?"

"I would love to."

Marie hugged Rogers and said, "Thank you for coming to see me."

Rogers placed a hand on her cheek and looked into her eyes. "Thank you for helping me all those years ago."

"You're welcome."

The rest of the family exchanged hugs and European kisses with Marie, then with Gavino, until it was just the two men facing each other.

"Thank you for everything, Mr. Gavino. Today and then."

Gavino nodded. "It was nothing."

"No. It really was not nothing."

The two men, the retired colonel and the retired partisan hugged, and kissed each other on the cheeks, and said goodbye.

Rogers took one more look over his shoulder. For a fleeting moment, Rogers saw the nine-year-old Marie. He blinked, then it was Marie, the grown woman who stood on the door step, her faithful black and white dog, Lila, sitting at her feet. Marie waved farewell. Rogers returned the wave and looked out the windshield.

As they drove away, he smiled.

Author's Notes

If you haven't read the book yet, you should stop right here, there are spoilers below.

To my readers: A heartfelt thank you! I find myself practically speechless—ironic, since I'm a writer—at the popularity of the Sgt. Dunn books. I'm further humbled by the wonderful emails I have received from you. For new readers, my email is at the end of the author's notes, and I really do read and reply to every single email.

While writing *Behind German Lines*, I envisioned the next book, this one, as yet not plotted and unnamed, taking place around the invasion of southern France, *Operation Dragoon*. At some point, I decided to drop Dunn and Saunders into Italy, thinking perhaps afterwards they'd be part of the invasion.

As you might imagine, I'm fairly well-versed with WWII history, but I still voraciously read about it. While doing research about the SS and the Gestapo in Italy, I came across an article: http://en.wikipedia.org/wiki/Sant%27Anna_di_Stazzema_massacre.

After reading it, I knew the third book would be about the true evil that permeated the Nazis at all levels, not just with Hitler, Goering, and Himmler. I was already familiar with the unspeakable tragedy of Lidice, Czechoslovakia from reading *The Rise and Fall of the Third Reich* (William L. Shirer) years ago. I highly recommend that you read it. I have read it twice, all 1,000 plus pages.

As ideas started to come to me, I hammered out a rough plot, which included a massacre of another village, not Ville Di Murlo. I talked to my wife about the plot, as I always do. When I hit the point about the massacre, her visible negative reaction told me what I had been feeling myself. Don't do it. Just don't. I thanked her and said I didn't *want* to write that chapter, and I didn't, not in any version of the story, not even as an experiment. Writers: pay attention to your gut instinct!

Some writers might be aghast that I chose not to put it in, but history is full of those terrifying true stories and my writing it in would not make the book better. However, as a storyteller, I believed the *threat* of it was fair game and would work. I hope you were really worried about Marie and the rest of the village.

A very special thanks goes to my friend, Greg Schluter, who allowed me to use his name for the hands-down most despicable character in all of my books, not counting Hitler and Goering. After reading *Behind German Lines*, Greg suggested I use his name in my next book as a bad guy. At the time, I was already plotting *Brutal Enemy* and replied, "How's a Gestapo agent sound?" He said that would be awesome and that he should be killed in the end. I said that was my plan for that character. I hope you enjoyed your character's demise, Greg.

I was surprised by the way the timeline for this book developed. I've always expected about a month of time to pass in each of the Sgt. Dunn books, since the first two were about that long, but as this one started to come to life, it became clear that it would be a shorter duration. I was fine with that and I hope you were, too. The story is only as long as it needs to be.

It's no accident that in all three Sgt. Dunn books, the local resistance members or partisans play a big part. This is because they truly did make a difference in the war and I wanted to display that. Having Dunn travel around Europe is slightly challenging in terms of language—too bad he isn't multi-lingual. I hope you liked the Martelli character, although I'm wondering how many more translators Dunn is going to need. Just kidding . . . sort of. I'm thinking ahead.

The village of Ville di Murlo is completely fictional, although its physical layout is in common with other Italian valley villages I found on Google Earth. The POW camp is fictional, but the location of San Giuseppe and the curious U-shaped river bend is real. You can most easily find it by map searching for Millesimo, Italy, then look to the east about three miles (a search for San Giuseppe yields too many locations).

The Hotel Nationale in Turin is real and it was the Gestapo headquarters for a time. Torture of prisoners took place in the basement. The villages that form the right triangle near the rail bridge targeted by Saunders are real. Potanza is fictional.

The Allied build up for *Operation Dragoon*, so named because Churchill felt "dragooned" into it, was indeed on Corsica and included about 100,000 men and all the equipment needed for them. General Truscott's personal details are accurate.

Gestapo Agent Schluter's discovery of Colonel Rogers' true identity is based on fact. The Nazis did have dossiers on some American servicemen. I first ran across this tidbit when watching a documentary about the Red Tail Squadron based in Italy. One of the pilots spoke of the time he was captured after being shot down in southern France. He was taken to a room and when the interrogator came in, he laid a binder on the table. Inside the binder were the pilot's high school picture, his high school information, his wife's name, and the name of his flight training school, plus other stuff, all gathered by German spies working in America.

Note: Items that are underlined below can be entered into a search window.

Thanks go to my technical advisor, Steven E. Barltrop, for suggesting two aircraft that made their first appearance in one of my books. Both are British: the Lysander, which was used heavily by the Special Operations Executive (SOE) for inserting spies, and the De Havilland Flamingo, which sadly really was a bit unlucky. The other aircraft, mentioned by Rogers' son, the Boeing 377 Stratocruiser, is a gorgeous airplane. Steve deserves credit for the idea of bringing Saunders into Ville di Murlo.

I didn't introduce any new weapons, except the Walther PPK used by the Gestapo. Until I researched it, I thought all Germans carrying pistols used the more famous Luger. I probably got this impression from all the World War II movies I've seen. If you're a writer: be sure to fact check.

In Pamela's storyline, the Queen Alexandra's Imperial Military Nursing Service is real and changed its name to Queen Alexandra's Royal Military Nursing Service in 1949.

The rescue of the sixty-two prisoners was not in the original plot. As I was writing the scenes leading up to what would have been the rescue of Rogers, I realized there was no way Tom Dunn would leave those men to their fate at the Nazis' hands. He simply *had* to rescue them. Raids on POW camps are real. Here's a Google list: POW camp raids. Here's one that was especially daring: <u>Operation Jericho</u>, although it was conducted by the RAF and not ground forces.

A few words on the tactics put together by Dunn on the fly. In both attacks, the POW camp and the ambush, surprise is such a big factor that it directly contributes to the success of the attacks. Without it, the outcome would likely be different. In order for me to write the scenes I had to create maps of each attack. The maps helped me know who was where and what they were doing, just like it was for Dunn. Although it took me days to get it right, unlike our quick-thinking hero, Dunn. As noted in the Acknowledgements, my friend, Robert A. Goerdt, SFC (U.S. Army, Retired) helped me with the tactics, specifically the ambush, which was quite complex. Rob was kind enough to review the attack for military accuracy. He asked some specific questions and then said it was good as is. However, any errors in my descriptions of the attacks, or elsewhere in this book, that you may find or suspect, are all solely my fault.

Lila, Marie's dog, is named for my eldest granddaughter's dog. Our Lila really does do a combat crawl as depicted in Chapter 27.

The Epilogue. About a month or so before I finished the book, the idea of taking Rogers back to Italy came to me. I wrote the epilogue pretty much as you read it in two days, which is a lot for me. It just seemed fitting for him, and us, to find out what happened to little Marie, who turned out to be one of my favorites. In case you're wondering, I also considered doing the same with Dunn instead, but for two reasons chose not to: I would be forced to reveal Dunn's future and I don't want to do that. I think we need to continue with Tom Dunn, and Pamela, on the journey through World War II, and perhaps someday, beyond. The other reason came down to Rogers being the one who interacted the most with Marie. I thought it was more emotionally charged and fulfilling for that story to be concluded.

I'm delighted to reveal that the fourth Sgt. Dunn book (sd4 - I call my books sd# until they have a title) is in the plotting stages as I write this note to you. I know the main event of the story and the subplots that will go with it. That's all I'm saying.

As for the dedication for my grandson, Elijah: count the number of syllables for each line, no, it's not Haiku. The first five is for George Brett's number, my family's long-time favorite baseball player. The rest will be self-evident.

I really would love to hear from you. Please email me at sgtdunnnovel@yahoo.com.

RM
Iowa
December 2014

Please consider following me on my blog and or Twitter to get up-to-date info on what's happening with upcoming books.

www.ronnmunsterman.com

http://ronnonwriting.blogspot.com/

https://twitter.com/RonnMunsterman
@ronnmunsterman

About The Author

Ronn Munsterman is an Information Technology professional of over twenty years. He loves baseball, and as a native of Kansas City, Missouri, has followed the Royals since their beginning in 1969. He and his family thoroughly enjoyed the Royals' return to the World Series in 2014. Other interests include reading, some selective television watching, movies, listening to music, playing and coaching chess, and photography. Visit his website for a list of his favorites. www.ronnmunsterman.com

He also writes short stories, two of which have been published, and they are available for free download on his website. His lifelong interest in World War II history led to the writing of the Sgt. Dunn novels.

Ronn does volunteer chess coaching each school year for elementary- through high school-aged students, and also provides private lessons for chess students. He authored a book on teaching chess: *Chess Handbook for Parents and Coaches*, available on Amazon.com.

He lives in Iowa with his wife, and enjoys spending time with the family.

Ronn is currently busy at work on the fourth Sgt. Dunn novel.

93083469R00202

Made in the USA
San Bernardino, CA
06 November 2018